D1252205

SHOVELING SMOKE

a clay parker crime novel

SHOVELING SMOKE

AUSTIN DAVIS

CHRONICLE BOOKS

SAN FRANCISCO

Copyright © 2003 by Steve Garrison and John Alexander.

All rights reserved. No part of this book may be reproduced in any form without written permission from the publisher.

This is a work of fiction. Names, places, characters, and incidents are products of the author's imagination or are used fictionally. Any resemblance to actual people, places, or events is entirely coincidental.

Library of Congress Cataloging-in-Publication Data:

Davis, Austin.

Shoveling smoke : a Clay Parker crime novel / Austin Davis.

p. cm.

ISBN 0-8118-4152-9

1. Trials (Fraud)–Fiction. 2. Horse farms–Fiction. 3. Texas, East–Fiction. I. Title.

PS3601.U86S47 2003

813'.6–dc21

2003009720

Printed in the United States of America

Designed by tom & john: a design collaborative

Composition by Suzanne Scott

Cover photo by Petography

Distributed in Canada by Raincoast Books

9050 Shaughnessy Street

Vancouver, British Columbia V6P 6E5

10 9 8 7 6 5 4 3 2 1

Chronicle Books LLC

85 Second Street

San Francisco, California 94105

www.chroniclebooks.com

Lawyers spend a great deal of time shoveling smoke.

– Oliver Wendell Holmes, Jr.

Good men must not obey the laws too well.

– Ralph Waldo Emerson

CHAPTER 1

JENKS, TEXAS, WAS NOT AS EASY to find as Wick Chandler had led me to believe on the phone. I headed north out of Houston on State Highway 59, switched to 69 at Lufkin, and spent two hours drifting through thick pine forests and fields of Bahia grass, most of which had been walked brown by cattle. None of the folks in the filling stations and convenience marts I stopped at could or would give me a coherent set of directions. "Jenks?" they said, a faraway look in their eyes as they pointed me down the road, usually back the way I'd come. The air conditioner in the Austin Healey gave out—I should never have installed one in that wreck of a car—and the last hour was godawful, with hot wind blasting through the open windows and the locusts in the trees making their damned clatter, as if the sky were unzipping itself from the ground. Finally I found it, a one-horse town with a two-block business district and a Dairy Queen. Jenks. My new home.

The office of Chandler and Stroud, Attorneys at Law, was a storefront operation on the main street, next to the Video Palace and the Bon-Ton House of Fine Apparel. Tired as I was and dressed in jeans, T-shirt, and flip-flops, I nevertheless decided to go inside and get the introductions over. I was curious to meet Gilliam

Stroud and Hardwick Chandler, the two lawyers who had offered me, sight unseen, a job out in the middle of nowhere, among the locusts and pine trees and cattle.

Stroud I knew something about. He had had a reputation in his early days, a long time ago. Chandler was an unknown quantity, a friendly voice on the phone. I was hoping the two of them would turn out to be wise old country lawyers. In addition to a job, I needed some wisdom.

When I walked in the office nobody was home. Country music played softly from a radio on the front desk. I went through the little reception room, down a hallway, looking through doors. There were three offices in a row, one virtually empty, but two with desks buried in papers and bookshelves crowded with a conglomeration of objects never before seen in a law office. There were burlap bags of what looked to be grain; shirt boxes trailing rumpled sleeves; giant plastic sacks of Butterfinger candy bars; enough fishing tackle to start up a shop; piles of hubcaps; a model of a sailing ship; garden hoses; plastic body parts—arms, legs, hands with pointing fingers; glass bottles of all shapes and sizes; maybe twenty-five pairs of boots, all bright orange with parti-colored cactuses on the sides; a beer cooler full of disassembled firearms; and dozens of rusty leather-and-steel contraptions that looked like they had something to do with either horses or nineteenth-century bondage. The place was part law office, part weird warehouse.

Back in the hallway, I collided with a giant wearing frayed denim overalls split from the crotch to the knee. I fell back from him, startled, and we stared at each other. The man's beard looked as if it had exploded, leaving clumps of spiky red hair scattered across his massive jaws. His T-shirt was stained nearly black at the neck and armpits, and a smell of sweat and new-mown grass rolled off him. His eyes were round and colorless. He was chewing something.

"I'm sorry," I said. "I didn't see you." The tall man looked at me as if I had spoken in Polish. His face was badly sunburned under his bill cap, the front of which read, in script, *Pascal's Wonder Wormer.*

"Is somebody helping you?" I asked.

He took a massive chew, held it, spoke: "Mr. Stroud told me to come in. He said I needed a easement." His voice was slow and thick, like asphalt liquefying under a July sun.

"I see." I glanced past him toward the reception desk. It was a little after ten o'clock in the morning. Where was the secretary? I pointed to the waiting room. "Why don't you go down there and sit, and we'll see if anybody turns up."

The big man kept staring. "Mr. Stroud said I needed a easement," he said. I excused myself and went to the receptionist's desk, where I thumbed through a Rolodex, looking for Stroud's number and trying to figure out how in hell a law firm could be deserted at ten A.M. on a business day, with a client waiting in the hall. At *S* I found three entries, two of them women's first names, the third, Sin Palace. So I tried *C* for Hardwick Chandler. Nothing but nonsense: *Che-Che, Cherry, Choo-Choo, Cosy,* and *Cutie.* No Chandler.

The phone rang. I picked it up.

"Hello?"

"You have ten seconds to come up with an alibi, you fornicating son of a bitch." It was a woman's voice, white hot. "And it better be good. You've seen what I can do with a razor!"

"You've got the wrong number, ma'am," I said. "This is a law office."

"That's eight seconds," said the voice.

The big farmer had wandered up the hallway in my wake. We shared a moment of silence: slow giant, crazy woman on the phone, baffled lawyer. "Three seconds!" said the phone.

The front door opened and in walked a tiny, stern-faced woman wearing a librarian's blouse, skirt, and sweater. Without a word she took the phone from me, listened for a moment, and hung up. She looked at the big farmer, the planes of her small face sectioned by deep worry lines.

"You go on home now, Mr. Randall," she said in a soft, sad voice that managed to convey authority.

"Mr. Stroud said I needed a easement," the farmer told her.

She took the giant by the arm and walked him to the door. "Come in tomorrow afternoon," she said. "Mr. Stroud will do that easement for you then." The big man shuffled away down the sidewalk just as the phone rang again. The little woman picked it up. "Attorney's office." She listened for a few seconds and hung up.

She turned to me. "You must be Mr. Parker." I nodded. She shook my hand and introduced herself as Molly Tunstall, the firm's secretary. She spoke to me with the same sweet gravity in her voice that she had used on the big farmer. "Please come with me," she said, and then she was hustling me out the door just as she had done Farmer Randall.

"Where are we going, Ms. Tunstall?" I asked.

"Please just call me Molly," she said as we walked past the Bon-Ton House. "I'm sorry to bother you with this on your first day with the firm, but there's no help for it. I can't find Mr. Chandler, and I need some assistance with Mr. Stroud." Suddenly she stopped walking and looked me over.

"Have you brought a suit with you?" she asked.

"I've got one in my car," I replied.

"Would you mind getting it? We'll find a place on the way for you to put it on."

"Are we going somewhere?" I asked, walking over to the Austin Healey and opening the trunk.

"Mule Springs," she said. "It's the county seat. Mr. Stroud has a trial set there this afternoon."

"We're going to trial?" I asked, pulling a garment bag out of the car's trunk.

"Soon as we collect Mr. Stroud," she said.

"Where is he?"

"He's over at the jail. We have to bail him out."

CHAPTER 2

THE JAIL WAS ONLY A BLOCK AWAY, a cinderblock lean-to attached to the city hall. Parked in front of it was an old black Continental, its vinyl top shredding with age. Molly unlocked its trunk and had me put my garment bag in it.

"What's Mr. Stroud been arrested for, Molly?" I asked.

"Let's just see how bad it is," she replied.

The jail's office was paneled in cheap plywood, the windows reinforced with chicken wire, the linoleum floor marbled with grime. Everything in the place, from the chairs to the air conditioner to the bailiff and his panzer tank of a desk, looked as if it had been pounded with a large hammer. Molly made arrangements with the bail bondsman, and then we sat on a bench under the buzzing fluorescent light waiting for Stroud to be brought out to us.

There was a framed photo on the wall next to me, showing a wet, stocky man in swimming trunks, grinning, with his fist down the throat of a whiskered, olive-and-flesh-colored nightmare the size of a six-year-old. Two other men were helping to hold the animal up.

"It's a beaut, ain't it?" the bailiff said to me.

"What is it?" I asked.

"Catfish!" he said. "A flathead. Sixty-four pounds. That's the sheriff caught it, over in Oklahoma. Sheriff's a noodling champ."

"I'll bet your day has taken a bit of a turn," Molly said to me.

"A bit of one," I replied.

I was actually thinking about another photograph, old, grainy, black-and-white, hanging on a wall in the Leon Jaworski wing of the Baylor Law School. It's a snapshot of the iron railroad bridge, long unused now, that spans the Brazos just north of downtown Waco. For generations that black-trestled bridge was the townspeople's favorite spot for taking the law into their own hands, and sure enough, spreading out through the foreground of the photo is the dark stain of an angry mob. Standing at the bridge's center are two sheriff's deputies, one with his arms crossed, one fingering his holster. Between them is the black man the mob has come to hang. The man has just been found not guilty in court of raping and murdering a white girl, the daughter of a local dry cleaner. At the end of the bridge, between the mob and the three men, is a tall, bulky figure in a black suit, facing down the crowd with a section of railroad trestle, which he holds in his hands like a club. The man in black is the acquitted man's lawyer, who, having saved his client in the courthouse, is now saving him outside it. The year the photo was taken was 1948. The lawyer was Gilliam Erasmus Stroud.

That photograph helped get me through law school. From time to time, as I struggled through civil procedure, contract law, torts, or property, I would stop in the hallway to look at the tall figure holding at bay the collected hatred of an entire Texas town, swinging a trestle for justice. That was the sort of lawyer I was going to be.

While at Baylor I learned only a little more about Gilliam Stroud's career. After coming west from Harvard, he had taught with distinction for some years at Baylor, then was appointed to a federal judgeship out in West Texas. I knew that he left the bench only a few years later to go into private practice. That was odd,

giving up a lifetime appointment. In fact, it was unheard of. I knew
nothing about his reasons for abandoning the bench or about his
subsequent career.

But I did know that he saved his man from the Waco mob,
and that there had been other moments for him like the one on
that bridge.

Noise of a scuffle came from the other side of the door leading
to the cells. An officer appeared and unlocked the door, but before he
could open it, he was pushed aside by a slack, massive shadow that
spun into him from behind and bounced into the waiting room.
The figure righted itself three feet from me—I caught a sweet-and-
sour gust of whiskey—and, turning back to the officer, spoke in a
deep, booming voice: "Fuck you and the horse you rode in on."

Stroud was dressed in a black suit three sizes too big for him.
He had the withered look of someone who had been burned
through by some terrible illness. His scrawny neck rose out of a
soiled collar to support a tiny, wizened head adorned with random
wisps of white, baby-fine hair and heavy eyebrows the color of lead
ingots. In shape, Stroud resembled a giant condor, with shaggy
plumage and a fragile, dwarfish cranium. His eyes were dying
coals. His breath was the breath of the dragon.

Stroud was so drunk he was molten. He was squinting in
an odd way, as if working hard to keep his eyes fixed on either
side of his nose. Molly took him firmly by the arm. The top of her
head only came up to the old man's shoulder, and together they
looked like a bizarre carnival attraction: an aging waif with a
trained condor.

"Get him home, Molly," said the bailiff, patting the old man on
the back, "he's had a rough night." Stroud whirled at the touch
and puffed his cheeks in and out. He opened his mouth to speak,
but apparently couldn't find any words. In his confusion, he
turned and saw me for the first time.

"Who in hell are you?" he asked. I was engulfed in a tidal stench of whiskey and decay.

"I'm your new lawyer, Mr. Stroud."

Stroud fell back as if he'd been struck in the face, then lurched forward again. I could see why Molly Tunstall had thought she would need help with her boss.

"My new lawyer," Stroud murmured, rolling the words around on a tongue the color of ash.

CHAPTER 3

THREE MINUTES LATER, I was driving Stroud's Lincoln Continental out of Jenks. Molly Tunstall sat on the passenger side, and the old man slouched in the backseat, staring at me in the rearview mirror, tufts of fine white hair floating over his skull. He had rheumy blue eyes that burned brightly despite the rheum.

"Clayton Parker," he said, the syllables rumbling like boulders down a mountainside. "I suppose people call you Clay?"

"Yes, sir," I said.

"Do I have to call you Clay?"

"Is there something you don't like about my name?" I asked.

He laughed and shook his head.

"Mr. Stroud," I said, swinging the car onto State Highway 69, "if there's something about me that you don't like, say so." I looked in the rearview mirror to give him back stare for stare, but he had disappeared from the mirror. He had fallen over as I turned the car.

"Is he all right, Molly?" I asked.

"He'll be fine," she said.

"I'm guessing from the look of him that he does this all the time."

"Oh, no," she replied. "You see, it's Tuesday, and Monday nights he likes to get out of the house." The little secretary explained that

Jenks is in a dry county, so when Mr. Stroud wished to visit a bar, he usually drove to one of the three or four that sat on the other side of the county line. For that reason, Molly said, the local constabulary tended to watch for him.

"Where the hell is Hard-dick?" Stroud asked from the backseat.

"He means Mr. Chandler," Molly explained. "Hard-*wick* Chandler."

I heard terrible wheezing from the backseat. Molly showed no trace of alarm. "He's laughing?" I asked. She nodded. In another moment, he began to snore.

The big car lumbered down the two-lane highway. "He asked a good question," I said. "Where is Mr. Chandler?" I wanted to know why the founder of the firm wasn't cleaning up after his partner, why it had fallen to Molly and me to do it on my first day on the job.

"Mr. Chandler is out of pocket," she said. Something about the way she said it gave me the feeling she wanted to say more, but she didn't.

"Will Mr. Chandler meet us in Mule Springs?" I asked.

"I doubt it," she said. "No, it's just us." She reached into the backseat floorboard, pulled up a worn leather briefcase stuffed with papers, and rummaged through it.

"I don't see how Mr. Stroud can function in a trial, drunk as he is."

"He's not drunk. He tends to tipple on the weekends, like I told you. But he's as sober right now as you or I." Molly pulled out of the briefcase a spray can of air freshener—Garden Mist—and made two or three passes with the can over her sleeping boss. The car became filled with the fresh, sweet scent of dewy flowers on a spring morning. Stroud continued to snore.

On the outskirts of Mule Springs, Molly had me pull into a Texaco station so that I could change into my suit in the men's room. I have always packed a complete outfit into a garment bag, and in this case, anticipating my first day in a new law firm, I had brought standard dress for the sort of lawyer I had, until recently, been: an associate in one of Houston's more prestigious firms. Imagine my surprise when the pair of Cole Haan oxfords that I thought I remembered slipping into the shoe compartment of the garment bag failed to be there. I had forgotten my shoes. It shouldn't have surprised me. Considering the state I had been in during the months since my fall from grace in Houston, it was a wonder I had remembered as much of my ensemble as I did. This lapse left me dressed in a black pin-striped Armani, a Canali tie, and flip-flops over my socks. Mortified, I walked out and got into the Lincoln.

"We have to stop at a shoe store before we go to the courthouse," I told Molly Tunstall as I started the car. She looked at her watch.

"I'm afraid we don't have time," she said. "We've got to be there in six minutes."

"We have to do something," I said, pulling the Lincoln onto the street.

"At least you've got socks," Molly said. "We'll be okay."

"Look, Ms. Tunstall, there's no way I'm walking into a courtroom dressed—"

"We can't be late, Mr. Parker," Molly said. "This is not a forgiving judge. And it's a murder trial."

"Jesus H. Christ," I said, my state of mind ratcheting up from mortification to panic.

To tell the truth, my experience as a trial lawyer was a little thin. Years earlier, when I went to work in Houston, I experimented with the trial branch of my firm and found I didn't have the knack for winning over a jury. I had the sweaty-palm problem, galloping drizzles, stage fright, call it what you will. Trial law is a performance art, like acting or playing the cello, except the stakes are a hell of a lot higher. Blow it once in front of a jury or a judge, and fortunes can be lost, lives destroyed. And it is so easy to screw up. All it might take is a nervous swallow or a scratchy throat or a joke that doesn't quite come off. During the few trials I actually worked, I became an insomniac, a zombie-eyed burden to my then-wife and my friends and, I feared, to my clients as well. Thank God I was good with figures, and my firm let me transfer to tax law.

When Hardwick Chandler called to offer me the job in Jenks, I remember a doubt floating momentarily before my eyes. I thought of asking him about the amount of trial work I might be expected to undertake. But I didn't. I needed a change, after all. I wanted to get out in the country, and I figured I could handle anything that Jenks, Texas, threw at me.

And now here I was, walking into my first murder trial. In flip-flops.

Molly filled me in on the case that, in a few minutes, Gilliam Stroud would have to be woken up to try. To make things even crazier than they had already been that morning, it was hell's own case. One spring afternoon three months earlier, on the poor side of Mule Springs, what they call "the acre," Jolene Biggs had watched as her husband, Lanier Biggs, was shot to death in his own yard by a man named Clifton Hardesty, Stroud's client. Hardesty had driven his pickup into Biggs's driveway, called Biggs out of the house, and then emptied both barrels of a shotgun into Biggs at point-blank range. Biggs had been unarmed and, for that matter, mostly undressed, wearing only a pair of shorts. Jolene had seen the whole thing from the front porch, not ten feet away. Biggs had bled to death on his own sidewalk.

After shooting Biggs, Clifton Hardesty had driven immediately to the police station and confessed. The district attorney was going for first-degree murder, premeditated, cold-blooded evil. Clifton Hardesty was guilty *in fact* of shooting Lanier Biggs.

Nevertheless, as was his right, Clifton Hardesty had pleaded not guilty.

The trial had started yesterday, and today Jolene Biggs, wife of the murdered man, was scheduled to testify.

Mule Springs looked a lot like Jenks, except there was a town square with one of those ornate, castellated redbrick courthouses in the center. I pulled the Lincoln into the courthouse parking lot and switched off the ignition.

"Molly, I'm sorry, but I don't think I can be of much help in this case. I haven't read it, I don't know any of the testimony."

"Mr. Parker," Molly said, "I'm not sure what Mr. Stroud will want you to do, but whatever it is, you don't have to worry about it. *He's* trying the case." She turned to the backseat and said, "We're here, Mr. Stroud. It's time to go to court."

Gilliam Stroud sat up, smiled at Molly Tunstall, and winked a red-rimmed eye at me. "Let's get 'em," he said, and climbed out of the car.

CHAPTER 4

THE COURTROOM WAS one of those old-fashioned, high-ceilinged outfits with a balcony and whitewashed walls and a giant Texas flag hanging above the judge's bench. There were maybe twenty-five onlookers, dwarfed in the wide, high emptiness of the room. As I followed Stroud and Molly down the center aisle, I noticed that Stroud walked with a slight limp but had lost all trace of the unbalanced swagger that had made getting him into his car difficult earlier that morning.

Stroud noticed my shoes. "Mr. Parker," he said, "you're not a member of any sort of sect, are you? Some outfit with its own dress code?"

Before I could answer we reached the defense table, where the defendant was already sitting. Clifton Hardesty was a scrawny, middle-aged man with a blond ducktail and deep pockmarks on his face. He was wearing what I assumed were his best clothes, a deeply wrinkled plaid sport coat, an orange pullover shirt, and jeans.

Molly Tunstall had brought the briefcase with her and now began to lay out stacks of papers and files on the table.

"Where've you been, Mr. Stroud?" Hardesty whispered.

"I have been rounding up experts to aid in your defense,"

Stroud replied in a loud voice, placing his hand on my shoulder. "Mr. Hardesty, allow me to introduce Dr. Clayton Parker. Please don't be alarmed by his choice of shoes. He is afflicted with a terrible case of athlete's foot and has to air his toes."

"Pleased to meet you, Dr. Parker," said Hardesty, who stood and offered me his hand, which was cold and limp. "Sorry about your toes."

"Wait a minute," I said. At that moment the jury filed in, followed by the judge, and everyone in the courtroom stood. I tried to back away from the defense table and take a seat next to Molly in the first row of the audience, but Stroud clutched my arm and, as the judge seated himself, guided me into the chair between himself and Hardesty.

"I'm not a doctor, and I don't have athlete's foot," I whispered to the old man.

"My mistake," he whispered back. "We'll sort it out later."

I noticed that a slender, hunched man sitting at the prosecutor's table in a Western-cut suit and bolo tie was staring at me. Stroud nodded at the man, who acknowledged the nod with one of his own. "Our prosecutor," Stroud whispered to me. "Nasty little prick."

As soon as the clerk had called the court to session, the prosecutor stood, pointed at me, and said to the judge in a reedy whine, "Your Honor, I wonder if we could have this gentleman identified. He may be a potential witness, and the State has invoked the Rule."

"Mr. Stroud," said the judge, "the State has invoked the Rule of Witnesses, so potential witnesses have to remain outside, out of the presence and hearing of the other witnesses."

Stroud rose, smiling. "Surely the Court will exempt an expert who must listen to the State's witness in order to rebut that testimony? He can't talk about what he hasn't heard, Your Honor."

I felt my throat going dry. Stroud was implying to the Court and the jury that I was a medical expert, a doctor of some kind.

We were defrauding the Court! We were going to be disbarred! The judge, an elderly, rumpled man who seemed to be trying to shake off the effects of a nap, looked me over. When his gaze reached my feet, he woke up all at once.

"Mr. Stroud," he said, "can you explain to me why your expert is not wearing proper shoes in my courtroom?"

"Bromohydrosis, Your Honor," Stroud said gravely. "It's a condition of the lower extremities. My colleague has been stricken with a serious case of it. His podiatrist insists on constant ventilation. I assure you we meant no disrespect to the Court."

The judge gave me a hard look, then shrugged and bid the prosecutor call his first witness.

"Bromohydrosis?" I whispered to Stroud as he sat down.

"A serious case," he replied.

I shook my head and started to tell him what I thought about feeding lies to a judge, when the old man shoved some black-and-white photos in front of me that choked my protest in my throat. The photos revealed a large man, naked except for boxers, lying facedown in an inky puddle.

"When you shake your head in front of the jury, be sure you're looking at these," the old man whispered. "And look concerned! You may be up in a moment. Don't piss in the on-deck circle, Tiger."

The State called Jolene Biggs, widow of the deceased. Mrs. Biggs took the stand and was sworn in, a large, doughy woman wearing a shiny green dress, her bright red hair unraveling from a bun on the top of her head. As the prosecutor coached her through her rehearsed testimony, Stroud slid a manila file over to me. In it were photos of Lanier Biggs, the dead man, on the coroner's table. They were shocking, not so much for the two terrible shotgun wounds in the man's stomach as for all the old, healed wounds. Smears of scar tissue, some waxen and smooth, some badly puckered, covered the body. It looked like Lanier Biggs had carried a scar for every day of his life. The body was big and well muscled, the face appallingly brutal: one eyebrow shredded by scars, a broken nose, a huge, truculent jaw. Lanier Biggs was nobody I would have wanted to meet in an alley.

"Why do you suppose our prosecutor hasn't offered these photos in evidence?" Stroud whispered.

By the time the prosecuting attorney turned Jolene Biggs over to the defense for cross-examination, she had explained, in a calm, disaffected tone, how she had watched Hardesty shoot her unarmed husband twice with a shotgun and then drive away. The prosecutor, giving a tug to the ends of his string tie, nodded to Stroud and said, "Pass the witness."

Stroud climbed to his feet, shuffled through some papers on his desk, picked up a blank sheet of paper and studied it. He walked, with the slight limp I had noticed earlier, to the center of the courtroom, trailing after him the vaporous, rainy-sweet scent of Garden Mist air freshener. He gave the witness a dignified bow.

"Mrs. Biggs, I am sorry for your loss."

That seemed to confuse the woman on the stand. "Beg pardon?" she replied.

"I'm referring to your loss of Mr. Biggs, the deceased. You must have loved him very much."

"Oh, yes, sir. He was my husband."

"Mrs. Biggs, were you ever afraid of your husband?" At this the prosecutor objected, saying it had no bearing on the case at hand.

Stroud withdrew the question. "Now, Mrs. Biggs, you have testified that you saw the defendant, Clifton Hardesty, drive into Lanier Biggs's driveway shortly before the shooting occurred, isn't that right?"

"Yes, sir."

"And Mr. Biggs went outside to speak to Mr. Hardesty, correct?"

"Yes, sir."

"And Mr. Biggs, your husband, made it very clear to Mr. Hardesty that he wasn't glad to see him, didn't he?"

The prosecutor objected, saying the question was not relevant to the facts of the case. Stroud explained to the judge that he was merely following the line of inquiry that the prosecutor himself had opened up, trying to reconstruct as thoroughly as possible the events leading up to and following the shooting. The judge overruled the objection.

In the next ten minutes there were to be several more objections from the prosecution, each more strident than the last, as Stroud coaxed facts from Jolene Biggs that the prosecutor had left untouched. It is customary for a lawyer to stick to yes-or-no questions when cross-examining a hostile witness, since an open-ended question might give the witness a chance to say something damaging. Stroud flicked his questions like a champion fisherman plays a fly.

"I take it," he said, "that your husband was angry with Clifton Hardesty for stealing from him?"

"No, sir," replied Jolene Biggs.

"Well, then, I suppose your husband was mad at Clifton for calling him names?"

"No, sir, nobody called Lanier any names."

"Then my guess is that Lanier got mad at Clifton Hardesty for beating him through the streets with a buggy whip?"

Jolene Biggs let out a surprised laugh. "Nobody hit Lanier with a buggy whip. That ain't why Lanier was mad."

"Then why was your husband mad?" asked Stroud, taking a chance.

"He was mad because it was his street."

The old man raised an eyebrow. "*His* street? What do you mean?"

The woman shrugged. "That's what he said. He always said it was his street, and anybody wanting to drive it better watch out."

Stroud had hit pay dirt. According to Jolene Biggs, her husband had appropriated two blocks of Jimpson Street in south Mule Springs as his own personal roadway. He had a habit of running with a baseball bat after cars that ventured down the street. Lanier had been especially angry with Clifton Hardesty, whom he had known since childhood. Mrs. Biggs was unable to say why, except that it had something to do with the shape of Hardesty's head.

"Lanier called it a walnut head," Jolene explained to Stroud. "He used to say you can't trust people with a head shaped like a walnut. It got him real mad sometimes."

"Mrs. Biggs, didn't your husband talk about doing violence to Clifton Hardesty?"

"Yes, sir. He said he was going to split that walnut head open, let the evil out."

"But Clifton Hardesty wasn't the only one whose head Lanier meant to open, was he?"

"No, sir. Lanier, he threatened everybody. All the time. He said there was lots of walnut heads in this town. Every day he saw more of them."

"Most people ran from Lanier, didn't they?"

"Yes, sir. Except those he hit with a bat."

"But Clifton Hardesty didn't run, did he?"

"No, sir."

"Clifton even pulled his shotgun down off the rack in his truck, didn't he?"

"Yes, sir."

"And Lanier Biggs, standing by the truck, saw that gun, just as clearly as you did from ten feet away, didn't he?"

"Yes, sir. He couldn't miss it. It was sticking out at him. Clif was trying to make Lanier stand still and talk, but Lanier didn't care. He cussed Clif, said he's going to kill him dead. And Clif was holding that shotgun on him. Lanier said for him to just wait there while he went and got his own gun so's he could kill him."

It was amazing. Stroud had found the right button to push, and the words tumbled out of Jolene Biggs.

"So Hardesty's shotgun didn't frighten your husband?"

"Oh, no, sir. Lanier had been shot before."

I watched the woman on the stand, trying to imagine what her life with this bullet-scarred maniac had been like. Stroud continued his cross-examination by leading Mrs. Biggs through what she had done after Hardesty had shot her husband and driven away. She revealed that Lanier Biggs, though gravely wounded, was still conscious and lying on the sidewalk, unable to move, shouting curses at the departing truck.

"And did you go to him, Mrs. Biggs?" Stroud asked.

"I asked him what should I do. He took a swipe at me, told me to go get an ambulance. So I got the car keys and drove off for the hospital."

"Did you take your husband with you?"

"No, sir. He was too angry for me to move him."

"So you left him and drove for the hospital, is that right?"

"Yes, sir."

"You must not have a phone in your house."

"No, sir. The power company cut it off."

"And nobody else on your block has a phone?"

"Well, sir, I suppose so."

"But you didn't go to anybody else's house to call the ambulance?"

"No, sir, I never thought of that."

"But you could tell that your husband was hurt, couldn't you?"

"Yes, sir."

"And hurt bad?"

"Yes, sir."

"So you went straight to the hospital, is that right?"

There was a pause before Jolene Biggs answered. "Well, no, sir."

"No, you didn't," confirmed Stroud. "In fact, you went somewhere else, did you not?"

"Well, I saw the 7-Eleven at Pine Street, a couple of blocks away, and I saw I needed some gas, so I pulled in."

"You stopped to get some gas?"

"Yes, sir."

"And while you were stopped, did you use the phone to call for an ambulance?"

"No, sir."

"Did you tell anybody at the store about your wounded husband? Did you ask for help?"

"No, sir."

"Didn't think of it, Mrs. Biggs?"

Jolene shrugged. "No, sir. I didn't think of it, I guess."

"So you pumped some gas and paid for it. Did you then drive to the hospital?"

"No, sir."

"No, you stayed in the store a while longer, didn't you?"

"Yes, sir."

"Why did you stay in the store?"

"Well, I was getting hungry."

"You were hungry?"

"Yes, sir."

"So you bought something to eat?"

"Yes, sir."

"Tell the jury what you bought, Jolene."

"A burrito."

"A burrito?"

"Yes, sir. A green chili burrito."

"A green chili burrito."

"Yes, sir."

"Any onions in it?"

"No, sir. I don't like onions."

"Neither do I. I assume the burrito you bought was frozen?"

"Yes, sir."

"So you had to heat it in the microwave?"

"Yes, sir."

"Did you eat the burrito?"

"Yes, sir."

"Where did you eat it?"

"In the store."

"I bet it was hot."

"Yes, sir, it was."

"Did you have to wait a bit for it to cool down?"

"Yes, sir, some."

"Do you remember how long you had to wait for the burrito to cool?"

"No, sir. Maybe a couple of minutes."

"Biting into a burrito that's too hot can really mess up your tongue, can't it?"

"Yes, sir."

"Did it fill you up, Jolene?"

"Pretty good. I didn't have no breakfast that day."

"Did you get a doughnut, too?"

She bristled at that. "No, sir. I did not get a doughnut."

"There was no time for doughnuts, was there, Jolene? Not while your husband was bleeding to death."

Jolene Biggs glared at Stroud. "No, sir."

"You had to get right to the hospital, isn't that it, Mrs. Biggs?"

"Yes, sir."

"But first came the gas."

"Yes, sir."

"Then the burrito."

"Yes, sir."

"But you passed up the doughnut."

"Yes, sir."

It was like a verbal ballet, or rather a tango, with the tall, black-frocked lawyer manhandling his disdainful partner across the floor. I thought the prosecutor or the judge would come down on Stroud for badgering the witness, but they didn't. They were too caught up in the dance.

"And forty minutes after your husband was shot, you finally made it to the hospital, didn't you?"

"Yes, sir. Something like that."

"That's almost an hour just to get across town. Didn't you know how serious his wounds were, Jolene?"

"Yes, sir, I did. I knew they was serious."

"Mrs. Biggs, did your husband ever use his baseball bat on you?"

The prosecutor thundered out an objection, but Stroud withdrew the question.

"Let's get this straight, Jolene: Your husband was shot, he was bleeding to death on the sidewalk, and you were thinking gasoline, burrito, and then hospital, in that order?"

"Yes, sir."

"But no doughnut?"

She gave Stroud a strange look that wasn't exactly anger but was a long way from grief. "No, sir," she said, "no doughnut."

"Pass the witness," said Stroud.

The prosecutor had no more questions for Jolene Biggs. Instead, he called his last witness, the county medical examiner. As he took the stand, Stroud told me to look straight at the doctor and roll my eyes every time he said something more than yes or no. The medical examiner testified woodenly about the death wounds and the agony that Lanier Biggs went through while he bled to death. As the prosecuting attorney passed the witness to him for cross-examination, Stroud whispered in my ear, "Now we get the deceased Mr. Biggs to work for us." There were gasps from the jury.

I was worried that the old man was about to call me as a witness. Instead, Stroud got the photographs of Biggs's nude, battle-scarred body accepted as evidence. He passed copies out to the jury and to the pathologist on the stand. There were gasps from the jury.

"Now, Doctor," Stroud began, "this spot here on the decedent's side—how would you describe this scar?"

The pathologist, a portly, middle-aged man with sixties sideburns and a handlebar mustache, studied the photo through thick-rimmed glasses. "Scarring of an old stellate punctate wound," he answered.

"Isn't there another name for this type of wound, Doctor, in layman's parlance?"

"Yes."

"What is that?"

"Bullet wound."

"Bullet wound?"

"Yes."

And so it went, scar by scar, from razor slash to stab wound to buckshot pattern, truncheon scar, chain marks, and handcuff tracks.

When Stroud got through cross-examining the pathologist, the prosecution rested its case. Stroud began the defense, and I received still another lesson in trial law. Stroud made no comment on any of the prosecutor's claims, no rebuttals. Instead, he merely put on witness after witness to testify to the homicidal behavior of Lanier Biggs. There were motorists who had been terrorized by the bat-wielding Biggs, bar patrons whom Lanier had put in the hospital for no discernible reason, except, perhaps, the shape of their heads. Stroud got policemen to testify to the difficulty of arresting

Biggs. A jail trustee explained on the stand how Lanier had once pulled an iron bar out of a cell door and bent it across the head of his cellmate.

The prosecutor tried to undermine the credibility of Stroud's witnesses, but he didn't have a chance. They were simply testifying to what they had seen and heard, and it was hard to shake the sort of memories that Lanier Biggs tended to leave with people. By the time Stroud was through, he had transformed Lanier Biggs from a murder victim into a nightmare.

At three-thirty, when the judge offered to postpone closing arguments until tomorrow, Stroud talked him and the prosecuting attorney into going ahead. Why the prosecution agreed was hard to figure. At that moment, Stroud owned the jury. It would have been in the prosecution's interest to let the images that Stroud had conjured up dissipate a little. But the prosecutor offered no resistance to Stroud's request. Maybe by then Stroud owned him, too, and the judge, and the court reporter, and everybody else in that big white room.

In his summation, the prosecutor did what he could: He reiterated the facts of the case, which clearly showed that Clifton Hardesty, from the safety of his pickup truck, had shot and killed an unarmed man at point-blank range. The prosecution argued that murder had been Hardesty's motive for driving to the Biggs home in the first place, and that the facts bore this out.

But I'm not sure how many of the jurors heard the prosecutor. If they were like me, they were trying to deal with the image that Gilliam Stroud, in his closing argument, had just drawn of a man so insane with violence that his own wife let him bleed to death rather than risk his recovery. Stroud invited us to put ourselves in Clifton Hardesty's place, sitting in the driveway of a homicidal maniac who had sworn to murder us for no reason and who had just ordered us to sit in our pickup, *sit right there,* while he went inside and got a gun. Which of us, looking into those hate-glazed eyes and seeing our own annihilation, would not have done as Hardesty had done? You see a rabid dog about to leap, a rattlesnake coiled to strike, you kill it.

Stroud asked the jury to acquit Clifton Hardesty on grounds of self-defense. Half an hour later, it did just that. Several of the jurors, when they filed out of the jury box, came over to congratulate Stroud. Clifton Hardesty, who had collapsed back into his chair at the announcement of the verdict, looked dazed as his children climbed over him and his wife cradled his head against her breast. The effort of keeping himself rigid throughout the trial had exhausted him.

CHAPTER 5

AS WE LEFT THE COURTROOM, Stroud made a point of shaking hands with the prosecutor.

"P.P., you've got to stop feeding me lunatics like Lanier Biggs," said Stroud. "It's no challenge."

"All I know," said P.P., in his high, thin whine, "is that it takes a lunatic to nail a lunatic. Mr. Hardesty was very lucky in his choice of lawyers."

P.P. was Paul Primrose, the district attorney for Claymore County. He was a tall, narrow-shouldered man who looked to be in his late forties. Everything about him, from his thinning hair to his high-dollar boots, was the color of dishwater, except the big chunk of turquoise in his bolo tie, which he continually readjusted with a nervous jerk of his fingers. Stroud introduced me as his new associate, late of a big firm in Houston. "Mr. Parker is a city lawyer," he said, "come to find a little peace and quiet in the country."

Primrose gave me a long and not very pleasant look, his mustache working in an odd way. He was chewing on the news that I was not a medical expert, as Stroud had implied I was in court, and that he had been suckered into keeping his questions to the pathologist tame from worry that Stroud's expert would refute his claims. It was a tough knot to digest, but he did it and, with an odd little swoop of his shoulder, offered me his hand to shake.

"I knew it," he said, winking at me. "I had a feeling you weren't a doctor. Glad to have you among us, Mr. Parker. But I don't know how much peace and quiet you'll have looking after your boss here." There was a stiffness about Primrose's manner that was off-putting. He apparently understood this and tried to make up for it by lunging a little forward when he shook hands or spoke, like a bank president trying to act as if he were at home among farmhands. The ruse only succeeded in making him seem more aloof.

"Sorry about your foot problem," Primrose said. "I can give you the name of a first-rate podiatrist here in Mule Springs."

I thanked him.

"Speaking of feet, are those new boots, P.P.?" Stroud asked. "They look like elephant skin to me. Now, how does a humble servant of the people afford to go around in elephant boots?"

"Clean living, Gill," Primrose answered. "I don't make much, but I don't spend it on liquor and whores." The DA's smile tightened a notch.

Stroud turned to me. "P.P. is as straight an arrow as you'd ever want to meet, Mr. Parker. You would do well to use him as a model of deportment."

We had reached the front door of the courthouse. Stroud offered to buy Primrose a drink, but the district attorney said he had work to do. "I'm sure Mr. Stroud will agree with me when I tell you, Mr. Parker, that even out here in God's country, evil never sleeps."

"P.P. is a Southern Baptist," Stroud explained. "A lay preacher, in fact. It's why he's such a damn good prosecutor, this being one nation under God and all."

"We would love to see you this Sunday down at the Grace Tabernacle, Mr. Parker," Primrose said.

I thanked him for the invitation, we shook hands, and he headed toward a flight of stairs.

"Self-righteous son of a bitch," Stroud muttered.

"He's really a Baptist preacher?" I asked. "With that voice?"

Stroud nodded. "The coldest-hearted bastard in the county. You'd better not be caught breaking the law around here, Mr. Parker. Not so much as a parking ticket. If Preacher Paul gets the goods on you, you'll think what happened to Christ on Calvary was a picnic. There are a lot of lawyers like Primrose out in these small towns whose pants we've pulled down so often they're dying to get a look at our drawers. That's why we hired you, son. You are here to help us keep our drawers inviolate."

By the time we reached the bottom of the courthouse steps, Molly had joined us, and the three of us headed for the car. "Son of a bitch, it's great to win," Stroud said, throwing his arm over my shoulder. "You were a great help in there, young man."

"I didn't do a damn thing except sit, Mr. Stroud," I reminded him.

"But you looked like you knew what you were doing. You have an affidavit face, Mr. Parker. That's worth a hell of a lot in front of a jury. By just doing nothing you came off better than that whore of a doctor bought by our Brother Primrose, who is up in his office right now eating his heart out, I promise you. You just sat there looking moral as a church, and we won. Sometimes that's all it takes.

"It doesn't always work, though, does it, Molly?" he continued as we approached the Lincoln. "Old Hard-dick hired us a lawyer a couple of years ago, one of those fundamentalist Baptist types, you know, with a rod up his ass and a Bible in each hand. Maybe he was proof against Satan, but he sure as hell couldn't put up with us." Stroud laughed. "Just coming to work in the morning gave him the galloping shits so bad that Wick started calling him the Brown Bomber. He's a missionary now, somewhere in Cambodia, I think."

He stopped suddenly, clutched my elbow. "You wouldn't be a Baptist, would you?"

I told him I was not a Baptist.

"Thank Christ," he said, walking on.

"Do me a favor, Mr. Stroud," I said to him. "Don't pass me off as something I'm not. Especially in front of a judge."

The old man gave me a look of sly appraisal. "Call me Gill," he said with a smile.

"Don't pass me off as something I'm not, Gill," I said.

"It was my understanding, Mr. Clayton, that you are moving to the country to transform your life, to pursue a sea change into something rich and strange. Let's assume the transformation has begun, that it began in Prosecutor Primrose's courtroom. Doesn't the fact that you're becoming something new mean that you don't quite know what you are at the moment?"

"I know I'm not a medical doctor, Gill."

"So," he said, turning to face me, "are we confronting a breach of ethics here? Did I step over the line back in that courtroom?"

The tone he had fallen into, I realized, must have been the one he had used on his students at Baylor Law. He clearly found my annoyance amusing, a fact that annoyed me even more.

"Did you actually hear me say you were a medical doctor?" he asked.

"It was the implication," I said.

The old man cackled. "Implication? I thought you were a lawyer, Mr. Parker. Or maybe you thought country lawyers only spoke mother's-milk truth? Tell me, my sandal-wearing friend, what is the first question a trial lawyer asks his client?"

I sighed. He was cueing me for a timeworn mantra taught to every first-semester Baylor Law student. "He asks, 'Are you guilty?'" I replied. "I know where you're going with this."

"And what's the second question he asks his client?"

"It's 'How do you want to plead?'"

"And what do these two questions, taken together, indicate about our legal system?" he asked.

"They mean that everybody, guilty or not, has a right to the best defense we can make."

"Regardless of truth? Regardless of justice?" Stroud asked with a smile, giving the words *truth* and *justice* the slightest twist.

"Just don't pass me off in any discipline in which I could not actually earn my keep," I said. "Let's leave it at that."

He laughed again, and offered me his hand to shake. "I promise to consult you the next time your proficiencies come up in conversation."

"What is this bromohydrosis that I have such a bad case of, anyway?" I asked.

"Foot odor," he replied.

Stroud's limp was becoming more pronounced, and as we reached the car he leaned on me a little more solidly. He was tired. Winning was hard work.

By the time we turned onto Highway 69 and headed for Jenks, he had begun to snore in the backseat. This time Molly drove, and we rolled grandly in Stroud's barge of a car through the late-afternoon haze that the heat had thrown over the pastures and farmlands. I peppered Molly with questions about the firm, about Stroud, and about the missing Hardwick Chandler. She gave each question the same grave consideration and chose her words with care.

"We usually operate in what I call medium chaos," she said. "That's different from total chaos, but not much."

"Tell me about the boss, Molly."

"I think it's best if you form your own conclusions," she replied. "You'll meet him soon enough. But you may have to meet him on the run."

We reached Jenks about six o'clock. The downtown area's single street was deserted but for my car. Molly pulled the Lincoln up beside the Austin Healey. "Thank you for your help today, Mr. Parker," she said. "I'm sorry we had to pitch you right in like we did."

"And me with a killer case of bromohydrosis."

"I hope you find your shoes," she said.

There was a perpetual sadness about Molly Tunstall's eyes, small and blue, and a forlorn strength in the set of her chin. I had already decided that she was my idea of a pioneer woman: She had been worn down to essentials, all her edges shaped by strong winds. The ruddy tinge to her skin and her high cheekbones made me wonder if there was some Indian blood in her.

Molly was planning to drive Stroud out to his farmhouse and asked if I would follow her in my car so that I could drive her back to town. I followed the Lincoln a couple of miles past the city limits to a dirt road that led, in three more miles, into the yard of an old farmhouse standing in a grove of live oak trees beside a stock tank. It was a big two-story frame house with a sagging porch and a carport, under which sat a battered Winnebago van and a tractor that seemed to have turned completely into rust. To one side of the carport was a sleek, new sky-blue Mercedes convertible, looking as out of place as a flying saucer amid the decay. The house and the shabby barn behind it could not have been painted anytime this century. There was an odor of rotting hay about the place.

A lone cow watched from behind a barbed-wire fence as Molly and I opened the back door of the Lincoln to help Stroud out of the car. It was harder than it should have been. While lying in the Lincoln's backseat on his way home, Stroud had been drinking. As I yanked him upright by the shoulders, he waved a silver and leather boot flask at me.

"Have a drink, my boy," he said. "You've earned it."

Stroud was in worse shape than he had been in at the jail that morning. It was all we could do to get him on his feet and start him toward the house, with his arms over our shoulders. He was breathing hard, and when we reached the stairs, he started to wheeze. The wheezing got worse—great, tortured gasps that didn't seem to find any air—until he produced from a coat pocket an aerosol inhaler, which he jammed into his mouth and triggered. The medicine revived him a little, and he leveled his heavy eyebrows at me.

"What's your name?" he asked.

"This is Mr. Parker," Molly told him as we half pulled, half pushed him up the steps. "He's a member of our firm now, Mr. Stroud. He just helped you win the Hardesty case, remember?"

"That's right," he said. "The lawyer with the bad feet!" He laughed and pulled free of our grasp, then froze, his gaze fixed on the blue Mercedes beside the dilapidated carport.

"She's here," he said. "I thought she'd be coming tomorrow."

"Today *is* tomorrow," Molly told him.

Stroud tiptoed to the window and peeked inside his house, then turned, holding to the wall for support, and stared at me. "Mr. Parker," he asked, "can you tell that I have been tippling?"

"It's pretty obvious."

He turned back to the window. "She's going to have my ass," he murmured.

"The horse isn't in the barn," Molly said. "She's out riding."

"Mr. Parker," Stroud said, "would you try that doorknob?"

I turned the knob. The door was not locked.

"Now would you go inside and see if there is anyone in the house?"

"She's out riding, Mr. Stroud," Molly said again.

"That horse can get out of the barn by himself," Stroud snapped. He was still peering through the window. "Go on, Mr. Parker."

I stepped into the doorway. "Who am I looking for?" I asked.

"You'll know when you see her," said Stroud.

"What do I say if I find her?" I asked.

"Say something to get her to go out the back door," Stroud urged. "Then I'll come in the front."

I walked into a large, gloomy room full of overstuffed furniture. There were no lights on in the house. The late-afternoon sun shone through a window whose drapes were lying in a heap beneath the sill.

"Call to her!" Stroud whispered.

"What's her name?" I replied.

"Sally."

I called. There was no answer. I walked through the front room, past a parlor outfitted in cheap vinyl sofa and chairs, through a dining room empty of furniture but littered with piles of books. Down a hallway was a kitchen unmodernized since the original inhabitants, with an iron pump poised above a dusty sink. Layers of shadow covered layers of dust. Despite the moaning of the wind about the roof, the air inside the place seemed shocked into stillness by a crushing sense of emptiness. It was a home for ghosts.

I walked back to the front room. "Nobody here," I said.

"Go upstairs!" Stroud hissed from the doorway.

"Mr. Stroud, this is stupid," I said, shaking my head and staring at the floor. I was about to explain that I had reached my limit of foolishness for the day, and that if he did not want this Sally-whoever to catch him drunk, then he'd better just not drink, when I felt a wind rush past me, caught a faint whiff of Garden Mist air freshener, and turned to see Gilliam Stroud loping like a crazed black bear up the stairway, his wrecked lungs shrieking at each step. He disappeared down a hallway, and I heard a door slam.

CHAPTER 6

————— •• ———◄•►——— •• —————

ON THE WAY BACK into town I quizzed Molly about the scene we had just witnessed. She told me the girl's full name: Sally Dean. Otherwise, she was not forthcoming.

"Well, what's the story, Molly? Is she his wife?"

"No."

"Girlfriend?"

"No."

"They don't live together?"

"No."

"She just shows up and rides his horse from time to time?"

"It's her horse. She just stables it at the farmhouse."

"Is she some sort of nurse?"

"That's not her job," Molly said.

"Then why was Stroud so scared that she'd catch him drunk?" I asked.

Molly thought for a moment before answering. "I guess you could say that she kind of nurses Mr. Stroud. He kind of looks at her as a daughter."

"Is that a bad thing?" I asked, because her tone suggested that maybe it was. Molly Tunstall struck me as the kind of person who didn't like to say anything bad about someone else, but also as a person who would never lie. And there was something about Sally Dean that she didn't want to say.

"All I know is Mr. Stroud hasn't come to the end of his drinking days. Until he does, nobody can help him."

"And Sally Dean is trying to help him?"

Molly shrugged. "Sally is a sweet girl. She's just got a long way to go." I could not get her to elaborate.

When we reached Main Street, I dropped Molly off in front of the law office.

"You know how to get to your house?" she asked me. One of the perks of the job was that I was to be given the use of a house, free of charge, for the first year of my stay, with an option to buy at the end of the year.

I recited the directions that Hardwick Chandler had given me over the phone.

"That ought to get you there," she said. She reached into the briefcase, which she was still carrying, and handed me a small envelope. "Here are the keys. The movers brought your boxes yesterday. They're stacked in the house."

"Thanks, Molly," I said. "Day one has been some day."

"A good day," she replied.

"Do you think it was the shoes?" I asked. "Maybe they're lucky. I could always wear them when we go to trial."

She smiled. "There's no such thing as luck. Just grace, and the work you do."

"Well," I said, shifting the car into gear, "we'll hit it for real tomorrow."

"Oh," Molly said. She reached back into the briefcase, then handed me a thick manila file with the name *Rasmussen* scrawled across it. "Speaking of hitting it for real, do you think you could look this case over before tomorrow? Mr. Chandler wants to talk to you about it as soon as possible. You might keep your lucky flip-flops on while you read," she added.

"Are we in trouble on this one?" I asked.

"I think so," she said. "Just about anything to do with Bevo Rasmussen is trouble."

"Bevo?"

"That's his name." I took the file from her, promising to read it that evening, and drove off to find my house.

I failed. After ten minutes of crisscrossing the same set of streets half a dozen times, I pulled over to the curb in a neighborhood of giant oak trees and tiny houses built of planks and shingles, shifted out of gear, and put on the brake. I was lost, but it was okay. I had expected to get lost. It wouldn't have mattered if I had tattooed Hardwick Chandler's instructions to my inner eyelid, I would still not have been able to find the house. I was born without a sense of direction. The gene for finding places does not reside in my DNA chain.

The wind had died away, and the early evening was still deadeningly hot. I got out of the car, unsnapped the Austin Healey's convertible top, pulled it down, took off my suit coat, and climbed back in. I would sit here by the side of the road, whistling for a breeze, until the voice inside me railing at my navigational incompetence—the usual voice, my oldest companion—died down, as it would eventually do. And then I would drive off and try again. As long as I could remember, this had been my pattern. I began silently repeating to myself the mantra that I learned to say in such moments: Enough wrong turns will get you where you're going. It was the way I had arrived in Jenks that morning. It was the way I had gotten to Houston, years ago. It was how I had found my way into and out of my marriage and my career as a tax lawyer. And I knew that it would be the way I would find my house.

"Lost?" said a voice beside me. I turned, and my nose bumped against the damp muzzle of a big gray horse standing beside the car. I was startled—for an instant I had the notion that the horse itself had addressed me—and then I heard deep laughter, woman's laughter, from the rider. "Sorry about Ed's manners," she said. "He likes to sneak up on people when he gets the chance."

"He does a fine job," I replied, squinting up past the horse's head. In the glare of the dying sun all I could see was a slender silhouette.

"Ms. Dean?" I said.

"Mr. Parker," she replied. "It's good to meet you. The boys have been expecting you."

"The boys?"

"Wick and Gill. Chandler and Stroud. The pillars of our legal community. So tell me, are you looking for your new house, or are you casing the town?"

"I'm just lost."

"What do you say, Ed," she said to her mount, "shall we help get the city boy home?"

I idled the Austin Healey slowly along beside her as she turned the horse into the neighborhood from which I had just emerged. Sally Dean was wearing jeans and a red-and-white checked shirt tied at the waist. A country girl out for a ride.

"I suppose little towns can be confusing to urbanites," she said. "No freeway exit signs to help you find your street." Her voice had a sardonic edge to it, a kind of challenge, but what kind, I couldn't tell. "I'm sure you'll enjoy the leisurely pace."

"I don't know," I said. "Day one has been anything but leisurely."

"You sat in on the Hardesty trial," she said. "I heard. Gill must have put on a real show."

"He sure did."

"Damn," Sally Dean said. "I lose again."

"You and Stroud make bets on his trials?" I asked.

"We have ever since I worked for the firm."

This was something Molly Tunstall hadn't told me. "You were an associate of the firm?"

She smiled down at me. "I was a gofer. I got things for them. But I learned a lot from them, too."

Ed's back end had come even with my seat, and I took a flick from the big horse's tail in my face. It made my left eye sting.

"What breed of horse is Ed?" I asked, rubbing horse dust out of my eye.

"Ed's an Appaloosa," she replied. "Do you know anything about horses, Mr. Parker?"

"Not much," I said, looking up at Ed's glistening gray bulk. "Aren't Appaloosas supposed to be spotted?"

"Ed didn't spot," she explained. "If he had spotted, he'd have been a show horse, and he wouldn't be out here with us today. Also his name would have been something else: Mama's Little Goldmine or The Sheik of the Seven Veils."

"I take it spots make an Appaloosa more valuable."

"To some people," she said. "But Ed does okay without his spots, don't you think?"

"So long as he finds my house," I replied.

We made an odd little parade, a girl on horseback leading a broken-down sports car, but the house, it turned out, was only two blocks away. I had passed it on my search.

"*Voilà*," said Sally Dean when we got there.

On the phone two days earlier Hardwick Chandler had spoken proudly about the housing part of the job package, reminding me how unusual it was for a law firm to provide its new lawyers with free lodgings. It was a two-story frame house, recently painted an agreeable shade of green, with yards in both the front and back, a couple of huge, shady pecans, and a screened-in porch running along the side of the house next to the driveway. Not bad.

I climbed out of the car, thanked Sally Dean for helping me find the place, and invited her inside for a drink of water.

"No, thanks," she said, "but Ed could use something." She threw a leg over her horse and slid off. She was riding bareback. "He likes the heat, but it's been a little hotter this afternoon than he expected."

There was a garden hose coiled under a faucet at the side of the house. "Do you mind?" Sally asked, handing me the reins. I took them and she went to the faucet and uncoiled the hose. When she turned on the water, the horse came over to her—leading me— and lapped at the nozzle. When the horse finished drinking, Sally spritzed water over his back. Ed put his head down as the water ran over him. We were enveloped in the acrid odor of wet horse.

"Gill told me a little about you," she said. "You're a tax lawyer?"

"I *was* a tax lawyer," I corrected her.

"In a big Houston firm. Then you burned out, and your wife bailed."

"Stroud's got the facts out of order," I said, "but that's about right." I was not pleased that my new boss was entertaining folks with my life story.

"So now you're going to be a jack-of-all-trades country lawyer?"

"I'll be whatever the firm needs me to be, Ms. Dean," I said.

She laughed. "You may be surprised to find out just what all that is. Sorry about your feet, by the way. Bromohydrosis? I'll get you the name of a good podiatrist."

"So you heard about that, too," I said.

"A lawyer in Armani and beach sandals? That sort of news travels fast."

"There's nothing wrong with my feet," I said, dangling a sandal off the tips of my toes, and I explained the real reason behind my sartorial courtroom gaffe.

"Nice socks," she said.

"What about you?" I asked. "You say you used to work for the firm. What do you do now?"

"I'm the administrative coordinator for the Northeast Texas judicial district," she said, and watched for my reaction.

"Wow," I said, impressed. "That's quite a step up for a former office gofer."

"Yes," she replied, "it is."

The district coordinator, usually called the D.C., helps to arrange schedules for all the judges who sit in a particular district. When a sitting judge wants to go on vacation or simply does not want not to hear a particular case, usually for political reasons, it is up to the D.C. to find a replacement judge. The coordinator keeps a list of available visiting judges, most of whom have either retired from the bench or been voted out of office. From this list the coordinator picks replacement judges.

It would not be a strenuous job, especially in a district as sparsely populated as the one in which Jenks sat, but it would be an important one. By being able to pick and choose visiting judges in the district, Sally Dean, onetime office assistant for Chandler and Stroud, had a major say in how business got conducted at the courthouses in the district.

"Where I'm from, there's usually pretty stiff competition for the coordinator's job," I said.

"It's the same here," she said. "And yet I got the job after working with Chandler and Stroud for only six months." She shook her head and looked at me quizzically. "Now, how ever did a law firm lackey rise to such heights so quickly?"

"Perhaps she was in the right place at the right time?" I suggested.

She smiled. "I suppose that's it. Or maybe she slept her way into the job?"

"I suppose we'll never know," I said. Whatever sort of chip

this girl had on her shoulder, I found that I really didn't want to knock it off. Not tonight, anyway. "So what's the administrative coordinator for the Northeast Texas judicial district doing riding the range on a steamy August evening?" I asked.

"Right now she's giving her horse a bath," she replied.

I watched the big horse let himself be doused, but mostly I watched Sally Dean. She was tall and slim with richly tanned skin, incandescent now with a slight sheen of water from the hose. There was a kind of dark light about her that made it hard not to stare. In a moment I determined that at least part of my fascination came from a slight asymmetry in her face: her eyes, deep green and widely spaced, were not quite level above the short thin bridge of her nose, and her smile tended to pull her mouth slightly to one side, as if she were savoring some paradox that had escaped you. There was an amused light in her eyes that flickered from a depth, like heat lightning. Her black hair, falling in curls to her shoulders, glistened. I made her out to be twenty-five, maybe twenty-six years old. All in all, not your run-of-the-mill judicial district coordinator.

"Some horses don't like this," she said as she played the water over the horse's flanks. "Ed loves it." She turned the hose straight up so that the spray flowered for a moment over her. "Oh," she said as the water hit her, "I can see why." She smiled at me. "How about it, Mr. Parker? You look like you could use a good spray." Before I could answer, she flicked her wrist, and icy pinpricks scattered across my face and shoulders.

"Hey!" I gasped. I grabbed her hand to stop her from spraying me again.

"Don't like it? It's spring water, Mr. Parker. Something you can't get in Houston, except out of plastic bottles with designer labels." There was that smile again, and that irritating little curl in her voice.

"I take it you have something against Houston," I said, letting go of her hand in order to rub water out of my eyes.

Sally turned off the faucet and rewound the hose. "I'm sorry," she said. "I don't get a chance to flirt with city boys very often."

I had not been flirted with in a long time, and it was having an effect. Sally came close to me, and a new scent cut through the odor of damp dirt that came from Ed. This one had something of the tropics in it, mingled with the smell of rain just before it falls.

She took the reins out of my hand. "How about a boost?" she asked. I cupped my hands and she stepped into them, lifting herself into place on the horse's back. She goosed Ed with her heels, and the big horse lumbered slowly off toward the street. I walked beside her.

"Call me Sally, by the way," she said, "unless it's business. Then Ms. Dean is fine."

"Do you think we'll be having business dealings?" I asked.

"There are lots of different kinds of business out here in the country." She looked down at me and winked. "You'll do all right, Clay."

"I seem to be getting along with Ed here," I said.

"That doesn't mean anything. Ed's a rotten judge of character. But I think the boys may have picked right this time."

"This time?" I said. "What do you mean, this time?" But Ed had increased his speed, and horse and rider were leaving me behind.

"Be patient with the boys," she called over her shoulder. "Just don't judge them by their spots."

"Or lack of," I said to myself as the big horse plodded down the street.

I went inside my new house and found it furnished in a mongrel sort of way, odd pieces throughout, as if from many different homes. But that was okay. My boxes from Houston had arrived and were stacked neatly in the living room. The three window units in the house—bedroom, living room, kitchen—weren't running, and the air was hot and thick and bitter with the smell of ancient cigarette smoke. I switched on all of the air conditioners and changed into a T-shirt and shorts, then went out to the car to get the file that Molly Tunstall had given me in the office, the Rasmussen file. Some perspicacious and benevolent individual—Hardwick Chandler, perhaps—had stocked the liquor cabinet in the living room. I poured myself a good-sized bourbon and, sitting at the kitchen table, opened the file, grateful to have something to do on this first night of my new life.

Right on top I found a letter from Rasmussen to Stroud, outlining the case. Some horses that Bevo Rasmussen owned had died in a fire started by lightning, and Rasmussen's insurance carrier was refusing to pay off on his claim. It was to be a big payoff, over a million dollars. Apparently, these Appaloosas had spots.

Rasmussen's letter, full of typos, painted a miserable picture: dreams dashed, a business ruined, a reputation at stake. Rasmussen had to have the insurance money as fast as possible. "The wolves are at the door, Mr. Stroud," he wrote. "You are the only man who can get me out of this mess." I noted that the letter had been written over a year ago. How desperate was Rasmussen now? Surely in all that time the wolves had gotten in and carried off the baby. I would have to read further into the file to find out what had happened. But I could feel my concentration slipping away, and in a minute I had to get up and move around.

I should have been exhausted after the day I'd had, but I wasn't. What I needed was something to do, something other than wade through the misery of the Rasmussen file. I had noticed a lawn mower in the garage. The lawn could use a trim. That's what I would do, mow my new yard as the last of the evening sun died away. Backyard as well as front. Who knows, maybe I would keep going after the sun went down, edging, pruning the shade trees, painting the trim in the dark.

I finished my bourbon and poured myself another, raising it in a toast to Hardwick Chandler, whose bourbon I was probably drinking. May he be a reasonable man, when he finally showed himself. I drained the glass—one toast per glass, a law school tradition—then poured another and toasted his partner, Gilliam Stroud, a badly wrecked man but an amazing lawyer, still swinging that trestle. I tried to picture myself at Stroud's age, both barrels shot, a giant, ruined condor of a man. I wouldn't make it all the way to condor. I didn't have the height or the weight. Barn owl, maybe.

I toasted Bevo Rasmussen, the poor son of a bitch, and his sea of troubles, against which Gilliam Stroud and Hardwick Chandler—and now I—had taken arms. Molly Tunstall said the case was trouble. Well, all right. Let's see what kind of trouble a body can get into in the country.

My sixth, seventh, and eighth toasts went to Sally Dean, with her beautiful skin and her ironic smile. What the hell had she meant, "They picked right *this time*"? How many other times had there been, how many other lawyers had "the boys" hired before me, and why hadn't any of them worked out? How often did Chandler or Stroud ask their new associates to do—or be—something they weren't? I could tell from our little chat about ethics in the Mule Springs parking lot that Stroud and I had different ideas about where the lawyer on the case draws the line. Or did we?

My mind was getting fuzzy from the bourbon. I toasted Stroud again, then toasted the ethics of my profession. The drone of the air conditioners filled the cooling house.

CHAPTER 7

DURING THE NIGHT the locusts found a way into my brain, and when I woke up shortly after dawn, they were packed under my skull, shrieking like a chainsaw massacre. Five aspirin and a freezing shower shook only a few of them out. I put on a suit I found hanging in a wardrobe box and went down to the Dairy Queen, where a tiny waitress named Lu-Anne smiled as she took my order and asked me how I was doing. I thought of telling her, really telling her, then remembered that this was my town now, and Lu-Anne, like everybody else, was a potential client. Young as she was, it occurred to me that, this being the country, Lu-Anne might well be working on her third marriage to her third snuff-dipping, longhaired, out-of-work truck mechanic husband and might need my help to get out of this union, too, at any minute. It doesn't pay to alienate potential clients.

After finishing the sausage-and-biscuit sandwich that Lu-Anne brought me, I drove to the office to meet Hardwick Chandler. He would have to fill me in on the Rasmussen case. I had not finished working through the file.

When I got to the office Chandler wasn't there. Molly Tunstall had not heard from him. Stroud wasn't in, either, but would be

soon, she said. This was my second visit to the only law office on the
business street of Jenks, and I had yet to see another lawyer in it.

"What goes on, Molly?" I asked. "I mean, these guys have
clients, don't they? They do practice law?"

"Mr. Chandler says he runs a nick-of-time law firm," Molly
replied. "Everything gets done that has to get done, but only in the
nick of time."

"By the seat of the pants?" I suggested.

"That's another way to say it, I suppose."

"What about the Rasmussen case?" I asked. "Are we going to
be in the nick of time on that one?"

The color in the planes of her face darkened. "I don't know
about that one. Maybe you can tell us."

I went back to my new office, the near-empty one, a windowless
room with cream-colored stucco walls, a desk, three chairs, and,
hanging on a wall, a copy of the famous black-and-white photograph of Clarence Darrow and William Jennings Bryan, sitting
next to each other during the Scopes trial. Bryan was squinting off
in the distance, as if trying to imagine what a wonderful day he
would have been having if only Darrow weren't there. On the desk
sat a phone, an intercom, and a wire in-basket full of files. I laid
the Rasmussen file next to the in-basket, sat down in the desk
chair, and swiveled back and forth for a moment. It was a livable
office, spare and quiet except for the soft hum of the building's
air conditioner.

Molly brought me a cup of coffee, and as I sipped it I leafed
through the files in the in-basket, confirming to myself that they
were the sorts of things I had expected to find in my new job:
wills, probate, minor civil cases, minor criminal cases, and divorce
and child custody suits. Abandoning the files in the in-basket, I
opened the Rasmussen file. There were a number of documents in
it that I had not gotten to the night before, copies of bills of sale for

the horses, insurance policies, letters to and from creditors, pleas for help written to Stroud. I read for forty minutes. All together, the documents told the story of a lawsuit gone horribly wrong.

Thirteen months earlier, Bevo Rasmussen had bought nine quarter horses from one Nyman Scales, a breeder in Tyler. The horses cost Rasmussen $978,000. He had borrowed a quarter of that money from the Farmer's Branch Bank of Tyler and another quarter from Nyman Scales, the seller. The rest of the money, $500,000, Rasmussen had put up himself. He pastured the horses in a rented section of land out in Claymore County, where he had built a barn, and he bought insurance policies on the horses that totaled just over a million dollars.

A month later, the barn on the rental property where the horses were stabled burned down in a lightning storm, and all nine horses were killed. This sort of accident was covered in the insurance policy, but when Bevo filed his claim, the carrier refused to pay off. Bevo retained Gilliam Stroud to file suit against the insurance carrier, but the carrier jumped in ahead of Stroud, filing its own action for a declaratory judgment, claiming that the horses had been intentionally killed by Mr. Rasmussen, who was, therefore, a fraud and a felon. If the carrier won its action, Rasmussen would not collect a cent. Worse, if anybody over in the district attorney's office was watching, our client would most assuredly be prosecuted for fraud, arson, and animal cruelty.

That was not the end of Mr. Rasmussen's troubles. Three months after the carrier filed its claim against him, the Farmer's Branch Bank of Tyler sued him to recover the $240,000 it had loaned him on the original purchase. About the only thing going for Mr. Rasmussen was that Nyman Scales, his other major creditor in the horse deal, had not sued him. Yet.

I had heard of the insurance carrier before, an Italian outfit based in Naples named Associazione Stromboli, one of the biggest insurers of high-dollar horses in the world. Savage, Carlock, and Gannon, my old law firm in Houston, had a half-dozen lawyers who specialized in horse insurance, horses being a not-uncommon phenomenon in Texas. One of these lawyers, Rita Humphrey, had an office on my floor. Occasionally, over lunch, Rita and I compared cases in our respective bailiwicks, and I remembered her mentioning Stromboli. I kidded her about suing a Disney cartoon villain— Stromboli being the name of the evil carnival owner in *Pinocchio*, of course, who threatened to chop up the little wooden boy with an axe. She reminded me that Stromboli was also a volcanic island off the Italian coast, as well as a kind of Italian meat pie. Stromboli, she explained, was all things to all people.

Actually, Associazione Stromboli was not a single company, but a Lloyd's-type syndicate made up of several insurance companies that shared both the premiums and the liability of big-money policies. Say a horse dealer in Amarillo wanted to insure his new thoroughbred with Stromboli for five hundred thousand dollars. Stromboli would write him a policy, divvying it up among different member companies of the syndicate, who agreed to assume a certain percentage of the liability in return for a proportionate amount of the premium paid by the dealer. The volume of business such a syndicate did was staggering, hundreds of millions of dollars a year, much of it from horse breeders and dealers in the American Southwest.

Since there are about as many types of fraud involving horse breeders as there are breeds of horses, Stromboli often found itself in court, sitting opposite lawyers like Rita Humphrey, who was no slouch. This meant that counsel representing Associazione Stromboli had to be mean. The lawyers Stromboli used most often in their Southwest cases came from the insurance wing of Slaven, Wortmann, Applegate, and Tice, a Houston firm. I knew about them. The SWAT team, they were called. There was nobody meaner. When I found the plaintiff's original petition in the Bevo Rasmussen file,

I crossed my fingers and turned immediately to the end of the pleading to find out who had filed it. The lawyer was someone named Warren Jacobs, and under his name was listed the name of the firm he worked for. Slaven, Wortmann, Applegate, and Tice. Sure enough, we were up against SWAT.

At the bottom of the documents in the Rasmussen file I came to the set of interrogatories SWAT had sent us, all ninety pages of them. They were pretty much what I expected, thorough and efficient. I could not find a copy of Stroud's answers, and I called Molly Tunstall on the intercom to ask her where they were.

"I don't believe Mr. Stroud sent any answers," she said.

"No, Molly," I replied, "these are the interrogatories."

"Yes, sir. I know what interrogatories are."

"Well, then, you know that Stroud *had* to have answered them. I need to see his answers."

Molly appeared in my doorway. "Mr. Parker, I don't believe Mr. Stroud answered the interrogatories."

I sat stunned, staring at Molly Tunstall, who looked sadly back at me. "Molly, that's not possible. It *can't* be."

Interrogatories are what keep the average lawsuit from lasting until the end of time. Each side sends the other a set of questions that have to be answered, vital questions. The answers reveal who your witnesses are going to be and what physical evidence you plan to introduce. Interrogatories illuminate the contours of the case. If both sides handle their interrogatories well, asking and answering questions skillfully, then there will be no surprises in court, only arguments based on information that both sides hold in common and use to their best advantage.

By Texas law, interrogatories must be answered within thirty days of receipt. If in that time you fail to respond to the other side's questions, you cannot during the trial introduce a single piece of evidence or ask a single question contemplated by the interrogatories. SWAT's interrogatories had been sent to Stroud ten months ago.

"Molly, if he hasn't answered the interrogatories, he can't put on a case."

"Yes, sir."

"Jesus, Molly. He's completely cooked."

The enormity of Stroud's dereliction dawned on me fully. I understood now what Molly had meant when she told me the Rasmussen case might mean trouble. She had been dealing in heroic understatement. We were dead in the water, deaf, dumb, and blind, unable to put on even the semblance of a defense. And what was worse, it was our fault. How in hell could Stroud have failed to get the answers to the interrogatories back? How could a man who was so deadly in the courtroom be such a screwup out of it?

"Get him on the phone, Molly," I said.

Molly flushed a deep red. "Mr. Stroud doesn't like to be disturbed out at the farm."

"I don't give a damn about Mr. Stroud's likes and dislikes. Get him on the phone." There was just a chance that the old man had scribbled his answers out at his farm and mailed them from there. There was a chance that rats had gotten into the file I had in my hand and eaten our copy of Stroud's response. Or maybe Stroud had sent the answers by smoke signal from the barnyard. Whatever he had done, or not done, I wanted to hear it from his own withered lips. And I wanted to do a little yelling. I started by yelling after Molly as she disappeared down the hallway:

"And where the hell is Hardwick Chandler?"

Stroud was responsible for the Rasmussen fiasco, all right, but Chandler came in for a giant share of the blame, too. The head of the firm should have been watching his partner's back. What sort of man would leave his practice, even for a day, in the hands of a senile, debauched derelict like Stroud? What did Chandler's sloppy business practices say about his sense of responsibility to his clients? I looked at the basket full of documents on my desk and wondered how many other cases I would discover that had been as terribly mismanaged as the Rasmussen case. Questions flooded my mind, questions I should have asked Hardwick Chandler long before I ever agreed to take the job. A voice in the back of my mind whispered: Too late, too late.

What timing! I had gone to work in a dysfunctional law firm just in time to watch it get hooted out of the Claymore County courthouse for simple stupidity. No doubt we would be slapped with a whopping malpractice lawsuit by Bevo Rasmussen, who would most likely be sent to jail the minute we lost the case. I thumbed through the file on my desk, wondering if Bevo Rasmussen knew that he was already twisting in the breeze. If he didn't, it wouldn't be long now. According to the file, we had a court date for *Associazione Stromboli v. Bevo Rasmussen* in Mule Springs in eight days. Molly Tunstall's anxiety over the Rasmussen case was justified. We weren't going to make the nick of time on this one.

"It don't look good, does it?"

A scrawny, longhaired little man was sitting in the client's chair across from me, smiling like a redneck leprechaun. Several teeth in his mouth were gold, and in one I caught the flash of a tiny diamond.

CHAPTER 8

THE LITTLE MAN might have been thirty or fifty. He wore a suit of shiny gray silk, with a dark shirt, white tie, and black Italian loafers. He would have looked like an extra in a *Godfather* flick— the guy playing the corpse, given the pallor of his skin and the wrinkles in his suit—except that his hair was out of character. Carrot-colored, it fell back from a receding hairline and reached his skinny shoulders in lank, unwashed locks. The hair and the two days' growth of stubble on his cheeks gave him away as a Texas kicker, a guy more at home in jeans, T-shirt, and running shoes than in Continental finery. He might as well have been wearing a bill cap with his Italian suit.

He reached over the desk and offered me his hand. Tattooed on the back of it was the blue-green tail of a reptile whose body must have been slithering up his arm underneath the shiny sleeve. He smiled at me, skin whitening as it tightened over a cheekbone that, some time past, had been badly broken.

"I'm Bevo Rasmussen," the little man said. "I've been wanting to meet you." I shook his hand and sensed something awry with the motion of his arm, like a lever with a bent connecting rod.

"My pleasure," I said.

"I understand you're a Houston man," said Rasmussen, crossing his legs. I caught a flash of metal from under his pants cuff. He had a razor in his sock! "Houston's a fine town. Wouldn't happen to know a judge down there name of Nebold, would you? A federal judge?"

I said I was not familiar with the name.

"Judge Nebold is a good man," Rasmussen said, smoothing the whiskers on either side of his mouth with a lazy gesture of his hand. "He has looked after one or two little affairs of mine in the past."

I could not imagine anything a federal judge might do for the shabby little buccaneer sitting in front of me except to pass sentence on him. Molly Tunstall had suggested that I would not like Bevo Rasmussen, and she was right. I found him ridiculous and repulsive. And I felt a little guilty about my reaction. He was, after all, my firm's client. *My* client.

Rasmussen held his hand up and flexed it so that the dragon's tail tattooed on the back of it writhed. "You got a good handshake," he said. "Strong. I can tell things about a man by his handshake." There was a pause, in which I was supposed to ask what he could tell about me.

"I see," I replied.

"I can tell you're a man to be counted on, Counselor. I can tell we're going to be friends."

"I hope so."

"Mind if I smoke?" he asked, pulling a pack of cigarettes out of a jacket pocket.

"Sorry," I said, "there's no smoking in the office."

"That's all right, that's all right," he said, pocketing the cigarettes. "It's not going to ruin a budding friendship. Say, tell you what. I'm not just a client, Mr. Parker. I'm the welcome wagon." He set a bottle of Jack Daniel's on the desk between us. "Cheers to your new job with Chandler and Stroud. I don't know if you're aware of the fact, sir, but Claymore County is dry. It's twenty-two miles round-trip to the nearest liquor store, which happens to be run by an associate of mine. You wouldn't happen to know where we might find some glasses, do you? We could toast your new job. You do drink, don't you?"

"I do drink, and I appreciate the welcome, Mr. Rasmussen, but it's a bit too early in the day for me to start."

"Call me Bevo."

"Let's forgo the whiskey, Bevo."

"Well, then, here's something you might like to try," he said, reaching into his inside coat pocket and bringing out a slim plastic package, which he tossed on the desk. Inside the package were shiny black patches of what I took at first to be boiled tree bark.

"Jerky?" I said.

"It's another one of my bidniss interests. That's genuine emu jerky. You know, the big African birds? That's the most nutritious food in the world. Bursting with protein. Mark my words, that little package is going to make some people around here rich. Do you like jerky, Mr. Parker?"

I hadn't eaten jerky since I was thirteen or fourteen, but I remembered liking it then. "As a matter of fact, I do," I told him. "Thanks."

The little man slapped a scrap of paper on the desktop. "My final gift of the morning," he said. On the paper was scribbled a name and a phone number.

"Nevah June Balch?" I read.

"She's expecting your call. Best herbalist in three counties," he said.

"Herbalist?"

He leaned forward and whispered, "For your foot problem. That bromohydroxy business. She'll clear that right up. Don't worry about the fee. It's taken care of."

I felt myself coloring. "Thanks, Mr. Rasmussen, but my feet are fine."

"Sure they are! And they'll be even better when Nevah June gets through with them. Trust me on this. You'll like her. She's a favorite of Mr. Hardwick Chandler's, too. She makes this salve helps him with his dandruff. Speaking of Mr. Chandler, I ain't seen his jolly face around the office this afternoon."

"No, Mr. Chandler isn't here," I said.

"Nor is Mr. Stroud, am I right?" he asked.

"Not at the moment."

"But you're here, ain't you," he said, smiling as if he had just proven a point. "You're here holding down the fort."

It seemed I had passed some sort of test. He sighed deeply. "You might not know it to look at me, Mr. Parker, but it's been hand to mouth for me lately. Hand to mouth. A man who's been wronged like me, a responsible man, a man of the community such as I am, it just plays fast and loose with his sense of purpose. Know what I mean? I mean, what's it all for if it can all be taken away from you quick as a bullet? What has the American dream come to?"

There was an oily confidentiality in his tone that made my hands feel clammy.

"Let's talk about my suit," he said. For a moment, I thought he meant the lumpy ensemble he was wearing, which was coming unstitched at the shoulder. "Unless I miss my guess, that's my file right there."

The *law*suit—he was talking about the case concerning his dead quarter horses.

"So tell me, what do you think my chances are?"

"Mr. Rasmussen, I have just begun to examine the file. I'll be happy to discuss your case with you after I have become thoroughly acquainted with it."

"Come on, Mr. Parker," Rasmussen insisted, "give me your gut feeling, right now. I'm a man who believes in gut feelings."

I told him that I didn't have a gut feeling yet, but that I would share it with him when it came to me.

In other words, I lied to him. My gut had been shouting at me for a good five minutes before Rasmussen appeared in my office. My gut told me we were going to be slaughtered in court, that he would never see any of his money, and that he would most likely be arrested and charged with burning his own horses. But I didn't tell him any of that, partly because I hoped against hope that I was wrong, but partly because I didn't want to see his reaction. Bevo Rasmussen was a weird, pathetic little man, but there was something else about him that was past pathetic. I didn't know exactly what it was, some sort of look in his eyes, perhaps. But it was disturbing. I wasn't exactly afraid of him. I just wanted him out of my office as quickly as possible.

"Mr. Parker." It was Molly's voice on the intercom. "I can't get Mr. Stroud on the phone. He isn't answering at home."

"All right, Molly," I said into the machine.

"Ho ho," said Bevo Rasmussen with an ugly leer. "So he's coming in, is he? I wouldn't be surprised if Sally Dean hadn't been wringing him out fit to die."

"What are you talking about?" I asked.

"Haven't you met Sally Dean?" he replied. "Never mind, you will." He shook his head and made a grunting noise. "Finest piece of tenderloin in the county, would you believe it? She drives all the way down from Mule Springs and cleans his plow for him. A sort of May-December romance, don't you see?" He shrugged. "Some people have peculiar tastes, that's all."

I must have been staring at him, for he winked at me and smiled. "Oh, I know everything that goes on around here, Mr. Parker," he said. "Everything. You might even say I keep the clocks in this town." He stood, produced a Panama hat I had not noticed before, and with a flourish settled it on his head.

With his next words something new crept into his voice. "Look that file over real good, Counselor. Stroud won't give me the time of day anymore, but I've got a sixth sense that tells me we're in trouble." The wheedling, the contrived affability were gone. In their place I detected the hint of a threat.

He leaned over the desk. "Those goddamn wops owe me a million dollars, and they're not gonna get away with pissing in my hat. Stroud may not have the marbles left to win this case, and God knows Chandler never had the brains in the first place, but you're a Houston man, a goddamn city lawyer." He cracked his knuckles and pointed at me. "You're it."

I could not believe it. My own client, this fractured little man, was trying to intimidate me.

"I know you'll do what it takes," Rasmussen said, the diamond in his tooth flashing as he smiled. He held out his hand for me to shake. "It'll be a pleasure doing bidniss with you."

Ignoring his outstretched hand, I stood up and was about to tell him what I thought of him and his lawsuit and his conjectures about Stroud and Sally Dean, when suddenly a grimace crumpled Rasmussen's face, and he clapped his hands over his ears. I felt it, too, a silent but palpable buzz, an invisible knife that cut for an instant through the hum of the air conditioner and sliced off the top of my skull. It was as if the air in the room had come apart along a razor-thin line. My vision blurred. An invisible cat danced its claws along my spine. The feeling lasted for maybe four seconds, then was gone. I had never felt anything like it.

"That son of a bitch!" snapped Bevo, storming out of the room. I stood blinking, probing my skull with my fingers to see if it had cracked.

"A word, Mr. Parker," said Gilliam Stroud, who had materialized in front of my desk, broad-shouldered, hands behind his back.

"Did you feel that?" I asked him. My temples were throbbing. "Was it a sonic boom?"

Stroud ignored my questions. "I guess you're wondering why you're here," he said.

"Mr. Stroud, there's something weird going on."

"Listen to me, son," he said. "You have a mission."

"You told me about it yesterday, remember?" I answered, closing one eye, then the other, checking my vision. "You said I was here to keep you from getting depantsed in court."

"That's one mission. There is another." Stroud spoke in grim tones, a mortician explaining a mistake in the billing. "You have been hired, Mr. Parker, to perform a rescue."

"A rescue?"

"You are here to rescue the founder of this firm."

"Hardwick Chandler? Rescue him from what?"

"From the perils of the flesh," Stroud intoned. "Nookie, my boy."

"Nookie?"

"Our colleague is addicted to women, and his addiction has left him poised upon the verge of ruin."

My brain had not stopped spinning. "Mr. Stroud, I think there's something wrong with the air conditioner in this building."

"When a noble man is destroyed, a little something dies in all of us. Don't you find that to be so?"

I studied the old man's face. Dizzy though I was, I recognized a summation speech when I heard one—or, rather, a parody of a summation speech, theatrical intonations and all—and it irritated me.

"Ask not for whom the bell tolls," said Stroud.

"I'll tell you what's going to ruin Hardwick Chandler," I said. "The damned interrogatories in the Rasmussen case. They're going to ruin all of us. Mr. Stroud, tell me you turned them in. Tell me you didn't forget to do that."

He hushed me with an upraised hand. "Later, son. We'll iron all that out later. Right now we have a far bigger problem on our hands. The salvation of a soul in need, a brother at the bar laid low by circumstance and a saucy eye."

"Oh, come on," I said. But I could not jolly him out of his hammy mode of Shakespearean regret. He loved Hardwick Chandler like a son, he avowed, and he couldn't bear to see his son destroy himself.

"Together," Stroud announced, "we shall exert so positive an influence as to rehabilitate a good man and a fine lawyer." Stroud produced from behind his back the bundle that he had been hiding. It was a pair of pants on a hanger.

"Go!" he said, thrusting the pants at me.

"Go where?" I asked, taking the pants.

Stroud reached across the desk and clapped a giant hand on my shoulder. "Go and rescue Hardwick Chandler!"

CHAPTER 9

IT TURNED OUT THAT Hardwick Chandler needed more than a pair of pants to be rescued. He needed a whole suit of clothes and a pair of shoes, all of which Molly Tunstall handed me on my way out the door. I wasn't to know the reason for the wardrobe until I arrived at the farmhouse out in the country close to Mineola where, according to Gilliam Stroud, Chandler was holed up, "sideswiped," said the old man, "by appetite." Stroud gave me directions that kept me wandering back roads for an hour, griping at the cows as I passed.

I was driving by a six-foot-high section of chain-link fence, wondering what sort of cattle needed such a barrier to prevent their escape into the woods, when suddenly I passed what looked like an emaciated child in a gray ball cap and shaggy parka, staring at the road from inside the fence with his hands tucked high behind his back and his elbows sticking out at a weird angle. I turned to get a better look and almost landed in a bar ditch. It was a big, ugly bird. Fifty yards further was a sign announcing that I was passing the Triple-B Emu and Ostrich Farm. Next to the sign stood another bird that looked too shaggy and too stout to be an ostrich. That must be an emu. The bird stood completely still, poised as if expecting me to paint its picture.

Ostriches had been a coming thing in Texas for some time, but this was the first ostrich ranch I had seen. Well, I thought, why not ostriches? Weren't they the biggest birds in the world, and wasn't this Texas, where big was an obsession? Maybe Texas farmers were breeding ostriches to take over as the state bird. I passed two other ostrich farms as I crisscrossed the countryside.

The locusts were going full blast when I finally found a place that fit Stroud's description, a little yellow house with lace curtains and bright lavender trim on the windows and eaves, the sort of place you knew at a glance would be crammed with country knick-knacks. The house looked deserted, but when I knocked at the door a curtain moved, and a man's voice asked me my name. I gave it, the door opened, and I walked in to meet Hardwick Chandler.

"About fucking time," he said.

He was a short man, five-ten, maybe forty-five years old, and plump as a football, with a tremendous throat bound tightly by three gold chains. He had short, curly red hair and pinkish, freckled skin, much of which I could see because the woman's silk kimono he was wearing was wholly inadequate to the task of covering his immense stomach. The only other thing he was wearing was a pair of handcuffs, which dangled from his left wrist.

"Hardwick Chandler?" I asked.

"In the flesh," he replied. Snatching the hangers out of my hands, he tossed the kimono on the floor and began to dress with frantic speed, the handcuff flapping around him. Chandler was so obese that when he moved, different parts of him seemed to vibrate on their own separate frequencies. The effect was one of immense energy being let loose all over his body. The pink-speckled roll of fat around his middle rippled in counterpoint to the flab of his

neck and his upper arms as he worked his trousers up one leg and
then the next.

"I had to break the damn bed," he said, holding up the dangling handcuffs. "She'll chew my ass good for that." He told me he'd
been in bed for four straight days with the woman who owned the
house, whose name was Deirdre. The only time Deirdre would
unlock him was when he had to go to the bathroom. They had had
a fight that morning, and Deirdre had walked out, leaving him
cuffed to the bed. I asked him what happened to the clothes he
had been wearing when he arrived.

"Maybe she took them with her, for spite," he replied. Then
he smiled. "Or maybe they just burned up. Things got pretty hot
in here."

His wrist where the handcuff hung looked badly chafed and a
little swollen.

"Are you okay?" I asked him.

"Love's a hurtin' thing," he replied. He slid the handcuff into
his shirtsleeve, followed it with his arm in a practiced motion that
made me wonder if this sort of thing had happened to him before.
When he was fully dressed, he stepped back into the front room to
get a look at himself in a mirror, then offered me his unencumbered
hand to shake.

"Wick Chandler," he said, as if the last three minutes had never
happened. "It's great to meet you, Clay."

After the introductions, our next order of business was to get
the cuff off his wrist. He told me that he had turned the house
upside down looking for the key, and sure enough, the place looked
as if a pack of wild dogs had been set loose in it. So we went out
into the backyard, where there was an anvil sitting on a couple of
cinderblocks. Nearby on the ground was a big axe. Chandler laid
his wrist on the anvil and invited me to strike the locked cuff with
the flat end of the axe.

"What if I miss?" I asked.

"Clay, there's a woman back in town that'll kill me sure as we're standing here if she sees me with these handcuffs on. Now, I hope you don't miss, but I'd a hell of a lot rather have a bashed hand than a slit throat."

I remembered the phone calls from the angry woman with the razor. "You know some dangerous women," I told him, taking careful aim with the axe.

"That's the only kind God makes," he replied.

CHAPTER 10

HARDWICK CHANDLER TALKED all the way back to town. His words came fast and high-pitched, with the vowels hemorrhaging in all directions, East Texas fashion. Talking was breathing to him; topic after topic tumbled out of him, each one dying away with the end of a breath, to be replaced by a new one unrelated to whatever had come before. He asked me questions about myself, my career, my law school days—we had both attended Baylor Law, though he had gone before me—and gave me no time to answer. He loved sports cars, he said, and expressed admiration for the Austin Healey, into whose passenger seat he was barely able to stuff his amazing bulk. He fiddled with all the instruments and ornaments he could reach, hunting with quick-silver fingertips for ways to unscrew or unsnap them. He offered to buy the car if I would name him a price, but before I could do so, he was asking me about the restaurants in Houston. He announced that he was a gourmet and loved a good meal almost as much as he loved the ladies. And that brought him back to his one recurring topic. Women.

"Women," he explained, "are my sole reason for living, my raison d'être. God help me, I love 'em. I love every single goddamn *part* of them." He turned toward me in his seat. "You ever noticed the backs of their knees? The *backs,* not the fronts. I love the backs of a woman's knees. I've never met a woman who wasn't ticklish there." He stuck his head into the slipstream and gave a rousing whoop.

"That Deirdre," he said, thumping the outside of the car door, "she could have been a contortionist!"

Gilliam Stroud was right: Wick Chandler was hooked on nookie. I tried to ask him about the other woman, the one on the phone with the razor, but he got in ahead of me with a joke. Had I heard about the old boy who went to the costume party naked on roller skates and said he was a pull toy?

What a contrast he was, with his rapid-fire speech and manic movements, to his partner Stroud, whose every utterance and gesture seemed carefully crafted, even when he was drunk. The only thing the two men's conversation seemed to have in common was the ring of insincerity. They were both born liars. Perhaps that was what had drawn them together.

Wick got onto the subject of ostriches. "You ever eat ostrich meat?" he asked. I told him that I had not. "It tastes a lot like roast beef, but it's got only a fraction of the cholesterol of chicken meat. There's not much about an ostrich that you can't use. You can make boots out of their skin, clothes out of their feathers. They're a fucking miracle."

Right now, according to Wick, it was a breeder's market, because there weren't any sizable herds. But one day there would be herds of ostriches bigger than any buffalo herd of the past. "Look out there, Clay," he said. "Imagine those hills black with ostriches."

It was difficult to picture.

"You can sell a live, fertile ostrich egg for almost a thousand dollars," Wick said. "A pair of breeding chicks can go for upwards of three thousand. Takes money to set up an ostrich farm. Emus are getting to be pretty big, too, though I can't see why, the shaggy bastards."

Wick explained that ostriches had become the preferred currency of the drug trade. "It's true, Clay," he insisted. "Look here, you're a tax lawyer. What happens to any transaction involving more than ten thousand dollars in cash?"

"A little bell rings at the IRS," I said.

"That's right. And that little bell can also wake up the FBI, the DEA, and lots of other alphabet police. So instead of handing your connection a big pile of dirty bills that can be traced, you give him a pair of ostriches. It's a weird world, isn't it? They're nasty creatures, ostriches. Bad-tempered sons of bitches. You ever seen anybody kicked by an ostrich?"

I had not.

"You don't want to, either. An ostrich can work you over like a prizefighter. I saw a guy take a kick one time like to have broken his pelvis. And he was holding a big flat board like a shield between him and the bird. I don't know how that ostrich got around the board. They only have two toes on their feet, and one of them has a nail on it that can open a man up like he's got a built-in zipper. You see that farm over there?" He pointed to another field fenced with chain link. This field was sectioned into long walkways, like in a kennel for show dogs. One of the birds was standing in a walkway, looking at that distance like a butler in gray livery. "That's Deirdre's farm. Well, it's Mike's farm. Deirdre and Mike Starns."

"So Deirdre is married?"

"Mike is the guy I saw get kicked. He doesn't really like the birds anymore, not after he found out how mean-spirited they are. He sold most of his ostriches and put the money into emus because they're not so testy. But even emus can kick the shit out of you. He spends a lot of time out of town now," Wick said. "He likes to fish. I go with him sometimes. Then sometimes, when he goes on one of his trout safaris, Deirdre calls me up, and we have our own safari."

"One of our clients introduced me to emu jerky this morning," I told him.

"Bevo Rasmussen," he said. "So you've met him already. Christ. He thinks he's going to become the emu czar of Texas."

"If that's what he wants, then why did he buy a bunch of horses?" I asked.

"The horses were a way to make money to buy the birds. It's a complicated plan, which he'll tell you in great detail if you ask. My advice is, don't ask. Bevo Rasmussen is a fucking snake. God almighty, I wish he'd never walked through our door."

I told Wick that the little man seemed more pathetic to me than deadly.

"Bevo isn't his real name," Wick said. "He got that name from stealing the big steer down in Austin. You know, the university's mascot." The University of Texas football team is named the Longhorns, and their mascot is a longhorn steer named Bevo. From time to time a rival university tries to steal the steer before a big game as a prank. For this reason, Bevo the steer is heavily guarded during football season.

"He did it on a bet," Wick said. "Some smart-ass Aggies down in College Station put him up to it. But he didn't just steal the steer. He took it to a butcher down in College Station and had it cut up into steaks and served to the A&M football team!"

"That's right!" I said. "I remember hearing something about that. About eight years ago? So that was Bevo?"

"Yep. The Aggies thought eating the Longhorns' steer would be a motivator, you know, get the juices flowing. Turns out that the UT fans were so mad over it, there was a riot at the game, and some people got hurt. The Longhorns beat the shit out of the Aggies that year. So I guess you could say the prank backfired. Most of Bevo's pranks do. Disaster follows that boy around."

"That makes him a jerk," I said, "not the devil incarnate."

"I suppose you've noticed that problem he's got with his arm, how it moves kind of funny?"

"I've noticed," I said.

"He got that in a knife fight outside a bar in Dallas with a Mexican that tried to run out on a coke sale. The Mexican outweighed Bevo by a good sixty pounds. He was one mean son of a bitch, but Bevo called him on the trick and had it out with him."

"It looks like Bevo got the rough end of it," I said.

"He got torn up, all right," Wick replied, "but the Mexican got himself dead. Bevo's a tough customer. He carries a razor in his sock."

I told Wick that I had seen it.

"How do you know so much about Bevo Rasmussen?" I asked.

"We've represented him a time or two before," Wick replied. "That Mexican murder? Gill walked him."

"But he did it?" I asked. Wick nodded.

"Listen," Wick said, "Bevo will probably talk to you, try to get you to do something for him."

"What kind of thing?"

"I don't know. Something. Anything. But don't do it. Don't listen to him. Everything the man tells you is a lie. And never turn your back on him."

"I take it you think Bevo burned his horses?" I asked.

"As sure as I'm sitting here," he replied.

I asked him if he knew about the screwup with the interrogatories in Rasmussen's case. He nodded.

"No problem," he said. "We can still petition the court to allow us to answer the interrogatories. All we have to do is come up with a good enough reason why we didn't take care of them in the first place."

"Have you got a reason?" I asked.

"Well, there was Gill's heart attack about nine months ago. We could use that."

"Stroud had a heart attack?" I asked.

"He did if we need him to."

"You mean, he *didn't* have a heart attack?"

"It depends," he replied.

"Either he did or he didn't, Wick."

"We can get old Doc Jessup to corroborate. Gill's gotten him off so many DWIs that the man would swear Gill died and came back from the dead if we asked him to."

"We would *lie* to the court?"

"Lie? Never. We just put our pre-existing condition in the worst possible light, to borrow a phrase from the insurance defense boys."

"You can't lie to the court, Wick."

"You're not listening, Clay." He grinned at me, but then he saw that I was not amused. "Clay, this is not tax-form bingo in Houston. You're an advocate, and you're in the country, boy. Things have their own way of getting done out here. Trust me. We can finesse this fuckup. In fact, there aren't many fuckups we can't finesse."

"Even if that means putting our licenses on the line?"

"Nobody's gonna take your license. Look, we don't misrepresent the law, we don't ignore it. We massage it. We fondle it, we squeeze it. We goose it and grease it till it fits." His plump, ring-laden fingers moved in the air, fondling the law. "Whatever works," he said with a shrug. "That's the motto of our firm. Whatever works."

I didn't much like that motto and told him so.

"If it's any consolation to you," he said, "Gill really does have heart problems. He could go at any minute." Wick snapped his fingers. "Like that."

"That doesn't surprise me," I said. I told him about bailing Stroud out of jail the day before.

"You don't know him, Clay," Wick said. "Not yet. He was a great lawyer once. Hell, he's still a great lawyer. He's the greatest man I've ever known. And he's got more ethical scruples than Billy Graham." I thought of Stroud's attempt to pass me off as a medical expert in front of a judge yesterday and glanced at Chandler to see just how I was expected to absorb this testament to the old man's probity. To my astonishment, there were tears standing in his eyes. He may not have been convincing me, but he seemed to be convincing himself.

"Stroud's the reason you're here, Clay," he said. "I didn't say anything about this during our phone talks. I couldn't. But I'm counting on you to help me with him. I hired you to help me get him back on his feet."

"What?"

"We've got to get him off the sauce. You're here to help me do that."

This I found interesting. Wick was giving me the same line about Stroud that Stroud had given me about him! So I was hired to be a nurse, not a lawyer. Stroud was hiring me to rehabilitate Chandler, and Chandler was hiring me to rehabilitate Stroud. I told Wick of Stroud's duplicate plan.

Wick shook his head, smiling. "You see what I mean?" he said. "That man is always thinking of somebody else. I'm telling you, Clay, he can seem like a prize son of a bitch, but he's got a heart of gold."

"I think you're both bananas, Wick," I told him. "I think the two of you are out of control."

"You're right, Clay. We're out of control. That's why we need you. We need a city lawyer to straighten us out. We've gone a bit loco lately, but we're not over the hill. You're young, you're smart, you've got energy. You could set us on the right track."

"There's nothing in my job description about conducting rehab for the partners," I told him.

"It won't be too hard, Clay, I promise. We both know we need to reform. We'll work at it. You show us what to do. Whip us into shape!"

I could not see either Stroud or Chandler letting himself be whipped into shape.

"Don't worry about Gill," Wick said. "He's got some good years left in him. If you could only see him in front of a jury."

"I have," I replied. "I assisted in the Hardesty murder trial yesterday."

"The Hardesty trial?" Wick said. He looked at his watch. "What day is it?"

I told him.

"Jesus," he said. "That Deirdre."

"Did you know we go to trial in the Rasmussen case in eight days?"

That spooked him.

"Eight days?" he said. "That's a pisser."

"How are you going to finesse that?" I asked.

"Well," he said after a moment's thought, "Gill could always have another heart attack."

CHAPTER 11

IT WAS AFTER ELEVEN and blisteringly hot when we got back to town. Wick asked me to drop him at his home, and I drove him to a low-slung redbrick house set well back on a weedy lawn only a couple of blocks from the office. There were two cars in the gravel driveway, a Dodge Ram truck and an old black Corvette convertible. When I pulled up to the curb in front of the house, Wick told me he had an idea how I could spend my first afternoon in the office. He had some client appointments that, thanks to his tryst in the woods with Deirdre, he no longer had time to meet. These were the clients whose files Molly Tunstall had stacked in the basket on my desk. Wick called them basket cases.

"We got a load of 'em," he said. "People get cranky when their world goes bad, and East Texas is just about played out. I'd handle them, but I've got work to do here. There's nothing really tough about the cases. Why don't you take my appointments, introduce yourself to some of the clients?"

"I'll do it if you'll go back through the Rasmussen case file so we can talk about it tomorrow," I replied.

"No problem," he said, straining to pull himself out of the car. "Leave Bevo's file with Molly, and I'll pick it up this evening. See,

Clay? I'm starting to reform already. I'll find us a miracle."

"Find us one that does not require anyone in the firm to have a heart attack," I said.

At the office Molly told me my first basket case was scheduled for one-thirty, which was two hours away. I asked her to get me the phone number for the office of the administrative coordinator for the Northeast Texas judicial district.

"So, city boy, how's the new job going?" Sally Dean asked when I got her on the phone.

"I need some legal advice," I told her. "Where's the best place for a lawyer to get some lunch in this county?"

"There's a pretty good place over here," she said, "but from what I saw of your sense of direction yesterday evening, I'm not sure you could find it."

"Perhaps if you loaned me your horse, he could lead me to it."

"Be here in twenty minutes," she said. "I'll have Ed saddled and waiting."

Sally's office was in Wyman, fifteen miles north of Jenks. I got directions from Molly and in twenty minutes parked the Austin Healey on a downtown street in Wyman, which looked pretty much like Mule Springs, Jenks, and most of the other East Texas towns I had seen. A two-story yellow-brick building housed the state and county legal services. The Judicial District Administrative Coordinator's Office, on the second floor, was impressive: cherry wood paneling, lush green carpet, expensive prints on the wall. Sally sat in a blaze of sunlight coming from the windows behind her and reflecting off the rich wood of the desktop. She was on the phone with someone who, I could tell, wanted to be very nice to her.

"How kind of you to think of me, Judge Howell," Sally said, motioning me into the room. "I'll see you this afternoon, then." She hung up the phone.

"Friends in high places?" I asked, taking a seat in a gigantic leather chair that threatened to swallow me whole.

"Judge Howell has been fishing in Alaska," she replied, "and he wants to bring me some salmon." She came around the desk and sat on its edge, close to me. The country girl of yesterday was gone: Sally was wearing a tailored business suit—sleek double-breasted jacket and short skirt in a black-and-white hound's tooth—black stockings, and high heels. Her black hair was pulled back and bound with a simple bow at her neck. She would have been at home in any boardroom in Houston.

"He's still fishing," she said.

"Hoping to catch you?" I asked.

"Fishing is Judge Howell's reason to live. His next trip is to some river in Africa. It would be a shame if the safari had to leave without him because he couldn't get a replacement to take his place on the bench."

"I've heard of people trying to bribe judges, but never the other way around."

She shrugged. "Half the judges I deal with want to take off their robes for a while, and the other half, the retired ones, want to put them back on. This office handles the whole show."

"But you can't just accept a gift from a judge, can you? Isn't that tampering or bribery or something?"

"A few fish from an old friend?" She idly pushed against the arm of my chair with the toe of her shoe, the muscles in her calf flexing in an interesting pattern. Her perfume had redefined itself from the evening before. Very subtly, I was enveloped in a scent that made me think of mangoes and Caribbean islands and sunlight sizzling on the brown skin of native girls. "Haven't you ever been slipped a few fish from an old friend, Counselor?" she asked, smiling.

"I didn't see Ed downstairs."

"That lazy horse, he must have run off."

"Then who'll show me the way to lunch?" I asked.

We crossed the street and entered an old-fashioned diner with red linoleum tabletops and little jukeboxes sitting on the table in every booth. As out of place as Sally looked in the joint—a high-gloss Wall Street ballbuster in a dusty luncheonette—she obviously felt herself at home. She exchanged greetings with the dozen or so small-town types and worn farmers in the other booths as if they were cousins. She introduced me to the clientele as the new man at Chandler and Stroud. That drew a round of whistles and some laughter. "New meat!" I heard someone say, and a wizened little man in a madras jacket and alpine hat stood up from a booth to make me an elaborate salute.

"From whatever frying pan you was in," he said, "I welcome you to the fire."

"Is everybody in East Texas a comic?" I asked Sally as we slid into a booth.

"I think you've impressed them," she said. "You've given them a new topic to keep them busy. They'll be figuring out whether you're brave or just crazy."

A waitress came over, and Sally ordered chicken salad sandwiches, the house specialty, for both of us.

"How many new guys have Chandler and Stroud had?" I asked.

"I'm not sure," Sally replied. "Four, since I've known the boys. No, five. But that last fellow hardly counted. He only survived about thirty-six hours."

"Why, Sally? What makes it so hard for the new guy?"

She gave me a long, appraising look. "Let me tell you a little story about your employers. Some years ago, when Gill was in a little better health, he was the high district attorney of this very county. Wick Chandler was the assistant DA. One week, God knows why, they decided to break a record for court appearances. In that week, they tried eleven jury trials and brought twenty-one cases to the bench. That's a total of thirty-two cases, all tried in one week."

"Amazing," I said. "Weird but amazing. What a train wreck that must have been."

Sally pointed a cautionary finger at me. "Wait a minute. Out of those thirty-two cases they got a total of thirty-one convictions. It would've been thirty-two, but one of the witnesses had a heart attack and died while testifying. The boys also broke the total-years record."

"The total-years record?"

"A court reporter figured this one out. You add up the total number of years in all the sentences handed down in the cases that you prosecute. During their week, the boys racked up a total of almost three thousand years for the thirty-one people they sent to Huntsville. That's a statewide record. During the same week, they drank almost as many bottles of Jack Daniel's as they sent people to the penitentiary. Ask Molly Tunstall if you don't believe me. She took out the bottles."

"You want me to believe they tried all those cases drunk?" I asked.

"Totally shitfaced. I think that's the only way they could have gotten through so many trials. Drink seems to speed Wick Chandler up—in more ways than one. You should also know that during that week Wick was assaulted twice, on the steps of that same courthouse right over there, by jealous husbands."

I shook my head, laughing. "You're good, Sally, but that's over the top."

Sally did not crack a smile. "The second husband had a gun. He shot at Wick but missed and hit their new associate in the thigh. This fellow had been with them for only about two months. He came close to losing his leg. As soon as he could walk again, he quit."

I stared at her hard, looking for a trace of her customary irony. "This is true?" I asked.

"Around here, it's called the week of Jack Daniel's justice. Ask anyone over in the courthouse about it. But you asked me why the new guys have always failed. I think it's a question of balance. Their gyroscopes just couldn't handle it. They couldn't find the right rhythm. They never learned when to duck." Now a smile crept into her eyes. "How's your rhythm, Counselor?"

"Better than my sense of direction, I hope."

The sandwiches came, and while we ate we made small talk. I found out that she was a local girl, having grown up in small East Texas towns; her mother was dead, and her father had a horse ranch a few miles outside Jenks.

"Why don't you stable Ed at your father's ranch?"

"Ed stays at Gill's farm, on the other side of town."

"How many horses does he keep?" I asked. It was hard to imagine the drunken old man taking care of a horse.

"Just one," she said. "Just Ed. He's part of a reclamation project I'm working on. I'm a closet do-gooder."

"You're trying to rehabilitate Stroud?" I asked.

"No, I'm trying to rehabilitate Ed. That horse has a terrible drinking problem."

Sally explained that she had placed Ed with Stroud, her former boss, in order to give the old man something to do out on the farm. "He gets morbid if he sits alone on his porch too long. And he starts to drink. Having Ed to look after keeps him on an even keel."

"He wasn't on a very even keel yesterday," I said, telling her about his arrest.

"How was he in court?"

"He was awesome," I admitted.

"You will never see him drunk when he's working," Sally said.

"I thought you said he spent Jack Daniel's justice week drunk."

"That was before he met Ed."

"You realize that there's a kind of father/daughter sound to all of this," I said.

"I guess I don't mind telling you," she said after a moment. "Gill helped me out a couple of years ago when he hired me. To qualify to become a judicial district coordinator, I had to have at least six months' job experience in a law office. The rules didn't say what kind of experience. I just had to work in a firm. I really wanted to be a coordinator, so I went looking for someone to hire me. Chandler and Stroud was the first firm I applied to. They hired me on the spot. Gill has been a mentor to me ever since. We keep each other sharp."

"That's right," I said, "you bet on Stroud's trials. What sort of wager did you two make on the Hardesty trial, if I may ask?"

"You may not."

"So that's how Stroud helped you out, by offering you a job?"

"It's a little more than that. I was sort of a rehabilitation job myself at the time. I don't want to go into it. Let's just say Gill gave me moral support at a time when I really needed it. He taught me a lesson or two about responsibility. Let's leave it at that."

"Gilliam Stroud taught you about responsibility?" I asked. It was my turn to sound ironic.

Sally finished her sandwich and wiped her mouth with her napkin. "You haven't been here very long, Mr. Parker," she said. "May I ask you to do me a favor?"

"Of course."

"Don't judge Gill Stroud too soon. That's what the other new guys did. You don't know him yet. Give him a little time."

"What about Hardwick Chandler?" I asked. "Will I have to give him a little time, too?"

She wrinkled her nose. "Maybe more than a little," she replied.

"So, let me get this straight," I said. "That sleeping-your-way-to-the-top remark you made last night, that was just a joke, right?"

"It depends on which of the local idiots you ask," she said. "Some folks will tell you that I slept with Gill Stroud to get my job. Others will tell you I slept with Wick Chandler. How sleeping with either of those two could have made me a district coordinator is something maybe you can figure out and explain to the rural population."

"So who *did* you sleep with to get your job?" I asked.

She laughed. "I can see we're going to have fun with you, Counselor."

Then it was her turn. She asked me questions about my life in Houston, my marriage, my reasons for choosing Jenks to start over. I did my best to answer them.

"So you're rehabilitating yourself," she said.

"That's right."

"And you're looking for your lost ethics."

"I guess so," I said.

"In East Texas."

"You think it's the wrong place to look?" I asked.

"I think it's the wrong *way* to look. I don't think you're going to find them in a *place*. It's not like they've tumbled out of your brain and are hiding from you out in the back forty."

"So you think I'm crazy?" We were crossing the street, heading back to her office.

She looked at me, smiling. "Maybe a little bit. But not enough to show out here."

I said good-bye to her at the door to her building and turned to go.

"Do you like salmon, Mr. Parker?" she asked.

"Why won't you call me Clay?" I asked.

"Do you like salmon, Clay?"

"I like salmon."

"How about contraband salmon?"

"That's the only kind," I replied.

"See you around." She smiled, disappearing into the doorway.

CHAPTER 12

THOUGH I GOT BACK to the office a few minutes before my first appointment, a couple of clients were already sitting in the waiting room, grumbling about being forgotten. For the next four hours I got acquainted with my neighbors, clients who had expected to see Hardwick Chandler and were suspicious of the new man. Most peppered me with questions, wanting to know who I was, where I was from, and why a man would leave a lucrative Houston law practice to live in a failing community out in East Texas.

I gave what counsel I could, but it was a different clientele from the one I had been used to in Houston. Instead of sleek executive types representing corporations looking for tax loopholes, I got cranky, ill-educated people mired in hatred, greed, hopelessness, and desperation, looking for a magic solution. Instead of Brioni suits and Gucci loafers and Rolexes, I saw Dickey work pants and Wal-Mart boots and Timexes. I worked on drawing up wills for folks who owned nothing, who parceled out poultry by the bird to their relatives. I counseled a man, out on bail, whose wife had accused him of sexually abusing their eight-month-old daughter and who confessed to me that he had done it and wanted to know if I could get him off for $212, which was all he had. There were clients wrangling about probate on inheritances already eaten away to nothing in court costs, mothers suing sons, small children held for ransom by divorcing parents. A parade of the disinherited moved through my office, a ragtag assortment of refugees bombed out of the running for the American Dream by their own or someone else's stupidity, laziness, self-absorption, or just plain bad luck.

A case in point was Judi Rae Box, my last appointment of the afternoon. Mrs. Box was a small, wiry middle-aged woman with pinkish hair growing in odd patches on her head, a gauze bandage taped above her left eye, and a cigarette cough that sounded like timber splitting. Her speech was fast, low-voiced, and violent. I kept having to stop her midway through blasts of invective and coax her back on track as she told her story.

Judi Rae's husband, Layton, a plumber, was having affairs. Judi Rae herself worked out of town, in Greenville, at the Durever Glove Factory, where for the last eleven years she had sewn the right thumb into tens of thousands of pairs of men's gloves. The repetitiveness of her job made her inward looking and difficult to cope with on her days off. This was the reason Judi Rae gave for the start of her problems with Layton. Because of her work-induced contrariness, Layton had gone on the prowl.

"I own up to being prey to foul moods, Mr. Parker," she said. "But just because I get a little testy, that don't give him the right to go whoring around on me, does it?"

Judi Rae and Layton fought about his infidelity. Sometimes the fighting turned violent. Last night, Judi Rae caught him on the phone with one of his girlfriends and hammered him in the face with the phone's base, whereupon Layton hit back with the receiver and opened a cut over her eye that took sixteen stitches to close. Hence the bandage. In spite of this battering, Judi Rae managed to grab him by the scrotum and stretch that tender flesh sufficiently to require a visit to the hospital emergency room. Layton was afraid that Judi Rae had impaired his ability to perform what he called his masculine duties.

"Masculine duties," she scoffed. "He was doing his masculine duties all over the county. You ask me, I was the one doing the duty."

Actually, they both went to the hospital, after which they both went to jail on warrants they swore out against each other. But the sheriff knew Layton and sent him home on personal recognizance in less than an hour, while Judi Rae stayed overnight and solidified her view of the world as a dark conspiracy directed at her. It was in this attitude that she had come to talk to Wick Chandler about getting a divorce. Wick had handled divorces for two of Judi Rae's daughters, as well as for her mother.

Great patches of Judi Rae's pink hair were missing, like divots in a golf course fairway. "You're looking at my head," said Judi Rae.

Embarrassed, I replied, "I really didn't mean to stare. Do you have a medical condition?" I was convinced that she was in the early stages of chemotherapy.

"It's Layton," she explained, tears brimming in her eyes. "The son of a bitch tortures me." She turned her head so that I could see the patches over her ear. "You see where he pulled out my hair by the handfuls? That cheating motherfucker."

"Your husband did this?" I asked.

"Damn right he did."

"Why, Mrs. Box?"

"Well, I had ahold of him."

"You were holding him?"

"I had ahold of his balls," she explained. "Any time he comes for me, I grab him where it hurts. You see these thumbs?" She held them up, and I saw that her hands were thick-muscled, mannish from her years of work in the glove factory. She made pinching movements with her thumbs. "These suckers can core an apple with one prod. And I'll guaran-damn-tee-you, I wouldn't have

turned loose of Layton's tender parts if he hadn't pulled my hair
out. He outlasted me that time."

"I understand," I said. "And you want a divorce."

"Mister, I want more than a divorce. I want everything he has
and everything he thinks he might ever get. I want you to get
those balls off him permanent. Folks I've talked to say I can clean
the son of a bitch out for beating me like he has and pulling my
hair out and whoring around like he's been doing and I've caught
him at. I want you to rip him up one side and down the other. You
can carve up whatever's left to get your fee."

Judi Rae did not have any money. She was going to pay us out
of the settlement. I explained to her that we would need a retainer
in order to take her case. Her face fell.

"How much?" she asked. I did not know. I told her that I would
find out and get back to her. She left, grumbling about men in
general and lawyers in particular, who, I heard her say as she
walked out the door, are men without dicks.

CHAPTER 13

I ARRIVED HOME to find a light blue Mercedes convertible parked at the curb in front of my house. The front door was unlocked, and there were cooking smells in the air. Sally Dean came out of the dining room, dressed in a black silk blouse and short skirt and holding out to me a bottle of white wine and a corkscrew.

"You said you liked salmon," she said. "We're about to see if that's true." I followed her back to the dining room, working on the cork. Candles flickered over an elaborately set table.

"Funny thing," I said. "I could have sworn I locked my door when I left the house this morning."

"I picked the lock," she replied from the kitchen. "I can pick just about any lock."

"Is that a useful skill in your line of work?"

She came in carrying a salad. "Don't tell me you've never wished you could pick a lock, Counselor." She shrugged, "It's just something my daddy taught me. How are you coming with that wine?"

I got it open at last and poured. She came over to me, and we had a toast.

"To your new life," she said.

"To picklocks everywhere."

We sat at the table.

"Where's Ed?" I asked.

"He had a date."

"The only thing I can figure," I said, "is that I have captivated you with my big-city charm."

She smiled. "I believe I mentioned to you a bet I had with Gill over his murder case."

"The bet you lost?"

She nodded.

"So this is the favor you owe him?" I asked. "You have to be nice to the new guy?"

"How's the salmon?"

As we ate Judge Howell's contraband salmon, Sally asked me about my first full day on the job. I told her about meeting Wick amid the ostriches.

"One of these days," she said, "Mike Starns is going to catch Wick in Deirdre's little bungalow, and it'll be good-bye, Wick." She laughed. "I can imagine the funeral. Two-thirds of the women in the county will be there, crying their eyes out."

I didn't want to talk about Wick Chandler. "Tell me the truth, Sally," I said. "I refuse to believe you've come over here and done all this just because Gill Stroud asked you to look after me."

She thought for a moment before answering. "I don't know, Clay. Maybe I feel I have a proprietary interest in you. I did rescue you yesterday. If it hadn't been for Ed and me, you'd still be out there looking for your house."

"I wouldn't give myself too much credit, if I were you," I replied. "It seems to me Ed did most of the work."

"Ed wouldn't have done a thing on his own. He wanted to pass you by, but I convinced him to stop. You just looked so lost, sitting by the side of the road in your little car. A city boy lost in the country. I guess you appealed to my motherly instincts. I have this need to save lost critters."

"Like Appaloosas without spots?"

She smiled, picked up the wine bottle, and filled my glass. "Drink up, Counselor. You need to be buzzed to do what we're going to do tonight."

My heart gave a little jump. "And what's that, Ms. Dean?"

She poured herself another glass and drank it down. "My mama was a Cajun. There's an old Cajun ceremony for christening a new house. It's supposed to keep demons out of it. I don't know that it works—to tell the truth, I'm not sure I remember the whole thing—but it seems to me you need all the help you can get. So we're going to cleanse this house tonight, Cajun style."

I was about to laugh, but there was a look in Sally's eyes that stopped me.

"You don't want demons in your house, do you, Clay?"

I gazed at my plate, trying to think of a witty answer. "Just how nice to the new guy are you planning to be?" I finally said, but when I looked up, she was gone.

"Sally?" She wasn't in the kitchen. I looked through the other rooms on the first floor with no luck. The wine had started to work, and for a moment I had the feeling that I had dreamed the salmon feast and the beautiful girl, but when I walked back into the dining room, there were the plates, the burning candles. I walked up the stairs calling her name.

The landing was ablaze with candles, a line of them on the carpet leading to the master bedroom. I followed them, a little jittery, images of B-movie cult sacrifices forming in the back of my mind.

Sally's clothes were scattered on the floor. From the bathroom came the hiss of the shower. I stood in the middle of the room, buzzed, waiting for whatever was going to happen next.

That old pit-of-the-stomach feeling of being lost, having lost control of my surroundings, was building. It was never far away, but this time there was little of the panic that usually accompanied it. During the year and a half since my marriage had broken up I had not dated, and now, suddenly, I seemed to be in two places at once: standing in a bedroom in Jenks, Texas, and crossing the International Date Line. Time was doing something strange, and I was too slow to pick up on what it was. Before I could figure anything out, the shower cut off, and Sally Dean came out of the bathroom, toweling her hair and wearing my robe.

"I hope you don't mind," she said, walking over to the dresser and pouring some Jack Daniel's into a couple of whiskey glasses swimming with ice. "That kitchen got me all sweaty, and the Cajun priestess has to be clean for the ceremony." She came to me, offered me a glass.

"Here's looking at you," she said, taking a drink from hers.

I felt dizzy standing so close to her, breathing in the humid warmth of her hair and skin. I took a step back.

"This ceremony," I said, "does it hurt?"

"Only if you do it right."

Sally pressed forward, backing me toward an armchair next to a dresser covered with lighted candles. And I let myself be backed, taking part in a slow, sexy dance, trembling from the effort to keep my hands off her.

"All this just to pay off on a bet with Gill Stroud?" I asked.

"Out here we take our debts seriously," she said. Her robe—my robe, silk, sea green—came loose, and I watched Sally's skin welcoming the unfolding of the robe, welcoming the light.

"Are you sure this is a Cajun ceremony?" I asked as we both unbuttoned my shirt.

"I'm supposed to pluck a live chicken now," Sally whispered. "I guess I'll have to improvise."

She must have unbuckled my pants, because they slid to the floor, throwing me off balance, and I fell backward into the chair. Sally Dean landed in my lap, with the robe down around her hips and the drinks spraying over both of us. The shock of the ice and the bourbon played over me and over her skin, which shivered, her nipples darkening, hardening.

"According to Mama, this will keep the willies off you," she said. She took one of the burning candles off the dresser and poured a thin stream of molten wax across my chest.

"Jesus, Sally!" The heat shocked me, and I tried to push her off, but only for a moment. Everywhere I put my hands, she was there.

CHAPTER 14

THE NEXT MORNING Sally Dean was gone when I woke up. Bevo Rasmussen was sitting in the armchair, sipping Jack Daniel's from one of last night's glasses. He was wearing faded overalls, work boots, stained T-shirt, and bill cap, and I saw that I'd been right about him: A farm hand's uniform fit his hayseed looks better than the Italian suit he'd had on yesterday. I could see more of the dragon tattoo that ran the length of his right arm, red, green, and blue. He smiled, showing me his jeweled tooth.

"How's it hanging?" he asked. I struggled to sit up on the bed, surprised by how much effort it took. I was exhausted, played out in every muscle and sore in peculiar spots. A few dried strips of candle wax crumbled off my chest as I moved. My skin felt as if it had been sandblasted. I touched my rib cage and winced.

Bevo chuckled. "Sally sure can take it out of a man."

"Get out of here," I said. He reached to the dresser, poured some whiskey into the other glass, and handed it to me.

"Hair of the dog," he said.

I took it from him and set in on the nightstand. "Mr. Rasmussen," I said, "if you're not gone in thirty seconds, I'm calling the police."

"Now, that's no way to talk to a client, Mr. Parker," he said, "especially one who's looking out for you like I am. Why do you think Sally came over here and did you fit to die last night? She sure didn't do it for her boyfriend Stroud. He'd be eating his liver if he knew. No, sir, she did it for me."

I stared at him.

"Yes, sir," he said, smoothing his mustache with a self-satisfied air, "we have spared no expense to keep the new boy happy."

"You're insane," I told him. "Sally Dean is a state judicial district coordinator. An officer of the court. There's no way in hell she would be mixed up with you." It was inconceivable. Sally Dean and Bevo Rasmussen were from two different worlds.

Bevo read my thoughts. "Before you go heaping any more dirt on my head," he said, "you better check your facts. Okay, Sally might not have greased you just because I asked her. But she'd have done it for her daddy, and her daddy would have gotten her to do it for me."

"Her father?"

"Nyman Scales. You know about him, if you've been reading my file. He's my bidniss partner."

I knew the name. Scales was the horse dealer from whom Bevo had bought his horses. I recalled Sally telling me that her father was a local rancher. She had not mentioned his name.

"Sally Dean is Nyman Scales's daughter?"

"That's right," Bevo replied. "And she does whatever her daddy tells her to. Always has."

"Wait a minute. Why are their last names different?"

"Dean was Sally's mother's maiden name. Sally had a soft spot in her heart for old Mom. Any more questions?"

The conversation was getting crazier. "All right," I said, "let's assume it's true, Sally is Nyman Scales's daughter. Why would Scales tell his daughter to go to bed with a stranger?"

He gave me a sneer. "Because Nyman is a friend of mine, and he wants to see me beat this lawsuit. And it's going to take a third lawyer, somebody who ain't on his last legs, like Stroud, or has his brains all in his dick, like Wick Chandler. Since my case started, there've been four new lawyers start up with Chandler and Stroud, and none of them lasted long enough to do any good. Nyman and me, we don't want to lose another one."

"Let me get this straight," I said. "You're saying that Sally Dean slept with me because her father wants to keep me happy defending you?"

"You have caught my drift."

"That would make Sally Dean a whore and her father a pimp."

He nodded smugly. "It's what we call teamwork."

"You don't know what you're talking about," I said.

"You don't know Nyman Scales," he replied. "And you damn sure don't know Sally."

I had never felt more contempt for any human being than I did at that moment for Bevo Rasmussen. It was contempt mixed with awe. What he was suggesting was so off the wall, so illogical, that I could not imagine a human brain capable of taking it seriously. Yet this twisted little man sat nodding at me as if expecting me to buy the whole load.

"You like the house?" he asked. "I had a little something to do with it, too."

I swung my legs over the side of the bed, and Bevo started up out of his chair as if he thought I might backhand him. On the bed lay my robe, the one Sally had worn last night. I put it on.

"Leave, Bevo," I said. "Get out of my house."

"I didn't come here to bullshit you, Counselor. I come to ask you a favor. I got some bidniss in Dallas tomorrow night, and I sure would appreciate it if you would ride along with me."

"Why?"

The little man shrugged, his left shoulder moving more fully with the gesture than his damaged right one. "Oh, for friendship, let's say. I think we should get to know each other better, you being my new lawyer and all."

I remembered Wick's warning. *Don't believe a word the man says. Don't do anything he wants you to do.*

"I'm not driving with you to Dallas, Bevo."

"Not even if it would help my case?" he asked.

"This trip is connected to Stromboli's lawsuit against you?"

"It just might be," he said.

"Why not get Wick Chandler to go with you?"

"The people I got to meet wouldn't be impressed with Wick. They might be with you."

I had an idea that I did not want to meet these people, and I told him so.

Rasmussen leaned close. "How about if I got Sally to come with us? You and her could have the backseat all to yourselves." He leered at me. "Ever come in a Cadillac, Mr. Parker?"

I chased him halfway around the chair that he had kept between us.

"Hold it, Counselor," he said. "There's something else I know. I know Stroud has bungled my case. He's blown it so big that I can clean him out in a malpractice suit. I might even be able to sink your whole firm. How would that be?"

I quit chasing him. He might be right, I admitted to myself. Thanks to Stroud's failure with the interrogatories, this little rat just might have us by the short hairs.

"Did you set fire to your horses, Bevo?" I asked him.

"I swear on my mother's grave, Mr. Parker, I didn't do it. My horses was fine last time I saw them. Jesus, look at all the shit I'm in now. Do you think I'd have brought all this trouble on myself?"

"Then why won't your insurance carrier pay off?"

"It's a conspiracy, Mr. Parker. There's folks out to get me. They don't want to see me better myself. I don't know who they are, but they're the ones behind it. I swear it's true." He was starting to whine.

I told him to call me that afternoon and I would tell him then whether I would go with him to Dallas. "But now I want you to leave," I said.

Bevo was visibly relieved that I had agreed at least to think about going with him. He walked to the bedroom door, then turned.

"I'd count it a real favor if you'd go, Mr. Parker."

"No more threats against the firm," I replied.

"I'm sorry about that," he said. "It just shows you how desperate I am."

A thought suddenly struck me. "Bevo, this trip to Dallas. Is it going to be dangerous?"

He laughed at that. "I don't know what you've been hearing about me, Mr. Parker, but I can tell it's all wrong. Hell, no, the trip ain't dangerous. Would I put my new lawyer in jeopardy? So how about it, will you come with me?"

"Call me at the office this afternoon, and I'll give you my answer."

He looked down at his feet, shaking his head. "You're a hard man to pin down, that's for sure. Think of Sally in the backseat," he said, winking at me, and he walked out the door.

A moment later I heard the front door close. I went into the bathroom to take a shower. After talking to Bevo Rasmussen, I felt I needed one.

Standing in the tub, I let the water run over me as I thought through recent events. Bevo Rasmussen's presence in my bedroom this morning suggested that the little ceremony Sally Dean and I had enacted last night, guaranteed to keep the willies off me, hadn't worked. I still had at least one willy to worry about, a diamond-toothed one, at that. This did not at all mean, however, that the ceremony had been without value. I probed a sore spot over my rib cage, remembering the release that had rolled through me, unstringing muscles and tendons, dissolving away the last of the old life. Nothing I could remember had ever felt so good as Sally Dean had felt the night before.

Sally Dean. Sally Scales. Sally Scales Dean.

It was beginning to look as if country law was a bit more complicated than I had anticipated. But one thing I knew was true, I told myself as I dried off from my shower. Sally Dean had some real fun last night. I had the bruises to prove it.

CHAPTER 15

HALF AN HOUR LATER I walked out of the house planning to get some breakfast at the Dairy Queen and head for the office. A tall, round-shouldered man in a knit sport shirt and bill cap was rolling my lawn mower—the one I had never gotten around to using on my first night in town—down the driveway toward a pickup. I asked him what he thought he was doing. He stopped and looked at me.

"I'm repossessing what's mine," he said, chewing on a dead cigar stump clenched in his teeth. He took the cigar out of his mouth and introduced himself as Glenn Lawson, owner of the hardware store in town. We shook hands, and I told him my name.

"You're the new lawyer," he said. "Sorry to hear about your feet."

"Thanks," I said. "They're better now."

"Well, Mr. Parker, how many people like me have shown up since you moved in?"

"People like you?"

"Creditors. Didn't you know that the guy who owns this place walked away from all his debts? He moved in, bought up a bunch of shit, furniture and tools and whatnot, and then just stopped paying on everything."

"Hardwick Chandler didn't make his payments?"

"Hardwick Chandler don't own this place," Lawson replied. "It belongs to that little squirrel dick Bevo Rasmussen."

"Bevo?"

Lawson nodded. "I was a fool for selling him this mower. If business hadn't been so damn bad, I'd have kicked his skinny ass out of my store. The little shit broke into my brother-in-law's warehouse a couple of years back and tried to steal a truckload of electronic stuff." Lawson bit down on the cigar butt and started pushing the lawn mower again. Then he stopped and said, "You can have the mower, if you'll pay for it. It's a handy machine, the best I've got on the floor. It's self-propelled. Three hundred and fourteen dollars, and that's my cost. You can't buy it for that at the goddamned Wal-Mart."

"Mr. Lawson," I said, "you're telling me Bevo Rasmussen owns the house I'm living in?"

Lawson chuckled. "I guess maybe old Hard-dick pulled one on you, son. Are you paying anything on it?"

"No."

"Well, that's a mercy," he said. "Though sticking you in a house that's apt to be stripped and foreclosed on is a low deal, even for Hard-dick Chandler."

So Bevo had told me the truth: He *did* have something to do with my being in this house. In fact, he had everything to do with it.

Lawson told me that Bevo Rasmussen had bought the house over a year ago, from an out-of-work geologist so desperate to leave town that he accepted Bevo's offer even though Bevo was an unqualified buyer, and an unsavory one at that. Bevo moved in, outfitted the house, then failed to make payments on most of the things he'd bought.

"The story is, he only made one or two mortgage payments on the house," Lawson said. "It was a HUD loan, you see, and when the mortgage company saw he wasn't making his payments and threatened to foreclose, he filed for some sort of HUD extension, and that stopped the foreclosure. HUD is so loaded down with cases that it could be another year or so before they ever get around to taking care of the mess Bevo made."

"So Rasmussen was living here for free?" I asked.

"That's right. There are people who do that, you know, buy a house knowing they aren't going to pay for it. They just stay in it until somebody kicks them out. Then they slink away in the night. Since the loan was unqualified, the house goes back to the first owner, along with the debt. The first owner gets the shaft."

"Is that what happened to the guy Bevo bought the house from, the geologist? Did he get the shaft?"

"He will if HUD ever gets around to looking him up. I don't know where he moved to. If I had sold my house to Bevo Rasmussen, I think I'd move to Mars."

"What you're saying is Bevo stole this house?" I asked.

"I suppose so," Lawson replied. "He stole the use of it, anyway."

"And now *I'm* stealing the use of it? I'm living in it for free while the mortgage debt piles up at the door of that geologist?"

"Ask old Hard-dick about it. Maybe he cut some sort of deal with the owner or the mortgage holder. He's great at finessing deals."

I planned to ask old Hard-dick about it, all right.

"Why did Bevo stop living in the house?" I asked.

Lawson shrugged. "So you could move into it, I guess. I don't really know, just like I don't know why he bought it in the first place. My brother-in-law thinks maybe he was just tired of being a lowlife. Maybe he wanted to go legitimate, join us happy people here in the middle class. My brother-in-law's an idiot. I think Bevo was working some dodge, and it caught up with him. I've heard he's got himself into some trouble with a drug dealer. Maybe he's laying low. You sure you won't buy this fine lawn mower here? You won't find a better deal."

"I'll think about it," I replied.

Lawson had rolled the lawn mower to his truck. He squatted, rubbed at a scratch in the mower's red paint. "If I could just sell three of these beauties to everybody in this town," he said, "I could get halfway out of debt."

"I'll pass the word, Mr. Lawson," I told him. We picked up the lawn mower and put it in Lawson's truck.

Lawson climbed into the truck's cab. "Good luck, son," he said. "If you see Bevo Rasmussen, do me a favor and kick his ass up his throat." He laughed. "No, don't do it. He'd find a way to sue me if you did."

At the Dairy Queen Lu-Anne gave me a cup of coffee and a smile, smacking her gum with the sound of a rifle shot. I asked her how she could chew gum at 7:45 in the morning.

"I got a lot of excess energy," she replied. She put down her coffeepot. "You see this hand? See how steady it is? It would be jumping all over the place if I wasn't working my gum." She picked up the pot and topped off my cup. "You'd have coffee all over you right now if I didn't have this gum in my mouth."

She talked me into trying a country ham biscuit. The Jenks Dairy Queen, she said, was the only one in the state that offered country ham, a delicacy smuggled in from Tennessee by a cousin of the owner. Country ham, she said, was different from breakfast ham. She was right: Country ham tasted like the boot sole of a worker in a salt mine. It was something to chew on while I pondered once again the ironies of life in the country.

"You're the new lawyer, ain't you?" Lu-Anne asked me as she refilled my coffee.

"What makes you think I'm a lawyer?"

"It's your suit," she replied. "You're either a lawyer or a banker, and we don't get bankers in here very often."

"Couldn't I be a doctor?" I asked.

She smiled. "Doctors dress like golfers. You know, knit shirts, loafers . . ."

"How about a mortician?"

"A what?"

"An undertaker."

"We only got one of them, and he's not hiring."

"You'd make a pretty fair detective," I told her.

"You're that lawyer with the bad feet," she said. "How they doing today?"

"Maybe I'm a famous movie director thinking about using this town as the setting of my new picture."

She laughed at that. "Come *on,* what kind of movie would you be making out here?"

"Science fiction," I told her. "It's all about an alien who gets trapped in a small town in Texas. Nobody knows he's an alien because he looks just like everybody else. But he's not like everybody else. The question is, will he go crazy in the small town or will he adjust and live a peaceful life among the earthlings?"

"What does the alien look like?" she asked.

"He looks just like everybody else."

"No," said Lu-Anne, "what does he look like for real, when he doesn't have on his human disguise?"

"He looks like a giant purple foot."

A few minutes later, as I got up to leave, Lu-Anne patted me on the shoulder. "You'll get used to them," she said.

"What?"

"Mr. Chandler and Mr. Stroud. You'll get used to them. We're all used to them. You just have to learn how to duck from time to time. But you'll make out all right." She smiled at me and went back behind the counter.

Hardwick Chandler had not checked in when I arrived at the office. "Did you know that the house I'm living in belongs to Bevo Rasmussen?" I asked Molly Tunstall.

"Yes, sir," she said.

"Well, I didn't know."

"I'm sorry, Mr. Parker. I'm sure Mr. Chandler was going to tell you."

I told her to buzz me the minute Mr. Chandler showed up.

"Lu-Anne at the Dairy Queen says I'll make out all right here," I said, "if I learn how to duck."

"That's good advice," Molly responded. I had hoped to get a laugh out of her, but she just gave me a woebegone look from behind her desk.

"You'll help me learn to duck, won't you, Molly?"

"I'll try, Mr. Parker," she said. Under those mournful eyes her face scrunched up, and I realized she was smiling.

CHAPTER 16

THE RASMUSSEN FILE LAY on Molly's desk, exactly where I had left it for Wick Chandler the previous evening. Apparently his attempt at reform had not yet gotten truly under way. Neither of the partners was in, so I took the file back to my office and read it through again, trying to brainstorm some way around the problem with the interrogatories. I got nowhere.

About eleven o'clock Molly called on the intercom to tell me I had a visitor. It was a tiny, round lady in a cotton sundress, cowboy boots, and a denim apron stitched with the phrase *I'm with Stupid* in red across the front. She introduced herself as Mrs. Nevah June Balch and placed a quart jar on the desk. The jar was filled with what looked like a meat stew. A hoof of some sort floated in it.

"It needs to be good and hot," she said. "And never mind the smell. It'll fix your feet in two days."

"Do I eat it?" I asked.

"Well, of course you eat it," she said, giving me a surprised laugh. "What did you think you'd do, soak your feet in it?"

I asked her how much I owed her.

"Don't you worry about that," she said as she left. "Bevo took care of this dose. If you need another one, we can talk."

"Thank you, Mrs. Balch," I called after her. For maybe fifteen minutes I sat watching the hoof floating around in the herbal stew. Molly came back and stood in the doorway.

"Would you like me to do something with that?" she asked, pointing to the jar.

"Thanks, Molly," I said. She picked up the jar and left.

Around twelve o'clock Wick Chandler stuck his head in my door. "How about taking a break?" he asked. Before I could answer him, he and Stroud swept into the room, grabbed me under the arms, and whisked me outside. Stroud's Continental was idling at the curb. "Quick," Chandler said, throwing open a door to the back-seat and pulling me toward it, "get in before we're spotted."

"Spotted by who?" I asked.

"Witnesses," said Stroud, who limped around and got into the driver's seat. Wick squeezed himself into the passenger's side.

"Where the hell have you been?" I asked him.

"I have been reforming my character, Clay, just like you asked me to."

"Where are we going?" I asked.

"Barbecue!" Stroud roared as he gunned the engine and we peeled rubber down the street.

"Boo's barbecue," Wick explained. "Best in Texas. Our treat, Clay. But we've got one little thing to do first."

Stroud drove like a B-movie gangster, swiveling the big car down city streets until they gave way to farm-to-market roads.

"You're going to kill us!" I said, hanging on in the backseat.

"You see, Clay," Wick said, "we've got to beat the ex-pilots to the Old Platte Road."

"The who?" I asked.

"We're on a mission, son," said Stroud, turning around to give me a sodden wink.

Stroud was very drunk, his withered head bobbing up and down like the head of one of those spring-loaded toy dogs in the rear windows of cars. He hummed tunelessly as we scorched down the road, his eyes incandescent with drink.

"Mr. Stroud, should you be driving?" I asked.

"Hell, no," he said, smiling at me in the rearview mirror.

"What sort of mission are we on?"

"Wait and see," he replied.

"So how are things going in the country, Clay?" Wick asked. "How's our new man doing?"

Bracing against the swerves, I let my employers know how I felt about the housing deal they had set up for me. Wick assured me that nobody was being hurt.

"What about the geologist who sold the house to Rasmussen?" I asked.

"He's in China," Wick explained. "He's making a million dollars looking for oil for the Commie government. Don't worry, Clay. We'll make any mortgage payments that devolve on him, if he ever shows up and HUD comes after him. We'll do right by him. I promise. It was Bevo's idea in the first place," he added.

"Bevo's idea? To give up his house?"

"He saw it as a way to work off some of what he owes us. We've got fees charged to him from a couple of years back."

"Where is Bevo living now?" I asked.

Wick shrugged. "Do you know, Gill?" he asked. Stroud ignored the question.

"I agree with Mr. Parker," the old man grumbled from the driver's seat. "You never should have cut that deal with Bevo Rasmussen. It looks like we're taking advantage of a client."

"He's your goddamn client, Gill," Wick replied. "I'm just trying to get some kind of remuneration out of him."

For a few minutes as we sped down a section road they bickered about which of them was to blame for their association with Bevo Rasmussen.

"The Stromboli lawsuit was a black hole from the beginning," Wick said. "You must have been whacked out of your mind when you took it."

"At least I was working," grumbled Stroud. "I wasn't out rooting around for poontang like the distinguished head of our firm."

They got into a fight about Wick's involvement with Mrs. Starns, the emu lady. "Every time I look up, there's another tart leading you around by the ying-yang," said Stroud. "Deirdre Starns tells you to piss in the wind, and you unzip and let 'er fly."

"At least I can control my stream," Wick said. "At least I'm not dribbling boozy piss out my pants leg every time I sneeze."

"Enough!" roared Stroud. The car swerved off the road, and for a moment I thought we were going over. Stroud regained control, and I let out a long sigh. Both of them looked back at me.

"We almost killed our new lawyer, Gill," said Wick, "on his third day on the job." They both thought that was hilarious.

Next to me on the seat was a battered rattan suitcase with which I kept colliding as the car zigzagged down the road.

"Jesus, Clay," Wick said, "be careful with that suitcase!"

"You don't want that thing to come open, son," Stroud told me.

"Why not?"

"Just don't fool with it," Stroud replied. I pushed it away from me on the seat.

"This mission we're on, does it have something to do with former pilots?" I asked.

Stroud thumped Chandler on the shoulder with a liver-spotted fist. "He's a quick lad, Mr. Chandler!" The old man laughed.

Stroud turned onto another road, bordered by cultivated fields on one side and a wilderness of high grass on the other. He slowed the car down, and Wick scanned the new road in both directions.

"I think we made it," Wick said.

Stroud stopped the car. "Mr. Parker," he said, "could I trouble you to set that suitcase on the side of the road?"

"Carefully," said Wick.

I opened the car door, reached over, and picked up the suitcase by the handle. Something heavy slid to the bottom of it, and I heard a muffled, low-pitched whirring noise. The suitcase pulsed with pent-up energy.

"Jesus, what's in here?" I said. "Is this a bomb?"

"Set it upright," Stroud instructed. "Hurry, son!"

As soon as the case stood on the asphalt, Stroud hit the gas, and I almost fell out onto the road as the Lincoln sped away. Stroud drove about fifty yards, then pulled off the road behind a thick grove of pines and oak trees that gave way to a sheer wall of grass and weeds over six feet high. He plunged the car into the grass, and we rocked crazily through the crackling stalks. In a few seconds the car stopped, and I could see that we had come to the other side of the grass patch, where a dirt road snaked along toward the woods.

"We're here!" said Wick. "What do you think, Mr. Stroud?"

"Let us try it before the bar," Stroud replied, shutting off the engine. They climbed out of the car and pushed their way back through the trail that the Lincoln had made in the grass. Mystified, I followed them toward the grove of trees until, just before leaving the grass, we came upon a wooden frame, maybe ten feet high, made of faded, rotting planks. It looked like a gallows. A wooden ladder was nailed to its side.

"After you, Mr. Chandler," said Stroud.

"After *you*, Mr. Stroud," Wick replied. Stroud climbed slowly, wheezing by the time he reached the top. I saw him put his aspirator in his mouth and trigger it. Wick followed him up the ladder.

"What is this thing?" I asked.

"A duck blind," Wick said. I climbed up after him. At the top was a narrow walkway and a bench, approximately five feet long, all made of planks. A waist-high railing bowed treacherously when I took hold of it. The whole frame wobbled whenever any of us moved. I sat down slowly next to Wick on the bench. Grass shoots and tree limbs had been fastened to the railing for camouflage. My colleagues peered through the foliage at the road, and so did I. There was the suitcase, standing at the side of the road.

"Are there any ducks around here?" I asked.

"Nope," said Wick. "We had the blind moved here last week."

"Why?"

"You're about to find out."

"God almighty, it's a hot one," said Stroud, taking out a hand-kerchief and rubbing the back of his neck. The blind was shaded by oak trees, but the air was heavy and hot. Locusts sang in the trees all around us.

"Boo did a good job of setting this thing up," Wick said.

"He might have gotten us some more shade," Stroud griped.

"What are we doing, guys?" I asked.

"We're here to prove a point," Stroud replied.

"You see, Clay," said Wick, "there's a gentleman of our acquain-tance who thinks himself an ace trapper but who is, in reality, a tenderfoot shithead of the first water."

"An animal trapper?" I asked.

"Hah!" bellowed Stroud. "The only thing he's ever trapped is his own ass."

"Captain Jack is one of the ex-pilots," Wick continued. "We're waiting for them now. They usually eat Boo's barbecue on Thurs-day, and they usually take this road to get there."

"Who are the ex-pilots?" I asked.

Stroud let out a grunt of pure disdain. "A support group for morons," he said.

Wick filled me in. It seemed that Jenks sat on the easternmost edge of what had been one of the prime recreational areas in East Texas. The interstates made travel to and from Dallas easy, and many wealthy city types had bought land and built houses by the small man-made lakes bulldozed into the greenery. In the early eighties, these urbanites mixed on the streets of the local towns with farmers and cattle ranchers and oilmen, who were doing pretty well back then. The small area towns boomed. But along came the late eighties, and business went bust for just about everybody. The locals lost their farms, cattle, and oil, and the little towns started drying up, Jenks included. All the urbanites put their country homes up for sale and went back to the city. All, that is, except for a group of airline pilots from Braniff and TWA who had built big houses among the hills west of Jenks and couldn't move back to Dallas because they'd all been laid off.

"Those nitwits getting fired was the best thing that could have happened to the friendly skies," Stroud said.

These ex-pilots, ten or eleven in number and wealthy from their years with the airlines, formed a roving pack of disgruntled outlaws who went through phases of middle-aged despair together. During what Wick called their Guns-'n'-Ammo phase, the ex-pilots hung out at a gun repair shop that Captain Jack, their ringleader, built on his land, where they would drink all day and shoot at anything that moved in the woods.

"Delmar Spruggs lost two cows that summer," Wick said.

"Idiots thought they were *bears!*" said Stroud, laughing.

Wick explained that in the spring of '92 most of the ex-pilots bought Harley-Davidson motorcycles and took to roaring through the streets of the local towns, raising dust and irritating the natives.

The Hells Angels phase of their therapy was cut short, however, by Gilliam Stroud.

Stroud was city attorney for Jenks then, and he prosecuted five of the would-be rebels for traffic violations stemming from a drunken parade they extemporized one Saturday afternoon in downtown Jenks. Gilliam Stroud was no reformer; in DWI cases he usually erred on the side of leniency, recognizing the folly of throwing stones from the porch of his own glass house. However, the arrogance of the cycling ex-pilots so incensed Stroud that he pressed the case hard and got the offenders a few days' jail time along with their stiff fines. Captain Jack's incarceration, brief though it was, damaged the enthusiasm of the whole group, and within two weeks they had sold their Harleys. Captain Jack and his boys had never forgiven Stroud his persecution of them. Stroud, for his part, delighted in trading insults with the ex-pilots, who were now also ex-bikers.

"I would have put them away for good," Stroud explained, "if only they weren't such fun to bait when you come on them in the wild."

"Look!" said Wick. Up the Old Platte Road came an enormous Range Rover, painted in camouflage colors. It passed our hiding place, and I made out the shapes of five men inside. The duck blind made a perfect observation post.

"It's our boys!" said Stroud.

"There's something weird about their faces," I said.

"It's camouflage paint," Wick explained. "They're into a survivalist phase right now. They all think they're Rambo, waiting for the end of civilization. I wouldn't be surprised if there aren't half a dozen assault rifles in that buggy."

"Let me get this straight," I said. "We're sitting here in this heat to play some sort of joke on a bunch of armed psychos?"

"It's not a joke," said Stroud, "it's a mission. We are here to dispense a little moral instruction."

Stroud explained that the last time they had found themselves together—in a bar, as usual—he and Captain Jack had gotten into an argument about which one of them knew more about the local fauna. Jack, who cured animal skins at his gun shop, fancied himself a trapper. He boasted that he had trapped the last bobcat in the county years ago, and Stroud had explained to him that he was full of shit.

"I take it you're a backwoodsman yourself?" I asked Stroud.

"Hell, no," he said, "I don't know a goddamn thing about the goddamn woods. I didn't even know what a bobcat looked like until I got hold of the one we put in the suitcase."

"There's a bobcat in that suitcase out there?"

"Yep," said Wick. "Burl Weeks caught it for us up around Quitman. We picked it up this morning."

"Evil-looking critter," said Stroud.

The Range Rover slowed when it reached the suitcase, then drove on by.

"Shit and damnation," said Wick.

"Wait a bit," Stroud said. A hundred feet down the road, the car stopped and, after a moment, began to back up.

"Hell," said Wick. "I forgot the camcorder."

"A client I had once played a trick like this on his wife's boyfriend," Stroud said. "There's something about a suitcase sitting all by itself on the side of the road makes it hard to ignore. Of course, that fellow put six rattlesnakes in his suitcase. And the wrong party picked it up, a couple of college boys from out of state. Ugly mess."

"You said you were dispensing moral instruction," I reminded him. "What's moral about this?"

"Any truth, son, is a moral truth," said Stroud dryly. "It is a moral truth that bobcats still frolic in these woods. Captain Jack needs to learn that truth."

The Rover stopped beside the suitcase. A door opened, and the suitcase disappeared. The Rover zoomed away.

"But they'll know it was you!" I said. "This Captain Jack will remember your conversation in the bar. They'll know!"

"I was under the impression that you were a lawyer, Mr. Parker," said Stroud. "There's a mighty big gulf between knowing and *proving*."

"This is the stupidest thing I have ever seen two grown men do!" I protested.

"Three," said Stroud, mocking me with a sly grin. "Three grown men."

Suddenly the Range Rover went into a skid and stopped, blocking both lanes of the Old Platte Road. All four doors blew open, and five camouflaged men tumbled out. One of them fell onto the asphalt surface, jumped up, and ran screaming into the grass on our side of the road. Two of the men had rifles and started shooting at the car. Sustained bursts of gunfire chewed up the sides of the Rover, shattering windows and blowing out a tire.

"See there," said Wick, "I told you they had automatic weapons!"

Another man started yelling at the riflemen, waving at them to stop shooting.

"That would be Captain Jack," Wick said. "It's his car." As soon as the rifle fire stopped, a small shape bolted from the front seat of the car and into the grass near where the screaming man had disappeared. One of the riflemen fired a burst after it but missed. The man who had run into the grass came running out, screaming at the rifleman. There was a fistfight on the roadside, which eventually involved four of the ex-pilots.

"I've seen enough," said Stroud. "Let's go get some barbecue."

As we climbed down, Wick asked his partner, "Do you think Captain Jack knew it was a bobcat?"

"I think he knew it wasn't a field mouse," Stroud replied. We reached the Lincoln, and Stroud got into the driver's seat. Wick and I pushed the car the few feet from the grass to the dirt road, which sloped enough for the car to run along a couple of hundred yards without power. We did not want the ex-pilots to hear us making our getaway.

"We'd better call Burl to come and trap the cat again," said Wick as we glided down the dirt road without power. "It might eat an ostrich."

"You promised you were going to reform," I reminded him.

"I know," he said sheepishly. "I guess I'd better start over."

CHAPTER 17

STROUD SEEMED TO HAVE sobered up a little during his vigil in the duck blind, but his hold on the road was still pretty loose.

"Can we talk about the Rasmussen case?" I asked, hoping to steady him. "What are we going to do? We've only got seven days until the trial."

"Fourteen days," Stroud said.

"I beg your pardon?"

"We have fourteen days until the trial."

"The file says seven," I said.

"The file is not up to date," Stroud said. "SWAT asked for an extension, claiming scheduling problems. We have fourteen days."

"That's a relief," said Wick.

"Not much of one," I countered. "Tell me, Mr. Stroud, is the file out of date in any other ways? Did you, perhaps, remember to send answers to the SWAT interrogatories and neglect to enclose a copy in the files?"

"No," Stroud replied. "The interrogatories are a problem."

"You aren't planning to plead a fake heart attack to get more time, are you?" I asked him.

Stroud glared at Wick. "I told you, Hard-dick. Never again!" he said.

"It was just a thought," Wick replied.

"I wonder what kind of scheduling problems SWAT had that made them ask for a delay?" I asked.

"They wanted an extra week to sharpen their axes," Wick said. "They plan to chop us into lawyer pâté."

A couple of minutes later Stroud pulled the big car into a gravel parking lot, next to a shack with a roof sagging under a buzzing, spitting neon sign that read THE SINGING PIG. It was a little after two o'clock, and the only occupants of the Singing Pig were the owner and his wife, Boo and Betty, a leathery little couple who looked as if they'd been smoked in their own smokehouse. Wick Chandler bellowed a greeting at them, and Stroud limped up to Betty, took her hand, and asked in his deepest, most splendid voice if he could compare her to a summer's day.

"You can tell me what you want to eat," she suggested in a dry voice, but there was an amused light in her eye. "The only way I'm like a summer's day is I'm hot and dusty."

While they bantered with Boo and Betty, I watched my employers from a seat at the lunch counter. They were a study in contrasts: Gilliam Stroud, cadaverous in his dusty, hollow black suit, swept through the tiny diner like an ancient king; Hardwick Chandler, a bloated lounge lizard in tight silk shirt, sport jacket, and glittering gold, bustled like a cartoon steam engine. They were as odd a pairing as I had ever seen, yet they seemed to share some wavelength that coordinated their behavior. Boo's was pretty much a self-serve eatery, and I watched Chandler and Stroud set up a table for the three of us, fetching tableware, napkins, bowls of condiments, squeeze bottles of sauce, with a perfect economy of motion. All the while Stroud crooned courtly endearments to Mrs. Boo, and Chandler, a sheen of sweat glimmering on his rosy jowls, interrogated Boo about the state of his beef and the likelihood of a customer's bringing home from the Singing Pig something worse than a stomachache after eating the pork ribs. It was as if Stroud and Chandler, king and fool, were two halves of a single intelligence.

When it was time to order, Stroud gave me a canny look and asked, "What will it be, Mr. Parker, beef or pork?"

"Pork," I said.

"Hah!" shouted Hardwick Chandler, who slapped the counter and ordered pork himself and beers for all of us.

Stroud ordered beef. Later, at the table, he told me that barbecued pork was how the South lost the Civil War. "Trichinosis destroyed the army of Virginia," he explained.

Waiting for our food, we sipped our beers and brainstormed the Rasmussen case. The wording of the Stromboli petition required SWAT to prove that Bevo had killed his own horses. According to Stroud, Bevo claimed to have an airtight alibi for his presence on the night the horses burned. He was in Tyler, spending the night at the ranch of Nyman Scales, the breeder who sold Bevo the horses. Sally Dean's father.

"We will depose Nyman Scales," Stroud said. "I have already arranged with all parties to meet with Scales at his ranch in Tyler on Monday morning."

"I've always wanted to see Scales's ranch," said Wick. "I've heard it's a land unto itself."

"This Nyman Scales," I said, "I take it he's a big operator?"

"The biggest," replied Wick.

"And he's really Sally Dean's father?"

"Did she tell you that?" Stroud asked.

"Bevo mentioned it." I told them a little bit about my morning chat with Bevo. A very little bit. From the way the old man's eyebrows had lowered like thunderheads, I gathered that now was not the time to discuss Bevo Rasmussen's peculiar theory about the Scaleses' father-daughter relationship.

"That's right," said Stroud, "Scales is Ms. Dean's father. What of it?"

"Nothing," I said. "Coincidence, I guess."

"It might be more than that," Wick said with a note of wistfulness, turning to his partner. "It just might save our asses, if only you'd ask her to—"

"Stop right there!" the old man said. "Nobody's asking Ms. Dean to do anything that even looks like a breach of ethics. Do you understand me, Wick?"

"But there's nothing unethical about it, Gill," Wick argued. "Hell, the judges themselves do it all the time, cozying up to her to ask for assignments. I don't see why we can't turn it around and ask her to help us out just this once. After all we've done for her." He turned to me. "Tell him, Clay. There's nothing wrong with simply asking if the district coordinator can influence which judge handles a particular trial, is there? In the interests of fair play?"

"I don't understand this sudden delicacy on your part, Mr. Stroud," I said. "It's not as if you never ask Sally for favors."

"What do you mean by that?" Stroud snapped.

I told him what Sally had said about the bet she had made with him over the Hardesty trial and how losing it had required her to act as a one-woman hospitality committee for the new guy. I didn't say anything about the Cajun house exorcism or the willies-prevention ceremony, but Stroud eyed me suspiciously, anyway.

"I may have asked her to check on you, Mr. Parker, but only as a professional courtesy," he said. "My request had nothing to do with any wager—and it sure as hell didn't break any rules of the court."

"So Sally Dean was lying to me about the bet?" I asked.

"Ms. Dean has a whimsical sense of humor," Stroud said. "Perhaps she was simply amusing herself."

I'll say, I thought to myself.

"There is no way Ms. Dean can replace a judge who doesn't want to be replaced, short of breaking a chair over his head and stuffing him in a closet," said Stroud. "Not that it wouldn't do most of them a world of good."

Wick sighed. "I'm sorry, Gill. I guess I'm going crazy with this thing. If only we hadn't drawn Judge Tidwell for the case."

The food arrived, three immense platters, along with another round of beers.

"Well, it's Tidwell, all right, so suck up and live with it."

Wick sighed. "Wrong Tit Tidwell," he said, shaking his head and biting into a huge, dripping pork rib.

"Wrong Tit?" I said.

"I told you, Gill," said Wick through a mouthful of pork. "I told you it would catch up with us, and now it has."

"What has caught up with us?" I asked.

Stroud and Chandler looked at each other.

"Never mind," replied Stroud. "Let's just say Judge Tidwell won't mourn as we go down the tubes."

We ate in silence for a while. Wick was right about Boo's barbecue. It may have been the best in Texas.

"Okay," I said, "so we'll get no help from the judge on the interrogatories. Which means we can't call any witnesses. Nyman Scales can swear himself blue in the face that he was with Bevo on the night the barn burned, and the jury will never hear it. So why are we deposing him?"

Stroud glared at me. "We are going to depose anybody we damn well please. Nobody can stop us from asking questions, and there are reasons, Mr. Parker, why we must do so."

"What are they?" I asked.

"For one thing," said Stroud, "we may uncover information that would allow us to prove gross misconduct by SWAT. If we do that, we can threaten the bastards with an ethical complaint to the bar, or even criminal prosecution. We may get them to back down."

"There's a one-in-a-million chance of that happening in a SWAT case, and you know it," I told him. "You're grasping at straws."

Fury flushed the old man's face. "All right then, goddamn it, we're going to depose people because that's all we *can* do. I prefer to fiddle while Rome burns. Satisfied, Mr. Parker?"

"No, Mr. Stroud, I'm not satisfied," I said, "but I am glad to be back in the real world."

"Where's the pathologist's report?" asked Wick. "At least we could see what kind of physical evidence they have."

Stroud told us that SWAT had not provided a report yet from the horse pathologist who investigated the scene of the fire. That was odd. Perhaps it was the reason they had asked for a delay. I wondered if maybe there would be an irregularity in the pathologist's report that we could exploit.

"No chance," Stroud replied, without looking up from his plate. "They're using Pulaski as their pathologist."

"Oh, man," Wick groaned, shoving his plate away from him on the table. "This just gets worse and worse."

"Stan Pulaski?" I asked.

A horse pathologist who specialized in arson cases, Pulaski was known by lawyers all over the world as the Sherlock Holmes of horse pathology. He had testified in hundreds of trials, and only a handful of his opinions had ever been successfully contested. I had read articles about him in the Houston papers and remembered comments from Rita Humphrey, my old office-mate, who characterized Pulaski as brilliant and detestable, an arrogant bastard completely convinced of his own infallibility. I knew that Pulaski often worked for SWAT and that, according to Rita, he fit right in. That was the worst thing Rita could say about anybody— that he or she fit right in at SWAT.

"He lives not too far west of here," said Wick. "Maybe an hour away. Has his own lab out in the country and a landing strip. He's always flying off to study dead horses. He's got his own plane."

Stroud told me that he had cross-examined Pulaski several times and didn't care for the job. "The son of a bitch is hard to crack," the old man said. "I have never done a proper job of it."

"Looks like you're going to get another chance, partner," said Wick.

"What if we get our own pathologist?" I asked. They both looked at me. "Right," I said, "we can't call any witnesses of our own. All we can do is cross-examine the plaintiff's witnesses."

"Wrong Tit Tidwell and Stan-the-Man Pulaski," said Wick, shaking his head. "Goddamn it, Gill, you fucked up bad this time."

Stroud handed his steak knife to Wick, and with both hands pulled his shirt open, pushing his tie aside, to reveal a yellowing undershirt and a sliver of pale, silver-haired skin. "Go ahead," said the old man, "plunge it in to the hilt. Perhaps my life's blood will erase my guilt."

"For Christ's sake," said Wick.

"Could Bevo have been set up?" I asked. "He told me there was a conspiracy out to get him. Maybe somebody else did burn his horses."

"It's possible," Wick said. "Bevo only has about five hundred folks who hate him. And those are the ones we know about."

"How can this scrawny little loser stir up so many people?" I asked.

"Don't let his size or his manner fool you, Mr. Parker," said Stroud. "There is not a nastier son of a bitch in the state of Texas than our Bevo."

"You sound like you know him pretty well," I said.

"Better than I'd like to," Stroud replied.

CHAPTER 18

"BEVO GOT HIS START out at the sale barns, kiting cows," said Stroud.

"Kiting cows?"

"It's like kiting checks," Wick explained. "You go to a livestock auction, buy cows with a check at one barn, take them to another barn and sell them for enough money to cover the check you just wrote at the first barn, with maybe a little bit of a profit. At barn two you buy more cows, load 'em up, take 'em back to barn one and sell them there to cover the check you wrote at barn two."

"Again with a little profit?" I asked.

"That's right. Back and forth. You do the same thing at barn three, barn four. You're kiting cows. A pro can do it all day. He never actually has any property at any of these sales, yet he's always rolling in money. Everybody thinks he's a wheeler-dealer because he's always got a bunch of cows, herds of 'em."

"And that's Bevo Rasmussen?" I asked.

"That *was* Bevo," Stroud said. "Until he got ambitious and decided to move up to horses. Mr. Parker, do you know anything about horse trading?"

"Not very much."

"As a country lawyer, and this being East Texas, you will have to learn something of the horse trade."

"It's a different world, Clay," said Wick, shaking his head. "People in the horse-trading business, they're not even human. I don't mean all of them, of course. Just the bad ones. The bad ones are some sort of crawling bug. You pick up a big rock and look under it, you'll see some horse traders there. We're talking the ass end of America, Clay. The fucking ass end." From the look on his face, I had a hunch that Wick Chandler had had dealings with horse traders.

Stroud ordered another round of beers, which Boo brought over. "You boys talking about Bevo?" Boo asked, clearing away the plates.

"Boo here is a relative of Bevo's," said Wick.

"I'm his great-uncle," Boo said. "At least I think that's what I am. See that gal over there?" He pointed to Betty, who smiled at us from behind the counter. "That gal is Bevo's grandmother's youngest daughter." He laughed. "Now, me being married to her, what does that make me?"

"An upstanding citizen of Claymore County," Stroud replied.

"You boys going to make our Bevo a rich man?"

"We'll be lucky to keep him out of prison, Boo," Wick said.

"Well, don't feel bad about it," said Boo, walking away. "Prison might be just the thing that boy needs."

"Spoken like a member of the family," Wick said.

Wick continued his description of the horse trade. "Horse traders make screwing each other a way of life, and they all expect it, and they all lie, all the time. They're goddamned vultures. They're worse than you can imagine, Clay. Would you agree, Mr. Stroud?"

Stroud took a long pull from his beer, his Adam's apple jerking up and down his scrawny neck. "I would say you are being kind, Mr. Chandler."

"It's so bad that they talk to themselves in a kind of code, because they know that no matter what a person is telling them about a particular horse, he's lying. Everybody connected with these guys is the same. The veterinarians are crooked. The people who document pedigrees are crooked. They manufacture bloodlines. They make up horses, down to the last details. They make millions of dollars with imaginary horses. They're artists, Clay. They're the goddamned Vincent van Goghs of the maggot world."

"But it's a step up from the cow-kiting business?" I asked.

"That's what Bevo thought," Stroud said, taking up the story. "Our Mr. Rasmussen wanted to graduate from the cow business to the horse business. But it's a big jump and, snake though he was, Bevo was a schoolboy compared to the horse crowd. But he was in a hurry to learn, so he apprenticed himself to a master of the crooked horse trade."

"Who?" I asked.

"Nyman Scales," said Wick.

"Sally's father," I said.

"Yep," said Stroud, his eyes shining. "Bevo's alibi for the night of the fire. And the man who sold Bevo the horses in the first place. He even loaned Bevo a quarter of the purchase money. And I would bet my partner's last dime that Nyman Scales fully expected Bevo to burn his horses and split the insurance money with him."

"It is widely believed that Scales sells horses to crooks who burn them for the insurance money," said Wick.

"So Scales is a crook?"

"Oh, Nyman Scales is not your run-of-the-mill crook," said Wick. "You recall what I said about breeders being artists? Scales is like that. Only he's better than an artist. He's a goddamned magician."

According to Chandler and Stroud, there was no moneymaking scam concerning horses or cattle that Nyman Scales hadn't run. Like Bevo, Scales had got his start running cow scams. One of his scams, the one that made him rich, had become a legend among local dairy felons.

Some years ago the government decided that there was an undesirable surplus of milk in the country and that the prudent way to end subsidies to dairies was simply to buy the dairymen out. Learning of the government program, Nyman Scales went to fifty or so different livestock auction barns and worked up a giant cow-kiting scheme, so that he accumulated a huge number of sales receipts on cows. With these receipts Scales convinced the government that he had a huge dairy, and so the government bought him out, paying the highest recent market price for all of Nyman's cows, not one of which had ever actually set foot on Nyman's farm. At the same time the government was buying Nyman's cows, he was still kiting them, so Scales was actually making money two, three, even four times for the same cow.

"All this for beasts he'd never pulled a tit of milk from!" laughed Wick. "Now, there's an artist."

According to Wick, Scales used the enormous profit he made from the government buyout program to buy more cows, with which he set up a *real* dairy in order to receive the government subsidies that were still being doled out to the few dairies that stayed in business.

"How could he do that?" I asked. "Didn't the government catch on?"

"You got a mighty high opinion of our government," said Wick. "Nyman's no fool. One requirement of the government program was that once you'd sold out of the dairy business, you had to promise not to go back into it for a period of five years, or else the government would put your ass in jail. So Nyman put all his dairy cows in the name of his daughter."

"In Sally's name?"

"That's right."

"So Sally Dean owns the largest dairy in the country?" I asked, astonished.

"She did," Stroud said. "But she gave it up. She got us to void the agreement for her. She disinherited herself."

"That's true," said Wick. "Scales had to hunt up some cousin from out of state to take over the dairy. As far as I know, nobody has ever seen this cousin. You ask me, he doesn't exist. It's just another one of Nyman's scams."

"That dairy must be worth a fortune," I said. "Why did Sally give it up?"

"Because she's through with her father," said Stroud.

So Sally really was the daughter of a country gangster! Rasmussen had been right about that. I began wondering all over again how much else of Bevo's crazy story was true. "She seems to have turned out pretty well," I said.

"She has indeed," Stroud replied.

"There was a time when nobody would've thought that," said Wick. "Old Nyman had her running scams like you wouldn't believe. Like she was born to it. It was his idea for her to become district coordinator. He thought she could slip him useful court information, maybe make sure he had a favorable judge if any of his schemes came to light and he went to trial. He bought off a couple of retired judges on Sally's list—just insurance, you understand. Nyman Scales thinks of everything."

Stroud hoisted himself to his feet. "There is *no evidence* that Sally Dean has ever once accommodated her father in that way, you son of a bitch!"

"Just because there's no evidence doesn't mean she hasn't done it," Wick replied. "I don't have the faith in our Sally that you do, Gill. Blood will tell."

The old man swelled up in a trembling rage, and for a moment I thought he might attack his partner. Then the air seemed to go out of him, and he sat back down and stared at the table.

"Let me get this dairy thing straight," I said. "Scales got the government to buy out an imaginary dairy and then used the money to build a real dairy, for which he's getting government aid?"

"One of the biggest dairies in East Texas," said Wick.

"Where does Bevo Rasmussen come into all this?" I asked. We were on our fourth round of beers, and I was beginning to feel a buzz.

"I'm getting there," said Wick. "As big a success as Nyman was in the dairy business, he became an even bigger success as a horse breeder and trader. Scales found that he could insure horses for huge amounts of money and collect on them if they died accidentally. All he had to do was figure out a scheme to use on the insurance people and then create an accident. It didn't take Nyman long to work out the details. He buys big-money horses—we're talking fifty thousand, a hundred thousand a horse sometimes—and farms them out to his hands or his business associates. He makes it look as if the men are actually buying the horses from him, but they're just a front operation. Nyman's really selling them to himself."

"I don't get it," I said.

"It is not difficult to figure out," Stroud replied. "Scales really does everything. He helps finance the horse, then works a side deal with the buyer to get more money when the horse dies."

I was feeling queasy, having eaten too much barbecue and drunk too much beer. How ironic that for the first time since my arrival in Jenks, my new associates were having a serious talk with me—were not trying to scam me in some way—and I was becoming too drunk to follow what they were saying. Once again, two steps too slow.

"So you're saying Nyman Scales set Bevo up with horses in order for Bevo to kill them and collect the insurance, some of which would go back to Scales?"

"That makes the most sense, Clay," Wick replied.

"But something's gone wrong, and the insurance company isn't paying off."

"Yep," said Wick. "It's my bet that Bevo bungled the kill. Did something to make the adjusters suspicious. The whole deal depends on the insurance company not making any trouble. If they stall, and the claimant is a small-time operator, like Bevo, in bad need of the insurance money, he can have some real debt troubles."

"And now Bevo's bank has sued him for the quarter million it loaned him for the horses."

"It never rains but it pours," said Stroud.

At that moment the door opened and five men walked into the Singing Pig dressed in army camouflage outfits, their faces streaked with sweat and with green and brown paint.

"Jesus H. Christ!" cried Wick Chandler. "Walking shrubs!"

"They look like frogs from Mars," said Stroud, his eyes glowing with savage glee. The camouflaged men stood inside the doorway, scowling at us.

CHAPTER 19

"**WE DIDN'T HEAR YOU DRIVE UP,**" said Wick. "Did you arrive in one of those Stealth bombers?"

"Don't just stand there, Jack," Stroud said, "come on in. Frogs have to eat, too." Stroud turned to Boo behind the counter. "Boo, fix up a mess of flies for Captain Jack and his amphibians!"

The ex-pilots sat down at a couple of tables next to ours. Despite their high-tech outfits, only one or two in the bunch looked as if they had kept themselves in good shape. Captain Jack was short and thin, with tufts of yellow hair curling out from under his camouflaged bill cap and a yellow mustache that glowed against the paint on his face.

"Are you boys practicing for Halloween or just the end of the world?" Chandler asked.

This was not the tack I would have taken. Chandler and Stroud, however, were having fun.

"We've come to use your phone, Boo," Jack said. "Our vehicle broke down a few miles back and we need a tow."

"The Range Rover?" Wick asked. "I hope it's nothing serious. You should see their car, Clay. My, it's a fancy one. It's all camouflaged, too, just like the boys here. When they stand in front of it, you can't see them."

"What happened to the car, Jack?" Stroud asked. "Maybe we can help fix it."

Captain Jack started to say something, then stopped himself. "Forget about it, Jack," said another commando. "Tell them the good news about Red."

Jack smiled at us, placing his hand on the shoulder of the ex-pilot sitting next to him. "That's right, you boys haven't heard. Red here's going to be made a deputy."

"That is big news," Stroud said. "Is it a county in Texas that's doing that, Red?"

"This one," said Red. "I'm going to be your new deputy, Stroud. Starting Monday."

"Well," said Stroud, "I know we'll all sleep better at night, Red. Knowing you're out there driving around looking for trouble."

"First thing I'm going to do Monday," said Red, "is file a report on Jack's Range Rover."

"The one that's broken down?" asked Wick.

"It didn't break down," Red said. "It was vandalized."

"Vandalized?" said Wick. "While you boys were driving it? Now, that's a feat. I suppose you got a look at the vandal?"

"We've got a pretty good idea who it is."

"Well, I wish you luck catching the scoundrel," Wick replied.

"Now that your buggy's been vandalized, Jack," said Stroud, "you aren't thinking of going back to riding motorcycles, are you?"

Jack came halfway out of his chair. Red grabbed his arm and pulled him back down.

"You should've seen these guys on their big old Harley-Davidsons a couple of years ago, Mr. Parker," boomed Stroud. "Ripping and roaring all around, running into trees, falling in the bushes . . . We had to take them to court to save their lives. Those motorcycles would've finished them off."

Captain Jack leaned forward on his chair and began to speak in a hoarse voice. "Tell you what we're gonna do," he said. "We're gonna wait till the bombs fall, and civilization goes to hell, people screaming in the streets, government a thing of the past. And we're gonna find all the lawyers and put 'em in a big fucking stock tank. And we're gonna fill that stock tank with gasoline, and then I'm gonna light it. And we're all gonna dance around the fire." He smiled a wicked smile at us.

"Where will you be waiting?" asked Wick Chandler, leaning toward him.

Confusion flashed through Captain Jack's eyes. "What?"

Stroud's deep voice kicked in: "You said you'd wait till the bombs fall. Mr. Chandler here is asking where you're going to be waiting. Will you wait out in the woods?"

The ex-pilot chewed on his mustache. "Yeah," he answered. "We'll be out in the woods."

Wick Chandler leaned even closer, until he was face-to-face with Captain Jack. "Because, I mean, if you're going to be out in the woods, I just wonder who'll be looking after Shirelle. Hell, Jack, that wife of yours is a real screamer, and if you're out Rambo-ing through the woods waiting for the bombs to fall, well . . ." Wick whispered something in Jack's ear, making an obscene gesture with his hand.

For a moment the survivalists stared at Wick's pudgy fingers. Then Captain Jack launched himself at Chandler. Before he could reach Wick, the air was sliced by that silent, brain-scraping screech I remembered from the morning before in the office. It cut through my senses like a cry sent up from the ghosts of a billion locusts, and the thought flashed through my mind that I'd hit the end of the trail—brain tumor! aneurysm!—but then I saw that Captain Jack was affected, too. His head jerked as if an invisible mallet had come down on it, and instead of connecting with Wick's throat, he landed on top of our table, scattering the empty beer bottles. With amazing agility, given his bulk, Hardwick Chandler slid sideways out of his chair like a matador, and Captain Jack skidded across the table and onto the floor. Before the little man could get up, Boo and a couple of the ex-pilots had hold of him.

"You boys better git," said Boo to us. "You can settle up the bill later."

In seconds, Stroud's big Lincoln was spewing gravel out of the parking lot of the Singing Pig. In the driver's seat, Wick Chandler powered his window down and whooped in the wind.

"Did you see me move?" he cried. "I'm a fucking ballerina. I'm James Bond!"

"It was nobly done," Stroud told him. From a chain around his neck he picked up a small silver whistle, streaked with white flecks. He must have been wearing it inside his shirt, because I had never seen it before. He blew the whistle, and again invisible locusts swarmed inside my head, and my vision blurred with the ghostly vibration.

"Son of a bitch!" I said. "Cut it out, Stroud!"

Stroud squinted at me, then nudged Chandler. "Our boy hears it!" the old man said. "He's got the call! I told you, Hard-dick. Dogs, morons, and the pure in heart." He studied me, wicked merriment in his eyes. "Which are you, Mr. Parker?" he asked.

"What the hell is that thing?"

Stroud held it up on its chain for me to see: a short, thin tube of silver, randomly inlaid with what looked like ivory chips.

"It's the voice of doom," he explained. "It's the final trumpet. You are privileged to be able to hear it. I can't, and neither can my esteemed colleague here."

"Captain Jack got an earful, though," Wick said with a laugh. "Caught him right between the eyes."

We were passing a yard with a couple of hounds lounging in it. "Slow down, Wick," Stroud said. He blew the whistle, and the dogs went crazy, scrambling against the chicken-wire fence, barking and baying.

"Jesus!" I said, clapping my hands to my ears as the big car resumed its speed. "Stop that!"

"Time's wingéd chariot," said Stroud, "at your back. Gaining on you. That's what you hear." He rolled the whistle between thumb and forefinger. He looked at me again, a fierce light in his eye. "The readiness is all, son," he said.

"You're scaring the new man," Wick Chandler told him.

CHAPTER 20

IT WAS ALMOST FIVE O'CLOCK when we reached the Jenks city limits. "Goddamn," said Stroud as Wick pulled up in front of the law office, "what is our idiot sheriff thinking of, making Red Meachum a deputy?"

"What if Sheriff Nye deputizes the rest of that bunch? Can you imagine all of the ex-pilots as lawmen? They'll come after us with torches in the night."

"If they come on motorcycles, we'll be safe," replied Stroud.

Wick and I got out of the car, and Stroud scooted over behind the wheel. "I'm going home, boys," he said. "We've done about all the good we can today."

Wick and I watched the big car drive away. "He gets tired pretty easy these days," said Wick. "You should have seen him a few years ago, Clay."

"He should lay off the sauce," I told him.

Wick clapped me on the back. "That's what you're here to help me do! We're going to dry him out, like I told you yesterday."

"And you should lay off other men's wives," I replied. "You are both going to kill yourselves if you keep going. His liver is going to fall out, and some husband is going to gun you down."

Wick smiled, gestured at the office door. "Then all this would be yours."

"I doubt it," I replied. "I'm not sure I'll hold out much longer than the last six or eight new guys. There's too much weirdness here, Wick."

"Weirder than city life? Come on, Clay."

"I don't think you guys can see it because you're part of the weirdness. You *make* most of it. But it's not just you. Jesus, it's everything about this place. It's Judi Rae Box. It's bobcats in suitcases. It's the pile of plastic body parts in a corner of your office. It's Bevo Rasmussen . . ."

"It's Sally Dean," said Wick, "that's what you got going."

"What makes you say that?" I asked.

"Sally on a horse is a lovely sight," Wick said. "I had a try at her myself a few years back. Got shut down in eight seconds flat."

"Tell me about Stroud and Sally," I asked.

"It's too hot out here," Wick said. "Let's go inside." We went into his office, past Molly Tunstall, who informed me that Judi Rae Box had called to say she had decided not to divorce her husband, Layton, yet.

"She said she would give him one more chance," Molly said. "If it doesn't work out, she figures she'll just shoot him and have done with it."

"Thank God for marriage," Wick said. "We wouldn't have much of a practice without it."

When we were seated in his office, Wick pulled out a bottle of Jim Beam and a couple of glasses and poured us both a stiff drink. It wasn't what I needed, but I took it anyway. I was beginning to see the appeal of staying buzzed in the country.

"What I said at lunch about Sally being a wild kid was true," Wick said. "She was brought in on a couple of charges when she was just twelve or thirteen—shoplifting, vandalism, that sort of thing. That's when we met her. Gill was county attorney then. He refused to prosecute her. Then we heard of a more serious charge, out west in Travis County. Apparently there was some sort of scheme in which she would sell a calf or a horse to some idiot farm boy and then Nyman would show up after the sale and claim the animal had been stolen from him. Nyman would have a sales receipt, of course. And nobody could find the girl."

"But wouldn't Sally have given the buyer some sort of title document? I can't imagine anyone buying an animal just on the say-so of a young girl."

"Sure, but the documentation Sally left behind never held up under a close look. Nyman's sales slip would always be better. We figured Nyman forged the papers Sally used. Anyway, Sally got picked out of a lineup, and it looked like she might be sent to the juvenile facility in Gatesville. Stroud put a word in someone's ear and got her off. It was a stupid scam, one of Nyman's worst."

"Sounds like she had a tough time of it growing up," I said.

"Yes, especially after her mother died. That was about the time Sally started acting up." Wick told me that Sally's mother died when she was thrown from a horse. "It was an accident, all right, but there were rumors about it."

"What do you mean?"

"Nyman might have had something to do with it."

"Nyman Scales killed his wife?" I asked.

"Nobody thinks he meant to do it. Rumor has it he was experimenting with killing horses for profit even back then. He had scraped up some money to buy and insure a show horse, then did something to it, lamed it in some way, planning to collect on the insurance. But his wife must not have known about it, because she took the horse out for a ride and wound up with a broken neck."

"Mercy," I said. "Does Sally know that her father might have had a hand in her mother's death?"

"Gill thinks she found out a few years ago, because that's when she started straightening out like she did. It looked for a time like she was running away from home. She went to UT, got a degree, set herself up in Mule Springs. She had her last name legally changed to Dean—that was her mother's family name. It looked like she was turning over a new leaf—that is, if you look at it from a certain direction, the one Gill favors."

"What's your read on Sally Dean?" I asked.

Wick finished his drink, poured another, and topped off my glass.

"Remember I told you that Nyman put the dairy in his daughter's name? Well, he did it right after she changed her name from Scales to Dean. Now, if Sally was changing her name as a way of breaking off with her father, why would he turn right around and make her owner of one of his biggest cash projects?"

"You're saying she may have changed her name to help her daddy rip off the government? But a simple name change wouldn't fool a one-eyed auditor with an IQ over six."

"Go find me a government auditor with an IQ over six, and we'll talk."

"But you also told me she severed her connection with the dairy, Wick. Why would she have done that if she was still in cahoots with her father?"

"She dumped the dairy just about the time she applied for a job in our firm. Think about it, Clay. She couldn't very well have been involved in dairy fraud while applying for the job of Northeast Texas Judicial District Administrative Coordinator, could she?"

In Wick's version of the Sally Dean story, Nyman Scales's daughter had never reformed at all. Instead, she was just covering her tracks whenever necessary as Nyman moved her from one scheme to the next.

"So Nyman cut her loose from the dairy scam so that she could get the job she's got now?" I said. "Tell me, Wick, how could placing

Sally as district coordinator possibly pay off for Nyman as big as keeping her on as head of the largest dairy in the country?"

"Easy. In the last three years alone, Nyman Scales has been linked, either directly or indirectly, to five megabucks lawsuits. The three that went in his favor netted him something over four million dollars. With the right judges on the bench, his batting average might have been five out of five. Think what it could mean to him to be able to pick his judge whenever one of his lawsuits went to trial. Sally could help him do that."

I was starting to get drunk again, for the second time that day. And it was a good thing, because Wick was beginning to make sense, and what he was saying would have depressed me if I had been sober.

"But Stroud says there's no proof that Sally has ever influenced a trial in her father's favor."

"And he's right. I'm just playing devil's advocate, Clay. I don't have any proof that Sally's bad. But the facts line up more logically that way. Besides, Gill is smitten. He likes to think that he's the reason why Sally reformed. In Gill's view Sally was a tool of her evil father when she came to work for us, but thanks to the patience and interest and sterling integrity of Old Lawyer Stroud, she saw the error of her ways and took up the administrator's job with a soul purged of sin. What a crock! Christ, think of the way he acted at lunch when her name came up. It should be obvious to you that he's in love with her."

"He loves her like a father," I suggested. "Like the decent father she never had."

"Horse hockey, Counselor. You can't be that drunk."

He was right. The idea of Gill Stroud as a model of fatherly decorum was ridiculous.

"And don't think it's platonic, either," said Wick. "Let me tell you, Gill has a knack for picking up girls. You won't believe this, Clay, but the old goat's batting average is better than mine."

"You're right, I don't believe you."

"I think they want to nurse him, or maybe mother him. Or maybe they want him to father them, if you know what I mean. When you go out to his farmhouse, take a look in the closet at the top of the stairs. It's full of cowboy boots. Women's boots. He likes his women to parade around wearing a pair of cowboy boots and nothing else."

I pictured Sally Dean walking down some stairs in an old farmhouse, dressed only in cowboy boots, as Stroud watched from the foot of the stairs, trembling with antediluvian lechery. No, it wasn't possible.

Unless the crazy story Bevo fed me that morning wasn't crazy, after all. What if Sally really was still in league with her father?

"Damn you, Wick," I said. "This has not been a good day."

"Love hurts, partner," he replied.

I got up to leave, my head humming from the whiskey, then remembered Bevo's request for me to ride with him to Dallas the next night. I told Wick about it, and about Bevo's threat to sue us after we blew the case if we didn't play ball with him.

"I guess you'd better go with him, then, Clay."

"But you told me never to do anything he asks me to do," I reminded him.

"He seems to have us over a barrel."

"You don't know why he's going to Dallas, do you, Wick?"

Wick thought for a moment. "He goes club hopping a lot, but he wouldn't need a lawyer for that. I don't know, Clay, maybe he's just trying to make friends with you. That or he wants to pump you for information about his case. He's convinced we're not telling him everything, the paranoid little son of a bitch."

"Are we?" I asked.

"Hell, no. I'm not, anyway. I don't know what Gill has been telling him."

"So I'll ride with Bevo, then," I said, heading for the door.

"I think it might be best," Wick replied.

"For the good of the firm?"

"For the good of the firm."

But it would not be for the good of the firm if, as Bevo prom-ised, he showed up with Sally Dean in the backseat of his car. If he came with Sally, I would knock his teeth down his throat. Diamond and all.

I went to the Dairy Queen for a hamburger. Lu-Anne was not there, but the little girl who waited on me must have learned her gum-popping technique from her. I sat in the booth long enough for the buzz from Wick's bourbon to transform itself into a dull, throbbing ache in my temples. Blood will tell. That's what Wick had told Stroud at lunch. Sally Dean was Nyman Scales's daughter, and Nyman Scales's blood was black.

I drove home as the last of the pink stain in the sky disap-peared and the insane chatter of the locusts began to fade. There was no blue Mercedes parked at the curb tonight. I unlocked the door, cursing the locusts.

Before I could find the light switch, I was struck on the head, and my legs went out from under me. Bright squares of light exploded in my brain. I don't think I completely lost consciousness because the lights stayed with me and I had a sensation of being dragged. The next instant, I gasped as cold water hit me in the face, and I could focus again. I was naked, dripping, duct-taped hand and foot to a kitchen chair in my bedroom. The nightstand from the side of my bed had been placed directly in front of me, its reading lamp beaming into my face, turning the room into fuzzy outlines. One of the outlines belonged to a big man with a beer gut. He wore overalls and a baseball cap over lank hair.

"Howdy," he said in a cheery Texas drawl.

CHAPTER 21

SOMETHING HAD BEEN CRAMMED into my mouth—
a sock, from the smell of it. My head got clearer, and I struggled
against the silver bands of tape but found I couldn't move at all, as
if I'd been welded to the chair. My feet and hands were becoming
numb from the constriction of the tape.

Ex-pilots! I thought, in a panic. Out for revenge over the Singing
Pig incident.

The big man sat down in a kitchen chair to one side of the
light. "We got to have us a talk, Mr. Rasmussen," he said. "You
know what it's about."

Mr. Rasmussen! The guy thought I was Bevo! Up to this point,
I had been somewhat detached from the proceedings. I supposed
I'd gone into shock. But Bevo's name brought me fully into the
picture. I hollered, trying to work the sock out of my mouth with
my tongue. The man in the ball cap pushed the sock back in and
halfway down my throat, so that I started to gag.

"Not yet, Mr. Rasmussen," he said. "You're not ready to tell me
yet. Not the truth, anyway. I've got to get you ready for the truth."
I could read the insignia on his cap: *CR*. Ball Cap was a Colorado
Rockies fan.

"Have you ever had acupuncture treatment?" he asked, untying a cloth bundle on the nightstand between us. "It's great for treating all sorts of problems. Arthritis pain, nicotine addiction, even some forms of cancer." He unrolled the strip of cloth to reveal a row of needles, varying in size, gleaming in the light from the reading lamp.

"Acupuncture can even cure dishonesty," Ball Cap said. He selected a wicked-looking steel sliver about six inches long and held it, point down, in his fist like a dagger. I noticed a fat silver thimble on the tip of his thumb. He scooted the nightstand away and moved closer, so that I could smell the beer on his breath, and held the needle over my leg, a couple of inches up from my knee.

"Don't worry," he said, "I've been trained by experts." His fist thudded into my leg, and when he withdrew it, I saw the needle embedded in my flesh. A ribbon of blood began to run down both sides of my leg. There was no sharp pain, but a tremendous ache, as if I had been hit with a sledgehammer.

"Well, what do you know," he said, "I missed the femoral artery. That's mighty lucky for you, Mr. Rasmussen. I nick the femoral, and you're a goner."

I stared at the silver pin sticking out of my leg, trying to focus my thoughts. Ball Cap was looking at it, too. "Weird, isn't it, sticking up like that?" he said. "Can't tell how deep it is or how far it has to go to come out the other side." He chuckled. "You ain't seen nothing yet. I brought two hundred of the little darlings! You can make the damnedest patterns with them!"

This isn't happening, I told myself. You're having a dream. Wake up! I squirmed against the tape and a burst of pain from my leg let me know that I was not dreaming. To my horror, Ball Cap picked up a second needle. This one he held at a slant, its point aimed at the center of my knee.

"I bet you feel that old dishonesty melting away, don't you?" he asked. He reached down to the floor and picked up a hammer.

"This one requires a little more force," he said. "Maybe after it, we'll try to talk."

Let's talk now! I shouted against the soggy knot of wool in my mouth. *Now! Now! Now!* But I could not talk, could not move, could only watch in horror as Ball Cap settled the point of the needle in the skin over my kneecap and brought the hammer back. At the last moment, I closed my eyes.

As before, there was a thud, but this time it was only heard, not felt. I opened my eyes to see Ball Cap drop the hammer and collapse behind the nightstand, knocking over the reading lamp as he fell. After the glare of the lamp, the darkness was total, but I could hear someone moving close by. There was the rippling sound of duct tape being pulled off its spool, once, twice, several times. My rescuer was taping up Ball Cap where he had fallen.

Finally the reading lamp was righted and, to my consternation, aimed into my eyes again. This was too much! I bellowed in rage and pain. A hand came out of the darkness and began pulling the sock out of my mouth, then stopped.

"I don't know," said Sally Dean's voice, "this opens up a whole new set of possibilities."

Sally turned on the light. "I was heading for the Quik Stop," she said, looking down at the man she had just decked. "Ed loves Little Debbie cakes, and Gill is all out of them." She was wearing a black T-shirt and cutoffs. Kneeling next to my wounded leg, she inspected the needle sticking out of it. "Good thing Ed's got a sweet tooth, wouldn't you agree?"

The bleeding seemed to have stopped. She touched the end of the needle, and pain shot up my leg. I hollered through the sock for her to ungag me, but she ignored me, going into the bathroom and coming out with a towel and a box of Band-Aids. She knelt again, grasped the needle with one hand while pressing down on the flesh around it with her other hand. Slowly she drew the needle out. It felt like she was sawing my leg off.

"Stop moaning," she said. "I can see you've never spent any time on a farm. I've pulled bigger splinters out of a rabbit's ass." She stanched the blood with the towel, then, with a smile at me, she bent down to the wound and licked at a runnel of blood.

"I always wondered what a man's blood tasted like," she said. She made a face. "God, how do vampires do it?"

I began to gag, and Sally reached up and pulled the sock out of my mouth. "If you start hollering again," she said, "I'll stick it back." The inside of my mouth felt as if it had grown a coat of hair.

"Get me out of this chair," I gasped. Sally was strapping a Band-Aid over the black dot of the puncture wound in my leg.

"You might have a doctor look at this," she said. "A tetanus shot might be a good idea." She smiled at me again, and there was something else in her eyes. "You look cute, all tied up in that chair."

"Sally, that guy was going to kill me."

Sally looked down at him. "I don't think so," she said. "If he was going to do that, he wouldn't have rigged up this light so you couldn't see him. I think he was just planning to scare you."

"He thought I was Bevo."

"Well, of course he did," Sally replied. "Who'd want to stick pins in *you*? There's probably a bunch of folks out there wouldn't mind ventilating Bevo."

I couldn't get over how calm Sally was, how nonchalantly she perched on the nightstand, as if it were the most natural thing in the world for her to sit chatting with a wounded man bound naked to a chair next to a thug she had just knocked unconscious. Maybe such high jinks were nothing new to the daughter of Nyman Scales.

"Looks like our little Cajun ceremony last night was a bust," she said. "We didn't clean out all the demons."

A thought hit me. "This is why Bevo was happy to loan me his house!" I said. "He must have suspected some enemy might come for him, and he let Wick Chandler move me in here to take a message. The son of a bitch set me up!"

"Sounds like Bevo, all right," Sally said. She knelt next to me. "Maybe we should try that ritual again. I've remembered some parts that I'd forgotten." She ran her fingernails up my unwounded thigh, raising goosebumps.

"Sally, for God's sake!"

"You know, Counselor, for a city boy you're really beginning to get into the swing of things around here." She kissed me on the kneecap.

Anger suddenly overwhelmed the frustration and embarrassment I was feeling. "You can stop this," I told her. "I'm happy enough, thank you."

"What do you mean?" she asked, kissing me on the neck and down my chest.

"Bevo thinks you're just keeping me happy so that I won't quit the firm like all the other new guys did and leave his case hanging."

She laughed. "Bevo is an idiot. If I wanted to help his case— and I don't—I could do it from the office. It wouldn't take more than a couple of phone calls, and—" She stopped kissing me. "Do you believe Bevo, Clay?"

All my speculations about her motives vaporized in the look she gave me. "Bevo's an idiot," I said.

But I had missed a beat—late again! Sally stood up. "So I'm screwing you for *Bevo*?" She gave a grim little laugh that was more of a shudder.

"He's an idiot, Sally. He's certifiable."

"That would make me a whore, wouldn't it?" She looked down at me and shook her head. "You're one smart lawyer. You have figured out that the Northeast Texas Judicial District Administrative Coordinator is part of a prostitution ring all set up just to keep you happy in your new job of defending assholes who burn horses for profit. In fact, you have deduced that the district coordinator is the head whore!" She went into the kitchen, and I heard cabinet drawers yanked open and slammed shut.

"Sally, give me a break," I called to her. "I'm sorry. It's been a very confusing couple of days." As she thrashed around in the kitchen, I explained that I had learned a little about the shady elements of her past and that what I learned had thrown me. "But only for a moment," I said.

She came back from the kitchen, her eyes flashing at me.

"So, it's a family business," she said. "I'm working for Nyman as well as for Bevo." She had a carving knife in her hand.

"You're not working for Nyman or Bevo or anybody," I replied, watching the knife. "I know that."

"Scales family escort service and horse exterminators," she said. "It has a ring to it. I'll suggest it to Nyman at the next family reunion." She started to saw with the knife at one of the lengths of tape that bound me to the chair, then threw the carving knife across the room. "The hell with you," she said. "You can get out of this mess yourself." She knelt to check the binding on her captured burglar, and I couldn't see her face. "So last night, you and I, that was just business?" she asked, yanking on the tape around Ball Cap's wrists hard enough to make the big man groan in semiconsciousness.

"That's Bevo's version. It's not mine."

"So you talked with *Bevo* about what we did last night?"

"I'm sorry, Sally. I made a mistake. Last night was not just business. It couldn't have been."

When she looked up from the floor where she knelt, there was no trace of anger or confusion in her eyes, but she wore a bitter smile. "All right," she said, "what if it was just business? Let's assume Bevo Rasmussen is right, for the first time in his life."

"Stop it, Sally."

"I'm a whore, and last night had nothing to do with the way I feel about you."

"Hold on!" I said. "The way you feel about me? Sally, we hardly know each other, and last night you were all over me!"

"The way I remember it, *you* were all over *me,*" she replied. Now there was hurt in her eyes, and anger. "I never saw a man as needy as you. It was screaming out of you, from the moment we met."

Sally rose up on her knees, looking down at the prone, tightly bundled figure of Ball Cap, who was beginning to squirm a little against his bonds.

"Well," she said, "if we've got two geniuses like you and Bevo in agreement, I guess my case is closed." She came to me on her knees. "I tell you what, Clay..." She slid her hand up my thigh and into my crotch. "Let's do some more business. Maybe I can make the city boy even happier." She was massaging me with long, practiced strokes.

"Cut it out!" I demanded.

"No, sir," she said. "I'm just a simple working girl doing my job." Strapped to the chair as I was, there was no way I could move to stop her. I willed myself not to respond. But I did respond, despite my mental commands, despite the shock and pain of the night and the fact that we had company.

"I mean it, Sally!"

She stood, undid the snap of her cutoffs, and slid them off. She was wearing nothing underneath, and she straddled me as her hand continued to work. Pain shot up my leg from the puncture wound, but the rest of my body did not seem to notice. Pulling her T-shirt off over her head, she offered my mouth a nipple. I took it.

A moment later, as she repositioned herself, the big man coughed. Sally reached down to her jeans on the floor and pulled out what looked like an old policeman's sap, a leather-covered finger of lead. I heard a thud, and the man didn't make another sound.

CHAPTER 22

WHEN SALLY GOT THROUGH with me in the chair, she phoned the police and told them there was a break-in in progress at my house. My hollering at her to hang up only added sound effects to the call. I pleaded with her to untape me before she left. "I've lost all feeling in my hands and feet," I complained.

She surprised me with a long, passionate kiss, then reached down between my legs and gave me a tweak. "Don't worry, boss," she said, "that there's the only organ that counts." She walked out of the bedroom with her clothes in her hand.

The two policemen who showed up at my bedroom door five minutes later took one look and immediately misconstrued the scene.

"I've heard about this," said the younger one, a skinny farm kid, as he ripped the tape off me. "They do this sort of thing to each other so they can get off."

The paunchy, middle-aged patrolman curled his upper lip in disgust. "All that yelling they do about wanting to be treated like normal human beings. We should just turn San Francisco into a big frigging jail and ship 'em all there."

"Look at my leg, Officers," I said. "That man was torturing me."

"I heard they do that, too," said the kid.

Neither one of the patrolmen would talk directly to me. I never quite convinced them that Ball Cap and I weren't lovers whose tryst had gotten out of hand, but I did get them to run the big man in, dragging him, groggy and still taped, downstairs to their patrol car. They called a doctor, who came over, gave me a tetanus shot, and told me that whoever treated my leg had done a good job. Though it was midnight, the doctor was dressed as if he were about to set off on a bass fishing weekend, right down to the utility vest and the floppy hat decorated with fishhooks. He was a crinkled little man with amused eyes.

"You and your boyfriend might want to lay off the sado-masochism for a while," he told me. "You don't want to hit an artery when you go stabbing each other."

I tried explaining that the police were wrong about what had happened, but I doubt I got through. He nodded, gave me some pills he said were painkillers, and left.

The painkillers did not kill much pain, and at seven o'clock the next morning, after a sleepless night, I sat in a booth at the Dairy Queen, looking at the chicken-fried breakfast biscuit Lu-Anne had talked me into trying. Wick Chandler walked in. He flirted for a moment with Lu-Anne, ordered a cup of coffee, and joined me in my booth.

"So," he said, "did you get your circulation back yet?"

"Who told you?"

"This is a small town, partner. When our police go out on a call and find a big, nasty burglar all trussed up next to a naked guy taped to a chair, well, that sort of news tends to get around. What did Sally hit him with?"

"How did you know Sally was involved?" I asked. I had refused to give the police the name of the woman who phoned in the call.

Wick heaved a gigantic sigh. "I didn't. You told me just now. The dispatcher said it was a woman's voice on the phone. I took a guess."

Lu-Anne came over to bring Wick his coffee and fill my cup. She smiled at me, and I felt my face flame with embarrassment as she walked away. News gets around in a small town, Wick had said. Did Lu-Anne, my only friend in this godforsaken place, know about last night, too?

"So," Wick said mournfully, after Lu-Anne had left, "you and Sally."

"Let's not talk about it, Wick." I asked if he thought Stroud had heard anything about my little adventure.

"If he hasn't yet, he will," Wick replied. "He might not figure out about Sally, though. Nobody else knows about her. You may get lucky. He may just think you're gay."

"Not funny."

"That tape thing," he said, "it looks like it would hurt." He had the notion that Sally and I had been experimenting with the tape before Ball Cap arrived, and he wanted a play-by-play.

"Forget it," I said.

"I won't pretend I'm not hurt," he said, "after all the time and effort I put in on that girl." So the look of concern on his face was there because Sally would screw the new guy and not him. "I wonder if she's playing some sort of mind game with me," he mused.

"That's it, Sherlock," I said, "Sally's fucking me to get to you."

"Jesus Christ, Clay, and you've been telling me to keep *my* pants buttoned."

"Let it drop, Wick." I told him one other thing that I had not told the police last night, that Ball Cap had thought I was Bevo Rasmussen.

"That fits," he said. "The police got a report on your boyfriend. They found his name on his driver's license and ran a check. His name is Kirby Nutter, and he's a damned nasty sort of guy."

Nutter was a Houston thug who had fallen in and out of jail since his late teens, usually for selling drugs but occasionally for assault and battery. Recently he had moved to Dallas, where authorities thought he was working as an enforcer for a local drug dealer named Deck Willhoit.

"Now, why would a Dallas drug lord be after Bevo Rasmussen?" Wick mused.

"I've got a more immediate question," I said. "What should I do about Kirby Nutter?"

Wick suggested I let him go, refuse to swear out a complaint against him.

"The guy was going to perforate my kneecaps, Wick!"

"He thought you were someone else," Wick reminded me.

"So I should let him get away with sticking pins in me because he's a moron?"

"Okay," he replied, "file charges. And you can testify in court about how Sally Dean saved your ass, and that means Sally, our district coordinator, will have to testify about what you and she were doing at your house at that time of night."

Wick had a point. And after the anger and humiliation I had stirred up in her the night before, the last thing I wanted to do was drag her into court and jeopardize her job.

"You boys look down in the dumps," said Lu-Anne, returning with the coffeepot. "You need some caffeine."

"When are you going to let me make you a will, Lu-Anne?" asked Wick. "Everybody needs a will. You have assets that I'll bet you don't even know about. I would be happy to find them for you."

"I don't know, Mr. Chandler," the girl said, pouring. "You got so many new lawyers, I may just let one of them do it."

"We've only got the one new man, Lu-Anne," Wick replied. "Mr. Parker here is not interested in drawing up wills for beautiful girls. He's got himself a girlfriend."

"What about that other one?" Lu-Anne said. "The one that's been coming in here in the afternoons."

I asked Wick if he knew of any law office opening up in town. He did not.

"What makes you think this new guy works for us, Lu-Anne?" I asked.

"I don't know," she said. "I guess I just figured he was with you guys because of the way him and that Bevo Rasmussen carry on."

"Bevo and another lawyer?" Wick asked.

"They're funny about it. He comes in and drinks coffee until Bevo Rasmussen shows up and orders coffee at another table, then they leave without talking to each other. They get in their cars and head out of town. It's like some spy movie. They've done it four or five times over the last few weeks. The last time was yesterday. I'm glad the guy don't work for you. If he thinks he's putting something over on me, he's too stupid to be much good in a courtroom."

Wick and I looked at each other. "You know about this?" I asked him. He shook his head. "Lu-Anne, did you ever talk to this fellow? You don't know his name, by any chance?"

"No, sir."

We asked her to describe the man.

"He's about five-ten, real nice suits, beautiful shoes. Maybe forty-five, forty-seven years old. Dark skin, like he's been laying in the sun. Real curly hair. He don't quite look American, if you know what I mean. Like he might speak some other language."

"Lu-Anne," I said, "you should work for the police."

"Come in and I'll do you a will for free," said Wick.

"Maybe I will," she replied. "I can count my own assets, though."

"What in hell is Bevo up to?" Wick asked after Lu-Anne left. "I bet the little shitbrain is already working on a malpractice suit against us."

"Wick, we don't know who this guy is," I said. "He's probably not a lawyer. Maybe he's a drug contact. Maybe he's Bevo's uncle."

"You can ask him tonight on your way to Dallas," Wick said.

"Shit, I forgot about that. I'm not feeling much like having a night out on the town with Bevo Rasmussen," I said, flexing my wounded leg.

"It would be a good time to find out about this unknown guy, Clay," Wick said. "Why don't you go?"

Wick talked me into going with Bevo. For the good of the firm.

CHAPTER 23

————— ◆◆ ◄◆► ◆◆ —————

I WENT DOWN TO THE JAIL to turn Nutter loose. Before I signed the nonprosecution affidavit, however, I asked to see him alone. When he was led into the tiny conference room, he was still wearing his overalls and his Colorado Rockies cap and seemed none the worse for his night in jail, except for a bandage peeking out from under the cap where Sally had hit him. He didn't seem glad to see me; in fact, his face showed no emotion at all, unless you could call sleepiness an emotion. He looked as if he had just been awakened from a nap.

Before the attending officer left the room, I stopped him. "Officer," I asked, "do you know Bevo Rasmussen?"

It was the farm boy from the night before. "Yes, sir," he said.

"Am I Bevo Rasmussen?"

The boy frowned, as if trying to make up his mind. "No, sir, you are not Bevo Rasmussen."

"To your knowledge, have I ever been Bevo Rasmussen?"

"Not to my knowledge."

I thanked the policeman and let him go. If Nutter understood that the exchange had been for his benefit, he gave no acknowledgment.

He sat sleepily, eyes half-closed, his elbows on the tabletop and his chin in his hands.

"I know you're dying to apologize for breaking in on the wrong man and sticking a pin through his leg," I said. There was no response. I sat down on the other side of the table from him. He had not yet looked at me directly.

"There might be a way you could get out of this, Kirby," I told him. "Without your boss in Dallas knowing anything about it. Interested?"

There was a flicker in Nutter's eyes, a slight nod of the head.

"Tell me why you were after Bevo Rasmussen."

Nutter snorted, shook his head as if to clear sleep out of it. He wasn't about to spill any company secrets.

I explained to him that I was working on a case involving Bevo Rasmussen, that I was in fact a lawyer in Rasmussen's employ, and that I had a good idea what last night had been about. I told Nutter that if he could confirm my idea, I would let him go without pressing charges. I stretched the truth a bit, explaining that any details he gave me would be privileged information about a client, and therefore I could not divulge it to anyone without being disbarred. Still no response.

"What will Deck Willhoit think of you getting taken down by a girl in the middle of the night while torturing the wrong man?" That took a moment to sink in. Then Kirby looked straight at me for the first time. I tried to find a clue in his eyes to the kind of hatred or insanity or psychopathy that would allow one man to split the kneecap of another—a stranger, who had done him no harm—with a steel needle. All I saw was a cloudy, bovine stolidity, as if the capacity to remember were missing. In a moment, Kirby shrugged.

"It's money," he said.

It was what Wick and I had guessed. Bevo owed the drug people eighty thousand dollars. Not a lot of money by drug-lord standards, but enough for a collection agent to visit. Hence Kirby Nutter's trip to Jenks.

"So Bevo has been dealing dope for you boys?" I asked.

"Hell, no," said Nutter. "He's too smart for that. He's been helping us out with a little cash flow problem."

Bevo had been laundering money for Deck Willhoit, the drug dealer. He was supposed to have used the drug money to buy cows, then sell the cows and put the proceeds in a bank account in Valley View. But Willhoit's money men had connections with the Valley View bank and were able to determine that the account balance was lower than it should have been. Suspecting a double cross, Willhoit called Bevo up to demand an amount of money that Bevo should have had readily available. Bevo stalled, was still stalling.

"What do you think Bevo did with the money?" I asked.

"I don't get paid to think," Nutter replied.

I let that pass. "Okay, what does your boss think?"

"He don't think about it, either. He's a very scientific man. He don't think unless he's got the data in front of him."

"Does your boss ever make guesses?"

"Oh, all the time. He guesses Bevo spent the money. He guesses Bevo fucked up."

That was my guess, too. Bevo was ambitious enough to use laundered drug money to finance his new career as a horse breeder. It took a certain amount of craziness to risk annoying the sort of guy that Deck Willhoit must have been, but Bevo had craziness to spare.

The strangest part of my conversation with Kirby Nutter came next: I found myself trying to argue him into getting his boss to give Bevo a little more time. I explained about Bevo's horse-breeding scheme, speculating that Bevo had intended to use the million-dollar insurance payoff on his horses to reimburse Kirby's boss. If the man in Dallas would hold off until Bevo's case was wrapped up, I said, it might be that he could recoup his money then.

"That's if you win the case," Kirby said.

"Check."

"And if you don't," the big man continued with a sigh, "I guess I get to visit this goddamn town again."

"We'll win, Mr. Nutter," I replied, doing my best to sound like I believed it.

As I spoke I tried to figure out why I was working to save Bevo Rasmussen, a man whom Kirby Nutter, for all I cared, could turn into a human pincushion with his steel needles. I realized that I was defending Bevo not because he was innocent, but because he was my client and I was his lawyer. My talk with Kirby Nutter was not much different from talks I used to have with IRS officers on behalf of desperate clients. The stakes seemed pretty much the same, and so, in a way, did the penalties. In fact, certain punitive methods used by the IRS made Kirby Nutter's ventilating procedure seem like Christian charity.

I thanked Kirby for his information and told him I would clear him with the police. As I rose to leave, I must have grimaced from the pain in my leg, which was still slightly swollen.

"Does it hurt much?" Kirby asked, showing real interest for the first time.

"A bit. It's getting better."

"Would you say it's a sharp pain, or more of an ache?"

I stared at him.

"I'm sorry," he said. "The fact is, I only just started using them needles. It's easier on me than hitting a guy with my fists." He held up his left hand, clenched into a loose fist. "Three of these knuckles are broke," he said, prodding them with his finger. "They feel funny."

"I don't want to know how you broke them," I said.

"No," he replied, "you don't."

CHAPTER 24

IT WAS SEVEN-THIRTY Friday evening when Bevo and I crossed the long bridges spanning Lake Ray Hubbard at the northeast edge of Dallas. Pleasure boats of all shapes and sizes dotted the lake, and although the boats were enveloped in evening shadow, sunlight still flashed on the billowing canvas of a parasailing skier floating high in the air half a mile away.

"That's not something I would want to do," said my traveling companion. "Parasailing is dangerous shit. Friend of mine took off in one of those outfits, got tangled up in some electric lines. No more friend."

Name something, anything, and Bevo Rasmussen had a friend who had seen it, tried it, bought it, swallowed it, ridden it, run over it, or shot at it. Bevo had on the sharkskin *Godfather* suit he was wearing when we met, and he popped his cuffs out of his jacket sleeves to show me his cuff links. They were little silver skulls with diamond eyes.

"Got them from the president of the Hells Angels," he told me. "He's a friend of mine. He give me this one, too." Bevo curled his upper lip in a lupine snarl to show me the diamond in his tooth. "That one's worth over a thousand dollars."

Bevo had friends in high places. "Places of respect," he said. "Governors, movie stars, drug lords, TV preachers. The cream of the crop. There's a writer whose name you'd probably know, wants to write my life up. He says he'd have to make it a novel, because nobody would believe it if he told it for the truth."

"Who's that other lawyer you've been talking to?" I asked, hoping to catch him by surprise. "Is he one of your friends?"

Bevo said he did not know what I was talking about.

"You know," I said, "the one you've been meeting in the Dairy Queen."

"Oh, him," Bevo said. "He ain't a lawyer. He's an architect. From Dallas."

"An architect?"

"Yep. I'm thinking of building me an estate outside of town, and I brought him down from Dallas to consult on which land to buy. It's hard finding just the right spot. I need a lot of western exposure. Mornings ain't my time of day, but I love a good sunset."

"Bevo, how much do you think you're going to clear out of the insurance money?" That question had been puzzling me. I knew at least half of the purchase money, around $500,000, had come from the Farmer's Bank in Tyler and from Nyman Scales, in roughly equal amounts. I did not believe the other half-million could possibly have come from his own pocket. Bevo was carrying a lot of debt.

"It don't matter how much I clear," he said. "It's seed money. All seed money. I got me a plan, Mr. Parker. In four years, I'll be the richest man in the state. No, goddamn it, in two years. Know how I'm gonna do it?"

"Emus?" I asked.

"Damn right," he replied. "I'm gonna be the biggest goddamn emu breeder in the Southwest."

He rattled on about the big birds for a while, telling me how much money could be made from them. "They lay golden eggs,

Mr. Parker. Pure gold. You should think of investing. Wick Chandler's gonna invest. Stick with me, I'll make you rich."

"I'll think about it," I said.

We had been driving down I-30 in Bevo's open-topped 1977 Cadillac Seville, and my ears were starting to burn from the hot wind whipping against them. The Seville was his nighttime car, he told me. He had a couple of daytime cars, too, but his nighttime car was for cruising. "Women love this car," he said.

"Looks to me like Sally Dean doesn't much care for it," I replied. I reminded him of his promise to have Sally Dean waiting for me in the backseat if I agreed to ride with him. Sally was absent.

"Sally couldn't come. I hope you don't mind too much."

I told him I didn't mind.

"Nyman and I'll get her to make it up to you, Clay. You can count on it. Do you mind if I call you Clay?"

"Yes."

"How's that leg?" he asked.

Every five minutes or so he inquired about my wounded leg, apologizing for the danger he had put me in by letting Wick Chandler move me into his house. "I swear, Mr. Parker, I couldn't feel worse about it. I almost feel like it's my fault."

"It *is* your fault," I told him.

"If it will make you feel better, you can stick a pin in *my* leg," he said. "Hell, you can stick two."

I told him I didn't want to stick a pin into anybody. He asked me if I would like him to kill the man who stuck me. "I'll kill him so you can watch," he promised. "I'll kill him with my bare hands. I'll kill him with his own goddamn pins."

Stroud and Chandler both had told me it was impossible to have a real conversation with Bevo, and two hours in the car with him had convinced me they were right. I tried to talk to him about the lawsuit, but all I could get was a smile and a wink.

"You just get Nyman Scales on the stand," he said. "We're going to depose Nyman on Monday, right?"

"Right, but Bevo—"

"Just listen to Nyman on Monday, and you'll know," he said. "I didn't burn those horses, Mr. Parker. Nyman's gonna save my ass in court, and we'll all go home rich."

"You think a lot of Nyman Scales, don't you?" I asked.

"Hell, Mr. Parker, he's my mentor," Bevo said. "He's made me what I am today."

It turned out that Bevo had almost as many stories about Nyman Scales as he did about himself. It was a clear case of hero worship.

"Wait till you meet him, Mr. Parker," he continued. "You'd never guess how rich he is. Most of the time he dresses like a farmhand. Talks like a Baptist preacher. He's got that lisp, you know, that soft little *s,* like a pass-the-plate evangelist. People around the county say butter won't melt in his mouth." Bevo laughed and slapped his leg. "Biggest operator in five states, and he sounds like a fucking preacher."

"You're admitting to me that Nyman Scales is a crook?" I asked.

"Show me a big man who ain't," Bevo replied. "It takes a little wheelin' and dealin' to get to the top. It's the American way. Shit, you know that as well as I do. You were a tax lawyer, for Christ's sake."

"If he's such a famous crook, why hasn't he been caught?" I asked.

"Because he's so damn smooth," Bevo replied. "He's been named in all kinds of schemes. He's been indicted three or four times. There have been investigations. But I'm telling you, he thinks of everything. He's too smart for the local law. For the feds, too, for that matter. He's a hero to the people around him. He's like an old-time gangster, you know. A big shot. You can't catch the big dog."

Bevo asked if I had heard the "rumor" about Scales and one Jim Ed Murphy, whom he described as the Dr. Frankenstein of horse veterinarians.

"Nyman had this highbred colt, see, a stallion he named Beelzebub's Ghost, that would have fetched a good price but for one thing. He didn't have testicles. Born nutless. Nyman got Jim Ed Murphy to manufacture a set of balls for the colt and stick them on with surgery."

"They sewed fake genitals onto the horse?"

"God's truth, Mr. Parker. The horse was impotent and sterile, but he had balls. Jim Ed did such a bang-up job on the plastic surgery that it could not be detected. That colt fetched a hell of a price, too."

"This is pretty deep, Bevo."

"If you knew anything about raising horses, Mr. Parker, you'd know that birth defects like that are not uncommon, and that they ruin an otherwise big-money stallion. Thanks to what he did for Beelzebub's Ghost, Jim Ed Murphy became a kind of hero. Breeders would come to him to get him to sew fake testicles onto their own shortchanged horses. He and Nyman made a lot of money at it. Of course, I can't prove none of what I've told you," Bevo said with a smile. "Nor can nobody else. We're just speculating about a highly successful gentleman. And I want you to know that all my bidniss dealings with Nyman Scales have been strictly on the up-and-up."

"Tell me, Bevo," I said, "would this highly successful gentleman of yours ever destroy a horse for money?"

"On my honor, Mr. Parker, he would not," Bevo replied. "That's a nasty bidniss that Nyman and me wouldn't have any part of. I can tell you, though, there's those that do. There's all sorts of things a person can do to make a horse die accidentally, Mr. Parker. One thing is to give a horse a big enough shot of potassium to cause a heart attack that can't be detected in an autopsy. Another thing is give a horse a concussion. There's seven or eight ways to do that so the horse will go into a coma. You have to destroy it then."

"I get the picture," I said.

"You can stand a horse in four buckets of water, wrap it in heavy-gauge wire, and then shoot electricity through it. Just plug it in. Zap!—a lightning strike."

"Okay, Bevo."

"I've seen a surgical knife," he continued, "a long, mean-looking thing, can make a horse look like it's got itself all caught up in a barbed-wire fence. It's so sliced up it has to be put down." He wrinkled his lip in distaste. "That's a bad one."

"This is some business you're in," I told him.

"It's just temporary," he replied. "Like I said, I plan to make my fortune in the big birds. This is where Nyman and me are alike, Mr. Parker. Okay, he's in horses and I'm planning to be in birds, but we are both men of vision."

We reached the broad belt of the LBJ Expressway circling the city. There was always a kind of moving traffic jam on LBJ, cars bumper to bumper, all going seventy-five miles an hour.

"Okay, Bevo," I said, "why are we here?" I had tried to get him to tell me the reason for our run to Dallas as soon as we started out, but he refused, saying he would explain when we got there. Now, as he pushed the Cadillac into the westbound LBJ traffic, Bevo smiled.

"We're running an errand for Wick Chandler," he said.

"That can't be," I told him. "Mr. Chandler says he hasn't spoken to you in weeks."

Bevo's smile widened. "Now, don't get upset, Mr. Parker. Old Hard-dick wants you to know how sorry he is for this little deception. He says you can chew his ass when we get back."

Wick had told me he did not know Bevo's motive for driving to Dallas. Wick had lied. Or else Bevo was lying now. For a moment

I tried to determine which of my two new acquaintances was a bigger liar, but I soon gave up.

"Don't be too hard on him," Bevo said. "The fact is, it never occurred to him to ask you to go along with me in the first place. It was my idea. When you told him I asked you, he did some quick thinking and figured it would be a good idea. You see, Mr. Parker, I'm running a little repossession service tonight. We're picking up something that belongs to Mr. Chandler. It's something he feels real strong about and, to tell you God's truth, he don't trust me with it. He's counting on you to keep me honest." Bevo laughed at that. "Mr. Chandler was afraid you wouldn't come if you knew what we was here to pick up. Don't worry, it ain't drugs or nothing like that. Hell, it would make more sense if it was." He asked me if I knew a Dallas lawyer named Dick Devereau.

"No," I replied.

"Devereau and Wick are old friends. They went to school together, I believe."

We had taken the Skillman/Audelia exit, made a couple of turns, and were now driving through one of those raw, undeveloped patches that spread through the outlying areas of all fast-growing cities like a bad skin graft. Here and there sat half-built shopping strips, housing developments, and industrial parks consisting of Quonset huts surrounded by dirt and transplanted, anemic trees. Not yet finished, the area already looked old and tired, dried out, ready to be blown away by the first strong wind. I had seen a lot of this sort of urban wasteland. It made up half of Houston.

"So we're here to pick up something from Devereau?" I asked.

"In a manner of speaking."

Bevo told me that, years ago, Wick Chandler had gone fishing in the Yukon. He had taken someone else's wife with him, who bought him a memento of their trip. Wick loved the gift and mounted it on his wall.

"What was it?" I asked.

"It's a . . . a dingus." Bevo scratched his head. "Hell, Wick told me what you call it. Now, what is it? It'll come to me." He resumed the story. "Last fall Dick Devereau come to Jenks to see his old buddy Wick and do some drinking. Well, sir, he stole the dingus right off Wick's wall. Took it back to Dallas and put it on the wall behind his desk in his office. Wick called him, wrote him, but he couldn't get Devereau to give it back."

"What the hell is this dingus, Bevo?"

We were driving slowly through a trailer park, Bevo trying to read the numbers on the sides of the trailers. He stopped the car and switched off the engine. "It's right around here," he said. He reached over and, opening the glove compartment, took out a tiny plastic vial filled with powdery white stones.

"Goddamn it, Bevo, if we'd gotten stopped by the police—"

"I'll be right back, Mr. P," he said. "You might not want to get out of the car." He disappeared into the shadows, leaving me to listen to the crickets in this Dallas trailer park telling me what a fool I was, something I had already come to understand. A couple of minutes later Bevo was back, carrying a thin pole at least six feet long, which he handed to me as he got into the car.

"What do you think!" he said, starting the Cadillac. "I said I'd get it back, and I got it back."

It was a long spiral of something like rawhide that had been heavily shellacked. I tried bending it and found it amazingly strong.

"Bevo," I said, "this is a—"

"Pizzle!" he said. "That's what Wick told me to call it. A whale's pizzle."

"It's a penis!" I said.

"Yep. A whale's dick." The thing felt clammy. I dropped the base of it on the floorboard and wiped my hands on my pants. We drove back toward LBJ with the pizzle sticking up out of the convertible like a crazy, corkscrewed aerial.

Bevo patted himself on the back for his detective work. He said he had staked out the floor of the high-rise where Devereau's office was located and made the acquaintance of one of the janitors.

"Took about twenty minutes," he boasted. "The Mex janitor *wanted* me to steal it. He wanted it gone. He said it's unholy. I think the man is Catholic." He laughed. "Devereau's going to explode when he sees his empty wall on Monday morning. He was more attached to this thing than Wick. Wick says Devereau got superstitious about it, started thinking it brought him luck when he went to trial. He even signed documents with the name Whale-Dick Devereau."

"Of course he did," I said.

"You get Wick to show you anything Dick Devereau signed in the last couple of months," Bevo replied. "The typing underneath will say Willard Dick Devereau, but you tell me what the signature says. I admit, it's hard to make out, but it sure ain't Willard Dick." Bevo laughed. "You lawyers are crazy fuckers."

CHAPTER 25

WHEN WE GOT BACK TO THE LBJ Expressway, Bevo went west instead of heading back toward home.

"Now where?" I asked as we worked through LBJ's six lanes of traffic.

"Just another errand," he said.

"For Wick?"

"This one's personal."

That was all I could get out of him for twenty-five minutes, until he pulled the Cadillac into the parking lot of a seedy club on Industrial Boulevard. I could hear rock music booming through the walls of the strip joint next to the lot.

"Would you mind coming with me this time, Mr. Parker?"

"I'm not interested in retrieving any more whale parts, Bevo," I told him.

"It ain't anything like that," Bevo replied. "Please, Mr. Parker. There's some friends I want you to meet. They'll be impressed with you."

We headed toward the club, but before we got to the door, a Mexican in pressed Levi's, boots, and a Western-cut sport coat came out from between the cars and stopped us with a motion of his hand.

"How's it hanging, Mig?" said Bevo.

Without answering, Mig led us to the back of the lot. Seven or eight men dressed like Mig were lounging around a big black Bentley Arrow. There was music coming from the Bentley, a ZZ Top blues tune, and dancing in the bed of a pickup next to the Bentley was a girl in a sequined mini-dress. The girl danced languidly, a stripper's motions, the sequins on her dress blazing in the light from the neon sign that rasped and sputtered out the name of the strip joint: THE SHOWTIME LOUNGE. As we walked toward the Bentley, the girl saw us, jumped off the truck, and ran away, and the men moved out to circle us.

"Are these the friends you wanted me to meet?" I asked Bevo.

"Just give 'em a chance," Bevo replied. "You'll like them."

One of the men, the one standing closest to the back window of the Bentley, was Kirby Nutter. He had traded in his good-old-boy clothes for a Western outfit like the ones the others were wearing, but he still had his Colorado Rockies cap on. He did not look happy to see me.

Bevo seemed as unconcerned as if he were at a Sunday picnic. He walked toward the Bentley until Mig stopped him. The men behind us moved up so near that I could feel breathing on the back of my neck. Bevo peered into the Bentley from fifteen feet away.

"Howdy, Deck," he said.

All I could see in the Bentley were shadows. A voice came from the backseat, a low-pitched drawl I could barely hear above the rock and roll.

"There's folks said you'd be late to your own funeral, Bevo. I'm happy to see they were wrong."

Bevo reached into his jacket, a move that caused consternation among the men around us.

"Easy, boys," Bevo said, pulling out a banded stack of currency. He handed the money to Mig. "Would you give this to your boss, Miguelito?" Bevo asked him. The Mexican walked over to the car and handed the money in. There was a moment of silence, then a woman giggled in the backseat.

"A drop in the bucket, Bevo," said the voice.

"A first installment," said Bevo. "I know I screwed up, Deck. But I'm going to make good. You know about my lawsuit." He pointed at me. "This here is Mr. Clayton Parker, one of my lawyers. He's the fellow took the message you sent to my house. He'll tell you for me."

"How do, Counselor," said the disembodied voice.

"How do," I replied.

"You're new, aren't you? Whereabouts you from?"

I told him.

"A Houston man," said Willhoit. "Bevo Rasmussen has confused me on one point, Counselor. He says you intercepted the message I sent him. Now, what exactly does he mean by that?"

Kirby Nutter was staring at me from his spot near the rear door of the Bentley.

"He means that your associate contacted me in Jenks, and I acted as go-between," I said.

There was a moment of silence. Sweat gleamed on Kirby Nutter's impassive face.

"My, my," said the voice. Then, after another silence: "I understand there was an altercation at the Rasmussen house. You must understand, Counselor, that my associate is new to the company. I trust he did not behave indecorously?"

Nutter went white. I realized that he must have lied to his boss about his visit to Jenks—God knows what kind of story he made up—and had just discovered that his boss knew about the lie. I wondered how Willhoit had found out, and how much he knew. Had he heard about Nutter's arrest, or about Sally Dean getting the best of his new thug? I had the feeling that I had walked into a kind of back-lot trial, and that Kirby Nutter's fate rested in my hands.

"I believe that you would have approved of your associate's behavior," I said. I told Willhoit that Nutter had found me at Bevo's home instead of Bevo and had made an honest mistake.

"I heard," said Willhoit, "that at one point in your discussion, my associate became incapacitated."

I replied that his man had indeed been temporarily immobilized by an associate of mine.

"An associate with great tits, is what I heard," said the voice. There was a round of hooting and laughter, and Nutter's face went from white to flaming red.

The fact that I was working to save the man who had tried to shatter my kneecap with a needle must have shifted my exhausted brain into a kind of overdrive. My fear melted away, and I chatted with Willhoit as if he were a judge I was trying to talk out of coming down hard on a first-offender.

"So Bevo moved you in and didn't give out a forwarding address?" Willhoit chuckled, and the focus of ridicule slid from Nutter toward me.

"Yes, sir," I said, one good old Texas boy to another, "Bevo left both of us out of the loop on that one. You didn't know about me, and I sure as hell didn't know about you." That caused more laughter.

"Mr. Rasmussen is a resourceful rascal," said Willhoit. "Quite a salesman, too. Do you know about our business transaction, Counselor Parker?"

I said I had not heard about it.

"Your client there sold me on the idea of getting into the cattle business. I entrusted him with enough money to set me up in a small way, and damned if that money didn't just disappear."

"That is unfortunate," I said.

"And that was over a *year* ago. I keep waiting for restitution, but all I get are promises. Where has all my business sense gone?"

"I'll pay you back double, Deck," said Bevo. "I said I would, and I will. Tell him about my case, Mr. Parker."

"Did you hear that, Counselor?" said Willhoit. "Your client claims he can increase my original investment two-fold. What do you think? Will you win the case?"

It occurred to me that I could end everybody's troubles right then just by telling the truth. I could tell this invisible cowboy gangster that we didn't have a chance in hell of winning, that Bevo wasn't going to get a cent for his horses, and then Willhoit would hang Bevo from the neon sign, and we could all go home. Chandler and Stroud would be off the hook for screwing up the lawsuit; the geologist, wherever he was, could reclaim his house without a fight, if he wanted it; and I could stop puzzling about the hold this little weasel of a man might or might not have over Sally Dean. What a calmer, saner world it would be, I realized, if I came clean.

"Yes, sir," I said, "we're going to win."

"Well," replied Willhoit, "it was my intent to kick a mud hole in your client's lying ass and then stomp it dry. But you think I ought to wait on the trial?"

"Yes, sir."

Suddenly a couple of the cowboys behind us took hold of Bevo and pinned his arms behind his back. Bevo fought, tried to speak, but one of the cowboys had an armlock around his windpipe.

"Wait a minute, guys," I said, stepping toward Bevo. I felt something sharp press against my spine.

"I wouldn't move, if I was you, Houston," the man behind me said.

"Don't worry, Counselor," Willhoit said, "I'll wait for the trial, but I want to hold some security this time. Kirby, go on over there and cut something off Mr. Rasmussen. He's got a razor in his sock. Use that."

Bevo's body jerked as if a current had shot through it, but he was still held fast. I saw red fury in his eyes. Kirby came over to him, glanced at me as if to say, Sorry about all this. As he reached down to take the razor out of Bevo's sock, Bevo kicked him hard enough in the temple to cause him to go down on one knee. After the sap that Sally had given him the night before, I was surprised that Nutter didn't pass out. He grabbed Bevo's ankle and ripped the razor out of his sock.

"Cut me something I can put on my key chain," Willhoit called. "Don't take something he can't live without, but make it something he'll miss." He had leaned up from the backseat of the Bentley to get a good look at what was about to happen, and I saw his face for the first time. Deck Willhoit was a ZZ Top wanna-be, all black sunglasses and thick, grizzled beard.

Two other massive cowboys had captured Bevo's ankles and were holding his feet on the pavement so that he could not move. The arm around his neck tightened, and a strained, gurgling sound came out of his mouth. Nutter, kneeling, was unbuckling Bevo's belt.

"Hold on, Mr. Willhoit," I said. "Let's trade."

Willhoit cocked his head. "What sort of trade?"

"I've got an antique in the car that you just might find more amusing than one of Bevo's body parts."

"I doubt it," Willhoit said. "But let's see."

I went to Bevo's car and retrieved the whale's pizzle.

"What the fuck is that?" asked Willhoit as I handed it in to him. It protruded several feet out the window. I told him what it was, and he inspected it, turning it in his hands. I could now see the woman in the seat next to him, a brunette in a glittery dress who ran her fingers along the rawhide spirals of the pizzle.

"How about it, babe?" Willhoit asked her. He made thrusting movements with it, and I had to duck to keep from being struck in the eye. This amused Willhoit, and he used the pizzle to knock the hat off a cowboy standing next to the car.

"Whoa!" he said. "That's some dick."

"How about it," I said, "a dick for Deck."

He thought that was hilarious, and so did his girl. "What do you say, Bevo?" Willhoit called. "Is this thing bigger than yours?"

"I'll tell you one thing," I said, "it'll make a hell of a key chain."

The brunette whispered in his ear, and he laughed again. "Okay, Counselor," he said, "you've got yourself a deal. Kirby, turn that little rat's ass loose."

Nutter let go of Bevo's belt. As he climbed to his feet, he gave Bevo a terrific punch in the stomach. Bevo doubled over and fell to the pavement, gasping for breath. Nutter handed me the razor.

"I owe you one," he whispered, patting me on the back as he walked past me. Nutter and the other cowboys got into a couple of cars.

Willhoit had his driver roll the Bentley a few feet closer to us, and the drug dealer prodded Bevo with the end of the pizzle. "One hundred and eighty thousand dollars, Bevo, due the day you get it. Wait one day longer, and you and the whale this thing came from can start your own lonely hearts club."

A hand thick with gold nugget rings came out of the Bentley's window.

"It's been a pleasure meeting you, Counselor," said Willhoit. "Maybe we'll do business together someday." We shook hands. "If you see Nyman Scales's daughter anytime soon, you tell that little girl to call her pappy. I know Nyman's been missing her."

I promised to deliver the message to Sally Dean, and the big car pulled away, followed by the two carloads of cowboys. The tip of the pizzle slanted out of the Bentley's back window, whirling and thrusting in the air.

"You shouldn't ought to given that dingus away," Bevo gasped.

He was on his hands and knees, trying to stand up.

"It was either that one or yours," I reminded him.

"That dickweed wasn't gonna lay a hand on me," Bevo gasped. I pulled him to his feet—he was amazingly light—and he bent over and vomited.

"This is the second time you've put me on the spot with your friend Willhoit," I said to him a few minutes later as I drove the convertible back toward the LBJ Expressway. Bevo was slouched in the passenger seat, staring at the dash. "Don't do it again."

"Willhoit's made a big mistake," Bevo said, flicking his razor open and closed. "A big mistake."

"It was a laundering scheme, right?" I asked. "You were supposed to use Willhoit's money to buy him some cattle, make him a real cowboy."

"I should have sold him on emus," Bevo said. "I coulda got more out of him."

"Instead of buying cattle, you used his money to help buy your horses. Which you then burned for the insurance money. What in hell were you thinking, Bevo? Didn't you know a guy like Willhoit would be watching to see what happened to his money?"

"I didn't burn them horses, Mr. Parker. Besides, I'm gonna pay him off with the insurance money."

It was time one of Bevo's lawyers fulfilled his ethical obligation to his client by spilling the beans. "Bevo, you can't win the lawsuit." I told him all about Stroud's screwup with the interrogatories, how it meant we could not call any witnesses. I explained that SWAT was going to eat us for breakfast. The news did not register.

"Stroud will fix it," Bevo said. "All we got to do is get Nyman Scales on the stand. Stroud can do that. Or else you can."

"Bevo, listen to me. We are going to lose. Scales can't get on the stand for us. Nobody can. You can't count on money from the lawsuit to pay off your debts. We just lied to your drug dealer. *I* lied to him. Jesus, why did I do that?"

My question seemed to surprise him. "You were representing me, is why you did it. That's why I brought you along. We just went to court, Mr. Parker. We went to Deck Willhoit's court, and we won. You did just fine, like I knew you would."

"We didn't win," I told him. "We bought some time with a lie."

"Whatever works," he said. The motto of our firm.

I asked him where he got the money he gave to Willhoit that night. "You told me you were living hand to mouth," I reminded him.

"Money ain't nothing," Bevo said. "Getting money ain't nothing. It's the principle. That's all that matters. It's the principle of the thing."

"Is it principle to lie to everybody you meet, Bevo?" I asked. "Putting me in that house when you knew there was a chance Willhoit would come after you, did you do that on principle?"

"Principle is sticking to a plan, Mr. Parker," said the little man. "It's putting together the best plan you can make and then sticking with it. You do that, you're a principled man. No Deck Willhoit nor fancy-ass SWAT lawyer nor the whole goddamn state of Texas is gonna fuck up my plan."

"So you're a principled man, are you?" I asked.

"Yes, sir, I am. Though I know some that ain't."

CHAPTER 26

IT TOOK THREE SOLID MINUTES of banging on Wick Chandler's door Saturday morning to get him to open up. When he finally did, he was in pretty much the same condition as when I had first met him: naked except for a robe, this time one of aquamarine silk. A black sleep mask hung around his neck, along with his gold chains.

"We need to talk," I said.

"Now?" he asked, in a voice husky from sleep. I pushed past him and into the front room.

It was like stepping into another dimension. Chandler had gone in for postmodern in a big way, colors that scorched the eye and lean, rippling furniture, some of which looked like interior parts of a big machine. The couch seemed to be melting; the coffee table crouched, ready to spring. The room could have been a display in a museum for mad decorators, if it weren't for the clothes scattered across the raspberry-colored carpet. Some of the clothing belonged to a woman.

"This is a bad time, Clay," Chandler said, rubbing sleep from his eyes.

"You're going to have to make do with only one penis, Wick. I gave your whale ornament to Deck Willhoit to stop him from carving up Bevo. Which is just as well, because if I'd gotten home with it, I'd be jamming it up your left nostril right now."

That woke him up a little. He offered me a seat on the melting couch and then sat on a tiny wire chair that looked as if it could not possibly support his bulk. I told him about the run-in with Willhoit and his cowboys.

"You ask me," he said, scratching his ear, "that was damned irresponsible of Bevo, to get you involved in his shady deals like that."

"Irresponsible of *Bevo? You* sent me to Dallas to fetch a god-damned mummified whale's penis!"

"You've got to understand, Clay. It's a valuable artifact," he said.

"I'm sure it is."

"It has a lot of sentimental value to me."

"I'm sure it does. I just don't want to hear about it."

"I'm real sorry, Clay," he said. "The last thing in the world I wanted to do was hurt your feelings."

"You didn't hurt my feelings. You almost got me killed by a drug dealer in a Dallas stripjoint's parking lot, but you didn't hurt my feelings."

"I don't think Willhoit would have killed you, Clay," Wick said. "It sounds to me like the two of you got along fine."

"I have a low tolerance for fetching whale parts in the middle of the night, Wick. I didn't sign on for that sort of work." I stood up.

Wick stood up, too. "Jesus, Clay, you aren't thinking of quitting, are you?"

I hadn't been, and now that he mentioned it, I found that fact surprising.

"Give me one reason why I should stay."

"The firm needs you, Clay. You don't know how much you've done for us in just the last few days."

"All I've done is lose your whale dick for you."

"You've sharpened us up. We were just drifting on the Rasmussen case until you showed up and got us to working on it."

"You're still just drifting," I said. "You're going to lose the case big time."

"You fit here, Clay. You don't think you do, but you do." He spoke about plans he and Stroud were mulling over to expand the firm. In five years, maybe four, we would all be rich. "Don't you want to be rich?" he asked.

"I'd rather be sane," I told him.

"All right, then," he said. "There's another reason for you to stay. Sally."

"She left me taped naked to a chair for the police to find, Wick. I'm not too sure Sally cares if I stick around or not."

"I think that shows a real interest on her part."

"Wickie?" a woman's husky voice called from down the hall.

"Just a minute, Clay," said Wick, scuttling down the hallway. I heard the low, muffled drawl of Chandler's voice, its tone ardent and cajoling. I noticed a garter belt lying under the coffee table, and next to it, an ivory-handled straight razor. Perhaps it was the razor lady I had talked to over the phone on my first day in the office!

He came back wrapping the flimsy robe tighter around his huge stomach. "Look, Clay, I'm sorry as I can be about last night. I should have told you about the pizzle, and Bevo sure as hell should have told you about the meeting with Willhoit. But let me ask you something: If you *had* known—if Bevo had come clean and told you he wanted you to go with him to keep him alive when he met his drug dealer—would you have gone?"

"Are you crazy?" I asked. "I'm no bodyguard. And I don't practice law in parking lots."

"I'm not asking you if it was *smart* to go. I'm asking if you would have gone to save your client's life."

I thought about that. "This is stupid," I said. "If Bevo had told me what he wanted to do, I'd have talked him out of it."

Wick shook his head. "You don't talk Bevo out of things. He was going to meet that man in Dallas, with or without you. And without you, there was a much better chance of his winding up at the bottom of Lake Ray Hubbard. Now, knowing *that,* would you have turned Bevo down?"

"I don't know, and here's the point, Wick: I wasn't given a chance to find out."

"You're right, partner. I'm sorry. No more crazy missions. I promise."

I drove home but felt too restless to go in. Instead, I drove to the office and tried to work on the Rasmussen case but found I couldn't concentrate. I kept wondering if Sally might show up at my house that morning—an unlikely possibility, considering that I had basically accused her of whoring for her father the last time I saw her. On my way home I went by Glenn Lawson's hardware store and bought back the lawn mower. I mowed and edged and trimmed.

As Lawson predicted, off and on throughout the day people showed up to repossess things Bevo had failed to make payments on. An unassembled satellite dish was taken away by a couple of husky guys in a van. They took the television, too, and the VCR. I helped three teenagers carry a fiberglass Jacuzzi out of the garage and lift it into a pickup truck. Everybody who came to take away merchandise offered to sell it to me then and there. They would give me a great price on it. Apparently, there were not many buyers of luxury items left in Jenks.

Later on I strolled through the business district of Jenks, an exercise that took less than fifteen minutes, and noted all the shops that had gone out of business. The people I met, most of whom greeted the stranger in their midst with an automatic "howdy," moved with a curious floating listlessness, as if their chests were hollow or they had been balancing something heavy on their heads for a long time. I compared these folks to the thousands I used to see every day caught in Houston's frenetic bustle—the downtown crowds pushing through jungle heat on their way to lunch at noon or the parking lots at five o'clock. There was not much similarity. Houstonians were harried, but they knew they were going somewhere. If the citizens of Jenks had someplace to go, they weren't in any hurry to get there.

About four o'clock I wandered into Glenn Lawson's hardware store for the second time that day, this time just to chat, and ran into Captain Jack and Red Meachum, our soon-to-be sheriff's deputy. They were buying a spring-loaded animal trap. I introduced myself, something I hadn't done on our first encounter at the Singing Pig.

"I hope we can clear up any ill feelings that might exist between you boys and the firm of Chandler and Stroud," I said.

Captain Jack turned to Meachum. "Do you have any ill feelings toward 'em, Red?"

"Nope," said Red, "I love lawyers. Lawyers just make my day." He smiled at me, and I understood Stroud's contempt for the ex-pilots.

"That's a mean-looking trap you got there," I said. "What's it for? Bobcats?"

Meachum shot me a suspicious look. "What would make you think it's for bobcats?" he asked.

I shrugged. They had also brought to the counter a half-dozen little evergreen-shaped car deodorants.

"Whatever you fellows do in your cars must really be pungent," I said.

Jack pointed a finger at me. "City boy, you tell those fat farts you work for that their day is coming."

Meachum tapped his friend on the arm. "Now, Jack," said the big man, "this lawyer wants to make friends." Captain Jack bit down on the rest of his speech.

"We'll have to go to lunch together again sometime," I said as they left the store with their purchases.

Lawson had watched the encounter from behind the cash register. "I see you've met our rehabilitation project," he said.

"What they lack in brains, they make up for in charm," I replied.

"The big one there is gonna be our new deputy," said Lawson. "He says he's gonna get the others deputized, too. Their Rambo phase must be over, or else they'd have been all camouflaged up. Could be they're starting a new phase." He shook his head. "We'll have to get old Hard-dick to name it for us. How's the lawn mower working out?"

I told him that I had already given the yard a makeover.

He laughed. "You can usually tell who the city people are around here. They have the nicest lawns. I guess it's hard for them to find stuff to do in this little town."

"What *is* there to do around here?" I asked.

"Well," he said, "you could fertilize."

CHAPTER 27

CHANDLER AND STROUD had planned a little welcoming party for me that night out at Stroud's place. Shortly after six-thirty I parked the Austin Healey in the yard of Gilliam Stroud's farmhouse. From his stall in the broken-down stable, Ed the unspotted Appaloosa watched me climb onto the porch. The front door was open, and Cajun fiddle music blasted through the house so loudly that the air trembled. I peered in from the porch.

"Well, lookee here," boomed Stroud from the shadows, "our wounded boy has returned to us! "

"Clay!" Wick Chandler hollered. "Get in here!" He danced across the room toward me, a Hawaiian shirt billowing over his massive paunch like a crimson sail. Wick's top half looked too heavy to be supported by the thin, blue-white legs that peeped out from under his aquamarine Bermudas. He was wearing black business socks and loafers. He thrust a longneck into my hand, motioning toward the kitchen. "There's pâté in there. Help yourself." Wick was a dervish, whirling and hopping to the music, a ruby blimp caught in a cyclone. He danced away, bumping into furniture.

The early-evening sun coming through the windows flung bright bands of light across the ancient furniture. Stroud was sprawled on a sofa in the room's deepest shadow. He got up and lumbered toward me, holding out his hand for me to shake.

"Welcome to Jenks, Mr. Parker," he boomed against the music. "How's the leg?"

I told him it was fine, though to tell the truth it throbbed a little.

"That's fine, that's fine," he said. "I'm mighty proud of you, boy. Anybody who'd take a darning needle in the leg for a client— such heroism."

He put his hand on my shoulder, smiling broadly and, I thought, mockingly at me. He was wearing a bright yellow shirt with intricate designs like figures on a Mayan ruin and white linen pants that looked as if they had been wadded up before he put them on. He looked like a shriveled Sydney Greenstreet on a beach holiday, his pale feet marbly against the dark bands of his sandals. With a shock I noticed that the big toe on his left foot was missing. That explained the limp.

"We've got a housewarming present for you," Stroud said, motioning toward a package on the coffee table. I set my beer on the table and unwrapped the package. It was a shiny nickel-plated revolver.

"Smith and Wesson model thirty-six," said Stroud. "Hope you don't already have one."

I wondered if the gift was a joke concerning my run-in with Kirby Nutter. But when I replied that I didn't own a gun, I got a look of genuine surprise.

"A Texas lawyer without a gun? Well, you've got one now, son. And it's a honey."

"There's a holster goes with it," said Wick, who had come up behind me, still dancing. "We're getting your name put on it. In a while we'll go down to the pond and you can shoot some snakes."

"Thanks," I said, not knowing what else to say.

We were joined by a slim blond woman who I guessed was in her late thirties, with a cloud of cotton-candy hair floating above the deep, leathery tan of her face and shoulders. It was Deirdre, the emu lady, dressed in a bright blue jumpsuit with sailor trimmings and a lot of cleavage showing. As we shook hands I wondered where her husband was. To my surprise, she told me.

"My husband Mike's off catching bass at Texoma."

"Is that so?" I said, smiling.

"Do you fish, Clay?" she asked, and now I saw that she was drunk.

"Not since I was a kid," I answered, but she didn't hear me, because another woman had walked up behind her and slipped an ice cube down her back. Deirdre whirled around and around.

"Get it out, get it out!" she shrieked. She managed to extract it herself, and she flung it at the other woman.

"Wanda Sue, I swear!"

Wanda Sue was blond and dark-tanned like Deirdre, maybe a little younger, and dressed in a sleeveless jumpsuit of white and green polka dots. The depth of their tans was a little shocking; these women had been seriously irradiated.

"This is Wanda Sue Lovell, my cousin," Deirdre said. "She's been dying to meet you."

I shook hands and smiled at Wanda, who smiled back and moved close. Wick danced over and scooped Deirdre into his arms. He bumped against me, whispered, "Sally's out of town," and danced away grinning at me as if to say, Well . . . I realized then that Wanda was to be my date for the evening. A second welcome-party surprise: first the gun, now Wanda.

"Nice gun," Wanda said. I was still holding the revolver. Wanda slid her dark fingers along its barrel.

I tried to think, but it was hard with the Cajun fiddle music making my vision blur. I figured I was being scammed again, but by whom? Was it just Wick, unhappy about my relationship with Sally and hoping Wanda would steer me in another direction? Or was Stroud in on it, too, which meant he knew about Sally and me?

"Do you like to shoot snakes?" I asked. I was hoping to talk Wanda into taking my place on the snake-shooting expedition.

"I've shot a few in my time."

We all went to the dining room, where a feast was laid out on two card tables set up amid folding chairs and dusty piles of books: beef ribs, baked beans, potato salad, and a relish spicy enough to take paint off siding. Before long I was on my sixth beer and feeling wobbly. Gilliam Stroud didn't seem to have much of an appetite. He sat distracted, glaring around the room. Was he upset about Sally and me? Had he heard?

Wanda, it turned out, was a dental hygienist and had a fund of stories about bad teeth. They made for unusual table talk. I continued to drink until the buzz from the beer muffled the screeching fiddle music. At one point, maybe in the kitchen, I remember Wanda telling me that I had good, strong teeth, but I don't recall what I had done with them to earn her approbation.

I kept on drinking, moving from beer to whiskey. Everything got blurry. There may have been a fire. I have a memory of Wick dancing like a maniac with Deirdre, spinning her round and round until both of them fell laughing onto the sofa in the front room. Deirdre landed on me, and in the scramble she turned into Wanda, who performed a dental examination on my mouth with her tongue. I had one hand caught in the top of her jumpsuit and one in the tight bundle of her hair when I started to black out.

Then my brain jolted hard, like a fastball thudding into a catcher's mitt, and a sharp pain peeled layer after layer of drunkenness away until I was awake and standing in the gloom of Stroud's parlor. Wanda writhed on the couch, her hands clapped against her ears. I could hear Deirdre shrieking from the floor behind the sofa. "Goddamn it, Gill!" Wick hollered. "Cut it out." The pain stopped, and in the silence—where had the fiddle music gone?—I could hear dogs howling, some from close by, some from far away across the fields. There was an old porch swing just outside the door, and from it came the creak of chains and a deep-voiced chuckle. Gilliam Stroud had blown his whistle.

I stumbled toward the screen door in a rage. I was going to make sure Stroud never seared my skull with his little toy again. The door wobbled, stuck in the frame. I yanked hard.

"Give me that whistle!" I yelled. Before I could pull the door open, Wick Chandler collided against me, pushing me away from the door.

"Wait, Clay!" he said. "You don't know about it. Listen to me." I pushed at him and grabbed for the door. The girls had gotten up, Wanda half out of her jumpsuit, and watched us struggle.

"Get away from me, Wick," I said. "I'm gonna make him swallow that thing." I wrenched the door open and stepped out onto the porch. Gilliam Stroud lay in the porch swing, head thrown back, snoring. It had taken him less than a minute to fall asleep. The whistle hung on its silver chain against the hieroglyphs of his shirt.

I wanted to yank the whistle off its chain and throw it as hard as I could. But looking at the massive ruin of the man, the utter collapse of him, I couldn't do it. The anger began to drain out of me. Wick came out and stood with me, watching his partner drift on the swing.

"You don't want to take it away from him, Clay," Wick said.

"Why does he call it the voice of doom?" I asked. Winded, we sat down on the edge of the porch. Deirdre and Wanda joined us, and while Stroud snored, Wick told us the story of the whistle.

"There's a pond on this property," he said. "It's over yonder. Gill and I used to go down there to shoot snakes. This was years ago, right after he moved here. He had been living somewhere down around Gonzales, just marking time since he left El Paso. His wife had died there."

"What did she die of?" asked Deirdre.

"Cancer, I think. I'm not sure. Gill doesn't talk about it. I think it's what ruined him. He gave up his judgeship right after she died. A federal judge stepping down. I never heard of it before."

Neither had I.

"He had a daughter, too," Wick continued. "A friend of mine out in El Paso told me that she turned out to be no good. She got into drugs in a big way."

"What happened to her?" asked Deirdre.

"She died, too, a year or so after her mother. Car accident in New Mexico, I think. Gill almost never talks about it. We've been partners going on seventeen years, and he has mentioned her to me maybe three times." He gave his dozing partner a long, puzzled look.

"How did you two wind up together?" I asked.

Wick shrugged. "Just weird luck. I heard about his wife's death and sent him a sympathy card. My old professor, you know? A couple of years later I got the craziest letter from him, asking if I thought East Texas had room for another lawyer. He didn't mention the lawyer's name, and I thought he was asking me to do him a favor, take on some kid out of law school who needed experience, that sort of thing. I wrote him back and said, Sure, send him on. Business was good back then, and I figured if the guy had a recommendation from Gilliam Stroud, he'd do fine. I didn't know he was talking about himself until he showed up in the Lincoln. He was pulling a trailer with everything he owned in it. It was an awful small trailer." Wick shook his head in wonder. "Gilliam Stroud, asking for a job from me. I wasn't his best student, not by a long shot. To this day I'm not quite sure why he chose me and Jenks."

"Maybe he was just looking for a way out," I said. It made sense to me. If Gill Stroud had wanted to bury himself, Jenks was a good place to do it.

"I made him a partner right off, of course," Wick said. "Jesus, I couldn't get over the way he had changed since the days at Baylor Law. I don't know how to describe it. It was like he'd been bitten in two, like something had dug in and scooped most of him out."

Wanda went into the house and came back with longnecks for the four of us. Wick took a long drink before continuing.

"Anyway, Gill liked shooting snakes. He built a cabin by the pond; it's about two miles over that way. We'd go out there with a cooler of beer and sit on the porch and shoot at the water. We could generally hit the pond. I don't know that we killed many snakes, but they by-God knew we were out there." He laughed. "One day we got really drunk and decided to play a fast-draw game. We strapped on pistols and nailed targets to a couple of pine trees, moved a ways off from each other, and let fly. We didn't put a single hole in either of those targets. We were really buzzed."

"You were lucky you didn't kill yourselves," I said.

"I thought about that later," Wick replied. "I noticed that some of Gill's shots were going wild. I mean *really* wild, snapping branches high off of trees. I looked around at him, and it looked kind of like he was fighting himself for the pistol. It was the strangest thing I ever saw, one hand fighting the other. He actually got the gun pointed at his skull a couple of times, and the second time, it went off, just missing him and singeing his hair. If you look hard, you'll see a little white scar over his left ear."

Wanda got up, tiptoed around behind the porch swing, and squinted at the side of Stroud's head.

"Wanda!" hissed Deirdre.

"Yep," Wanda whispered, "there it is." She came back to the group. "Well, I'm *sorry,* Dee-Dee," she said to Deirdre, "but I'm the sort of person likes things proved. It's there, all right, just the tiniest little scar."

"We were shooting .22 target pistols," Wick said. "If we'd been shooting anything else, the man wouldn't be here with us today. You should have seen him, half-bald, black gunpowder on his face, and that red welt running across his skull. He was blinking like a baby, like he'd just been born."

"What did you do?" I asked.

"I went crazy. I ran for him, got my hand on the gun. And it was like there were three of us fighting for it, me and Gill and whatever it was inside him that had made a grab for it in the first place. We fought for what seemed like five minutes before the gun went off again. The bullet hit him right in the joint of his big toe. It damn near tore it off."

Wanda reached out to touch the empty spot on Stroud's sandal. Deirdre swatted her hand.

"That sent him into shock, and I was able to get him into the Dodge and drive to the clinic. The doctor there said he couldn't do anything but take off what was left of the toe. But Gill didn't want any part of that. He raised hell, threatened to sue if the toe came off. We wound up going to Dallas in an ambulance, with Gill swearing and thrashing around, in spite of all the painkiller they gave him. He was a sight, hair all standing up, that big scar on his scalp, and the powder that had bit into his face and wouldn't wash off. It looked like his brain had exploded inside his head. A surgeon at Parkland tried to save the toe, but he couldn't do it. Gill was under anesthetic, of course. When he came to, there was hell to pay."

"Wick," I said, "what does this have to do with the whistle?"

"I'm coming to that. When he found out the toe was gone, he asked for it back. Can you imagine that? He wanted the remains. The surgeon said he couldn't have them; they were long gone. Gill roared at him, said he would sue him and his hospital and the whole damn town if he didn't get his toe back. Finally he wore them down, and they gave him a prescription bottle with some tiny bone fragments in it and something that might have been a toenail. If you ask me, there was no way to know if they were really Gill's toe bones or bones from a rat's ass, but Gill took them and sent them to an Indian silversmith he knew in El Paso." He pointed at the whistle hanging from Stroud's neck. "You see those little flecks of white in there? Toe bones."

"God almighty," said Wanda. She tried to move in for a closer look, but Deirdre grabbed her arm and yanked her back down.

"You are a scandal," Deirdre scolded.

"The silver isn't really silver," said Wick. "It's white gold. It's his wedding band, and his wife's. I asked him why he did that, why he would make such a godawful trinket, and he told me something strange. He said his little accident with the gun—he called it an accident—taught him the last lesson he ever had to learn. He said he had already learned that other people could die, but he hadn't believed it of himself. He said his little accident taught him that he could die, too. Now he blows his whistle to teach his lesson to others."

He turned to me. "That's why he calls it the trumpet of doom, Clay. He says it's an intimation of mortality. He says the sound it makes is death laughing at us, laughing at us through his toe bones, laughing inside our skulls. It's death, saying life is short. He says he's taught his lesson to all the dogs in the county and now he's working on the humans."

"That's the saddest thing I ever heard," said Deirdre, her eyes welling with tears.

"I think it's a crock," Wanda said. "I think you're yanking our chains, Wick Chandler."

Wick shook his head. "I don't know," he said, "I can't hear a thing when he blows it. I guess that means I'm going to live forever."

The snoring stopped, and Stroud's head jerked upright. "Sally!" he cried, coming out of his sleep. His eyes focused slowly. He saw us all sitting at his feet, looking up at him.

"What happened to the party?" he asked.

"I think it's about played out, Gill," replied Wick.

"Well then," said Stroud, "we need a benediction." He raised the whistle to his lips and blew. The girls hunched their shoulders, my mind flapped like a window shade in a gale, and from all points of the compass came the mournful howling of dogs.

CHAPTER 28

ABOUT ELEVEN O'CLOCK I said good-bye to Wanda Sue and the other partygoers and drove home in fragile condition from the beer-and-whiskey combination. As I left, Wanda kissed me on the cheek and offered to clean my teeth for free anytime. On Sunday I slept until almost noon. I got up, with my head thundering, and called Wick to remind him that we were to pick up Stroud at eight o'clock the next morning and drive out into the country to depose Nyman Scales at his ranch. Wick was groggy on the phone. I had woken him up.

"I'm pretty wrung out," he said. "That Deirdre."

I reminded him of his promise to reform. He did not want to be reminded. I asked him if there had been any word on Stroud's attempt to get relief from the judge on our failure to answer the interrogatories.

"Not as of last night," Wick said, yawning. "There won't be any relief, Clay. Not from Wrong Tit Tidwell. There's bad blood between him and Gill going way back. It was Gill that gave him his nickname."

"I don't want to hear about it," I said. "Jesus, Wick, is there anybody in the East Texas judicial system that you guys haven't pissed off?"

"Maybe a few court clerks here and there," he said.

I suggested that he get out of bed and do something to try to save his law firm.

"What is there to do, Clay?" he asked. "We haven't seen a single piece of evidence from the plaintiff; we haven't even got that goddamn Pulaski's pathology report. We have a client who won't listen to us and lies every time he opens his mouth. And now we're deposing people who won't be allowed to testify, either in person or by deposition, for God's sake. You tell me what I can do, Clay, and I'll do it."

"I don't know. Would you comb back through the file? Maybe we missed something we can use."

Wick promised to review the file as soon as his head stopped pounding. I hung up and called Stroud but got no answer. We had not gone over the questions that he would ask Scales at tomorrow's deposition, but I supposed that was okay. According to Bevo, there was only one question that mattered—his whereabouts at the time of the fire—and Scales already knew what to say about that.

I was not looking forward to the deposition, although Wick had told me that Nyman Scales's operation was worth seeing, a state-of-the-art horse ranch, complete with a genetics lab. Also, it would be our first look at the other side's hired guns, the trial lawyers from SWAT.

A deposition is a pretty formal affair. Both parties to the action have to be present, as do their counsel and the court reporter. Only the judge and jury are missing, but the testimony from a deposition can be used in evidence at the trial, subject to objections. I did not relish the prospect of sitting there watching the SWAT people smirking at us while Gilliam Stroud asked his useless questions. So what if Scales could place Bevo at his place on the night of the fire? Scales was not going to get the chance to testify, and the judge wouldn't let us use the deposition. And even if he did, all

Scales's testimony would show was that Bevo did not actually start the fire. SWAT might—and probably did—have evidence linking Bevo to whoever lit the match. Bevo could have helped us by giving us the names of his accomplices, but he continued to proclaim his innocence, despite the fact that no one, not even his lawyers, believed him.

The sad fact was, we didn't know what SWAT had on him. Since Stroud had never sent over his own interrogatories, SWAT was under no obligation to send us any information on their case. We had no idea what sort of evidence they would present. It would be the O.K. Corral, with SWAT as the Earps and us as the Clantons. The only significant difference was that, in the real gunfight, the Clantons got to use live ammunition. We would be firing blanks.

I tried to think of something to do on the case, but Wick was right, there was nothing else, except get braced for what SWAT would do to us. My brain had still not worked its way out from under the rock I seemed to have set on it the night before, so I took some aspirin and tried to go back to sleep. At three o'clock I showered and went down to the Dairy Queen for a late lunch. As I was parking the Austin Healey, a man came out of the restaurant who matched the description Lu-Anne had given us of the "lawyer" who had been meeting secretly with Bevo. He got into a big black Lexus and pulled out of the DQ parking lot as I walked in.

"That's him," Lu-Anne said, "your competition. You missed Bevo by about four minutes. You ask me, I think they're heading out of town to meet somewhere."

I ran back out to my Austin Healey and took off after the Lexus. The car was too far ahead for me to see it, but it had left a fine haze of dust hanging in the air east along Main Street, heading out of town. I lost the trail at the last asphalt cross street before the roads turned to dirt. There was too much dust in the air to make a guess as to which road the Lexus had taken.

"Too fast for you?" Lu-Anne asked as I walked back in the DQ.

"If I'd taken you along, we wouldn't have lost them," I replied.

There were no other customers. Lu-Anne explained that I had missed the Sunday lunch crunch and was too early for the after-Sunday-night-church crowd. I told her to surprise me with something good to eat and slid into a booth.

I had seen that man before. In Houston, although I could not remember exactly where or in what context. Lu-Anne was right: He looked like a lawyer. He was a lawyer. But who the hell was he?

I figured it out just as Lu-Anne came to my table with my lunch. As she put the plate down, I jumped out of the booth.

"It's just chicken fried steak," Lu-Anne said.

"Antoine Duett," I said.

"What?"

I sat back down and tried to eat the lunch Lu-Anne had brought me, but my appetite was gone.

This was serious news. Antoine Duett was indeed a Houston lawyer. I remembered my old colleague Rita Humphrey introducing us once in the lobby of the building where our firm had its offices. He was not one of Rita's favorite people, she told me later. More a dirty-tricks operator than a practicing lawyer, Duett performed nasty little jobs for other law firms. He tracked down reluctant witnesses, encouraged unreluctant witnesses to change their minds, and helped with the general shuffling of opinion and evidence that often goes on behind the scenes of a trial and can sometimes shake up even the most open-and-shut cases. People like Duett are the CIA and the KGB of the big firms. Some lawyers see them as a necessary evil. Some would like to round them all up and stick them in a gulag.

I knew one other thing about Antoine Duett of Houston. Although he kept no legal connection with any firm, he had an office in the same building as Slaven, Wortmann, Applegate, and Tice. Bevo was holding secret meetings with the enemy.

CHAPTER 29

I DROVE TO WICK'S HOME, rang the doorbell, then beat on the door with my fist. No Wick. When I got to Stroud's farmhouse, about four-thirty, Sally's blue Mercedes was parked in the yard, and Sally was out in the stable, going over Ed with a brush. She was wearing jeans and a workshirt tied at her waist. A country girl again.

I went into the stable and stood awhile, watching Sally work the brush methodically down the horse's side, and tried to think of something to say. "Hot day," was what I came up with.

"I want to thank you," she said, without looking at me, "for not turning me in to the police."

"There's no law against refusing to untape a man from a chair."

"There's one against prostitution," she replied. "You could have shut me down, and I'd have had to fall back on my day job."

So it was going to be like that.

"I'm looking for Bevo," I said. "Do you know where he is?"

She shrugged. "You could ask Gill, but he's probably still asleep."

"Maybe I'll wake him up."

"You might try, but I should warn you, he sleeps with a loaded gun. I know, because my daddy pays me to service him from time to time, just like I do you."

I went up to her, took the brush out of her hand, and spun her around. "How long are you going to keep this up?" I asked. There was a sharp, painful tug at my waist: Ed had clamped his teeth on my belt and was apparently trying to expel me from the stable. I pulled free, and he showed me a grin full of gigantic teeth.

"This is Ed's hour," Sally said, "not yours. You're lucky he didn't get you by the tenders."

I handed the brush back, and she continued grooming the horse.

"I saw Deck Willhoit in Dallas a couple of nights ago," I said. "He told me to tell you your father misses you. I guess you'd better check in."

The only sound for a while was the rasp of the brush as it moved down Ed's flank. "Deck is my uncle," she said at last. "Not by blood, but by business. He and Nyman were partners years ago. They probably still are, in ways that would interest the FBI if they only knew where and how to look."

She moved around the horse and began to work Ed's other side. "I've been trying for a couple of years now to decide whether or not to have a talk with the feds, see if I couldn't point them in the right direction. Selling out your own father is a harder thing than you might think, even for the daughter of Nyman Scales. But you and your idiotic guesswork the other night have just about made up my mind for me."

"You've kept up with your father's business activities?" I asked.

"According to you and Bevo, I *am* one of my father's business activities." She laughed. "You and Wick and Bevo and Gill, half the judges in the county, and my father, too, old crafty Nyman. You're all working so hard to come up with an angle on me. I can see the gears running behind your eyes. It would be funny if it weren't so pathetic."

"Come on, Sally."

"This may surprise you, Counselor, but I've never known *exactly* what my father is up to. Oh, I've known for years that he was up to no good, and God knows, I did some odd things for him when I was young. But he always kept me as much in the dark as possible. And he never told me the truth. He doesn't know how. Even when I was busted for fraud—I was fourteen at the time— and Gill got the charges dropped, Nyman insisted to me there had been a terrible mistake. For a while he said he was working up a lawsuit against the county for arresting his little girl. Keeping quiet might have been his way of protecting me, but more likely it was because he didn't want anyone, even his daughter, to have enough on him to cause him to worry. So, no, I haven't kept up with him. But lately I've been doing a little checking. From the questions he asks me about my judges' schedules, I think I've figured out which of the bastards he's bought. That information might be of help to some DA. I'm beginning to think that I could put Nyman away."

She kept working on the horse, methodically, carefully. "Did you ever have a pet, Counselor? Did your mommy and daddy ever get you a dog or a cat or some little rodent, or maybe a turtle?"

"I had a dog," I replied.

"When I was young, Nyman used to give me pets. Not dogs or cats. Larger animals. Sometimes a calf, sometimes a half-grown horse. He usually did it after he'd been away from home for a couple of weeks or a month, with Mama wondering where he was, curs- ing him under her breath. She really was a Cajun witch. I think she tried spells on Daddy. Maybe they are what made him such a son of a bitch. Maybe they kept him from being worse than he is. Or maybe they just annoyed him; there is a rumor that he killed her."

"I've heard it," I said.

"It's a lie," she said flatly. "Who told you, anyway? Wick Chandler?" She laughed. "He's been sore at me ever since I refused to do with him what I never should have done with you."

"Sally—"

"Anyway, Daddy would finally show up after one of his absences, with an animal in tow, and he'd sit me down and give me a big hug and make a show of giving me a pet. 'It's all yours, baby,' he'd say. 'You can name her and raise her as your own.' And I'd do it every time. I'd feed them and brush them and do whatever else it took to keep them healthy. But I learned never to get too involved with my pets, because I knew that someday I'd come home after school and my colt or my calf would be gone. It had run away, Nyman said. He had looked everywhere for it. He thought maybe someone had stolen it."

She sighed. "It took me two or three years to figure out what was happening. My father was giving me his special stock, those animals he was saving for some particular scheme, some get-rich-quick experiment. When I was a little older, I would try to find out what happened when my pet-of-the-moment disappeared. Usually it had been sold—I found where Nyman kept his bills of sale—but sometimes it had had an accident. Little Buttercup had run into barbed wire or gotten struck by lightning."

"I'm sorry, Sally," I said.

"You'd think a man as clever as Nyman would be smarter about his own child. He seemed to think I would never catch on to what he was doing. Or maybe that I just wouldn't care. Well, I did care. I just didn't know what to do about it. You see, Counselor, in a way, you and Bevo were right about me. I was the most special stock of all. I could do tricks without having to be maimed or killed first. Nyman taught me a lot of them. It was petty thievery mostly, in the beginning, but it got more complicated after Mama died. Nyman said it wasn't wrong because it's every man for himself out there. 'It's a fallen world,' he'd say. 'But we don't have to fall along with it.'"

"Sally, you don't have to tell me any of this."

"You asked me once why I keep Ed here instead of at Daddy's place. Do you think you can figure out why now?"

"I guess, maybe, an unspotted Appaloosa wouldn't have much value to Nyman," I said.

"Except as tinder," she replied. "Well, Ed is going to live into old age. Gill and I are going to see to that." She put the brush on a shelf and washed her hands at a faucet. "Do you really need to see Bevo?" she asked.

"I have a few questions that need answering."

"Come on, then. I'll take you to his hideout." She walked out of the stable and climbed into her Mercedes.

"So you know where he lives?" I asked as I got into the passenger seat.

She switched on the engine. "A girl always has to know the whereabouts of her pimp."

CHAPTER 30

SALLY DROVE EAST out of the yard along a road that was nothing more than a couple of wheel ruts running through knee-high grass. The little car did not have much road clearance, and it crested the waves of grass like a speedboat. I realized it was a good thing that we hadn't taken my car, because the Austin Healey would have surely run aground.

"Nice car," I said.

"If a girl takes care of herself in this line of work, she can make some money."

"Look, Sally I want to—" A bump in the road bounced me up against the car's roof, and I bit my tongue hard enough for pain to ring like a bell in my mouth.

"You better buckle up," Sally said. "I'd hate to bring you back with a broken neck. Bad for business."

We bucked on for about five minutes, sometimes through fields with no wheel ruts at all, until we arrived at a brick-and-shingle cabin sitting beside a large pond.

"Is this Stroud's shooting spot?" I asked.

"It used to be."

Though badly run down, Stroud's cabin was a pretty sophisti-
cated piece of work, with a fireplace, a garage, and a screened-in
porch running the length of the cabin's front. Square holes bordered
with elaborate wooden frames had been let into the screen at a
variety of heights.

"The holes are for shooting at snakes in the pond," Sally
explained. Bevo's Seville was not in sight, nor were any of the other
cars he claimed to own. We walked across the porch, knocked, got
no answer.

"Does Stroud know Bevo is living in his cabin?" I asked.

"Bevo's a real entrepreneur. Cows, horses, whores. There's a
connection there, don't you think?"

"You left out emus," I said.

"He's branching out into the big birds?" she replied. "That little
man is full of surprises."

Sally told me that Bevo had been a hanger-on at her father's
ranch back when she used to crash there. "He thought he was hot
stuff because he was selling invisible cows." She shook her head.
"When he found out who I was, he made a dozen different kinds
of moves on me, all of them hopeless. He was like a mangy puppy
rubbing up against my leg. But he wasn't really after me. He was
after Nyman. He wanted Nyman to turn him into a big-time horse
dealer. I left the ranch about the time Nyman started noticing him.
It surprised me to learn that Nyman had sold Bevo some horses.
Bevo always seemed like such a lightweight."

"They're big pals now," I said. I told her that Bevo was counting on Nyman to save him at tomorrow's deposition out at the
Scales ranch.

Sally shook her head. "Nyman used to be a better judge of scum."

I tried the door. It was unlocked, and we went inside. The front
room of the cabin was a mess of strewn clothes, half-eaten TV
dinners, and bedsheets. It looked like Bevo had been sleeping on

the couch. There was a big table that stood not quite chest high with some odd-looking machines on it, some of them clamped to the table's edge.

"Are these for drugs?" I asked, pointing to the machines.

"They're not Bevo's," Sally said. "They're Gill's. They're for loading bullet casings. He and Wick used to make their own bullets." She pointed under the table to a huge plastic sack of what looked like black sand.

"Gunpowder?" I asked.

"Walk lightly, city boy," she said, "that stuff is pretty old. You don't want to set it off."

"Sally, tell me about you and Stroud."

She sat on the stool in front of the loading table and took a brass casing out of a paper sack. "Gill showed me how to do this once," she said. "Let's see if I can work it without blowing us both up." She fitted the casing into a recess in one of the machines clamped to the edge of the table.

"It's a simple story," she said. "Gill rehabilitated me. After I graduated from college I went into a tailspin. I think I was having an allergic reaction to being Nyman Scales's daughter, though I didn't know that's what it was." She took some gunpowder out of a small crock and filled a metal funnel on the top of the machine. "I had an apartment in Mule Springs, but I was out at the ranch all the time. Nyman had me change my name legally. It was all part of a scam to fool the government about who owned his dairy. I didn't care. I was into drugs, antidepressants mostly, mixing them with whatever I could find in the liquor cabinet. Nyman didn't notice. He still saw me as his trained pony. At the time, I still was. I would listen to him, knowing everything coming out of his mouth was a lie, and yet I would nod and smile and do what he told me to do." She shook her head. "What makes people do things like that, Counselor? How can a person just consign herself to hell?"

"He's your father, Sally," I said. She put up a hand as if to bat the words away.

"The judicial coordinator's job came open, and Nyman thought it would be great having someone he could use in the office, someone to feed him inside information. So he found out what the requirements were—college degree, six months of work in a law office, the ability to count to ten. He told me to go get a job with some lawyers. I remembered the time Gill got me out of jail, so I went there. He hired me on the spot. God knows why. I looked like a reanimated corpse with the shakes. But then, so did Gill. He hired me, and Wick went along with it."

"And Stroud straightened you out?" I asked.

"Let's just say that Gill Stroud did not treat me like a trained pony. He was the first man I ever met who dealt with me like I was a human being."

"And then he fell in love with you?" I asked.

"That's one version."

"What's your version?" I asked.

Sally turned a crank on the side of the machine and sent a small amount of powder into the casing. She set a cone of lead in another fitting in the machine and used a lever to stuff the cone into the top of the casing. She tossed me the bullet.

"That's for a .38 special," she said. "It'll fit the gun that the boys gave you last night and which you forgot when you went home, I assume because Wanda Sue Lovell had got you thinking about dental hygiene."

"Sally."

"My relationship with Gill Stroud is my business. Mine and Gill's. Can you accept that, Counselor?"

"I guess I'll have to," I replied. "But after you straightened out, you took the district coordinator's job, anyway."

"That's right. I let Nyman pull the strings, and I got the job."

"Why?"

"I figured doing an honest job in that office was the best way to show my father that he'd better train another pony, because this one had gotten away from him."

"And you haven't been helping him out?"

Sally looked at me in exasperation. "No, Counselor, I have not been helping Nyman. He's asked, all right, lots of times, and every single time I've shut him down. Daddy's little girl isn't Daddy's little girl anymore. What's more, if I ever get proof—solid proof—that he has killed an animal for money, I'll go after him any way I can."

I remembered Stroud thundering at Wick in Boo's barbecue shack that there was no evidence of wrongdoing on Sally's part as judicial district coordinator, and I felt one of the knots in my gut begin to loosen. The old man was right about Sally—and I suddenly realized that she was the one thing in the world I had most wanted the lying old charlatan to be right about.

"And yet," I said, moving toward her, "here you are, whoring for Bevo Rasmussen."

She stared at me for a moment—just long enough to see that, for the first time, I had gotten the jump on her. She shrugged, a faint smile on her lips. "I guess it's my bad blood," she said. "What can I do?"

"I think you need a lawyer," I said. She got off her stool, backed slowly along the table as I approached.

"Why would I need a lawyer?" she asked, letting me back her against the wall.

"Legal services," I replied. "Maybe something to do with duct tape." I reached to kiss her, but as my lips brushed hers she pushed me away.

"No, damn it," she said, "I'm mad at you." She poked me in the chest, and it was my turn to be backed along the wall. "I cooked you dinner, I exorcised your house, I saved your kneecap, I provided you with truly amazing sex, and you called me a whore. Jesus, I get crazy just thinking about it. No, sir, I've got no more pity for the poor city boy."

"Pity?" I said. "You left me taped to the goddamned chair!"

"You deserved it," she replied. She started to say something else, then her gaze went past me into the room beyond.

I turned and looked into the room. It was packed to the ceiling with boxes. I switched on the light and saw that the boxes were for electronic equipment of all sorts—television sets, stereo amplifiers, speakers, CD players, phone answering machines, faxes. There must have been a hundred thousand dollars' worth of boxed goods, all stacked neatly as if in a warehouse.

"Bevo is fencing stolen goods," Sally said. She began to laugh. "Like I said, the little shit is full of surprises."

CHAPTER 31

SALLY DROVE ME BACK TO STROUD'S, and I ran upstairs to tell the old man about the stolen goods warehoused in his cabin. They would create quite an embarrassment if the police found them. And as of tomorrow, the police would include among their ranks an ex-pilot with revenge on his mind. I yelled Stroud's name.

"Be careful," Sally called after me.

The old man wasn't in his room. He wasn't in the house.

"Damn," said Sally. "That means he's headed for the county line."

Jenks was dry, and the nearest bars were in Claymore County. According to Sally, Stroud often slipped out and drove himself to the Claymore County line, coming home hours later in a lolling, weaving tour that had made him infamous in the small towns along State Highway 11. "Folks down there call him the road warrior," Sally said.

"He wouldn't get drunk tonight," I said, "not with a deposition tomorrow."

Sally shook her head. "I've seen him drink himself half to death the night before a murder trial." And so had I, it occurred to me:

The morning before the Clifton Hardesty trial, Stroud had been boiling drunk when I helped Molly Tunstall bail him out for DWI.

"He says drinking helps him see things he wouldn't see sober," Sally explained. "The finer points of the law are hiding at the bottom of the glass, he says."

I phoned Wick Chandler's home and got no answer. "Damn it," I said to Sally, "Wick is supposed to be going over Bevo's case file."

"Wick Chandler is going over Deirdre Starns," Sally replied. "Or maybe Joyce Littler or Bobbie June Gilroy. Inch by inch."

I got in my car and headed back to town, miffed that neither of my colleagues seemed to be taking their looming courtroom disaster seriously. On the way home I stopped at the office to pick up the file that Wick Chandler had told me he was going to review. To my surprise, Molly Tunstall was at her desk working on the computer.

"On a Sunday, Molly?" I said, standing in the doorway to her office.

"It's this new word processor," she explained. "I don't have time during the week to figure it out." She sat hunched in front of the keyboard, frowning at the screen.

"It's too bad your bosses don't have your dedication," I told her. There must have been a good deal of disgust in my voice.

"Mr. Chandler and Mr. Stroud tend to do business in funny ways," she said, "but the business gets done. If Mr. Stroud has a big trial coming up, he might go fishing for a couple of days before it starts."

"Or go drinking," I said.

"Mr. Chandler usually hunts up some female companionship. It may look to you like they're just not paying attention to the case at hand, but it's always on the back burner. Sometimes the back burner is better than the front burner."

"Sometimes?" I asked.

The lines around Molly's mouth and chin tightened. "It doesn't always work."

"Is it going to work for Bevo Rasmussen?" I asked.

She looked mournfully up at me. "I couldn't say."

"How long have you been with the firm, Molly?"

"About eight years."

"Has it always been like this? Have they always flown by the seat of their pants?"

She thought for a moment. "There have always been ups and downs, I suppose. Things might have been a little smoother when Sally Dean worked here. She really was a help. I think Mr. Stroud tended to drink less back then. At least when he came in to work he was in better shape."

"He cleaned himself up for her?" I asked.

Molly nodded. "When she left, the drinking got a lot worse. Then Sally started spending time at the farm. She moved her horse up there. It seems to have done Mr. Stroud some good."

"So you don't dislike Sally?"

Molly looked at me for a long moment. I could tell she was trying to make up her mind about telling me something.

"My husband and I had a farm out west of town. This was before I came to work here. One afternoon Roy came back from a stock sale down in Pickton with a milk cow he'd bought from a teenaged girl. He had paid a little more than we had agreed on for the cow. He was a bit embarrassed about that. But he said he had done a good deed. The girl needed the money. He said I'd have been proud of him. The next week, the sheriff came out to tell us that the sale hadn't gone through. The cow was really owned by a farmer out toward Mule Springs, and the ownership paper the girl had was fraudulent. We wound up losing the cow and the money Roy had paid. It made a hole in our budget for quite a while."

"I take it the girl was Sally?"

"I didn't know who she was at the time. Three years later, after Roy had died and the farm was up for sale, I got a knock at the door. It was a girl, asking if I was Mrs. Tunstall and wanting to see Roy. When I told her Roy was gone, she handed me an envelope with cash in it, told me she had come to make restitution for the cow, and started to leave. I asked her to stay and made some tea. We had a nice talk. That was how I met Sally Dean."

"She paid you back for the cow," I said.

"Every dime. I'm not sure, but I think she paid everybody back that she had cheated. She impressed me back then as somebody on a mission. She didn't know me from Adam, but she stepped right up and admitted what she did and apologized for it. I liked the way she took responsibility for herself. In this office you don't see a lot of people who are willing to do that."

"True," I said.

"I'm sorry if I gave you the impression that I don't like Sally. That isn't true."

"It's okay, Molly," I said. "I'm sorry about Roy."

"Me, too."

I got Molly to give me Sally's home number, and after I drove home I called her but got no answer. I left a message asking her to let me buy her dinner, and then went to work rereading the Rasmussen file. I had found it at the office—Wick had not touched it—and for three hours I studied the documents again: the bills of sale for the horses; the declaration sheets for each horse, physical descriptions of the horses on which Stromboli based the insurance policies; the three-way barrage of letters from Bevo, Stromboli, and Stroud; Stromboli's petition against Bevo; and, of course, SWAT's unanswered interrogatories.

I noticed that a new document had been added: On Friday Stroud had filed a motion addressed to the Honorable A. C. Tidwell, presiding judge in the case, asking that the deadlines for answering and for requesting answers for interrogatories be extended. The ground Stroud gave for the request was gross incompetence on the part of the lawyer of record—himself. So he had not used the heart attack. What a lot of pride he must have swallowed to draft that motion. I hoped the judge was the sort of man who could rise above personal animosity and grant relief.

I went to sleep on the couch reading the file. Sally never called me back.

At three A.M. my phone rang.

"You've got to help me, Clay." It was Wick, whispering and out of breath. There was a lot of static on the line.

"I can barely hear you," I told him.

There was shuffling, and when he spoke again, the static had cleared a little. "Clay, do you remember that little house where you picked me up the other day?"

"The house where your girlfriend handcuffed you to the bed?"

"There's a dirt road about fifty yards beyond the house. I need you to drive down that road about a hundred feet and stop the car. Do you think you could do that?"

"Tonight?" I asked.

"*Now!*"

"So Mike Starns came home from his fishing trip a little early, did he?"

"Listen, it'll take you maybe twenty-five minutes to reach that spot. I'll be waiting for you there. One more thing, Clay."

"What?"

"When you turn down the dirt road, would you switch off your headlights?"

"Jesus, Wick, is he after you?"

"In a big way, partner," he said, and the line went dead.

CHAPTER 32

IT WAS A MOONLESS, HUMID NIGHT. Wick had under-estimated the time it would take me to reach the turnoff in the Austin Healey. On my way there I scanned the road ahead and behind, looking for any vehicle that might be looking for me, but the countryside was deserted. I turned onto the dirt road, which disappeared into the woods, and switched off my lights. The world went black. This wasn't going to work; I could not keep the car on the road in such total darkness, so I turned on the parking lights and crept forward.

"Wick!" I whispered out the open window.

Something flitted across the dim glow of the parking lights. It looked like a giant piebald bat with a horribly distended stomach. With a leathery flapping of its wings the creature pulled desper-ately at the passenger door.

"For God's sake, unlock it!" the figure cried. Its face was masked. I reached over and let it into the car. "Jesus, Clay, are you trying to get us caught?" Wick was wearing black bikini briefs, a black cape, and a glittering black mask, and that was all. His snow hill of a stomach heaved as he fought to get air into his lungs. I could see scratches on his pale skin, some of them bleeding.

"What the hell?"

"Go!" Wick yelled. "Go, go, go!" I hit the accelerator and took off down the dirt road.

"There's a crossroads in half a mile that'll take us back to the main road," said the big bat in the passenger seat.

"Are you all right, Wick?" I asked.

"Maybe he didn't see me," Wick gasped. "Thank God Deirdre's got better hearing than me. She had me out the back door with seconds to spare. She threw me the phone and locked the door. I just wish to hell she'd thrown me my pants."

"So you don't know for sure if Mike Starns is looking for you?" I asked. "Jesus, Wick, he'll know your car!"

"It's at home. Deirdre drove last night. But he's got to be out here, Clay," Wick said. "He's not very smart, but, hell, my clothes are all over the house, and the way Deirdre's made up . . ."

We turned left onto another dirt road and found ourselves driving alongside a tall chain-link fence.

"Are those headlights?" Wick cried, looking behind us.

"I can't see anything," I told him. Wick panicked. He reached over, switched off the parking lights, and grabbed the steering wheel.

"Faster, Clay!" he yelled as we fought for the wheel. The little car left the road and bounced through grass at maybe fifty miles an hour. I slammed my foot down on the brake, and the car fishtailed to the left, smashing into something springy that yielded to the weight of the car, snapping and singing like a piano hitting pavement after a seven-story drop. The engine died as the car came to a stop. I found myself crumpled in the floorboard, gasping for breath, with a terrific pain in my ribs. We were upright, though canted at a steep angle.

"You okay?" I asked. There was no answer. I looked over and saw that Wick was gone, his door open. He must have been thrown out of the speeding car, and as I struggled for breath, my mind formed a terrible picture of Wick Chandler sprawled in the grass, dying, in his Batman outfit. Then I heard the sounds of a scuffle. I raised up painfully and peered through the windshield. Two shadowy figures were wrestling in the starlit meadow. One, the bat, seemed to be getting pummeled pretty badly. I heard blow after blow landing on soft flesh, and Wick's panicked voice raining curses.

"I'm coming, Wick!" I hollered, afraid Mike Starns would beat him to death before I could pull myself out of the car. My door would not open, so I began to climb across to the passenger side, when it occurred to me to flip on the car's lights. I did so, and for an instant both antagonists froze in the headlights' glare. Then Wick's assailant disappeared, jumping straight up, out of the light, with a rustle of its shaggy wings. There was a thump as it landed on the car's hood, and then the big bird was loping down the dirt road, kicking up little puffs of dust in the heavy night air.

"Where'd he go?" asked a dazed and battered Wick. He sank to the grass and ran his hands over his face. "Jesus," he said, "he kicked the shit out of me."

"Congratulations, Batman," I said, "you just got beaten up by an emu." I climbed out of the passenger door, gasping against the pain in my ribs, and helped Wick to his feet. We inspected the car, which had smashed into the fence circling Starns's ostrich farm and was now sitting on a fallen stretch of chain link. Aside from a crumpled rear fender and a jammed door, the Austin Healey seemed okay. When I crawled back in and turned the key in the ignition, the engine started up. Wick limped around and got in, and we rolled off the chain link.

"Do you think we could travel for a while without the lights, Clay?" Wick asked. I told him to shut up, and neither of us opened our mouths, except to groan, until we reached town.

Fearful that Mike Starns might be waiting for him at his place, Wick asked if he could sleep on my sofa. I drove us to my place, found him sheets and a pillow, and went into the bathroom to take a look at my ribs. There was a purplish shadow under my arm that hurt when I prodded it, but in general the pain was subsiding, and I could breathe without difficulty. When I came out of the bathroom, Wick was sitting on the sofa, putting a Band-Aid over a particularly nasty scratch on his forearm.

"I almost pulled my goddamn arm off in a thicket," he told me. In his bedraggled cape and briefs, he looked like a parody of a comic-book crime fighter. He was terribly skinned up from running through the woods, and his arms and legs were a mottled mass of bruises.

"Well, Wick," I said, "so much for reform."

"I think it has something to do with my thyroid," he said. "I've been meaning to get it checked."

Gathering up the pages of the Rasmussen file, I dropped them next to him on the couch.

"I'll go over it before I go to sleep," he promised.

"Sleep light tonight, Wick," I said. "There's an emu stalking you."

I went to bed and drifted off to sleep, wondering if a phone call would summon me to the jail before dawn to bail out my other boss.

CHAPTER 33

A SAFFRON HAZE BLANKETED the fields early the next morning as I drove Chandler and Stroud out to the Scales ranch for the deposition. We were in Stroud's Lincoln. The old man had made it back from the Claymore County bars the night before without incident, so far as he remembered. Now he lay in the backseat with his battered briefcase on his chest and his knees in the air. He looked like a corpse squeezed into a coffin too short for him.

Wick Chandler slumped against the passenger door in the front seat about three-quarters dressed: His suit was on him, but nothing was buttoned or zipped. Earlier that morning, after I had driven him to his house to clean himself up, he discovered that various parts of his body were so swollen with pain from his night in the woods that he could not fasten his clothes. "You're going to have to cinch up when we get to Scales's ranch," I told him as we drove.

"I'll be dead from pain and shame before we reach Tyler," he replied. "I am already losing feeling in my extremities." It was like driving an ambulance full of crash victims who were slipping away.

"Gentlemen," I said, "we need to talk about our client." I told them about Bevo's Dairy Queen assignations with Antoine Duett, the SWAT dirty tricks man. "Bevo's talking with the enemy," I said. "Anybody know why?"

"I wish I could die right now," Wick moaned. "I wish this door would open and I would fall out on the road and die."

A spindly leg wobbled over the seat-back, the toe of its shoe feeling along the passenger-side window above Wick's head. "If I can reach the latch with my foot, I'll accommodate you," Stroud said.

Wick swatted the shoe wavering in the air over his head. "That's right, ridicule a man in pain," he whined.

I told them about Bevo's second career as a receiver of stolen electronics.

"Bevo's got stolen goods out at my cabin?" Stroud said, sitting up in the backseat.

"This isn't good," said Wick.

"What do you think would happen if Officer Meachum were to stumble on Bevo's illegal warehouse?" I asked. "It could mean jail time for you, Gill."

"Clay's right, Gill," said Wick. "Deirdre says the ex-pilots are up to something. What if they're planning to raid the cabin?"

"How would Deirdre-of-the-emus know what the ex-pilots are doing?" I asked.

"Her husband, Mike, pals around with them when he's not out fishing or cursing his birds. Deirdre sometimes passes me information. That Deirdre's a good old gal."

"I hope things didn't go too rough for her last night," I said.

"Deirdre can handle Mike," Wick replied. "She kicks harder than those damn birds."

"One crisis at a time, gentlemen," said Stroud. "Let's concentrate on the Rasmussen case, shall we? We've got Scales to depose this morning, and tomorrow we depose Pulaski in Mule Springs."

"Maybe we should have hired our own pathologist," I said. "Maybe Pulaski missed something."

"That's entirely possible," replied Wick. "I'll tell you something not everybody knows about our Mr. Pulaski. Stan-the-Man writes a mean report, and he reads it like he's Orson Welles playing Sherlock fucking Holmes. He oozes confidence on the stand. But the fact is, Stan Pulaski is an idiot."

"That son of a bitch needs his bag split and his leg run through it," grumbled Stroud.

"You see, Clay," said Wick, "Pulaski didn't get his reputation as a hot-shot pathologist by being brilliant, but by being for hire. You can't testify in over four hundred cases and always be right. Pulaski is as crooked as Nyman Scales, or Bevo Rasmussen, for that matter. You can bet he slants his reports."

"Then why hasn't he been caught?" I asked.

Wick laughed. "Why isn't Nyman Scales in jail?" he replied. "Why is Paul Primrose allowed to prosecute cases? Why is Tidwell a judge? Because that's the way things work, Clay. The system takes care of itself. I thought you would know that, coming from Houston."

"Even if Pulaski missed something and we caught him on it, the jury wouldn't care," said Stroud. "I've never seen a jury that didn't love Pulaski. He flashes them his big shit-eating smile, and they buy his report just because he's so goddamned smooth."

"Suppose we had gotten a pathologist," Wick said. "We couldn't get him on the stand. The interrogatories, remember?"

"And there's no chance of help from the judge?" I asked.

Wick shook his head. "Not for us. Not from Wrong Tit Tidwell."

"All right," I said as we rolled through the fields toward Tyler, "tell me how Tidwell got that nickname."

Wick explained, "A few years ago we handled a divorce for a woman who had just given birth to twins."

"Moe and Flo," said Stroud. "Ugliest little stumps I have ever seen. I believe the parents were related."

"Anyway," said Wick, "the parents had separated before the children were born, and right after the birth, the mother filed for divorce."

"Irreconcilable differences," Stroud said.

"There was a custody fight over the twins," said Wick, "and it was complicated by the fact that both of them were allergic to cow's milk. The mother was breast-feeding them every three hours or so, one on each side. Gill went to court to get temporary custody for the mother until the divorce could be heard."

"A. C. Tidwell, the presiding judge, considers himself a mental giant," Stroud explained. "Most of our judges consider themselves mental giants. There should be a home for mental giants out here."

"Here's the kicker, Clay," said Wick. "Tidwell awarded the boy to the father and the girl to the mother. He split them up."

"So the boy wouldn't be able to be nursed by his mother," I said. "Wouldn't he have died?"

"Yep," said Wick. "Either from malnutrition or an allergic reaction to store-bought milk."

"The wisdom of Solomon," said Stroud, cackling in the back-seat. "Of course, I filed an appeal. I also contacted La Leche. Know who they are?"

"Aren't they an action group for breast-feeding women?" I asked.

"That's right," Wick replied. "They're a national organization, you know. They showed up by the hundreds at the appellate court when Gill argued the appeal. The appellate court reversed the decision of the trial court and sent the case back to Tidwell."

"That's where the court of appeals judges made their mistake," Stroud said. "They should have spelled out in plain English what they wanted Tidwell to do. But they didn't, and old A.C. took the reversal to mean he'd given each kid to the wrong parent. So to fix things, he reversed his own ruling, gave the little girl to her daddy and the boy to the mother."

"You're joking," I said.

"Gospel truth," Stroud said. "I appealed again, on an emergency basis. This all happened in less than thirty-six hours, you understand. This time the breast-feeding folks took the story to the networks."

"The *Today* show sent a crew down here," said Wick. "Tidwell wouldn't talk to them."

"A.C. got reversed again, of course," said Stroud. "This time around, the court told him to let both kids stay with their mother."

"I don't believe Flo or Moe actually missed a meal," said Wick. "Anyway, from then on, old A.C. was known far and wide as Wrong Tit Tidwell."

"Our relationship with him soured after that," Stroud said.

"You shouldn't have called him a syphilitic idiot on national television, Gill," said Wick. "I think that's why he's so down on us."

"That could have something to do with it," Stroud agreed.

CHAPTER 34

A FEW MINUTES LATER we topped a rise, and the vast green roofs of the Ninth-Man Ranch spread out below us.

"Mother dog, that's a big place," said Wick.

The Ninth-Man was the size of Jenks and much better organized. Giant hangarlike buildings sat amid neat rows of stables. On all sides were rolling pastures, some divided into exercise fields, some into neat little pens, each with a corrugated tin sunroof, for individual horses. Wood fences ran out past the pastures, securing even more land beyond. The whole ranch was painted a bucolic green, and the paint looked fresh. On the roof of the largest building was painted a complicated stick figure, in white. "I take it that's the ninth man," I said.

"Check out the torso," Wick said. The long, squarish body of the figure was composed of lines making up the roman numeral IX.

"Nyman Scales was the ninth of nine children," Wick explained. "Apparently it was a litter of boys, and the parents ran out of names after number eight. Nyman's real name is Ninth-Man Scales. Over the years, it's gotten rubbed down to Nyman."

"Weird," I said.

"Yes," said Wick, "but functional."

People were bustling among the buildings, trucks unloading, forklifts buzzing in and out of storage sheds, men leading horses along the graveled roadways that surrounded and connected the buildings. Little green golf carts hummed down the gravel roads.

To one side of the wrought-iron gate leading into the compound stood a statue of a colossal rearing stallion, perhaps three stories high. The stallion was built of red brick and framed by a huge golden horseshoe, with the name of the ranch stamped on its arch.

"This must be horse heaven," said Wick as we drove past the brick horse. Behind it sat a wood-frame Victorian-style house that would have seemed enormous anyplace but here. I parked the Lincoln in front of the house; we walked up onto the porch and rang the bell. An attractive young woman in jeans and a checked workshirt greeted us, saying that we were expected, and that Mr. Scales was waiting for us in the laboratory. She took us outside to one of the green golf carts and drove us past several of the big barns to a one-story brick building with a picture on its side of a cartoon cow smiling and saying "Moooooove over, Mother Nature!"

"What do they do in here?" I asked the girl.

"It used to be a dairy genetics lab," she said. "Now we work on horses."

"Better horses for better living," said Wick.

She let us off at the front door. I knocked, and the door was opened by a tall, wiry man in frayed overalls, workshirt, and a short-brimmed felt hat badly faded from wear. He looked like one of those lean-faced, desperate men in photographs from the Dust Bowl of the thirties, with pale-blue eyes haunted by hunger and mad visions. The ninth man. Stroud shook hands with him.

"Gilliam Stroud," said Scales. "We meet again."

"Long time between drinks, Nyman," replied Stroud.

Scales shook hands with Wick. "Mr. Chandler," he said, "I understand you are interested in pricks."

"Only those I represent," said Wick. "Aside from my own, of course."

"Bevo tells me you just lost a favorite wall ornament down in Dallas." Scales took from behind the door a smaller version of the corkscrewed stick that I had given to Deck Willhoit in order to keep Bevo intact. "I'm afraid this one is not as long as the one you lost. It's from a bull, not a whale. But I would like you to accept it as a gift, with my compliments."

The pizzle was intended to be a walking stick: A flap on one end was shaped into a handle. Wick balanced the stick in his hand, gave a couple of slashes with it through the air.

"Thank you, Nyman," he said. "It's a fine replacement."

Bevo had told the truth about Scales's mastery of the preacher-boy *s*. Every word he spoke was carefully crafted and uttered with the intimate sincerity of a country parson comforting a stricken parishioner.

"We're all friends here," said Scales, flashing a scruffy smile. There was a feral quality to it that reminded me of Bevo's smile, but I saw no diamonds in any of Scales's teeth.

Wick introduced me to Scales, and we shook hands. It was like sticking my hand in a trash compactor.

"Bevo has mentioned you to me. He says you and my daughter are getting to be friends. You might tell her to pay her old man a visit one of these days." Scales winked at me.

A chill crept up my spine.

"This way, gentlemen," Scales said, conducting us down a hallway.

The secretary's office that we entered was crowded with people sitting on folding chairs, drinking coffee. We shook hands with the court reporter, a ferret-eyed little woman who clutched her stenographer's machine and kept eyeing the door. Scales introduced us to Vincenzo Laspari, a representative of Associazione Stromboli, who had flown in from Naples for the deposition. Laspari, a trim little man in an Italian suit, gave me a chill smile and a formal handshake that, together with his silence, served to increase the cultural distance between us. The man seated next to Laspari, and rising now to meet us, was Warren Jacobs, counsel for the plaintiff. Jacobs was maybe forty-five, tall and rangy, with wisps of sandy hair combed across his forehead. He looked exactly like Rita Humphrey once described the typical SWAT lawyer: a vampire who played a lot of racquetball.

We shook hands with Jacobs, whose every movement seemed spring-loaded with confidence. He professed it an honor to meet Gilliam Stroud. "Mr. Wortmann of our firm asked me to convey his regards. He speaks very highly of you. He says you taught him everything he knows about tort law."

"Jimmy Wortmann," said Stroud. "Do you remember him, Mr. Chandler?"

"I believe I do," said Wick.

The old man gave Jacobs a suspicious look. "You're telling me Jimmy Wortmann made *good?*"

Jacobs cleared his throat. "He is one of the senior partners of our firm, sir."

Stroud turned to Wick. "You hear that, Mr. Chandler?" he said. "Jimmy Wortmann made good."

Wick held out his palm. "Pay up, Mr. Stroud."

Stroud pulled a crumpled five-dollar bill out of a pocket and handed it to Wick. "Who'd ever have thought that kid would have amounted to a rat's ass?"

"I did," Wick said, pocketing the bill. "I had Jimmy Wortmann pegged for a rat's ass the minute I met him."

They had worked the joke so smoothly that it took Jacobs a moment to catch on. His eyes narrowed, then he smiled at Stroud. "Mr. Wortmann told me to watch out for you. I can see why."

Scales unfolded chairs for us, and we sat down. Our arrival had interrupted a chat, which now resumed, about the many ways in which horses were murdered for profit.

"A fellow up near Gainesville stuffed Ping-Pong balls into the nostrils of his horse," said Scales. "You may not know, Mr. Parker, that a horse cannot breathe through its mouth."

"I didn't know that," I replied.

"The horse died, all right, but the owner hadn't thought up a way to explain how it could have died by asphyxiation in an open field." Scales chuckled. "He tried to argue that the horse was so badly scared by a crop duster plane, it forgot to breathe. I swear, some of these old boys aren't as smart as the horses they kill."

There was another knock at the door, and Paul Primrose, the Mule Springs district attorney, walked into the room, along with a uniformed policeman.

"Howdy, folks," said Primrose in his high-pitched whine. "What have you got going here, Mr. Scales, a prayer meeting?"

"Holy shit," said Wick.

CHAPTER 35

"HOWDY, PAUL," said Nyman Scales. "This is a nice surprise. You fellas come on in and have a seat."

"Primrose?" said Stroud, rising from his chair. "What in hell are you doing here?"

Primrose smiled as he shook hands with us. He was wearing another string tie, this one with a bolo of clear plastic in which a scorpion was embedded. He introduced his companion, who was the assistant deputy sheriff for Claymore County.

"I was down here on business when I heard about the deposition," he explained. "You don't mind if I sit in, do you, Gill? After all, the horses we're talking about were killed in my county. I've got an interest in this case."

"I most certainly do object," Stroud said. "This little get-together already looks too much like an undertakers' convention to please me. You just go take care of your business and let us attend to ours."

There was a knock at the door. It was Bevo, the last participant, wearing his sharkskin outfit. He had gotten his lank hair trimmed a little, but he still looked like a hayseed in a stolen suit as he clapped Scales on the back and apologized for being late. He shook hands all around, flashing his diamond tooth in his wolf's smile.

"Well, Mr. DA," he said, shaking Primrose's hand. "I haven't seen you since you tried to pin the murder of that poor Mexican fella on me. Sorry I couldn't oblige you."

"It's okay, Bevo," Primrose said with a washed-out smile. "You will one day."

Bevo wanted to let the DA and the policeman sit in on the deposition. "It's time they found out I'm innocent." But Stroud insisted that Primrose and his deputy sheriff stay out. Under the court's rules, one side has to give the other written notice of the intent to include persons other than the parties and their lawyers at a deposition. Jacobs had not sent such a notice, and Primrose had not gotten the court's permission to attend. The DA knew he would be excluded if Stroud objected. Primrose waved wanly as Scales led the rest of us to another, much bigger room in the genetics lab.

In the center of the concrete floor lay a massive slab of what looked like black marble. Above it a jointed metal arm, rigged with pulleys and steel cables, reached into the room through a hole high in the wall. The arm ended in a wicked-looking metal claw, which hovered over the center of the slab. The slab was slightly concave, and there was a drain in its center.

"Homey place you got here, Nyman," said Wick.

"You folks have a seat," Scales said. There were folding chairs arranged in a couple of rows to one side of the slab. As we sat down, Scales pushed a button on the wall, and with a low hum the slab began to rise. Scales let it reach the height of a desk, then pushed another button, and the slab stopped moving.

"Mrs. Mears," he said to the court reporter, "you might like to put your steno machine on the table."

The reporter clearly did not want to have anything to do with the marble slab. "I'll be fine right here," she said, balancing the stenographer's machine on her lap.

"I don't blame you," Scales said. "I suppose it's a kind of creepy place. We sometimes use the table to gut large animals." He pointed to the metal claw and winked at Laspari. "There's a way to make that thing act just like a human arm." Laspari nodded at him, and I wondered if the Italian understood English.

Scales sat on the marble slab while Wick got the deposition going by asking him the standard identifying questions. Then Wick turned to the case.

"Mr. Scales," he asked, "do you know Mr. Bevo Rasmussen?"

"I do," said Scales.

"Will you describe your business relationship with Mr. Rasmussen?"

"He bought some horses from me."

"Would you characterize your relationship with Mr. Rasmussen as a cordial one?"

Scales smiled. "All my relationships are cordial."

"Ask him about the night the horses died," hissed Bevo. Turning to me, he smiled and said, "I want to get out of here quick as possible."

"Mr. Scales," said Wick, "has Mr. Rasmussen ever spent the night at your home here?"

"Yes, sir, he has."

"Did he do so on the night of July the fourteenth of last year?"

Scales squinted into the distance, as if trying to remember. "No, sir, I don't believe he was with us that night."

I stared at Scales. We all stared at him.

Wick cleared his throat. "Let me ask you again, Mr. Scales, did Bevo Rasmussen spend the night of July fourteenth of last year at your house?"

"Nope."

"Are you aware, Mr. Scales, of what happened on that night?"

"Wasn't that the night Bevo's horses burned up?"

"Yes, sir."

All innocence, Scales gave Wick an apologetic smile. "Well, then, I'm sure Bevo wasn't with us. I remember reading about that fire in the papers the next morning and saying to old Pete Taliaferro down at the stables how sad the whole thing was, Bevo being so strapped for cash and all, and now he didn't even have his horses. Pete was of the opinion that Bevo might have had something to do with the fire, but I told him I doubted the lad would stoop so low."

There was a crash as Bevo's chair flipped over. Bevo had launched himself at Scales.

"You lying son of a bitch!" Bevo hollered. He had one hand on Scales's throat while the other was reaching toward the boot where he kept his razor. An instant later he was flying through the air. Scales had simply picked him up and thrown him. Bevo landed on top of Laspari, the Stromboli agent. Laspari cried out as his chair collapsed under him, but the moment he hit the floor, Bevo was up and racing for Scales again, his razor in his hand.

"I'll tell 'em," Bevo hissed. "I'll tell 'em everything, you fucking backstabber."

Scales looked at him quizzically. "You seem to have me mixed up with somebody else, Bevo," he said. Bevo cut at Scales with the razor. Scales grabbed Bevo's hand and cranked it hard, sending the razor flying. As the rest of us watched, frozen, Scales gave Bevo four fast blows in the ribs with his other fist, and Bevo crumpled. Scales picked up his scrawny assailant by the lapels of his sharkskin suit and placed him in the shallow depression of the marble slab.

"That claw up there could do you a world of good," Scales said. Keeping a grip on Bevo's throat, Scales flipped a toggle on the side of the marble slab, and a rigor passed through the long metal arm above them. Pushing buttons on the side of the slab, Scales caused the claw to open and descend. Bevo fought Scales's grip but could not break it.

"Look here, Wick," Scales called over his shoulder, "I'll show you how to make a walking stick like the one I gave you."

The rest of us finally found ourselves able to move. Jacobs bent to help Laspari to his feet, while Wick and I jumped to the table. I took hold of Scales's arm to break his grip on Bevo's neck. I might as well have tried to shatter the marble table with my forehead. Under Scales's workshirt his muscles were steel cables. He turned and gave me a dry smile, his blue eyes dancing with deadly amusement.

"Let go of our client, Mr. Scales," I said.

With a wink, Scales released Bevo. "I don't take well to being jumped," Scales said, and he walked out of the room, closing the door behind him.

For a moment Bevo lay gasping for breath, his hands at his throat, then he was off the table and running for the door Scales had just gone through.

"Come back here!" he screamed.

As he reached the door, it opened. The deputy sheriff from Mule Springs pushed Bevo back into the room, raised his revolver, and pointed it at Bevo's forehead.

"Bevo Rasmussen," he said, "you're under arrest."

Bevo stared at the muzzle of the revolver. "What for?" he asked.

"Arson."

"Just a minute, Deputy," roared Stroud, limping forward. "You have no jurisdiction here!"

Paul Primrose came out from behind the deputy and handed Stroud a document. Stroud read it, then crumpled it and threw it on the floor.

"I told you I was here on business, Gill," Primrose whined, his face glowing with righteous irony.

"I'll have him out before you can say grace at supper tonight," Stroud told him.

"You'll have to drive to Mule Springs to do it," Primrose replied. "Cuff your prisoner, Deputy."

The policeman shoved Bevo up against the wall and handcuffed his hands behind him. As he led Bevo out, the deputy began reading him his rights from a small card.

"Get me out, Mr. Stroud," Bevo hollered as he disappeared down the hall. "I got things to tell you."

Warren Jacobs and Vincenzo Laspari walked up to us at the door. "Well, Mr. Stroud," said Jacobs, "you East Texas folks sure know how to show visitors a good time." Smugness oozed out of both men's smiles. We had been set up.

"If I find out you've had anything to do with the incarceration of my client, Jacobs," said Stroud, "nothing little Jimmy Wortmann learned at Baylor is going to save your ass."

"See you tomorrow, gentlemen," said Jacobs as he brushed past us. "We have another deposition in the morning. I hope you manage to make it as amusing as this one has been."

CHAPTER 36

THE SHOCKS IN STROUD'S Lincoln were old, and as we tried to keep up with the patrol car taking Bevo to Mule Springs, the Lincoln bucked along the heat-rippled asphalt like a barge barreling down rapids. It was sixty hilly miles to Mule Springs from Tyler. Our friends in the patrol car were ignoring the speed limit, and before we had gone ten miles, they were so far ahead of us that we no longer glimpsed them as we crested the little hills.

"You've let them get away!" cried Wick, who sat in the passenger seat next to me.

"We know where they're going, Wick," I reminded him. "I'm not giving some state trooper the chance to run us in for speeding." Sure enough, a couple of miles later we passed a black-and-white waiting in ambush on the road's shoulder. Wick waved at them as we drove by.

From the backseat came a bitter laugh. "You can bet your grandmother's ass Primrose set that up," said Stroud. "The pious little shit."

"You know why Primrose wants to beat us to Mule Springs," said Wick. "Bevo's going to get damaged in handling."

That surprised me. "You don't really think they would rough him up, do you?"

"The Mule Springs cops hate Bevo," Wick said. "They've been chasing him for years, but he's always slid loose. Now that he's theirs, they'll want to leave an impression on him."

"Serves him right," said Stroud. "He's been lying to us from day one. In fact, Mr. Parker, slow down. Let's give the Mule Springs police plenty of time to get to know our stalwart client."

An hour later, when we saw him in a cell in the Mule Springs jail, Bevo looked as if he had witnessed a cattle stampede from underneath.

"He resisted when we took his fingerprints," said the deputy who unlocked the cell door.

"Like hell I did!" said Bevo, who jumped up from the bunk and took hold of the cell bars. "They knocked the diamond out of my tooth, Mr. Stroud. Look here." He hooked his mouth open with two fingers and thrust his face at us.

"We got his diamond," said the deputy. "It's in an envelope with his other stuff. He can have it when he leaves. *If* he leaves."

"We're gonna sue your ass," said Bevo. "You have violated my civil goddamn rights. It was three against one!"

"I would hush if I were you, Brother Rasmussen," said Stroud, sitting down on the end of the bunk. "They may take it into their heads to re-insert that diamond."

"This is America, goddamn it," huffed Bevo, throwing himself on the opposite end of the bed from where Stroud sat. "It ain't the Soviet-fucking-Union." His left eye was closing, and evidence of a nosebleed was caked across his face and down one sleeve of his shiny jacket. He kept running his tongue across the empty socket in his tooth.

"Bevo," said Wick, "why do you think people keep beating you up?"

"The world is against me, Mr. Chandler," Bevo replied in a voice mournful with self-pity. "They hate to see an honest man better himself."

"Is that what you've been doing by lying to us?" I asked him. "You've been bettering yourself?"

"Like I told you, Mr. Parker, I got a plan. You stick to a plan, the plan will see you through."

"You'd better let us in on the plan, Bevo," said Wick, "before it beats you to death."

"I must admit, there seems to be a flaw somewhere," Bevo replied.

Bevo explained his plan. It was pretty much what we had thought. He had gotten Nyman Scales to set him up with high-dollar horses that would die in a fire so Bevo could claim the insurance money.

"After I paid off all the horse debt and the start-up money I owe Farmer's Bank and that son of a bitch Nyman Scales, I figured to have cleared a little over one hundred and twenty thousand dollars," he said. "That was gonna be seed money for my emu ranch."

"But Stromboli didn't roll over, did they?" Wick asked.

"No, sir, they did not. Scales was wrong about that. He said my case was small potatoes to Stromboli. That's why we went with the goddamn wops in the first place. He said they wouldn't read the claim twice, and I'd have my money before the last horse cooled."

"But Stromboli sued you, and now Scales is not going to lie for you," Wick said, "and your ass is cooked."

"But Scales *did* lie," Bevo said. "I did spend that night at his ranch. I really didn't torch those horses, Mr. Chandler. I don't know how many times I have to say it. I didn't burn 'em. I was gonna do it, I think, but they went up before I had the chance."

"What happened to them, then?" I asked.

"Nyman said it was probably lightning. It really does happen, you know; a barn gets zapped every once in a while. But now I figure Nyman himself did it. It's not like he hasn't burned horses before." He shook his head. "Nyman Scales sold me out." His voice broke on the last word. "He said I was like a son to him, and he sold me out. Him and his whore of a daughter."

"What makes you think Sally was in on it?" I asked, glancing at Stroud, who sat staring at the floor.

"Nyman told me," Bevo said. "After Stromboli shut me down, Nyman told me to sue them. He said Sally would fix it so's we'd get one of Nyman's judges." Bevo got up and started to pace, a tricky feat in a small cell with three other men in it. "Then I discovered that she was playing hide-the-candle with the city boy here, and I figured Nyman had figured out another way to use her, to make sure you renegades didn't run off another associate."

There it was: If Stroud had not guessed at my relationship with Sally before, he knew about it now. Yet the old man sat motionless on the bed, staring down at the floor, as if he had not heard Bevo.

Bevo snapped his fingers. "Hell, I been wrong all along. Sally wasn't fucking you to keep you on the case. She was spying for Nyman!" He pointed at me and hooted. "She was tickling information out of you and giving it to her daddy so's he could jump me like he just done. Jesus H. Christ, why didn't I see it coming?"

"Sally was sleeping with me in order to spy for her father?" I asked. "Bevo, that makes no sense."

"It makes as much sense as anything else that's happened since I bought those horses. Every goddamn thing that could go wrong has gone wrong. Even my own lawyers are working against me." He was whining now.

"We're not working against you, Bevo," Wick said. "But it's hard to defend a client who lies every time he opens his mouth."

"You're calling *me* a liar?" Bevo replied. "What about you, Hard-dick? What about the interro-whatchamacallits, those little questions you were supposed to send back to SWAT and forgot to? When were you planning to let me know this old man here fucked up my case? Mr. Parker's the only one of you that's come clean with me, and I figure that's just because he's new and hasn't learned how to play the game your way yet." He grinned his wolf's grin. "Calling me a liar. Shit."

"Why would Nyman Scales want to see you go down?" I asked him.

"Competition, Mr. Parker," Bevo replied. "That's the only reason I can see. Nyman Scales has got a swelled head. He thinks he's the greatest thing since barbed wire. And here I come along, with a plan for a bird ranch that would make me the biggest show in East Texas. I think he was just jealous. He double-crossed me so's I would never outdo him."

"That's a hoot," said Wick.

"You people with your talk about lying and morals and ethics," Bevo said, shaking his head. "You sound just like Scales, do you know that? He's always talking ethics, shit like that, and here he's sold me out. He's as slimy as an otter's cock." He stopped pacing, took hold of the bars, and heaved a gigantic sigh. "I'm the only man I know has got an ounce of principle."

"How much principle did it take to conspire with Stromboli's lawyers without telling us?" I asked.

Bevo looked at me blankly. "I beg your pardon?"

"You've been talking to Antoine Duett, haven't you, Bevo?"

"Who?" Bevo asked.

"Cut the shit, Rasmussen. I caught the two of you leaving the Dairy Queen yesterday afternoon, and I know you've met several times. Why are you holding secret meetings with the dirty-tricks man from SWAT?"

"All right," he replied, "it's true, I've spoken to Mr. Duett once or twice. But that was just self-protection. I wasn't selling out my case. I wasn't selling you guys out. Honest, Mr. Parker. I was just trying to help."

Bevo explained that he had contacted SWAT to offer them a deal in return for settling the Stromboli case against him.

"I told them I had enough information to nail the biggest insurance crook in the country. That's worth something to a big insurance law firm like SWAT. So they sent Antoine Duett down to see me about making a deal."

"Who did you snitch on?" I asked.

Bevo rolled his eyes. "Why, Nyman Scales, of course. He's the Al-fucking-Capone of insurance fraud in Texas, maybe even the whole country. He's got dozens of jobs like mine working all the time, and nobody can nail him in court. He's been keeping SWAT busy for years and costing Stromboli millions."

"So you were selling out the man you just said was like a father to you?" I asked. "*That's* principle, all right."

"Didn't Scales just do the same thing to me?" Bevo snapped.

"Yes," I agreed. "He sold you out this morning. But you didn't start meeting with Duett this morning. You were double-crossing Scales long before you knew he was double-crossing you."

"It don't hurt to have a backup plan," Bevo replied.

"So you think you've got the dope on Scales?" Wick asked skeptically.

"Only enough to send him away for a thousand years," Bevo replied. "I didn't tell Duett no more than half of what I got. I got horse killings, rigged birth certificates, counterfeit bills of sale, doctored horses, if you know what I mean—"

"And you've got hard evidence to back you up?" Wick asked.

"I'm no goddamn detective," Bevo said. "Let them find it on their own. I can tell them where to look."

"Bevo," Wick said, "if you don't have hard evidence, you don't have shit. *Everybody* knows the stories about Nyman Scales. But there's no evidence. Scales is too smart to leave any. He's famous for staying clean. Let me ask you, did Duett ever agree to a deal with you?"

"Not yet," Bevo replied. "But it was in the works. We were going to meet next week and work something out."

Wick shook his head. "SWAT wasn't going to deal with you, Bevo. They were fishing for information about our case, jerking your chain. You just thought you were fucking Scales. He'll turn out to be the tush hog in this deal."

"We'll see, won't we?" Bevo sneered. He went back to pacing. He began muttering about Nyman Scales and Sally. "I'll get him. Soon as I'm out of here. I'll strap him to his goddamn table, see how he likes it. Him and that cunt Sally."

Stroud, who had been brooding silently all this time, suddenly lunged off the bed, caught Bevo by the throat, and slammed him against the wall between Wick and me. The old man held Bevo off the ground while Bevo pulled desperately at the big liver-spotted hands that had cut off his wind. Wick and I were trying to loosen Stroud's hold, when our commotion brought the jailer to the cell.

"Now, boys," the jailer said, watching calmly from the other side of the bars, "you probably shouldn't ought to choke your client like that." Stroud let go of Bevo, who slumped to the floor, both hands at his throat.

"Miss Dean was not working against you, Rasmussen," said Stroud, between gasping breaths, "if only because you aren't worth working against. You aren't worth a cup of cold piss, and I regret the day I ever took you on as a client."

He motioned for the jailer to open the cell, and when he did, Stroud limped down the hall without another word.

"That old man tried to kill me," Bevo said, staring wide-eyed at the departing Stroud.

"That's the fourth attempt I've witnessed in less than a week," I reminded him, "and the second one today. You've sure got a way with people, Bevo."

CHAPTER 37

WE CAUGHT UP WITH STROUD in the parking lot. "Aren't we going to bail him out?" Wick asked.

"Let him rot," Stroud replied. "Let Primrose do what he likes with him." The old man turned to me. "Mr. Parker, give me my car keys."

"We can't just leave him, Gill," Wick said. "He's our client. He's a prick from hell, but he's our client."

The two of us finally convinced Stroud that we should get Bevo released. The justice of the peace had already set bail at twenty-five thousand dollars, but when we called the only bondsman in Mule Springs, we found that he would take nothing but cash, and the three of us together had nowhere near the twenty-five hundred he wanted to post the bond. One of us would have to drive back from Jenks with the money.

"It's Primrose," said Wick as we headed home. "He must have called the justice of the peace and got him to set the bond so goddamned high. Otherwise we could've gotten Bevo out with postage stamps. Hell, they don't set bonds that high on capital murderers in this county."

"Straight is the way," said Stroud in the backseat, "and narrow is the gate."

"Primrose isn't even a real Baptist," Wick griped. "He was Episcopalian until he found he couldn't get elected without the Baptist vote. So he switched religions."

"They're just different denominations," I said. "They're not different religions."

"Have you ever been to a Baptist service out here, Clay?" Wick asked.

It was vital to get Bevo out of jail. If SWAT discovered that he was stuck behind bars, they would go to trial and we would be even worse off, naked in front of a jury with no client in the courtroom. We agreed that Wick would get the bail money from the bank and drive it back to Mule Springs while Stroud and I stayed at the office to work on the Pulaski deposition set for the next morning. We went through the drive-in teller at the First National Bank for the bail money, then Wick insisted that we accompany him to his house while he got his car. He was worried that Mike Starns, Deirdre's husband, might be planning a little surprise for him, and he thought there might be safety in numbers. When I pulled up in front of his house, Wick got out and walked slowly across the yard, peering in the front windows.

"Check under the car," Stroud called from the Lincoln's backseat.

Wick squatted down, balancing his stomach on his knees, and looked under the wheels of his Corvette.

"Emus like to hide down there," Stroud told him, chuckling.

"If this car blows up on me halfway to Mule Springs, you remember to tell that joke at my wake," Wick replied, struggling to his feet.

Stroud handed the envelope from the bank through the window. Wick took it, looked at it for a moment. "Twenty-five hundred dollars," he said. "I wonder what the chances are of Bevo ever paying this back?"

"About the same as our winning the case," Stroud replied.

As Wick climbed into the driver's seat of his Corvette—it was a tight squeeze—I remembered something I had meant to grill Bevo about before the deposition blew up on us. "Wick," I called out of the Lincoln's window, "when you spring Bevo, tell him to get all that electronic stuff out of the cabin. If he doesn't do it soon, we might be bailing Gill here out of jail next."

"I'll tell him he has twenty-four hours," said Wick, "or else we'll turn him in ourselves."

Back at the office, I sat in the conference room reading through the Rasmussen file for the fifth or sixth time. Stroud sat at the other end of the conference table and stared at the wall, doom raying out from under his iron-gray brows.

"Have you got a plan for the Pulaski deposition?" I asked.

Stroud shook his head. "It'll take all day, and it won't be pretty. I'll ask the son of a bitch a thousand questions, mostly details about the fire, and hope that some of his answers don't square. I doubt that will happen, though, Mr. Parker. I have questioned Stan Pulaski on the stand maybe five times and never cracked him, never even come close. He's crooked, I'm sure of it, but he's so convinced of his own righteousness that the jury thinks he eats, breathes, sleeps, and shits truth. Examining the good Dr. Pulaski is like examining Mount Rushmore." He sighed. "Wick's right. We need a copy of that report, and I fucked up. There doesn't seem to be much I'm good for anymore."

"That's not what Wick said."

But Stroud had dived into the sea of self-pity. "Mr. Parker," he said, "promise me that the next time I fuck up, you'll use that gun we bought you to put me out of my misery."

"I don't know where it is," I told him.

"It's at my place. I'll see you get it back."

"There's an old picture of you in the Baylor Law building," I said, "You're out at the Waco bridge, swinging part of a train trestle, saving your client from a mob."

"That wasn't me," Stroud replied.

"It was you, all right."

"I was drunk."

"You weren't drunk."

Stroud gave me a black look. "I didn't take you for an ass-kisser, Mr. Parker," he said.

"I didn't take you for a mewling, self-indulgent, pathetic sack of shit, Mr. Stroud," I replied. For an instant his eyes flashed murder at me, then the anger went out of them, and a half-smile played across his face.

"Looks like we were both wrong about each other," he said.

"Looks like," I replied.

There was a knock at the door of the conference room. It was Molly Tunstall with cups and a pot of coffee.

"So how about it, Molly girl," Stroud said as Molly poured, "have you ever seen a case as badly screwed up as this one?"

Molly thought for a minute. "There was the Greiner case last year. That one was pretty bad."

"Yes, but I wasn't the cause of the trouble then. Have you ever seen a case that I screwed up like I've screwed up this one?"

"I have never seen a case that could have been handled better than you handled it, Mr. Stroud. I have seen you lose cases, but never because of something you did."

Stroud reached over and patted the hand that held the coffee-pot. "Thank you, Mrs. Tunstall. But I'm afraid we're about to reach a new low."

Molly started to say something, thought better of it, and left the room.

"Why couldn't that little moron have fallen into the fire with his horses?" Stroud muttered. He had begun to finger the little silver whistle hanging around his neck.

"If you blow that thing, I'm walking out of here," I told him.

He smiled. "So you don't think it's time to play taps over this mess of a case?" he asked.

"Is there a chance that Bevo's telling the truth about not starting the fire?"

"There's a chance," replied Stroud. "There's also a chance pigs will learn to fly. I wouldn't want to bet money on either possibility."

"Why would Nyman Scales sell Bevo out like he did this morning?" I asked.

"Are you sure he did? We only had Bevo's word that Scales would help him. We don't know if Scales ever really promised Bevo anything."

"Then why would Bevo have told us Scales would save him?"

"There's no honor among thieves, Mr. Parker. Maybe Scales promised to lie and then thought better of it for some reason."

But that scenario did not explain, at least to my satisfaction, the utter blind fury of Bevo's attack on Scales in the horse lab. There was shock and pain mixed in with Bevo's rage, more emotion than there would have been if Scales had simply refused to lie for him. Bevo's was the anger of a born liar who had finally told the truth and then seen it undercut by a better liar.

And if Scales had lied at his deposition, then there really was a conspiracy to hang these horse murders on Bevo. And Nyman Scales was behind it.

Suddenly Stroud changed the subject. "I want you to know something," he said, his gaze fixed on the wall. "Bevo is dead wrong about Miss Dean. She is not a spy. She is not a whore. She is my protégée. That's all she is. My protégée and my friend."

It was an abdication speech: Stroud was renouncing any emotional claim I might have thought he had on Sally, and when he was through, the old man shot me a glance that told me not to open my mouth for a while. It was just as well, because I did not know what to say. We sat in silence.

The phone rang. I answered. It was Warren Jacobs, the SWAT lawyer.

"Put it on the speaker," Stroud said. I did, and Jacobs's voice, oozing condescension and mock concern, filled the room.

"I think that maybe tomorrow's deposition could be dispensed with, gentlemen."

"He wants to grind our noses into the manure," Stroud whispered. Then he asked, "Why don't you want us to talk to your pathologist, Warren?"

"I'm just trying to save you some trouble, Gill. As you can see from the written report, Dr. Pulaski has done his usual professional job on the... oh, that's right, you haven't seen the report, have you? You never asked for it, did you?"

"We'll have Dr. Pulaski fill us in tomorrow at the deposition," I said. "Now, Mr. Jacobs, if you'll excuse us—"

Stroud shook his head at me. "Never cut off a talkative enemy," he whispered.

"Who's that doing your talking for you, Gill?" Jacobs asked.

"That's Parker, our book lawyer from Houston," Stroud replied. "You met him this morning at Scales's place, remember?"

"Well, Mr. Parker, welcome aboard," said Jacobs. "Why don't I just read some of this report to you? Maybe that would help cut your book work down a little."

Intimidation was a SWAT specialty. Jacobs was trying to demoralize us. Stroud set his chin in his hand and closed his eyes. "Be our guest," he said, "you shit-eating son of a bitch."

"What a sad story," said Jacobs, "all these beautiful horses, penned up and set on fire." He began to read from the section of the report that described the horses before and after they were killed.

"Here's Shannon's Misfit, a strapping sorrel mare, one hundred thousand dollars' worth of pampered horseflesh, reduced to a thighbone, some hide scraps, and a box of teeth... Wow! Hey, guys, did you know your client chained the stalls so the horses couldn't kick their way out? He chained them in and doused them with kerosene!"

Stroud rubbed his temples, let out a strained sigh.

Jacobs read descriptions for a couple of the other horses, potential champions, and told us what was left of them after the fire.

Suddenly Stroud's head snapped up, a look of surprise on his face. He reached across the table, pulled the dec sheets out of the Rasmussen file, and scanned a few of them.

"I'm not boring you boys, am I?" Jacobs asked.

"Not too much, Warren," said Stroud. "Read on." He slid the dec sheets across the table to me and whispered, "Read along!" Jacobs began to recite the vital statistics of After the Goldrush, an Appaloosa stallion, reduced to half a rib cage, a fetlock, and some patches of charred skin.

But something was wrong. In his grade-school scrawl, Bevo had described After the Goldrush on the dec sheet as a roan mare, not an Appaloosa stallion. I read back through the dec sheets for the other horses Jacobs had described, and I looked up at Stroud. "They're different!" I whispered, sliding the pages back to him.

"Warren," Stroud said, interrupting the lawyer's oration, "would you start over again on that horse?"

There was a pause, then Jacobs said, "I beg your pardon?"

"You just told us that After the Goldrush was a stallion, is that correct?" Stroud asked.

"Correct."

"That's very curious," said Stroud, "since the dec sheet I've got here says that he was really a she, and not an Appaloosa, but roan. How do you explain the discrepancies, Warren?"

There was silence on the line for a moment.

"Are you there, Warren?" Stroud asked.

"Yes," came the answer, in a voice that had suddenly lost its

coat of oil, "I'm here. I'm sorry, boys. It looks like I've been reading from a different report."

"A different report?" I asked. "How many did Pulaski write?"
There was a shuffling of papers on the other end of the line.

"Yes. I apologize, gentlemen. It seems I've been reading the
report for another case I'm working on. I have several at the
moment, and I guess my secretary just got careless. She handed
me the wrong file."

"So you were reading from another case, is that it, Warren?"
Stroud asked.

"I'm sorry," Jacobs said. "I realize it was not very professional
of me."

"If you're reading from a different report," asked Stroud, "then
why do the horses in this other case all have the same names as
Bevo's horses? That's a hell of a coincidence, Warren."

There was a very long pause. "Yes," replied Jacobs, "it's hard
to account for."

"Could it be that there is some irregularity in the pathology
report for Bevo's case?"

"No," said Jacobs, "there is no irregularity. It's just a simple
mistake. I—"

"I'll tell you what, Warren," Stroud said. "I'm going to subpoena
every single goddamn note that your pathologist took on the Rasmussen case, and we're going to find out how Sherlock Holmes Pulaski
managed to guess wrong on the sex and color of every single horse
he *says* was killed in the fire. Now, what do you think about that?"

"Well," said Jacobs, "it would be a waste of time, but you boys
do what you have to do. It's a shame, though, to see Gilliam Stroud
grabbing at straws, resorting to pathetic little tricks."

"You didn't just make up those descriptions to tease us, did
you, Warren?" Stroud asked. "SWAT hasn't started hiring novelists
to try their cases, have they?"

"What the hell do you mean by that?"

"It's simple, Warren. Somebody's switched horses. Now, was it you or Pulaski?"

"Go fuck yourself, Stroud."

"I think I'd rather fuck your pathologist, Warren. See he gets to the Mule Springs courthouse at eight o'clock tomorrow morning."

"Listen to me, if you boys try to argue that—"

"Can't hear you, Warren," Stroud said, "the connection is breaking up." He reached over, punched a button on the phone, and the line went dead.

Stroud sat back in his chair, spread his arms, and began to sing in a booming *profundo:* "'Amazing grace, how sweet the sound / That saved a wretch like me!' Sing with me, Mr. Parker!"

"I'm not much of a singer," I said, staring at him.

"Not even when God almighty pours out his blessings on the heads of his children?"

"I didn't know he'd done any pouring," I replied.

"Let this be a lesson to you, son. Cockiness is one of the seven deadly sins." He laughed. "Didn't you hear what our worthy opponent just said? Somebody screwed up somewhere, son, and that may just save our asses!" He got up and limped down the hall, singing.

CHAPTER 38

THREE HOURS LATER, Stroud and I were on the road again, driving west in the big Lincoln toward Greenville on State Highway 11. "Careful, Mr. Parker," Stroud warned. "The highway patrolmen on this stretch of road know my car, and we can't afford to be stopped now." In the canted light of evening, the hills were lengthening, the deep green of the pines taking on shadows. "We want to hit him right after supper," said the old man. "People tend to put their brains on hold about then."

We were on our way to shake down Stan-the-Man Pulaski, veterinary pathologist extraordinaire. Stroud felt that if we surprised him tonight with questions about the discrepancies in his report, he might become flustered enough to tell us something useful.

"Pulaski is Jehovah on the stand," Stroud said. "But it's hard to be Jehovah when you're caught off guard in your living room."

"But how off guard will he be?" I asked. "Won't Jacobs have already told him about his talk with us?"

"Of course. And if I'm right, if the good doctor really did screw up the necropsies, he'll be getting sweaty, trying to pull a story together. But he won't expect to have to tell his story until tomorrow morning. Trust me, Mr. Parker, we'll be a big surprise."

"The surprise may be on us," I reminded him. "Jacobs may have done what he said. He may have just picked up the wrong report."

Stroud laughed. "We've got him, Mr. Parker. You heard him on the phone. That was the voice of someone seriously nonplussed."

"Nonplussed?"

"Can't you feel the change in the wind?" Stroud added, "God is on our side. We're living in a state of grace."

"I don't get it," I said. "How did Pulaski screw up? Could he have gone to the wrong fire?"

Stroud hooted. "Jesus, I wish he had! What a great story that would make. It would be the end of him in this state. But no, Mr. Parker, he must have found the barn, all right. There wouldn't have been more than one to go up in flames that night. We would have heard."

I was surprised when Stroud told me that neither he nor Wick Chandler had ever visited the site of the fire. "Why would we have gone out there?" Stroud said. "We're no experts. Besides, the fire happened months before Bevo brought us in on the case. By then there would have been nothing left."

Stroud explained how Pulaski went about examining the site of a fire. "First, he shovels and sweeps the site down to bare earth and six inches beyond. Then he carts off the ashes in buckets and crates that he numbers to correspond with a grid he draws over a diagram of the site. Finally, he winnows it all down to a few jars of stuff. That's what he brings to the trial to ram up the other side's ass."

"All right, then," I said, "what happened with the report?"

Stroud hummed tunelessly for a minute. "I am beginning to see it, to smell the rottenness of it. The parts are coming together. Let it percolate a little longer, Mr. Parker. Let me keep it on the back burner awhile."

"Molly Tunstall said you liked the back burner."

"I'm a great believer in it," he replied. "The back burner and

God's grace." He started singing "Amazing Grace" again, thumping the dash in time. "'I once was lost, but now am found, / Was blind but now I see.' Grace, Mr. Parker. Sometimes that's all you have to fall back on."

"I didn't know you were such a believer, Mr. Stroud."

"I'll believe in anything that wins the case. If it takes God to do it, then I'm a goddamn deacon."

Traffic picked up a little as we neared Greenville. "Farmers," said Stroud, watching the taillights of the pickup ahead of us. "I was raised on a farm. A big one. Hated every minute of it. I swore I would get away, make a name for myself. And now here I am, living in a run-down farmhouse, making wills and getting divorces for farmers." He laughed, shook his head. "God surely has a sense of humor."

When we reached Greenville we turned onto State Highway 57 and drove toward McKinney. About the time the sun disappeared in front of us, Stroud told me to start looking for a turnoff. "It could be tough to find in the dark."

"Have you ever been to Pulaski's place before?" I asked.

"Once. He hosted a get-together of the East Texas Bar Association. It's a fancy house with a pool and a couple of big barns and a landing strip that he keeps smooth as a putting green. The whiskey flowed that night, and if I recall correctly, the lieutenant governor and some of his buddies staged a three-legged race on the runway and tore out some grass. Pulaski got a little put out. He's a very serious fellow."

"Do you really think he's crooked?"

"A horse pathologist, Mr. Parker, is the ripest virgin in the whorehouse. Everybody wants to corrupt him. If you're in the horse business and are crooked, as you very probably are, you practically have to have an animal pathologist in your pocket. Stanislaus Pulaski has testified in over four hundred insurance fraud cases. In three hundred of those, he was hired by SWAT. Now, you tell me, are there scorch marks on his pudenda, or what?

"So you think he's been bought by SWAT?"

"It's a foregone conclusion."

We got all the way to McKinney, having missed the turnoff. "Jesus wept!" Stroud cried. "Turn around, Mr. Parker. We'll try again."

On our second pass we found the road, drove about five miles down an asphalted lane, and then a couple of miles on gravel through a pine forest, coming at last to Pulaski's compound. The house sat on a rise, with the barns in a little valley behind it and the landing strip at the bottom of the valley. There were two vehicles in the driveway, both Jeeps, but no lights on in the house or the barns.

"Does he have a family?" I asked.

"Divorced."

"Maybe there's nobody home," I said, pulling to a stop behind one of the Jeeps.

"Yep," said Stroud. From his tone of voice, I gathered he was not surprised.

We got out, went to the front door, rang the bell. We rang again. Stroud knocked. "Stan," he called, "come on out, you lying, thieving son of a bitch."

"Jesus, Gill," I said. "Take it easy."

Stroud cocked his head, listening. All I could hear was the whisper of a soft wind and the crickets taking up where the locusts had left off at dusk. It was a dark night, no moon, the stars dimmed by a low-lying haze. Stroud was only a gaunt shadow as he limped to the side of the house.

"Come on, Mr. Parker," he said, disappearing toward the back. I followed him along the side of the house, past the swimming pool, a green glow in the darkness, to a sliding glass patio door.

Shards of glass crackled under our feet: The door had been smashed. From somewhere inside the house came a faint beeping.

"A break-in," I whispered. "That noise must be the burglar alarm."

"Yep," said Stroud. "It's coming together. Stan, you stinker, you."

"Let's get out of here," I said, taking the old man's arm. "The burglars may still be inside."

"If they are," said Stroud, "they'd better be ready for a fight."

Stroud shook free of me and, before I could stop him, walked through the jagged hole in the door.

"Stroud!" I hissed, sticking my head through the hole in the glass. It was pitch black inside the house.

I jumped when Stroud's voice boomed in the darkness next to me. "Go get my flashlight out of the trunk," he said.

"This is burglary!" I replied.

"Hurry, Mr. Parker. I imagine the police are on their way."

I ran to the car, fumbled in the darkness for the trunk key, opened the trunk, and found the flashlight. Stroud was waiting inside the door when I got back.

"We have to find the study," he said, switching on the beam. We were in a kind of solarium, full of hothouse trees and exotic plants. Walking through the house, we saw evidence here and there of vandalism: smashed picture frames, lamps knocked over, a mahogany entertainment center in the den cleaned out of all its electronic components. But the house was not in terrible shape.

"Very neat burglars," said Stroud. We found the study, a big cherry-paneled room in the center of the house. Stroud switched off his flashlight and turned on the overhead light. In one corner of the room sat a computer work desk with wires sprawling across its top and no computer; in another, a small bookshelf had been knocked over, with books strewn on the floor around it.

"What are we looking for?" I asked.

"Something we won't find, if I'm right about this little operation." There were papers scattered throughout the room. Stroud picked up a few and scanned them, then went to the big cherry-wood desk in the center of the room and looked through a couple of drawers. "I would bet Bevo's whole insurance policy that we won't find a single page relating to his case in this room," said the old man.

"We don't have time to look," I replied. The beeping of the burglar alarm was making my skin crawl. Perhaps six minutes had passed since we drove up to the house. How long would it take the Collin County sheriff to answer Pulaski's alarm?

"Look here!" cried Stroud, kicking at a cardboard box big enough to hold a good-sized television set. Across the side of the box was stenciled the name *Rasmussen*.

"What's in the box, Mr. Parker?"

I knelt and opened the top. There were several Mason jars containing little piles of whitened ash. Plastic freezer bags held fragments of bone and charred flesh. There were plastic boxes of microscope slides and three small pails full of debris, wadded-up paper, scorched links from a metal chain, bent nails.

"Bevo's horses, is my guess," I replied.

"Pick up the box!" Stroud said.

"Why?"

"Pick it up, goddamn it, or I'll do it myself."

I folded the top closed and picked up the box.

"Now what?" I said.

"What do you think? Go put it in the car!"

"We can't do that!"

"Move!" the old man snapped.

"Do you know how many laws we're breaking, Stroud? We're stealing. We're tampering with evidence. We're—"

"That's right, Parker, and if you don't move your ass, we're going to get *caught*."

I set the box back down. "Mr. Stroud, this is wrong."

"Fine," he said, "it's wrong. Just get out of here, then."

"The cops will be here any minute!" I reminded him.

"Let 'em come!" said Stroud. "Let 'em carry me off in chains. Let me waste away in prison, a martyr to your goddamn notion of ethics. And when I die, you can lower me into the ground with your lily-white hands."

"Jesus," I said.

"I don't recall much about law in the city, Mr. Parker, but out here we try to win our cases. Now, you have a choice. You can either leave that box on the floor, in which case I'm not budging until the police come and arrest me, or you can pick up the goddamn box and we can get out of here and maybe save the case and our law firm to boot."

Stroud sat down in Pulaski's office chair and crossed his arms.

"You're not moving?" I asked.

"Not without the box."

"They won't arrest you, Stroud. They'll wonder what you're doing here, but they'll know you didn't break in. You're not a burglar."

"Maybe so," the old man said. "Though it won't exactly help our case for me to be found here. But if we get out of here in time, and we take this box with us, we can turn this case around." He paused for a moment, then said, "You wanted a new life in the country, son. Well, here it is, tied up in a bow for you. Let's just win this case, and we can thrash out the morality of it tomorrow morning."

I looked at Stroud, and I looked at the box. I thought long and hard. And in the end I carried the box to the car. I broke the law big time. As I stumbled back out through the darkness, listening to the Mason jars clinking in the box that I held in my hands, I tried to convince myself that I had given in only to save this cracked old man from embarrassing himself and his firm—my firm—by being caught at the scene of a crime. But I knew that was a lie. The fact was, I wanted to win the Rasmussen case, and this was the only way I could see to do it. So much for rediscovering a sense of ethics in the country, I thought as I closed the trunk.

When I got back to the study, Stroud had the phone receiver in his hand and was dialing a number from his address book.

"Now what?" I asked.

"Keep quiet!"

I heard a muffled click as the line connected, then a voice, unintelligible from where I stood. Without a word, Stroud put his whistle to his lips and blew. I staggered out of the room, my spine jumping as if zapped by a current. The whistle kept attacking my nerves until I had made it back outside, and even standing away from the house, I felt the skin dance on the bridge of my nose. I thought seriously again of just getting in the car and driving off, leaving the old man to fend for himself. The appeal of that idea grew as minutes passed and Stroud did not appear. Then the high, thin whine of a siren reached me, and I ran to the house to pull Stroud out by his collar. We collided at the broken patio door.

"The police!" I said.

"Let's vamoose!" he replied.

By the time I had the Lincoln's engine started, we could see gleams of light cutting through the trees from the dirt road that led to Pulaski's house. Our escape route was blocked.

"Let's go visit the barns," Stroud suggested. Without headlights, I drove down the gentle, shadowy slope of the valley toward the farther of the two barns, a Quonset building that, I figured, must serve as the hangar for Pulaski's plane. Behind the building was a stand of evergreens and, passing nearby, a small road that ran alongside the landing strip. I was heading for that road when the flashing lights of a squad car appeared on it, about a mile ahead of us, cresting the top of the valley.

"Trapped like rats!" Stroud said.

I turned the car into the grove of evergreens and got out.

"Where are you going?" Stroud asked.

"They may find the car, but they don't have to find us," I replied. He got out, too, and we ran for the barn. There was a small metal side door, locked, but with a glass panel in the top half of it. I used the butt of Stroud's flashlight to smash the glass, and we got inside before the patrol car reached the barn. We stood panting in the darkness, waiting to see whether the police would catch sight of the Lincoln or drive on up to the house. Stroud, starting to wheeze, took his inhaler out of his pocket and dosed himself.

"I hope they catch us," I said between gasps. "I want to tell them we got caught because you spent five minutes blowing your goddamned whistle into the phone. That whistle's going to be exhibit A in your sanity hearing."

Stroud switched on the flashlight and swung it through the room. "This is a happy place," he said. We were in a long, narrow, high-ceilinged room, lined on all four sides with shelves that were loaded with Mason jars. The jars contained ash, like the ones in the Rasmussen evidence box. A superfine haze of dust hung in the air, making the flashlight beam a solid, glowing shaft as it played along the sides of the jars. Under the shelves were numbered bins full of plastic freezer bags, each wrapped around bone fragments or other horse parts. Close to me at one end of the room were a couple of refrigerators. I thought about opening them, then changed my mind.

"It's the elephants' graveyard of horses," I said. "There must be half a ton of defunct tissue in these jars."

"Put all the parts together," said Stroud, "and you would have one hell of a horse."

Every surface in the room was coated with shaggy grit. I could feel it under my shoes. Stroud broke into a shuffling dance step.

"The old soft shoe," he said with a chuckle that turned into a sharp, barking cough.

"Put out the light!" I cried as the sheriff's car drove past. It missed the Lincoln and rolled on up the slope. Stroud and I crept out of the barn, got into his car, and without headlights I drove up the valley road. At the house on the hill behind us, spinning lights from three patrol cars raked, red and blues, through the darkness.

CHAPTER 39

"**HOW MUCH DO YOU KNOW** about the horse insurance business, Mr. Parker?" Stroud asked.

"Not much."

We were less than half an hour from Jenks, and I was still numb with relief over our escape from the McKinney police. Stroud had been cogitating quietly in the passenger seat, the look on his face suggesting he was shifting something from the back burner to the front.

"It's pretty cut and dried," Stroud continued. "You buy a horse, you apply for an insurance policy on it. The carrier sends you a form to fill out describing the horse in detail, from its dollar value right down to the fuzz on its ass."

"The dec sheet," I said.

"Correct. You fill it out, usually by hand, send it to the carrier, and some scribe in the carrier's office attaches the policy to it and files it away."

"And you think something happened to the dec sheets when Bevo sent them to Stromboli," I said. By then the same thought had occurred to me.

"That's right. One of the wop secretaries could have attached Bevo's dec sheets to the wrong insurance policies. It wouldn't be the first time a mistake like that was made. Think how many policies show up in one day at a big outfit like Stromboli. Hundreds. A couple of years back, a friend of mine, Dallas Goode, got his policy back from a carrier out of Philadelphia. Dallas took a look at the contracts the carrier returned to him and found out he had insured six performing Shetland ponies instead of the brood mares he'd bought." Stroud laughed. "He said he'd rather have had the Shetlands, for all the good he got from those mares."

"You're saying Stromboli accidentally mixed up the dec sheets and attached the descriptions of somebody else's horses to Bevo's policies?"

"I'm saying that sort of thing happens. Maybe it happened to Bevo. Bear with me here. A month after he buys them, Bevo's horses are killed in a fire, and he sends in his claim. Stromboli contacts SWAT, and SWAT sends Pulaski to investigate and write the necropsies. Stan-the-Man does his usual thing, pours the horses into his little jars, takes the evidence back to the lab. Now, here's where things get interesting. As a matter of course, Stromboli would have sent Pulaski a telex with all the relevant information about the horses: their ages, their sex, potential productivity, and, of course, their money value. Suppose that Pulaski, being the cocky son of a bitch that he is, does a half-assed job of analyzing the evidence. Or, better, doesn't even look at the stuff in the jars. After all, he's got the Stromboli telex giving him all he really needs to know about the horses. What if he writes up his necropsies solely on the basis of the info Stromboli sent him?"

"Without comparing the telex information to the physical evidence?" I asked.

"That's right."

"What sort of pathologist would do a thing like that?"

"A no-good, lazy-ass pathologist who thinks he's God. Don't forget, Mr. Parker, Pulaski has a reputation for never being wrong. His word is law. Nobody contests him anymore. He thinks anything he does is right."

"But that's stupid!" I replied. "It's like a coroner basing an official autopsy on information from the dead guy's insurance carrier."

"That's exactly what it's like. And don't think *that* doesn't happen, either!"

"So Pulaski's report is completely screwed up, and nobody checked it until today?" I asked.

"Nobody felt the need to look at it. After all, it's from Sherlock Holmes Pulaski. He might not even have given a copy to Jacobs until the last day or so."

"What you're saying is, SWAT didn't take this case seriously."

"No," Stroud replied, "what I'm saying is, they treated it as routine. And anytime you allow the law to become routine, it can jump up and bite you between the buttons, as I have cause to know." He stretched, scratched himself with a self-satisfied air. "It seems, Mr. Parker, that both parties to this particular suit have been remiss. Our adversaries, however, have proved themselves a little more remiss than we."

"Too bad this is all just speculation," I said.

"Is that all it is?" Stroud asked. "Why do you think there was a break-in tonight at Stan Pulaski's house?"

"You think there's a connection?"

"I asked you what *you* think," replied Stroud, the old Baylor law professor. "Let's see if you have a country lawyer's powers of deduction."

"Or invention," I countered.

"Or invention," he said, smiling.

I thought for a moment. "All right. Let's assume the report really is screwed up. That would explain the sudden change in Jacobs's tone of voice on the phone today. Don't forget, he was nonplussed."

"Nonplussed?" Stroud said. "He was abashed, Mr. Parker. He was seriously disconcerted."

"Okay, he was abashed. He's got two problems. First, how to stop you from making good on your threat to subpoena all of Pulaski's notes. Second, how to fix the bogus report without the court ever getting wind of the problem."

"And what is his solution?"

"Well, apparently, it isn't simply to come clean and fix the report."

"With Gilliam Stroud on his tail? He's got no chance of that. I'll scream foul. I'll argue they were manufacturing evidence to work some sort of scam on our poor, innocent client. Before I'm through, I'll have the jury believing Pulaski himself set fire to those horses. And Warren Jacobs knows it."

"All right, then. I guess Pulaski sets up a break-in at his own house, in which the burglars take the stereo, the TV, the computer, some cheesy paintings—oh, yes, and the pathology report for Bevo Rasmussen's suit! Then, since the original report is missing, Pulaski will petition the court to let him write a new report based on the physical evidence he has collected."

"You have earned your weight in chitlins, Mr. Parker," he said. "What do you think of my little scenario?"

"Pretty far-fetched," I replied. "Who's going to believe burglars would steal a pathologist's report?"

"There was a beautiful eel-skin briefcase lying on Pulaski's desk. No—ostrich-skin! The nasty thieves could not resist it. Unfortunately, it happened to contain all of Pulaski's papers on the Rasmussen case."

"Come on!" I said. "Are you telling me there would be only one copy of Pulaski's report? What about the copy Jacobs read from this afternoon on the phone?"

Stroud's smile widened. "In light of the aspersions we cast upon it, Jacobs gave it back to Pulaski so that Stan-the-Man could check its accuracy. It was in the briefcase with Pulaski's own copy."

"Who in the world would buy this story?" I asked.

"Judge Wrong Tit Tidwell, for one," said Stroud. "If Pulaski told Wrong Tit that Martians ate his report, Tidwell would smile and nod."

"Let's see," I said, "incompetent pathologists, corrupt law firms, vindictive idiot judges, impossible scenarios. Seems country law works pretty much like city law."

"Now, Mr. Parker, do you see why we took the evidence box?"

"You wanted to spend the next five to fifty years of your life behind bars?" I asked.

"Don't go ethical on me at this late hour, son."

I did know why we took the evidence, of course. "Without the physical evidence, Stan-the-Man cannot turn in a credible report. He would have to base his findings only on his memory. But he investigates so many fires a year that it would be impossible for him to reconstruct one fire, over a year old, totally from memory," I said. "You would rip him to shreds on the stand, Wrong Tit Tidwell notwithstanding."

"Very good, Mr. Parker. And can you think of any other reason why we took the box?"

"Spoliation," I answered.

"Excellent!" he said.

The doctrine of spoliation holds that if you are party to a lawsuit and evidence is destroyed or lost while in your possession, it is presumed the evidence is unfavorable to you. The doctrine was originally intended to protect litigants in product liability cases. In such cases one lawyer or the other used to send the product in question—an oven, a seat belt, a watch crystal—back to the manufacturer for testing. In the course of such testing, the product was often unavoidably destroyed. This was unfair to the other litigant in the case, who now could not conduct his or her own tests. To protect this second party, the court, invoking the doctrine of spoliation, instructs the jury to presume that the destroyed evidence is unfavorable to the party who had it destroyed.

What this meant in our case was that the disappearance of the evidence box would count heavily against Stromboli. Add spoliation to Pulaski's inability to submit a pathology report, and it would be next to impossible for Stromboli to win. Bevo would get his money.

"Jesus!" I said. "We've beaten SWAT!"

"Amazing grace, Mr. Parker," said the old man. "We are imbued."

"It's not grace, Mr. Stroud. The other side screwed up worse than we did."

"Sounds like grace to me."

"Let's just see if we're imbued tomorrow morning," I replied. "If you're wrong about Pulaski's report, Jacobs is going to clean our plow."

"Clean our plow." Stroud rolled the syllables around in his mouth. "A nice rural image. You're catching on, Mr. Parker."

As we neared Jenks, Stroud had me circle to the road leading out to his farmhouse. "I want to take that box of dead horses out to the pond and sink it," Stroud said. "Pulaski will figure out that his burglars didn't really steal the box along with the briefcase. He may put two and two together and start wondering if we somehow had something to do with it."

"That's a long shot, isn't it?" I said.

"Yes, and it's giving Pulaski credit for brains that he just doesn't have. Still, I want to make sure that if he comes snooping over here, there's nothing for him to find."

"Good idea. Destroy the evidence," I said, feeling even more like a criminal than I had when I carried the box to Stroud's car.

Turning into the meandering dirt road that led to the house, I noticed flashes of what looked like heat lightning in the sky ahead of us. As we got closer, the flashes became more intense. Beyond the house, in the direction of the cabin, a reddish glow pulsed in the sky.

"I think maybe we just drove out of the state of grace," I said.

CHAPTER 40

I STEERED THE LINCOLN through the tall grass toward the valley where the cabin lay. Now we could see smoke straggling upward in the distance.

"Bevo Rasmussen is burning down my cabin!" Stroud cried. "That's the last straw!"

Suddenly another car loomed in the grass, coming at us fast. It swerved aside, missing us by inches. The driver was only a blur, but I could tell that the car was a police car. In the next instant, something exploded against our windshield, and light seared my eyeballs. When I opened my eyes again, we were topping the hill overlooking the cabin and pond. With my vision clouded by the explosion's afterburn, I could see nothing but dark shapes in the landscape and sudden blooms of sparks as other explosions erupted in the valley. I heard the explosions going off amid the popping of small-arms fire and the snarl of men's voices shouting in panic. Rockets whined and shrieked.

"The dogs of war!" cried Stroud.

"I can't see," I told him.

The old man reached over and yanked the steering wheel. "Give her some gas," he said. I did, and Stroud steered us across the top of the valley to a stand of pine trees about a hundred yards from the cabin. "We'll be safe here, I think," he said. I switched off the headlights and the ignition.

We sat under the trees in the car, with the valley sloping away in front of us. As my eyesight came back, I could make out distinct shapes. The cabin was still there—it had not been set on fire—but a patch of grass behind it, maybe half an acre, was burning, the flames lapping low to the ground, churning out black smoke. In front of the cabin, a battle was going on. Half a dozen cars, three of them black-and-whites from the Jenks Police Department, were swarming in the space between the cabin and the pond. Men leaned out car windows to shoot rifles and handguns at the cabin.

As we watched, two of these cars collided head-on and bounced back from each other. I heard a voice say, "Shit, Red, let me drive." One of the cars spun off again, but white steam billowed from the hood of the other. It was finished. Three men tumbled out of it, waving frantically until a car stopped and picked them up. Two other cars sat on the slope of the valley, one smoldering, the other lying on its side in a ditch. The smoldering car was Captain Jack's Range Rover. I could see bullet holes dotting its flank, and I wondered if they were new or if they dated from the afternoon of the bobcat ambush.

It was an oddly unfocused battle. The men in the cars were pouring ammunition into the cabin, yet there was no visible activity inside it. The clearing where the cars bounced around seemed to be the center of a mortar attack, yet we could hear no incoming shells; every few seconds a spot of ground or a bush would belch upward in a thundering explosion.

The top of the Lincoln was hit by what sounded like bullets. "Incoming!" I yelled, kicking my door open and sliding out onto the ground. Above me, there was laughter. I looked up but saw only foliage until an arm high in a tree waved at me.

"Where are you hit, Clay?" It was Wick Chandler's voice. "Get that man into triage." Something bounced off my forehead, and I picked it up. A pebble. To considerable snickering from above, I stood up and discovered that I had parked the car next to a duck blind identical to the one on the road to Boo's barbecue shack. The people in the blind had tossed pebbles onto the Lincoln's roof.

Stroud limped past me and began climbing the ladder. "Let me see!" he cried eagerly. I followed him up. On the platform we found Wick, Bevo, and Boo himself. Wick and Boo were watching the battle through binoculars.

"Glad to see you, Mr. Stroud!" said Bevo. "I didn't want you to miss my little party."

"They've come to arrest you, Bevo!" I told him. "They must know the place is full of stolen goods."

"Stolen goods?" said Bevo. "Where'd you get a notion like that, Mr. Parker?"

"Somebody give me some binoculars," Stroud said. Wick handed him his, and the old man stared through them.

"I'm sorry, Gill," Wick said. "Maybe I shouldn't have bailed Bevo out, after all. They've shot up the cabin pretty bad."

"Bevo," said Stroud, "the fee you owe us for getting you out of that drug deal last fall?"

"Yes, sir?" said Bevo.

"It's forgiven. All right with you, Hard-dick?"

"Sure thing, Gill. You're not mad?"

"It's beautiful," said Stroud. "It's the most beautiful thing I've ever seen." He lowered the binoculars and to my astonishment I saw tears in the old man's eyes.

Bevo explained that he had been setting up the ex-pilots for weeks. "Bunch of assholes," he sniffed.

"Tell 'em about them guys bustin' up our still," Boo suggested.

"Two stills, Uncle Boo," Bevo reminded him. "Don't forget

that one over by the Five-D Ranch a couple of years ago. It's getting so you can't take a shit in the woods without one of them idiots tripping over you."

"So you weren't fencing stolen goods?" I asked him.

Bevo gave me his wolf's smile. "All them boxes stacked in the cabin is empty. Let's just say I planted some hints, and sure enough, old Jack and his pals came sniffing. Red Meachum deputized 'em this morning. Guess where they went to plan the raid?" He clapped his uncle on the back.

"The Singing Pig?" I asked.

"They come in for lunch," said Boo, beaming at us. "I heard every goddamn thing they said. Boy howdy, they hate you, Mr. Stroud. They was planning to catch Bevo with a load of goods and then knock down your door. They got a search warrant." A jagged nicotine laugh barked out of the little man. "I hope they like what they found."

Bevo reached down and picked up a small metal box with a crank handle and posts for connecting electric wires. "Give me another one, Uncle Boo," he said. Boo ripped a piece of tape off the duck blind's guardrail, then handed Bevo the ends of two wires that had been secured under the tape. I saw that the wires led down one leg of the platform, into the darkness. Several more pairs of wires were taped to the rail. Bevo wrapped the two leads around the posts on the box, then handed the box to Stroud.

"Would you care to do the honors?" Bevo asked. Stroud took the detonator. Bevo pointed to a dried bush fifty feet from the cabin door. "Now, wait for a car to get close, and crank that sumbitch."

Stroud clutched the box, his hand on the crank, until one of the patrol cars veered toward the bush. He gave the crank a swift turn, and the bush burst into flame. The driver jerked the steering wheel to miss the explosion, and the car rose on two wheels, balanced precariously, then crashed down on all fours again.

Stroud howled. "It's Christmas! It's my fucking birthday!"

"Boo is a man of hidden talents," Wick told us. "He did most of this with that old black powder we kept in the cabin. That and some leftover fireworks."

"Where'd you learn explosives, Boo?" I asked.

"Seabees," he said. "Out in the Pacific. Nineteen and forty-four. I blew up an entire island once. An aye-toll. 'Course, it's good to find a use for the old skills, now and then."

"I don't understand why they don't just get out of their cars and charge the house," I said. "Nobody's in there."

"That's not what they think," said Bevo. "We had the lights on, till those guys shot 'em out. And every once in a while, we give 'em a burst of machine-gun fire."

"How?" I asked.

Bevo handed me another box, like the first one. "Want to shake 'em up? It's only firecrackers."

I took the box, cranked the handle.

In a few seconds a series of flat, popping noises stuttered out of a cabin window, accompanied by occasional sparks.

"Sounds like an M-16," said Wick.

"Try that one," Bevo said to me. I cranked the handle on a third box, and a comet's tail screamed out of a cabin window, bouncing twice in the valley grass before bursting into a mass of silvery tracers that arced and died in the air.

"That must have been what hit the Lincoln," I told Stroud.

"If we only had Roman candles," the old man replied, "we could hold them off for a week."

"These idiots are gonna catch on pretty soon," Bevo said. He turned to his uncle. "How many charges we got left?"

Boo shook his head. "Only one or two. There's one over to the side of the house. Then, of course, there's the house itself."

"You wired the cabin?" Wick asked.

"Of course," said Bevo. "When you do a job, you do it thorough."

"I didn't know about that, Gill," Wick apologized.

But the old man was watching through the binoculars. "Blow it up, burn it down," he said. "This is its finest hour."

Bevo and Boo worked on the detonator box for a moment, then handed it to Stroud.

"Mr. Stroud," said Bevo, "I'm sorry for our little set-to in the jail today. I was crazy from the way those cops had been beating on me."

"All is forgiven, Bevo," replied the old man. He cranked the handle on the box, and the front wall of the cabin blew out, the roof collapsing and catching fire. Debris spewed into the night sky. The force of the explosion made the duck blind wobble.

"Good one, Uncle Boo," said Bevo.

"Makes a man kinda sentimental," Boo replied.

CHAPTER 41

THE NEXT MORNING Pulaski was late for the deposition. We sat in the courtroom waiting for him, Stroud next to Bevo at the defendant's table. Stroud hummed his tuneless song and winked at the court reporter, a young woman who would not smile back at him. Stroud looked a little worn but was still in high spirits from the night before. It certainly had been an interesting evening. Shortly after the roof of Stroud's cabin collapsed, Sheriff Nye had arrived on the scene. He de-deputized the whole smoldering troop of ex-pilots and threw them in jail around ten P.M. "Those boys will be walking softly around us for a long time to come," Wick had said that morning as the three of us drove into Mule Springs. "Gill had to use higher math to explain to Nye the kind of lawsuit we could file against the city."

Wick was the picture of health and energy, his ruby throat swelling above a crisp collar and a striking silk tie. "Nothing like a little nighttime jamboree to clear out the cobwebs," he whispered.

Vincenzo Laspari, the Stromboli company representative, was seated at the plaintiff's table cultivating a look of genteel boredom. Next to him sat Warren Jacobs, cool and collected. Jacobs's self-possession worried me. How could he look so calm if his case was in shreds? I voiced my concern to Wick, who shrugged and looked uneasy, too.

"So you're from Naples, Mr. Laspari," Stroud said.

"Yes," returned Laspari.

"What sort of weather they having out there?"

"It is very hot." Laspari gave Stroud a half-millimeter smile and a slight nod of dismissal, as if to signal the end of their conversation.

But Stroud would not be shaken off. "Hotter than here?" he asked.

"No . . . Perhaps as hot."

"What about the humidity?"

"The . . . ?"

"You know, the water in the air. They must have humidity in Naples."

"Ah, *l'umidità.* It can be bad."

Stroud nodded at the Italian, and there was a moment of silence.

"Too bad it's falling into the sea," he said.

"I beg your pardon?"

"I say it's too bad Naples is falling into the sea."

"You are thinking of Venice, Signore Stroud."

"You're right, Mr. Laspari. My apologies."

The baiting continued, Stroud rattling off skewed snippets of tourist lore, Laspari correcting him, his Continental reserve beginning to fray a little. Finally Pulaski arrived, to the relief of all in the room. A tall, broad-shouldered man with a distinguished head of amber hair going picturesquely gray at the sideburns, he resembled Stewart Granger in one of his African movies, right down to the khaki safari jacket.

Stroud saw him first, leaped to his feet, and walked up the aisle to shake his hand. "Stan-the-Man," he said, conducting Pulaski to the chair placed for him in front of the judge's dais. "How's it hanging?"

Stroud's joviality seemed to confuse Pulaski, who sat down slowly in the chair. He looked around the room until his eyes fell on Warren Jacobs.

"Mr. Jacobs," Pulaski said in a low voice, leaning toward the SWAT lawyer, "might I have a word with you?"

"Okay if we start, gentlemen?" Stroud asked, making a show of looking at his wristwatch. "We've already been here awhile."

"By all means," Jacobs replied.

"Warren," said Pulaski, rising from his chair, "I need to speak to you."

There was an edge in Pulaski's voice that escaped Jacobs's notice. "I don't think we should keep these good people any longer than we already have, Stan," Jacobs replied.

Pulaski sat back down. "Very well, I have an announcement to make." He spoke disdainfully, as if angry at everyone in the room. "Last night my house was broken into. Whoever did it took a number of items, including all my notes on Mr. Rasmussen's horses."

"Burglars?" said Stroud. "My, my. That's a shame, Stan. But you still have your report, I trust?"

"That's another thing," Pulaski said. "They—the burglars—took my report, too."

"They took your report?" asked Stroud. "But you must have copies, Stan."

"The burglars took all the copies."

"All the copies?" Stroud asked. "How could that be?"

Pulaski shrugged. "I'd collected them all together. That's how."

"But Mr. Jacobs read to me from a copy of the report yesterday," Stroud said. "What happened to that copy?"

"If you will recall, Mr. Stroud," interrupted Jacobs, "I told you I was not reading from the Rasmussen report. I had meant to—"

"Oh, that's right, Warren. You picked up the wrong report by mistake. You're working on so many, you just got a little careless."

"That is correct," Jacobs replied, coloring deeply. "I gave my copy back to Dr. Pulaski yesterday afternoon, so that he could check it for errors." Jacobs looked at Pulaski. "Are you saying, Stan, that my copy is stolen, too?"

"Yes, that's right," Pulaski said. "All gone."

Stroud walked up to Pulaski's chair, cocked his head in disbelief. "You're telling us, Dr. Pulaski, that thieves broke into your home and stole a *pathology report?*"

"That's not all they took, of course," Pulaski said. "They got my stereo, my VCR, my fax machine—"

"But why would they take a pathology report?" Stroud interrupted.

Pulaski swallowed. "It was in a very expensive briefcase. I assume the burglars were after the case."

"Was it a leather case, Mr. Pulaski?" asked Stroud.

"Yes."

"What kind of leather, do you recall?"

"Ostrich."

Stroud walked back to the table. He winked at me.

"We're wasting time, Gill," Jacobs said. "In view of this unfortunate event, may I suggest that Dr. Pulaski be allowed to reconstruct—"

"*My* suggestion, Warren," said Stroud, "is that Signore Laspari contact his employers in Naples to tell them to drop their lawsuit and pay my client the full amount of the claim."

"Now, hold on, Counselor," Jacobs said, rising to his feet. "The break-in is a tragedy, to be sure, and we sympathize with Dr. Pulaski. But losing the documents is no more than a minor inconvenience as far as our case is concerned. I'm sure Judge Tidwell will give us time to reconstruct the pathology report."

"Reconstruct the report?" said Stroud. "You mean rewrite it? After all this time has passed since the fire? How could anyone, even the immensely talented Stanislaus Pulaski, reconstruct it? I don't know, Warren, sounds fishy to me."

"It should be a simple matter," Jacobs continued. "After all, Dr. Pulaski still has the physical evidence, the remains of the horses. That should be enough, in Dr. Pulaski's capable hands, to establish the necessary facts, cause of death, and so forth."

Pulaski cleared his throat. "I don't have the physical evidence," he said, looking down at his feet.

"I'm sorry, Stan," Stroud said, "I didn't hear you. Would you repeat that?"

"I said, I don't have the physical evidence." He raised his eyes and met Jacobs's shocked gaze. "It was stolen, too."

"All of it?" Jacobs asked.

"Yes, of course, all of it. It was all in one box. The thieves took the box. It's gone."

There was a moment of silence.

"Any other bright ideas, Warren?" Stroud asked.

"Just a moment," Jacobs said. "I need to confer with Dr. Pulaski."

"I'll tell you what you need to do, Warren," said Stroud. "You need to think about the doctrine of spoliation. What's worse, your fumble-fingered expert here cannot possibly hope to make a credible reconstruction of the fire. Then you need to think about the counter-claim I'm going to file against you and your client as soon as we get out of here today."

Stroud walked toward the plaintiff's table, behind which Laspari sat, eyeing the old man in horror. "The facts are, Signore Laspari, that your company dragged my client into this protracted and expensive litigation without a single piece of physical evidence on which to base their case. Your company has failed to deal with its own customer in any semblance of good faith. Thanks to the cost of defending himself against your spurious charges, my client has lost his house and its furnishings. The mental anguish he has endured has been intense. We're talking really bad faith, something folks down here don't like to see. Something that used to make them itchy for a rope."

Stroud hovered over Laspari like the angel of death. "Pay my client what you owe him, Signore Laspari, or I'll file a claim for bad faith settlement practices that will make you think twice about ever setting foot in the New World again!"

CHAPTER 42

WICK HAD CRANKED UP the stereo in his office and was dancing down the hallways, singing along in a gravelly rhythm-and-blues grunt. He stopped in front of my door. "Catch, Clay," he said, tossing me a dripping bottle of Chihuahua beer. The bottle slipped through my fingers, thumped on the desktop, but didn't break. He tossed an opener next to the bottle.

"There's pâté in my office," he said, bobbing like a buoy in rough seas. "It's Mexican, made from the livers of geese fed on grain soaked in mescal. Eat and you will see visions."

"I'm seeing one now," I replied, watching him gyrate.

It was only twelve-thirty, but we had closed the office following Laspari's capitulation in the Rasmussen suit. The vision of Stroud in the courtroom that morning, looming over him with lightning in his eyes, had proved too much for the dapper Italian. Against Jacobs's white-faced protest, Laspari agreed to file a motion to dismiss Stromboli's lawsuit and to pay Bevo the face value of his policy, $1.2 million. Stroud pressed Laspari into agreeing to send a certified check, made out to Chandler and Stroud as trustees for Bevo, that very afternoon by courier, an unprecedented move.

"The sooner the better," Wick had told Laspari, "considering the wrong done to our client."

"Nice doing business with you, Warren," Stroud had called to Jacobs as the SWAT lawyer hurried from the courtroom, hot on the trail of Stan Pulaski, who had slipped out ahead of him.

The firm's fee for the settlement would come to $360,000. Not bad, considering that a day earlier we had not had a prayer of winning the case.

"It was a religious experience," Wick had said as we drove out of the Mule Springs parking lot, "like beating a full house with two deuces and a cat turd." He sat silent on our drive home, stunned, I think, by the victory. But as soon as I'd parked in front of the office, he came alive.

Now, in my office doorway, he shuffled through a flab-punishing disco lounge breakdown. "I'm happy as a dog with two dicks!" he hollered, his shirt buttons threatening to pop. As Molly Tunstall edged by him with some files in her hand, he caught her and danced her down the hall.

I was working on some papers for another case; in the last few days the pile of documents in the basket on my desk had grown. What with the bass throbbing through the walls and Wick shaking the foundations of the building, I was having a hard time concentrating. I picked up the bottle of beer and rolled it across my forehead. The cold felt good.

"It works better if you flip that little silver thing off the top and stick the end in your mouth." It was Sally, sitting in the client's chair. She reached over the desk, took the beer out of my hand, popped the cap, and after the shaken beer had spewed half its contents on my rug, took a long, slow swallow.

"That's how you do it," she said. "What are you looking at?"

"You are the most beautiful administrative judicial district coordinator ever to drink a beer in my office during work hours."

"Hey, I'm on my lunch break," she asked. "Cut me some slack."

"Have I got a story for you," I said, getting up and coming around the desk.

She set the beer bottle on the desk and stood up. "Wick's trying to get me to dance with him out there. I thought I'd come in here and see if I might get you to show me how they do the two-step in Houston. That is, if you can dance with bad feet."

"Let's see if I can," I said, putting my arm around her. We two-stepped around the desk.

"So, Counselor," she said, "how does it feel to win your first case in the country?"

"I didn't have much to do with it," I replied. "A little breaking and entering, a little burglary, that was it." As we danced I told her a bit about what had happened last night at Pulaski's house and then at Gill's snake-shooting retreat.

"So how do you feel about all these backwoods antics?" she asked. "I wonder if life in the country is agreeing with you."

"I'm dancing, aren't I?"

We two-stepped until Wick cut in on me. Then he and Sally danced, then Sally and Stroud, until Sally's lunch hour was all danced away, and she drove back to Wyman.

About two o'clock Bevo showed up at the office, dressed in a new shark-skin suit and driving a Lexus that resembled the one Antoine Duett had been driving when I tried to tail him from the Dairy Queen two days earlier.

"What do you think?" he asked, dragging us all out to look at the car. "Don't it show me off to perfection?" He smiled. One tooth winked in the afternoon sun.

"I see you got your diamond back," Stroud said.

"They just bonded it back on, no problem. Wealth sticks to me."

"The settlement hasn't even come in yet, Bevo," I said, "and you're already spending it?"

"This ain't as frivolous as it looks," Bevo replied. "This is my company car." He handed all of us business cards with an engraved picture of a big shaggy bird, and words that read:

— FREEBIRD ENTERPRISES —
The Wings of Emus

"You know, gentlemen, emus are the future of East Texas."

"If that's the case," muttered Wick, looking at the card, "I'm moving."

"You couldn't do better with that three hundred thou I just made for you than invest it in this little enterprise right here."

We were saved from the rest of Bevo's sales pitch by the arrival of a small red car out of which came the messenger, a young man in the uniform of his carrier service. Stroud signed a paper on a clipboard, and the messenger handed him an envelope and left.

"I wasn't sure Laspari would come through," Stroud mused.

"After your performance this morning?" Wick replied. "You could have doubled the settlement."

"Come on, come on," said Bevo. "Open her up."

Stroud opened his penknife and, with a flourish, slit the edge of the envelope. He pulled out a folded piece of blank paper, out of which a check fell on the sidewalk. The old man picked it up.

"Amazing grace!" he said, turning the slip of paper around in his hand so we could read it. It was a $1.2 million check, made out to Hardwick Chandler and Gilliam Stroud, trustees for Bevo Rasmussen, signed by Vincenzo Laspari.

"No shit," said Bevo, snatching the check from Stroud. "Amazing grace."

The actual arrival of the check proved an anticlimax after the office party. Stroud showed no inclination to burst into song, and Wick declined to dance. There was talk of what to do with the check. Bevo wanted to cash it immediately and take his share. Wick tried explaining to him that there wasn't that much money in both of Jenks's banks put together. But Bevo insisted that Chandler and Stroud accompany him to the bank to see what could be done. To my surprise, they agreed.

"Maybe it'll get him out of our hair," Wick told me. Molly had joined us outside the office, and she and I watched the three of them walk across the street to the First National Bank of Jenks.

"Have we ever settled a case this big before?" I asked Molly.

"Never a single one this big," she said. Then she added, giving me her odd near-smile, "Maybe you've brought us some luck."

Molly went inside, but I sat on the fender of Bevo's Lexus and watched the Jenks traffic go by. A cloud had obscured the sun momentarily, tempering the glare, and the heat felt good after several hours of office air-conditioning. From the trees wafted the billowing song of the locusts. A pickup went by with a middle-aged couple in it, both wearing baseball caps. They waved at me as they passed. I waved back and found it a pleasant thing to do.

I might have sat on Bevo's fender for the rest of the afternoon, communing with the locusts and solidifying my new position as the waving lawyer of Jenks, but the front door of the First National Bank burst open and Bevo, Wick, and Stroud sprinted out of it. Bevo reached the car first, yanked open the driver's door, and leaped inside.

"Get off!" he hollered at me. Chandler and Stroud reached the car and climbed in. I scrambled into the backseat just as the car lurched backward out of its parking slot. With a screech of the tires, we were heading out of town.

Winded from his run to the car, Stroud was sprawled in the seat next to me, his chest wheezing like an antique furnace. Pulling his inhaler from his pocket, he gave himself two jolts of medicine.

"Goddamn," he gasped, glassy-eyed and pale, "goddamn."

CHAPTER 43

"**THERE WAS A HOLD ON THE CHECK**," Wick panted, fighting for breath in the front seat. "Notice of forfeiture. Primrose did it."

"The DA seized the check?" I asked.

"I'll kill him," Bevo said. "I'll cut his fucking heart out."

"That pious cocksucker," said Wick. "He's looking for a way to screw us out of the money."

"How can he do that?" I asked.

"RICO," Stroud replied.

"Oh, shit," I said. "All right, Bevo, what have you been up to?"

"Me? I ain't done nothing, goddamn it. I'm pure as a newborn."

"Save it," said Stroud as the car tore down the road to Mule Springs. "We'll know when we get there."

The Racketeer Influenced and Corrupt Organizations Act allows the government to confiscate anything suspected of having been either used or obtained by a criminal during the commission of a crime or as a result of a crime. A man suspected of driving the getaway car in a robbery could find his car taken away from him and sold. Simply put, RICO is a way for the government to steal from people who may or may not turn out to be guilty of a crime.

The federal version of the act proved such a smashing revenue bonanza that many states set up their own RICO acts. The money forfeited goes into private "law enforcement" budgets, and district attorneys can tap into the money without having to account for it to the public.

Now it seemed that Paul Primrose, the DA of Claymore County, was using the Texas RICO act to confiscate Bevo's insurance settlement. All Primrose had to do was think up a way to implicate Bevo and his settlement in a crime that had taken place within his jurisdiction. Since Bevo's horses had died in Claymore County, Primrose would not have had to work very hard at sketching a case.

Bevo was out of the car almost before it careened to a halt in the courthouse parking lot. We ran after him into the building, rode an elevator to the office of the district attorney. Bevo had taken the stairs and beaten us. When we arrived he was leaning over the DA's desk, ranting and shaking his fist in Primrose's colorless face. Stroud swept into the room, grabbed the back of Bevo's collar, and yanked him into a chair.

"Thanks, Gill," said Primrose in his dry whine. "I thought for a moment I was a goner." He adjusted his bolo tie coolly, nodded at us. "Good afternoon, Mr. Parker, Wick. I was sort of expecting you boys."

"I don't know what you think you're doing, Primrose," said Stroud, "but I hope you keep it up."

"I appreciate your support," Primrose replied. "It's always gratifying when good works are recognized."

"I hope you keep it up, because I would sort of like to own this courthouse, and that is exactly what I'll do after I get through suing you for violating my client's civil rights."

Primrose pushed a button on his intercom. "Helen? See if you can get Clyde to step in here for a minute, will you? I think he's in the basement." He leaned back in his chair. "Why don't you boys all have a seat?" There was only one other chair in the room besides the one Bevo was in. I tried to steer Stroud into it, but he shrugged me off, so I took it.

"Mr. Primrose," I asked, "what is your legal basis for seizing the Rasmussen settlement money?"

"I'd have thought a big-city attorney like you would know the answer to that, Mr. Parker," the DA replied. "RICO, of course. We have reason to believe that Mr. Rasmussen here is guilty of fraud, and the settlement being the fruit of his criminal activity, we're confiscating it."

"There's not a case you can make against Bevo," Wick said. "This is stealing, Primrose, pure and simple."

Primrose's mouth was hidden by his drooping dishwater mustache, but his eyes were crinkling in a smile. It was the smile of the righteous. "No, Mr. Chandler," Primrose replied, "these are the wages of sin. We are relieving your client of the wages of sin."

"Bullshit," Stroud said. "It's not going to work, Paul. You've got nothing on Bevo, and unless you release the check right now, you will soon have less than that. Not only are you not going to be able to keep the money, but I'm going to grind your pompous dick in the dirt. I will take you to court and crucify you worse than Jesus Christ had it done to him. I'll take your name off this door and put my own on it. We'll have bingo in the courtroom every Wednesday night."

A deputy in a tall white Stetson appeared at the door. "Hey, Paul," he said.

"Hey, Clyde," said Primrose. "Wick, Gill, I think you both know Clyde. Mr. Parker, this is Clyde Fortinbras, our sheriff. Clyde, that fellow in the chair over there is Bevo Rasmussen. Have you got something for him?"

"I surely do," said Clyde. He handed Bevo a couple of papers, which Bevo squinted at before handing them to me. One was a copy of the notice of forfeiture that had prevented Bevo from claiming his money. The other one was an arrest warrant.

"Mr. Rasmussen," said Fortinbras, "you're under arrest. The charge is racketeering. I need you to come with me, sir."

The fury I had seen once or twice before in Bevo's eyes was there again. His hand slipped down toward his ankle, but before he could reach the razor, I took hold of his wrist. "That's not going to do you any good," I said, slipping the razor out of his sock.

"What did I tell you, Mr. Parker?" said Bevo. "It's a fucking conspiracy." The sheriff tapped him on the shoulder, and we both stood.

"You'd better get started back to Jenks, Gill," said Primrose, "if you want to get bail money before the bank closes. Too bad the forfeiture includes your fee, or you could dip into that."

"P.P., are you sure you are a saved man?" asked Stroud. "Are you certain you have been washed in the blood?"

"Why, yes, Gill, I am a Christian."

"Well, gird up your loins, because you are about to walk through the valley of the shadow." He turned, and the whole troupe of us was filing through Primrose's door, when the DA stopped us.

"You might enjoy this as you drive home," he said, placing a small tape recorder on his desk and flicking it on. It was a taped conversation between two men, one of whom was unmistakably Bevo, and the other, I realized in a moment, had to have been Antoine Duett, the SWAT dirty-tricks lawyer with whom Bevo had tried to make a secret deal. It was a very clear recording—the wire Duett had been wearing must have been very high-tech—and Bevo's voice, oozing self-importance, filled the room.

". . . flipped the switch and that horse starting sparking and shimmying like Christmas. I never saw anything like it. Smoke coming out its ears. I thought it might buck itself clear, but it just stood there shaking, and then it fell over. The worst part was the smell, of course. It ruined my clothes. Remember to stand upwind. But I got to tell you, there's better ways to manage a lightning strike."

We stood transfixed, listening to the tape, until Primrose switched it off.

"The Lord giveth," he said, "and the Lord taketh away."

CHAPTER 44

"**SON OF A BITCH,** you can't trust nobody!" said Bevo. "None of it's true, Mr. Stroud, I swear! I was just shooting the shit, was all. I never zapped no horse."

"Where did you get that tape?" Stroud demanded of Primrose. The DA tossed a manila envelope on the desk. Stroud picked it up and examined it. There was no return address, no mark of any kind.

"My secretary found that envelope taped to the door when she came in this morning," said Primrose. "There was nothing inside it except the tape. I just assumed it was left by a concerned citizen doing his part to clean the riffraff out of our county." He said he did not recognize the other voice on the tape, but that he would begin searching for him in the foreseeable future. "Unless you would like to tell me who he is," the DA said to Bevo.

All heads turned to our client, whom the sheriff had just cuffed. "Well," said Stroud, "are you going to tell him?"

"Mr. Stroud, I was just shooting the shit with the guy, honest. It's a fucking conspiracy to get me."

"From the tape it sounds to me like you got yourself, Mr. Rasmussen," said Primrose.

"Maybe we can cut a deal," Bevo suggested. "What'll you do for me if I name the man on the tape, Mr. District Attorney?"

"I'll tell you what I'll do," said Primrose. "I'll give you the best cell in the basement. Now, how's that?"

"Bevo, it's no skin off his ass if you don't talk," Stroud said. "He's not after the other guy, unless that guy's got a million dollars he can be screwed out of, too, right, P.P.?"

"You want a deal, Bevo?" Primrose asked. "I have one for you. Don't fight the seizure. Let the court take the money. Hell, there's a good chance we'd get it, anyway. You do that, and this tape may just get lost."

"That's extortion!" thundered Stroud. "Highway robbery! We piss on your offer."

"Why don't you let your client talk for himself, Gill?" Primrose suggested.

"Because I'm his lawyer, you moron," Stroud snorted.

But Bevo was thinking. "You're saying if I give up the insurance money, I walk?"

"No, Bevo," Wick replied. "He's saying you *might* walk. It's possible you could give up the money and still wind up in jail."

"Is that true?" Bevo asked Primrose.

Primrose arched his eyebrows. "I doubt that would happen."

"See?" said Wick. "You don't want to trust him."

But Bevo, standing next to the sheriff in handcuffs, was crumbling. "This is fucking unreal," he said. "I can't do time, guys."

"Our client needs to sleep on your offer," I told Primrose.

The DA shrugged. "Fine with me, Counselor. I'll give him twenty-four hours. If he doesn't give up his little friend by then, the deal's off."

The sheriff took Bevo downstairs and put him in the same cell he had been in the day before. Bevo was pacing again, kicking at the bars each time he got to the end of his brief circuit. Chandler, Stroud, and I sat on the bed.

"So what do I do, boys?" he asked. "You're my fucking lawyers. How do I get out of this?"

"The thing that burns my chops is that this is just for spite," said Wick. "SWAT didn't have to do this. The case was over. Warren Jacobs just didn't want us to get the money."

"Bevo," I said, "why in hell were you telling Duett about electrocuting a horse? You deliberately incriminated yourself in front of a SWAT lawyer!"

"I don't know. It just kind of happened. I was dealing dirt on Nyman Scales, you know, trying to cut a deal on the Stromboli case. . . . Hey, that's right! Most of the stuff on that tape is about shit that Scales done. Why don't they go after him? I was just doing my patriotic duty, helping 'em get the goods on a low-life horse thief."

"I promise you, Bevo," said Stroud, "you didn't tell them anything about Scales they haven't already heard. Scales has beaten those raps before. No evidence, remember?"

"Then why'd they come after me?" he cried. "I was just blowing air, Mr. Stroud, honest. None of that shit happened. I was just trying to make that lawyer think I was hot stuff. You know how you get when you start spinning tales? That's what I was doing. And he was eating it up. Duett thought I was Jesse James."

"So he just sort of coaxed that story about electrocuting the horse out of you?" I asked.

"That's what's so bad!" cried Bevo, close to hysterics. "*I* never electrocuted no horse. That was Nyman Scales that done that. I just sort of stole that story and put me in it." He took hold of the bars, and his whole body sagged. "And now I'm gonna go to jail over shit that Nyman Scales done!" He whirled to look at us. "You said they got no evidence on Scales for that stuff, right? Well, they got no evidence on me, either!"

"Just your taped confession," I reminded him.

"Shit, you guys could beat that," Bevo said.

"Maybe," said Wick. "If you could be believed. Or even if anybody anywhere had any use for you at all. But nobody can stand you, Bevo. You've pissed off too many officials of the law. It would be hard to beat your freely given confession in a trial, even if you were Billy Graham, which you aren't." Wick sighed. "And God knows what would have happened to our money by then."

"*My* money," said Bevo.

"Primrose will spend it to put Bibles in the cells," Stroud muttered.

"I can't do time, Mr. Stroud!" Bevo said.

"Primrose doesn't want to send you to jail, Bevo," I told him. "He's just trying to get hold of the money."

Stroud stood up and signaled for the guard to let us out of the cell. "Don't agree to any deal Primrose makes you," he told Bevo. "Do you hear me? Don't agree to a thing until you hear from me. If you do, I swear to God, I'll kill you myself."

As we got into the elevator, we heard Bevo moaning in his cell, *"I can't do time!"*

CHAPTER 45

WICK DROVE US BACK to Jenks in Bevo's Lexus. The loss of a three-hundred-thousand-dollar fee had plunged him into a foul state of mind. "There goes Barbados in August," he said, "and Deirdre in a string bikini."

"How were you planning to get her off the emu ranch without her husband finding out?" I asked.

"Starns would never know she's gone," Stroud said from the backseat. "He hasn't caught that bird you two let loose the other night. I imagine he'll still be chasing it in August."

"Primrose!" Wick spat out the name. "That fucking hypocrite. Did you know he's a lay preacher, Clay? He preaches all over the goddamned county. Saving souls for Jesus. A whited sepulcher, that's what he is. It's enough to make me give up being a Baptist!"

"You're a Baptist, Wick?" I asked.

"He's lapsed a bit," replied Stroud, "but he's not gone yet. As many men's wives as Hard-dick runs through, he can't afford to give up God completely."

"I imagine Primrose is telling the truth about the tape, though," I said. "Duett or somebody else from SWAT probably left it at the door, just like he said."

"True," said Stroud. "P.P. is an asshole, but he doesn't have the nerve for a real criminal conspiracy." Stroud seemed more bemused than angry at the turn of events.

It was almost four o'clock when we got to town. Wick headed for the bank's drive-through teller window, but Stroud had him take us to the office instead. "No bail-out for Bevo?" asked Wick, parking in front of the door. "Suits me fine."

Wick shuffled into the office ahead of us, head hanging low, hands in his pockets. Molly Tunstall was sitting at her desk, typing. She gave us her look of deep concern as we came in.

"Molly," Wick said, "get Reverend Blankenship on the phone. Tell him we've all resigned from the Baptist religion until they excommunicate Paul Primrose."

"Before you do that, Molly," said Stroud, "dial Warren Jacobs's office for me. Let's see if we can catch him before he goes home. Put it through to the conference room."

"Good idea," said Wick, "let's make an obscene phone call."

The phone rang. Stroud pushed a button and transferred the call to the speakerphone.

"Afternoon, Warren," said Stroud.

"Well, well, Gill Stroud," the lawyer replied. "I'm glad you called. I left the courtroom without congratulating you on your stroke of good fortune."

"Why, thanks, Warren. Pulaski's burglars really saved our ass. You should give them a bonus."

"What a card."

"Listen, Warren, do you happen to know a fellow named Antoine Duett?"

"Duett?" There was a pause. "No, I don't believe I've had the pleasure."

"That's odd. He has offices in your building."

"It's a big building, Gill. I doubt I know half the people we employ, much less who rents space down the hall."

"But you would know Duett. He's the dirty-tricks boy your firm sent to undermine our case. Remember? The spy who held secret meetings with our client, which he seems to have taped?"

"Spy? Tape? I'm sorry, Gill. It sounds like you've gotten into some bad Scotch."

"So you're saying you don't know Antoine Duett?"

"You're catching on. I do not know the man."

"And you know nothing about the seizure of Bevo's settlement money?"

"The money was seized? By whom?"

Winking at us, Stroud filled Jacobs in briefly on our afternoon.

"Oh, dear," said Jacobs, "how unfortunate for you. I guess Bevo loses, after all. That should teach him not to play with matches."

"I've got a hunch, Warren, that you're up to your buttocks in shit on this."

"Are you sure that's a hunch, Gill? At your age it could be wind or senility. Now, if you'll excuse me, I've got some work to do."

"Before you go, let me tell you about one of my hunches that just paid off. I had a hunch that the break-in at your man Pulaski's house might not have been so random as Pulaski wanted us to believe."

"Oh?"

"So I did a little checking, and, by golly, the phone company has proved me right."

"I have no idea what you're talking about," Jacobs replied.

"You might want to do a little checking on your own. I'll expect a call from you tonight between seven-thirty and eight. If you don't call, I'm taking my little hunch—and Pulaski's phone records—to the FBI."

"A hunch isn't going to save Bevo's money, Stroud."

The old man switched off the phone. "Boys," he said, "we're finally getting down to the licklog."

CHAPTER 46

THE FIVE-D STEAKHOUSE, five miles from town, was a series of shabby, interconnecting shacks that sprawled under a thick stand of evergreens next to a small lake. Going in, I hit my head on the doorpost, and as my eyes teared up from the smart, I noticed a sign posted on the wall opposite the door that read HURTS, DON'T IT?

"Barbarian humor," said Wick, clapping me on the shoulder.

"I noticed you didn't warn me," I replied.

According to Chandler and Stroud, the Five-D was the only eating establishment within sixty miles of Jenks that cooked a decent steak. Stroud had offered to prove to me the truth of this contention, so at six o'clock that evening the three of us found ourselves seated at a linoleum table in a tackboard lean-to next to the salad bar, waiting for our steaks to arrive from the kitchen. It was a slow night, which suited me fine, since the flooring of our little room did not feel all that secure to me, and I believed that the weight of an extra party or two might sink us.

Stroud, in high spirits, raised his glass of iced tea and offered a toast, "to the law," in which we all joined him.

"Enjoy your steaks, gentlemen," said the old man. "But remember, we must be back at the office by seven-thirty."

"Or not," said Wick. He smirked unhappily at his partner, who faced him across the square table.

"Mr. Parker," Stroud said, "we are about to discover whether I am a genius or a senile idiot."

"Can we vote now?" Wick asked.

"Mr. Chandler has become temporarily deranged from the loss of a great deal of money," Stroud explained to me. "It remains, then, for you to make my case for me."

"Me?" I said.

"Of course, you. You're the only one left to represent me. Surely you see the method in my madness?"

At that moment, I did not see much of anything.

"Let us retrace some of our steps," Stroud said. "Do you recall our visit to Stan Pulaski's house last night?"

"I believe I do," I said.

"Did anything of interest happen there?"

"We became felons," I replied.

"Anything else?"

"We narrowly escaped being arrested with stolen property in the trunk of your car."

"Anything else, Mr. Parker?"

"You made a phone call," I said.

"Exactly!" said Stroud, slapping the table with his palm.

And at that moment, I caught on. I saw Stroud's gamble, realized the nature of the trap he was trying to spring. It seemed flimsy to me, yet the simple fact that I saw it—that I had finally figured something out—gave me a feeling of relief that was almost dizzying. Maybe I would not have to spend the rest of my life two steps behind.

"So, what do you say, Mr. Parker, am I a genius or a candidate for the bone orchard?"

"I am not competent to answer that question, Mr. Stroud, but I do know one thing that you are."

"What is that?"

"You're a whistle-blower."

A self-satisfied smile creased his pallid face. "Well done, Mr. Parker."

"What the hell are you talking about?" Wick asked.

"The phone call, Wick," I said, "the one your partner made from Pulaski's study when we broke in last night." I turned to Stroud. "You crafty son of a bitch," I said to him. "You called SWAT!"

Stroud's eyes gave off a crocodile glint. "Jimmy Wortmann's office, to be exact," he said. "The phone company records will show that at the time of the burglary, a call was placed from the scene of the crime to a SWAT office."

"SWAT would have one hell of a time explaining that," I said. "But I've got a question. Why did you blow the whistle into the earpiece?"

The answer came from Wick. "You haven't heard that thing come through a phone line, have you, Clay?" he said. "It makes a noise on the line that everybody can hear. Like Ma Bell is melting."

"I had a hunch that's what it was," I said. "The big firms usually have a taping system that records calls coming in after business hours, which means there's a chance that they've got the whistle on tape. If they do, it'll sound like something very odd has happened to a phone conversation on Jimmy Wortmann's line."

"It would sound like something's been erased," said Wick.

"At least it will give pause to any law enforcement agency that hears it," Stroud said.

"So the call was insurance," I said. "You were betting SWAT might pull something at the last minute, and you found a way to give us some hidden leverage."

"That's right." Stroud turned to Chandler. "So, Hard-dick, has our new associate made my case?"

Wick raised his glass of iced tea in a salute to his partner. "God-damn dry county," he said. "This ought to be champagne."

CHAPTER 47

THE STEAKS ARRIVED. As we ate, Stroud explained why he thought SWAT would find the phone call he placed from Pulaski's house alarming.

"SWAT is the top firm in the country for horse insurance litigation. What if they have a way to know for certain which cases they take on are genuine and which are crooked? What if they're in league with someone who can tip them off to the crooked claims, even hand them the evidence needed to beat the suit? An arrangement like that would guarantee them a phenomenal win-loss record in handling big-dollar lawsuits, and, after all, winning is what keeps that steady stream of business coming in from big insurance firms like Stromboli."

"You're saying SWAT has its own crook squealing on the crooks around him," Wick said.

"It would have to be a superstar horse dealer," Stroud said, "somebody who brokers a lot of horse deals in the course of a year. Somebody who knows all the ins and outs of the business. A real horse magician."

"Somebody like Nyman Scales," I said.

Stroud nodded. "Nyman must set up twenty or thirty big buys a month. All these horses get insured, and most of them live out their lives as God intended. But horses do die, they get hurt, so a percentage of these horse deals will end in an insurance claim. Some of the claims are legitimate, of course, but some aren't."

"Quite a few aren't," Wick said.

"Our magical dealer knows which claims are legit and which ones aren't," Stroud continued. "He knows because he's the one who sets up the horse accidents, too. He sells the horses, then he zaps the horses."

"All for a percentage of the insurance take," I suggested, "and some kind of kickback from SWAT."

"Mr. Parker, what do you think of that rib eye?" Stroud asked.

"It's excellent," I replied.

"So our horse dealer is in a position to feed information to SWAT about any claim coming from one of his crooked partners," Stroud continued. "SWAT could then decide which of these lawsuits to win and which to lose. They would need to keep a balance, deliberately losing some suits and winning others. That way they could satisfy a percentage of Nyman's partners as well as their own clients, the insurance carriers. And that's the point—to keep the giant carriers like Stromboli happy. The name of the game is billable hours."

"Billable hours," Wick murmured. "The numbers must be staggering."

"But what about the crooked lawsuits SWAT decides to win to keep its average up?" I asked. "In those cases Scales would be selling out his own partners."

"Exactly," said Stroud. "You've just seen it happen to Bevo."

"But wouldn't these people scream bloody murder?"

"What do you think Bevo's been doing?" asked Stroud. "Nyman Scales has been surviving these kinds of accusations for years.

Some of the people he chooses to do business with are lowlifes like Bevo, people so crooked they can't pee in a straight line. What judge or jury is going to listen to them when they say they've been double-crossed by the biggest horse dealer in East Texas? Hell, Mr. Parker, Nyman probably put half the judges on the bench."

"I'll be damned," said Wick. "So Bevo really didn't burn his horses. He was telling the truth!"

"It's a possibility," Stroud replied. "Scales could have sent his boys to do it and make it look like it was Bevo. Or maybe Bevo did it himself. We'll probably never know."

"If you're right," I said to Stroud, "it's an amazing setup. Your call from Pulaski's house would scare the hell out of them."

Stroud nodded. "The phone records will show that SWAT got a call from the burglars during the robbery. Jimmy Wortmann won't run the risk of the law seeing those records and catching on to their operation."

"My guess," said Wick, "is SWAT will be falling all over itself to kiss our ass. Whoever calls us tonight is going to be wearing asbestos lips."

"That's quite a turnaround, Mr. Chandler," said Stroud. "As I recall, not ten minutes ago you were ready to ship me off to the rest home."

"I can't argue with genius, Mr. Stroud," said Wick.

We got back to the office at 7:15 and sat in the reception area by the front door, waiting for the phone to ring. Wick made a run to his house to pick up some bottles of champagne in the event that Stroud had guessed correctly about SWAT's response to his threat.

"What if I was wrong?" Gill asked as we watched Wick drive away.

"Then we'll have a more urgent reason to drink," I replied.

Stroud sat on the edge of Molly Tunstall's desk, staring out the window into the darkness. He looked tired and shriveled.

"I hope I will not insult you, Mr. Parker, if I ask whether you know the difference between being found not guilty of a crime and being innocent of it."

"Of course I know the difference," I replied.

"One may be found not guilty by a jury, and yet be guilty of committing the crime."

"Is this conversation leading somewhere?" I asked.

"That case you reminded me about the other day," he said, "the one in Waco."

"I remember."

"The fellow I got off. The black fellow. His name was Harms. Joseph Harms. The jury found him not guilty."

"I know that."

"What you don't know is that Joseph Harms was not only found not guilty by the jury, he actually *was* not guilty."

"That's a good thing, then," I said. "You saved an innocent man."

"I saved him for about a week, Mr. Parker. Harms moved out of Waco as soon as he could. But he didn't move far enough. The trial had gotten a lot of publicity throughout the South, more than Harms realized maybe. Anyway, six days after his acquittal, his body was found hanging from a tree down in East Louisiana."

I thought of the picture hanging in the Baylor Law building, the shadowy figure of the acquitted man and the tall man with the trestle in his hands, trying to keep him safe. "You did your best," I said to him.

"Ethics and justice," he said. "Let me tell you about ethics and justice. About a week after Harms was killed, the Waco sheriff's office arrested the dead girl's father and charged him with the killing. And guess who defended him?"

"You?"

"That's right. And I got him off, too. Want to know how I did it?"

"I wonder if I do."

"I convinced the jury that Harms did it. Harms was dead, killed by folks who thought he was guilty. I just let that grassroots feeling work for us. The DA in the father's case put a young criminalist on the stand who was really green. I turned him inside out. I could have gotten him to swear that the Easter Bunny had killed the girl. But Harms was handier. I refocused the light on a man who couldn't be tried again for the crime."

"Whatever works," I said.

"I was besotted with vanity," Stroud replied. "In those days I thought I could do no wrong. It pleased me to play with the law like that. I could have gotten Judas Iscariot off for fingering Jesus."

"At least you got the dead girl's father off."

Stroud smiled grimly. "Like I just said, Mr. Parker, sometimes there's a difference between being found not guilty and being innocent."

We both sat looking out the front window at the empty street.

"Maybe I'll retire," Stroud said, "hang up my whistle."

"I don't know about the retirement part," I said, "but the whistle should definitely go."

Wick came in, hugging half a dozen bottles of chilled champagne to his chest. "My tits are freezing," he said as he set the bottles on the table. He handed me one. "Open it for us, Clay. We might as well get braced."

There were no glasses in the room, so he and Stroud went to find some. While I sat on the edge of the table peeling the leaded wrapper off the top of the bottle, Sally walked in.

"I wondered what sort of trouble the boys were leading you into," she said. "Turns out it's simple alcoholism." She watched me work on the champagne cork. "You seem to be bottle impaired, Counselor. You aren't having any more luck than you did with that beer bottle yesterday." She came over and sat next to me. She was wearing her country-girl outfit, jeans and a T-shirt. I figured she had been out to Stroud's place to check on her horse.

"How's cousin Ed?" I asked, setting down the bottle.

"He sends his regards. He wants to know if—"

I kissed her hard on the lips. It surprised her.

"You wondered whether country life is agreeing with me," I said. "Well, it is, but I have something to say."

"Go on."

"It's just this. Once and for all, I'm sorry for any idiotic thing I've said to you in the last few days. I'm through asking questions, Sally. I'm tired of always being too slow, and the only way to catch up, it seems, is just to stop thinking altogether. So I don't care anymore. I don't care if you rustled stock when you were in diapers. I don't care if your mother was a Cajun witch or if your daddy is the biggest gangster in Texas. If you want to go after him, fine, I'll help you. If you don't want to go after him, that's fine, too."

I kissed her again. This time she helped. "I don't want to know anything else about your family or about your business or about your past. I don't want to know anything about you and Gill or you and Bevo or you and the pope. I don't want to be out-guessed, I don't want to be pinned down. All I really want is to take things a day at a time. And I want another kiss."

I would have gotten it, too—I could see it in her eyes—but the phone rang. Wick burst into the room, scattering paper cups, followed by Stroud, who slowly walked to the table and switched on the speakerphone.

"Well?" he said.

"Gill, it's Jimmy Wortmann. How do you want to handle this?"

CHAPTER 48

IT MUST HAVE BEEN A WILD NIGHT for Jimmy Wortmann and his associates. Gill demanded that Wortmann find a way to get the charge against Bevo dropped and Bevo driven back to Jenks by noon the next day, or else he, Gill, would go to the grand jury with the damaging phone record. He also demanded that the RICO hold on the Stromboli check be lifted by the time of Bevo's arrival in Jenks. We found out later that a whole raft of SWAT lawyers, including Jimmy Wortmann himself—the *W* in SWAT— descended on Paul Primrose's office at eight o'clock the next morning. Primrose was not there, he and Judge Wrong Tit Tidwell having teed off half an hour earlier at the Mule Springs Sportsman's Club. Primrose and the judge had reached the fifth hole when the SWAT lawyers found them and whisked them back to the courthouse.

There Jimmy Wortmann related a sad tale. It seemed that Warren Jacobs, one of SWAT's most brilliant associates, had, in the course of handling several high-pressure cases, become emotionally unstable. For reasons nobody could fathom, Jacobs had developed an intense hatred of Bevo Rasmussen, whose defense counsel had just outmaneuvered the ailing attorney in a recent lawsuit.

Smarting from that defeat, the lawyer initiated a plan to send Rasmussen to prison.

Wortmann explained to his mystified audience how the tape on which Rasmussen bragged about committing certain crimes was rigged: The voice that sounded like Bevo's belonged to an actor whom the demented lawyer paid to read from a script while he himself supplied the other voice. The sick man then delivered the tape anonymously, counting on Primrose to do his duty. The plot was only discovered late the night before, when Jacobs, the unfortunate associate, was relieved of his duties and sent to a hospital for a rest. SWAT was very, very sorry for any inconvenience their firm had caused the DA's office, but they felt they had to come forward in order to prevent a terrible miscarriage of justice. Bevo Rasmussen, Wortmann explained to Primrose and Judge Tidwell, was an innocent man.

It could not have played very well. Primrose would have demanded to know why, if this crazy story were true, Bevo had admitted to taking part in the taped conversation when it was played for him in the DA's office. I don't know how Wortmann got around that, or around the other holes in the story, but one thing I had learned in the new life was that there is no story told in the country without a few holes in it, some big enough to drive a hay baler through. That's true about stories told anywhere, of course. I had known that back in Houston—I was a tax lawyer, for God's sake. I guess I had not wanted it to be true in the country. Put me down for an idiot.

In any event, Wortmann finessed his sloppy story. An exasperated Judge Tidwell ordered Primrose to release Bevo and unfreeze the check. Primrose had to drive to Jenks himself to deliver the original of the order dismissing the RICO forfeiture. We saw his Buick sliding into a parking space across the street in front of the bank at eleven-thirty.

"That's one unhappy Baptist," Wick said, watching through the blinds as Primrose trudged into the bank.

A few minutes later, Bevo showed up. For the second time in two days, he, Chandler, and Stroud walked across the street and into the bank to cash the settlement check. I sat again on the fender of Bevo's Lexus, waiting for them to come out, wondering if I would need to dive into the car again for another wild ride through the blistering heat to avert some new catastrophe. To tell the truth, I don't think I would have minded much.

Maybe it was something in the water, or the effect of thumping along so many country roads, or the craziness of Bevo's case— or Sally, late last night, after we drove off in her Mercedes and found a roll of duct tape in her glove compartment—but I was beginning to think that country life was the right move for me.

True, it had not turned out to be quite the bucolic retreat I had imagined. In the last week, I had been threatened, stabbed, tied up, lost in the woods, and attacked in a diner. I had met drug dealers and horse thieves, I had survived a car crash, outwitted police, witnessed a fistfight between a man and an emu, burgled a house, and participated in a pitched battle won with firecrackers. I had careened in and out of the dim gray border regions of the law. And I had gotten shockingly, magnificently laid, on more than one occasion. I wondered what the next week would be like. Sitting on the fender of the Lexus, I waved to my neighbors as the locusts in the trees tried their best to give me a clue.

Then the three of them were out of the bank, heading toward me, and I saw that, for the moment at least, there would be no more mad dashes. I asked if they had seen Primrose while they were in the bank.

"He must have been hiding under the counter," Stroud replied. "Too bad. I was going to invite him over for a drink."

Bevo waved his cashier's check at me. "You're gonna have to

treat me different now, Mr. Parker. I'm a rich man.'"

"Remember what I told you, Bevo," said Wick. "I'd stay out of the county for a while if I were you."

"Scales ain't coming after me," Bevo said. "It would be bad for his bidniss if I disappeared so soon after the deposition."

"On the contrary," said Stroud. "He might think it *good* for his business. He surely knows you were selling him out to Duett. He's probably even heard the tape. I wouldn't think he'd take kindly to that."

"Thanks for your concern, gentlemen, but I can look after myself," Bevo said.

"At least now you can pay Deck Willhoit what you owe him," I said. "That should give you some comfort."

"I already paid him," Bevo said. "Me and him are friends again. I'm gonna get that whale-dick back for you, too, Mr. Chandler, if I have to steal it myself."

"Do me a favor, Bevo," said Wick. "If you get caught, don't mention my name."

"You say you've already paid Willhoit off?" I asked.

"Like I told you, Mr. Parker, it's no trouble getting hold of money." The little man shook hands all around, opened the driver's door, and climbed into the Lexus. "Gentlemen, I thank you for your services. If I ever get in another scrape—"

"*When* you get in another scrape," Wick interrupted.

"Okay, *when* it happens, you're my first call."

"You don't know how happy that makes us," said Wick.

"Say, Bevo," I called. "Wick and I have been thinking of driving over to take a look at your burned-down barn."

"We've been thinking what?" asked Wick.

"Old time's sake, you know, now that the case is over. We've never even seen the place. Can you give us directions, Bevo?"

Bevo looked at me for a long moment. "Sure, I can do that, Mr.

Parker. But you don't want to drive all that way. There's nothing there anymore. I haven't seen it myself in almost a year. You're liable to drive right by and miss it."

"All the same, Bevo," I said, "we'd like to head out there and tell the neighbors what we got for your horses. I think it might surprise them."

I looked into Bevo's eyes and he into mine for maybe ten seconds. Then he gave me that wolf's smile of his and shook his head. "How'd you figure it out?" he asked me.

"Figure what out?" asked Wick.

"I'll be damned!" said Stroud.

"It was a lot of things," I said. "Your paying off Willhoit before you got the settlement check, of course. But there was always something a little fishy about the money. Even cooking the numbers like you did, the scam just wouldn't have been worth the risk, after paying off all your debts, unless—"

"Unless what?" asked Wick.

"Unless there were never any horses to begin with!" Stroud said. He shuffled over and gave me an exultant slap on the back. "You're a quick study, Mr. Parker."

"I was wondering if any of you hot-shot lawyers would figure that out," said Bevo. "Damn if it wasn't the new guy."

"Wait a minute," said Wick, squinting dubiously at me. "You're saying there were no horses?"

"No flesh-and-blood horses," I explained. "But they were there on paper. I think what clued me in for sure was the glimpse Gill and I got of Pulaski's horse mausoleum. All those little plastic bags, neatly arranged and labeled, just waiting to be used in an arson scam."

"You're scary, Mr. Parker," Bevo said. "That's what happened, all right. Nyman sold me seven dead horses. He called 'em pre-burned. Pulaski picked 'em out—he and Nyman have been in bidniss for some time. Old Nyman told me what to write on the dec sheets, and we were in bidniss. I only paid Nyman seven hundred dollars up front, a hundred a horse, even though it says on paper that he loaned me a quarter of a million."

"All right, now," said Wick, "if that's true, then why didn't Pulaski just choose remains of seven more horses from his morgue the night he discovered the evidence was missing?"

"Because no other horses would have matched the descriptions on the original dec sheets," I replied. "The case had become so smelly by then that he knew we would hire our own pathologist to verify his findings. When our pathologist's report didn't match his, things would have gotten even more embarrassing."

"So the insurance money reimbursed you for the bogus quarter-million loan from Scales," Stroud said to Bevo.

"Right. Only, like I say, there wasn't no quarter-million loan from him, since there wasn't no horses. I was supposed to pay Nyman fifty thousand out of the settlement, when I got it." Bevo winked at me. "I don't think I'll do that now."

"And the money you borrowed from the Farmer's Branch Bank, you've had that money stashed all the time?"

"Yep. That's another quarter mil." He laughed. "If only I could have found a way to snooker you out of your fee, I'd have walked off with the whole pot. As it is, I made close to nine hundred thousand on the deal. Not bad, considering I never even had to burn any horses."

"A little more effort went into it than that," I reminded him. "Don't forget, Deck Willhoit almost gelded you that night in Dallas. And you came close to going to prison."

"You lying little rat's ass son of a bitch!" Wick said, a note of awe in his voice.

"It's the principle, Mr. Chandler," Bevo explained. "You get a plan, you stick with it. That's what I done, and it sure as hell worked."